Romantic Suspense

Danger. Passion. Drama.

Vigilante Justice
Jacquelin Thomas

The Marine's Deadly Reunion
Loretta Eidson

MILLS & BOON

VIGILANTE JUSTICE
© 2023 by Jacquelin Thomas
Philippine Copyright 2023
Australian Copyright 2023
New Zealand Copyright 2023

First Published 2023
First Australian Paperback Edition 2023
ISBN 978 1 867 29819 9

THE MARINE'S DEADLY REUNION
© 2023 by Loretta Eidson
Philippine Copyright 2023
Australian Copyright 2023
New Zealand Copyright 2023

First Published 2023
First Australian Paperback Edition 2023
ISBN 978 1 867 29819 9

MIX
Paper | Supporting
responsible forestry
FSC® C001695
www.fsc.org

Published by
Harlequin Mills & Boon
An imprint of Harlequin Enterprises (Australia) Pty Limited
(ABN 47 001 180 918), a subsidiary of HarperCollins
Publishers Australia Pty Limited
(ABN 36 009 913 517)
Level 19, 201 Elizabeth Street
SYDNEY NSW 2000 AUSTRALIA

Cover art used by arrangement with Harlequin Books S.A.. All rights reserved.

Printed and bound in Australia by McPherson's Printing Group

Vigilante Justice
Jacquelin Thomas

MILLS & BOON

Jacquelin Thomas is an award-winning, bestselling author with more than fifty-five books in print. When not writing, she is busy catching up on her reading, attending sporting events and spoiling her grandchildren. Jacquelin and her family live in North Carolina.

Visit the Author Profile page
at millsandboon.com.au for more titles.

The fathers shall not be put to death
for the children, neither shall the children be
put to death for the fathers: every man
shall be put to death for his own sin.
—*Deuteronomy* 24:16

Prologue

Legs planted wide and nostrils flaring, he stood on a hill, watching as a family gathered to lay their loved one to rest below him. His gaze was intense and unblinking. Sounds of people sobbing floated up to where he stood. He didn't know the deceased or any of the mourners. He didn't even care about them.

In this moment, it felt strange being here in Atlanta—he'd never wanted to come back to this place that was filled with nothing but bad memories.

"You okay?"

He had been too lost in thought to hear his brother's approach.

Pointing at the aging headstone, he said, "She's been dead thirty-two years today. I was six and you were only four."

"I know. I thought it was supposed to g-get easier with time. At least that's what people s-say."

"Yeah, that's what they say… They lied." A vein in his neck pulsed. "I can still remember that night. Begging her to let us stay home with her. She forced us to go with Dad. Said it was his weekend. Then coming home and finding her body…" She'd been bloodied and beaten. They'd been too young to know that she'd been raped, too.

"There wasn't anything we could've done. I b-barely remember wh-what happened. I only know what you told me." His brother spoke slowly to lessen his stutter, which grew worse when he was upset or anxious.

He gestured wildly in his anger. "Maybe not, but we could've tried to do something. You don't remember because I protected you from as much of it as I could." He had been tormented by guilt all these years, living each day with a dreadful sense of failure. It wasn't enough for the police to have found the man responsible for her death.

He recalled the day James Ray Powell was apprehended—three months after his mother's murder. It was all over the television. As they escorted the serial killer out to a waiting police car, he was laughing.

That's what I remember most. The laughing.

He drew in a few slow breaths to steady himself.

But the rage remained—it was a kind of cold fury that refused to leave. He'd never be rid of it until he dispensed the justice Powell deserved.

"Are we doing the right thing?" his brother asked.

"He took our mother away from us. We takin' his family from him. Tell me now if you're having second thoughts."

"N-naw…"

"Ya sure?"

"I'm good. Let's just get this d-done so I can focus on some other stuff. I've been thinking about my future. Got some plans in the works."

"Like what?"

Shrugging, his brother said, "I'm not ready to t-talk about it."

"Okay, whatever…" he said. "I found Ezra Stone. He don't live too far from here." He eyed his brother. "You with me on this, right?"

"Yeah. How m-many times I—I gotta reassure you. All we got is us."

They descended the hill, their steps muffled by the brown carpet of grass as they walked towards the faded yellow lines of the empty parking lot.

"Ride with me. I'll bring you back to your car."

They got into the car, started the engine and drove off.

They rode in silence for a while, the only sound coming from the radio playing hip hop music.

"You ever find out what happened to Pops?"

"Naw… It's pretty obvious that he abandoned us a long time ago."

"That ain't right," his brother said. "Something happened to him. His body just ain't been found."

"You can hang on to that dream, but the truth is that people out here don't care 'bout nothin' but they own lives. That's why we gotta take care of stuff ourselves."

When he glimpsed a police car a few vehicles behind them, he slowed down, cruising carefully down the street. He didn't want to risk getting a speeding ticket or even drawing attention to themselves.

Ten minutes later, he pulled into a parking spot near the corner. "That's the house right there."

They watched a man walk out of the house toward an old Cadillac. He unlocked the door and leaned inside. He appeared to be searching for something.

"That's him. Ezra Stone ain't changed a bit. Just got older."

"Old and gray," his brother responded. "He used to have m-more weight on him. At least that's how I remember him."

As he watched their target, he felt hot fury surge upward, threatening to explode.

Soon…

The thought of what they had planned appeased him. Temporarily. But his rage would return.

"We'll come back tonight," he announced.

"I'll be ready."

"It's time to make them all pay."

Chapter 1

James Ray Powell is a cold-blooded killer. He stole the lives of so many women, leaving their families devastated and heartbroken. It is only right that he feels what we feel—the loss of a child, a wife, a mother, a sister… I won't stop until I erase every single member of that killer's family. This includes you and your daughter.

Everleigh Sanderson Taylor stared at the letter in her trembling hand, reading it again, allowing the words to wrestle their way into her brain. A chill dashed down her spine at the mention of her little girl. Rae was only five years old—an innocent in all this. Six months ago, Everleigh's world changed when her mother told her about the circumstances surrounding her conception. Deloris died a few days later on the first day of June.

Two weeks after her mother died, Everleigh received an offer from a small university in Charleston. She'd accepted the position as a professor of psychology, seizing the opportunity to build a new life for herself and Rae. A month after her mother's funeral, Everleigh left Savannah, Georgia, to escape her past and start fresh on Angel Island, located off the coast of South Carolina. She was no stranger to grief. Just one year prior to losing her mother, Everleigh's husband died, leaving her a widow at thirty. With both gone, the Hostess City of the South no longer felt like home.

Starting over in a new city brought hope, promise and no drama. She and her daughter were about to spend their first Christmas on the island. Everything had been going well, until today.

Her thirty-second birthday when she retrieved the letter from her mailbox.

She glanced down once more at the typewritten note in her hand, the words jumping out at her, the tone accusing and judgmental. It had been originally sent to her mother's home, then forwarded by the current occupants to her new address. According to Deloris, the only people who had known her father's identity were Deloris's parents, but clearly, there was someone else who knew the secret.

Who would want to hurt her and her child?

Her mind jumped to Wyle Gaines, a smooth talker who'd befriended Deloris at the hospital where they worked. He'd spent a lot of time with Deloris, even taking her to doctor appointments, cooking and staying with her whenever Everleigh had to work. Perhaps her mother had confided in him, which would explain how he knew the truth.

Everleigh had never cared for the man, but was unable to convince her mother that Wyle couldn't be trusted. When she'd put the house up for sale after her mother's death, he'd made an offer to purchase it at a substantially lower price than what it was worth.

When Everleigh refused him, Wyle became angry. He even claimed that Deloris had promised the house to him shortly after she got sick. Her mother had never mentioned this to Everleigh and she didn't believe a word of what Wyle said. She ended up blocking him and threatened to call the police if he continued showing up at her door or her mother's home unannounced.

In the end, Everleigh rented out the house,

choosing to keep the property. Was this his way of getting back at her for not letting him have her mother's house?

Everleigh bit back the overwhelming streak of panic she felt, refusing to allow her fear to spin out of control until she had a reason to be fearful.

She picked up her coat and purse, and headed out the door. Everleigh was going to the police precinct in Charleston. Declan Blanchet, a fellow professor at the university, was also a criminal investigator. She didn't know him well. Until now, they hadn't had any real interaction on campus other than general faculty meetings. She'd heard from some of the other staff that he was a decorated police detective, having been in law enforcement for fifteen years.

Everleigh turned up the heat in her car. She wasn't sure if the sudden chill was due to the wintry weather or the feeling of dread coursing through her veins.

She pulled into the parking lot of the Charleston police precinct. Everleigh sat in the car, debating whether she really wanted to see this through, to open this Pandora's box.

Five minutes later, she strode with purpose through the doors, walking up to a large desk that was separated from the public by a glass partition. While waiting for someone to assist her, Everleigh could hear sirens blaring from outside the building, competing against the anonymous voice coming through an intercom system. Behind her, the doors opened and closed in rapid succession.

"How may I help you?" a young woman in uniform asked. Her hair was braided down and pulled back into a bun.

"I'd like to speak with Detective Declan Blanchet. I work with him at the university."

"Your name?"

"Dr. Everleigh Taylor."

"Please have a seat over there, Dr. Taylor," the officer directed. "I'll let him know that you're here."

"Thank you," Everleigh said.

She sat down, her back straight. Her body was filled with tension.

Relax.

Everleigh went through a series of relaxation techniques while waiting to meet with Declan.

After all, the letter could turn out to be Wyle's idea of a cruel joke. He'd vowed to make her life miserable after she refused to sell him her mother's house. She reminded herself that until she knew the threat was real, there wasn't anything to worry about.

Her body however, revolted at the thought that he could be so cruel.

Forty-year-old Declan Blanchet's dark eyebrows rose to attention when he learned the woman requesting to speak with him was none other than Dr. Everleigh Taylor. She was the new professor in the psychology department. She was also extremely attractive and reserved, keeping mostly to herself whenever she was on campus. They'd said hello a few times, but hadn't interacted much otherwise.

He couldn't imagine why she'd come all the way to the precinct in Charleston to see him. He knew that she lived on Angel Island, two blocks from another colleague, Robin Rutledge, and the island had its own police department.

Declan walked past a couple of officers chatting over the sound of a microwave beeping in the break room.

"What's up, Blanchet?" one of them asked.

"Same thing, different day," he responded with a chuckle.

Declan peered through the locked door before walking out. Everleigh was dressed in a pair of gray designer jeans and a black turtleneck beneath a black wool coat. On her feet were a pair of leather loafers. He liked a woman who knew how to dress to accentuate her curves. Her hair was styled in the usual neat bun at her nape. Her skin was the color of smooth chocolate and free of makeup. Normally, she wore black-framed glasses, but not today.

He walked up and asked, "What can I do for you, Professor Taylor?"

"I think someone wants me and my daughter dead," Everleigh stated, getting straight to the point.

His jaw dropped. *I couldn't have heard her correctly.* "Excuse me?"

She handed him a piece of paper. "This letter was forwarded to me by the people renting my mother's house in Savannah. I have an idea of who might have sent it, but I'm not sure."

Declan's eyebrows shot up as he read the note, and he looked at Everleigh in disbelief. He led her to a deserted office, weaving through cubicles until they came to one with its door shut tight.

Inside, Everleigh spoke, almost too quietly for

him to hear. "I found out six months ago that James Ray Powell is my father," she admitted.

He jolted. She didn't have to explain who the notorious serial killer was.

"My mother was one of his victims. She escaped with her life, but I was the result of the attack. She never reported it, and she told me that no one outside of her parents knew what happened. I think she may have told this guy. He spent quite a bit of time with her during her final days."

Declan swallowed his disbelief that someone as evil as Powell could've fathered a woman like Everleigh. The man had raped and murdered as many as thirty women…maybe more. James Ray Powell began terrorizing Atlanta, Carrollton and a few other surrounding cities in Georgia in the mid-eighties. He was finally apprehended June 1990, six months before she was born.

"Who was the letter addressed to?" he inquired.

"My mother," she responded.

"It's possible that the letter is most likely referring to the two of you—mother and daughter."

"I had considered that," Everleigh said. "But

this guy knows my mom is gone. Besides, she isn't related to Powell by blood—just me and Rae."

"We should consider all options. If it's not him, then I have to admit that I'm baffled," Declan said. "This is the first case I've heard about of a person seeking justice against a serial killer by going after the family members."

"So you don't think it's just some sick joke?" Everleigh asked.

"It's possible," he responded, though he had some reservations about the idea. "Have you told anyone about Powell?"

"No. It's not something I'd discuss—I'm disgusted by the very idea of that killer having fathered me. But this man…his name is Wyle Gaines. He worked at the hospital with my mom. He went out of his way to befriend her, although I never trusted him… Anyway, after she died, Wyle kept asking for different things—saying that she promised he could have them, including her house. He knew I'd never just sign it over to him, so he offered to purchase it for half of what it was worth. Wyle got very upset with me when I wouldn't sell to him."

"Did you ever feel threatened when he was around?" Declan asked.

"Not really," she responded. "Irritated mostly. But Wyle promised that he'd make life miserable for me."

"Do you think your mother told him about Powell?"

"It's entirely possible," Everleigh stated. "I'd like to think she wouldn't have told him anything, but my mother was under a lot of medication toward the end. She would say random things and she talked about Powell a lot in her final days."

He was surprised how calm Everleigh appeared to be about this situation, although he suspected that deep down, she was shaken.

"Detective Blanchet, I came to you to see if you can help with proving that this was sent by Wyle," she said. "It's crazy to think that there's someone out there who actually wants me dead because of a man I've never even met."

"Are you sure your mother never reported the attack?" Declan asked. "I believe there were only three victims known to have survived, but there is always the assumption that there could be more."

"According to what she told me, my mother

left Atlanta that same night and never reported
it. She said that she didn't know the identity
of her attacker until after he'd been arrested."

"I'll investigate to determine if this is a real
threat, or if this Wyle person is playing a sick
prank on you," he said.

"I have no idea why he'd do something like
this," she murmured bleakly. "It won't change
my mind about my mother's house." Everleigh
reached up and pushed away a dark, wavy ten-
dril of hair that had escaped. "Thank you, Detective. I appreciate your time. I have to do
whatever I can to protect my daughter."

"Please, call me Declan." He thought for a
moment. "Is there anyone else who might hold
a grudge against you? Have you ever been contacted by Powell himself?" The notorious killer
was in prison for life, but he might try to contact those he believed to be family.

She shook her head. "I don't think there's any
way he could know about us."

"Okay. I'll check out every avenue, including
Gaines and Powell. We'll see what turns up."

"Only if you call me Everleigh," she responded with a smile. "As for Powell, I'd really like to leave him out of this. I don't want
him to know about me, but especially about

my daughter. I would never allow him into our lives."

"I'll be discreet. And, Everleigh, I want to assure you that nothing is going to happen to either of you under my watch," Declan said as he escorted her outside the busy precinct. "Does Wyle Gaines have your current address?"

"We weren't speaking at the point I'd decided to leave Savannah, so I didn't tell him anything. This letter was sent to the old address and forwarded to me here." Everleigh pulled the folds of her coat around herself to ward off the cold blast of wintry air. "Declan, thank you again. I wasn't sure if I should bother the police, in case it turned out to be nothing but someone ranting. But since we're colleagues, I thought it wouldn't hurt to ask."

He zipped up his black leather jacket. "My thoughts are that we don't need anyone else involved right now. I'll look into this personally."

"Please let me know as soon as you can if you find anything. Good or bad. I need to know everything."

"Okay. I'll let you know what I find."

Everleigh handed him a business card. "I wrote my home number on the back."

Declan watched as she walked briskly to her vehicle, unlocked the door and slid inside.

He hoped that the note she'd received would prove to be nothing, but he wasn't holding his breath.

Chapter 2

It was still hard to digest the news of Powell being her father in addition to her grief. On top of that, Everleigh had to deal with Wyle's attempt to further manipulate her. Once Declan provided her with solid proof that it was him, she intended to petition the courts for a restraining order against Wyle. She was grateful Declan had agreed to look into the letter.

Everleigh wasn't so aloof that she didn't notice the outline of Declan's lean, muscular frame and long, powerful legs. His shaved head, warm mocha complexion, neatly trimmed mustache and beard… His face could have placed him on the list of the top ten most handsome men in the world.

In another life, Everleigh could appreciate a man as good-looking at Declan, but after losing her husband in the line of duty, she'd vowed to never give her heart to another *pro-*

tector type. She couldn't afford to put herself or Rae through another loss like that.

Everleigh made it back to the island in time to pick up her daughter from kindergarten.

"Hey, Mama," Rae greeted when she climbed into the back seat of the SUV. "Happy birthday! I made you a card."

Her heart warmed over her daughter's thoughtfulness. Rae was like her father—they preferred to make cards for special days like these. "Thank you, sweetie. Give it to me when we get home."

"Okay."

"How was your day?" Everleigh asked, looking into the rearview mirror. She waited patiently for Rae to secure her seat belt.

"Good," the little girl responded, her thick spiral curls covering her face.

Halfway down the street, she inquired, "Hey, where's your cap?"

"In my backpack," Rae answered. "I was about to get it out when you came."

Everleigh smiled to herself. Her daughter hated wearing caps and looked for any reason not to do so.

Ten minutes later, they were home. Once inside, Everleigh turned on the house alarm—

it was something she normally didn't do until bedtime, but this letter had her spooked.

"Rae, do you remember what to do if we have uninvited visitors or I say Barbie's in trouble?"

She nodded. "I'm supposed to hide in my toy box—the one in the closet.

I use the phone in the toy box and call 911," Rae recited. "I tell the police we need help, then leave the phone on so they know where to find us."

"Now, remember that phone is only for emergencies," Everleigh reminded her. "I know how much you love playing games on my cell. I don't want you pulling it out for a quick game or two." She made a mental note to check the battery life. She kept it charged regularly.

"I know, Mama."

When she was growing up, Deloris had enrolled Everleigh in karate, and she'd eventually earned a black belt. She understood now why her mother had been so concerned that she was able to defend herself.

"Mama, where are we going to eat?" Rae asked.

"I was thinking we'd just stay here."

"But we always go out for your birthday dinner."

"I thought we'd try something a little different," Everleigh said. "And we don't have to wait to eat birthday cupcakes because we'll already be home."

Rae beamed. "Yeah… I like that. But I still want to go out for my birthday dinner. I'll go get the menus out the kitchen drawer."

Grinning, she responded, taking a seat on the sofa to remove her shoes. "I know and that's fine." Rae's birthday wasn't until May, and Everleigh figured by then this mess with Wyle would be over. At least it was her fervent hope.

Anger washed over her in that moment. She didn't like having something like this hanging over her head. Her husband was gone and so was her mother. Everleigh's faith had gotten her through those heartbreaking losses, but how much more did she have to endure?

Rae interrupted her thoughts when she burst into the living room. "I hope we're ordering from Wings and More."

Everleigh's eyebrows rose in surprise. "You *want* hot wings?"

Nodding, Rae said, "You said it was your favorite place and it's your birthday."

She planted a kiss on her daughter's forehead.

"You're such a sweetheart. I appreciate your thoughtfulness."

Everleigh placed their order, then stood up saying, "I'll make some veggies to go with our wings."

"Spinach," Rae suggested while skipping around. "I want spinach."

"Okay, sweetie. That's what we'll have. You know…you love vegetables but you don't like veggie pizza."

A grimace on her heart-shaped face, Rae responded, following her mother into the kitchen.

"Mama…some stuff don't go on pizza. Not good."

Everleigh smiled in amusement before opening the refrigerator for the container of spinach.

Just under an hour later, they were seated at the dining room table eating.

Everleigh checked her phone several times. She didn't want to miss a text or a call from Declan.

"I like the lemon-pepper ones best," Rae said.

"I thought you really liked the honey-bar-becue wings."

"I do, but today I like this one best."

"You take after your grandmother," Everleigh

said, a smile on her face. Deloris's mood often determined the flavor of her wings. She would order the sweet-chili or mango-habanero wings whenever she was happy and in a good mood. When she was upset about something, Deloris wanted naked wings. Whenever her mother felt daring, she would order the Nashville-hot or ghost-pepper wings.

"I wish Grandma and Daddy could be here with us, but I know they're in heaven having a party for your birthday."

Everleigh eyed her five-year-old daughter in awe. "I believe they are," she responded softly.

Rae finished off a wing, then asked, "Do you think God eats cupcakes?"

"Hmm… I'm not sure."

"I bet He does, Mama. Everything good and sweet comes from Him. That's what Daddy used to say."

Everleigh blinked back tears. "Your father was supersmart."

Rae nodded in agreement as she picked up another wing.

After they finished eating, Everleigh said, "Go wash your hands while I get the cupcakes."

"Don't forget that you have to blow out the candles first," Rae responded as she left the table. "And I have to sing 'Happy Birthday' to you, Mama."

She put cupcakes on each of their plates and stuck a candle on top of hers.

"I'm back," Rae announced, holding up her hands. "Clean."

"Good job, sweetie."

Everleigh blinked back tears as her little girl sang, "Happy birthday to you, happy birthday to you, happy birthday to yo-o-u-u... Happy birthday to you..."

She bent down to blow out the one candle.

"Did you make a wish?" Rae asked.

"I did."

Rae gave her the card she'd made. "And I have a present for you."

"You do?"

Rae grinned. "Yeah. I made it." She pulled a small box out of her pocket. "I wrapped it myself."

"You did a fabulous job."

Everleigh's eyes watered all over again when she saw the beaded bracelet her daughter made for her. "Oh, sweetie... I love it. And it's my favorite color. Purple."

"My friend and her sister helped me with it. Her sister makes them all the time."

She pulled Rae into her embrace. "You've made this birthday the best one *ever*. Thank you, my darling girl." Everleigh refused to allow anything to completely ruin this day for her.

When they readied for bed later that evening, she said, "I want you to sleep with me tonight."

"Yay!"

While Rae took her bath, Everleigh did another walk through the house, making sure the windows and doors were all locked.

Everleigh checked the alarm again, since she'd turned it off briefly to accept their delivery order, then went back upstairs to her room. She checked the Taser in her nightstand drawer and the one stashed away inside a drawer in her bathroom.

She took a deep breath and forced her body to relax. She silently recited Psalm 91, then whispered, "Lord, I'm trusting You to keep us safe." Everleigh paused a moment, then added, "I hope You won't let me down again."

Declan sat in his office at the precinct, staring at the computer monitor the next morning. He was conducting a search on Wyle Gaines. The man had a couple of complaints for drunken behavior but no convictions. Another complaint came up. He was accused of taking advantage of an elderly woman. The family had filed a report that he'd swindled their elderly mother out of a large sum of money. However, when police had queried the woman, she'd admitted that she'd given the money to Wyle as a gift and refused to press charges.

Declan concluded that Wyle was most likely after the house and financial gain. He didn't doubt that the man would try to use fear tactics against Everleigh after she'd refused to give into his demands. But would he send a death threat?

He read the letter once more. The tone was chilling.

Somehow, Declan didn't believe it came from Wyle. He continued his investigation by calling the hospital where he worked.

"Savannah Memorial Medical Center…"

"I'd like to speak with Wyle Gaines."

"I'm sorry, but he doesn't work here anymore."

"When did he leave?" Declan asked.

"Five…six months ago. I'm not sure. Did you want to speak with someone else in the IT department?"

"No thanks. I'm a friend of his. We hadn't

talked in a while. I'm in town for a few days and wanted to touch base."

"Oh, okay. Well, I'm sorry I can't be more help."

"It's fine," he said, then hung up.

"Where are you, Wyle Gaines?" he whispered.

For now, Declan decided to take the investigation in another direction.

He searched Powell's parents.

Ray Thomas Powell died a year after his son's arrest. The killer's seventy-year-old mother had died eleven months ago—Declan was relieved to see it was due to natural causes.

The next find, however, cooled his blood several degrees. Powell's oldest sister had been murdered in her home three months ago to the very day. Declan strongly considered the possibility that her death was simply a coincidence until his research led him to two other relatives in different cities also found dead in the past eight weeks—their deaths had been ruled homicides, but were unsolved. Both had arrest records, so again, it could just be a tragic happenstance. Besides, the methods of murder were different. The sister had been strangled. One of the relatives had been killed by gunshot, while the other had been bludgeoned to death. "No obvious connection between the murders," he whispered.

He checked to see whether any of the victims had received letters similar to Everleigh's. There wasn't any mention of it in the news. Declan hadn't expected there would be—it was not something he'd share with reporters if he was investigating the case.

Declan conducted a search through the National Integrated Ballistic Information Network to see if there were any matches to the bullets found at one of the crime scenes.

Next, he called and spoke with the investigators on all three murder cases. Declan decided to deliver what little information he'd found to Everleigh in person. He had been left with more questions than answers. He wished he had more definitive news for her.

Declan left his office shortly after one o'clock and drove to the university.

During the spring and summer months, the quad was covered in vibrant green grass criss-crossed by decorative pavers. Wooden benches were spaced along the pathway. He strolled past bike racks and plants in large pots toward a building with a decorative archway. However, the cordgrass was now a beautiful coppery brown.

Despite the biting December chill in the air, students sat outside alone or in groups; some walked to and from classes, oblivious to their surroundings. Banners hung over the pathway to the building next door.

Declan entered through the doors of the social-sciences building. He found Everleigh in her office.

"Good afternoon," she greeted when he knocked on her open door. "C'mon in."

"G' afternoon," he responded.

"Were you able to find anything out?" Everleigh asked when he sat down. "I know it's probably a long shot." She trained her eyes on him as if eager for information.

"I've found some concerning information. This may be more than the prank we'd hoped." Keeping his voice low so as not to be overheard, Declan said, "Powell's sister was murdered three months ago—she was strangled. Two other relatives in the last eight weeks. They all lived in different cities. The second victim—a cousin— was shot a couple of times. The third was involved in an altercation involving a woman a few hours before he was found bludgeoned to death. I spoke with the detectives on record for all three cases and was told that there weren't any letters found at the scenes."

Anxiety captured her body in a tight grip. "Do you think I was the only person who received one?" she asked.

"It just means they didn't find them. Still, there's a strong chance that those deaths could be random killings."

"And Wyle Gaines?"

"Your instincts about his motives toward your mother were on point. He manipulates and steals from women. There's no record of violence or threats. That being said, he could be behind this letter."

Everleigh rose to her feet and walked over to the window, then stood with her back to it.

"What do you think we should do?"

"I think it's best if we treat this threat as real."

She gave a stiff nod. "So what do I do now? I have classes and my daughter has school…" Her voice quavered, her body taut with dread.

"Have you seen anything out of the ordinary? Anything that may have stood out to you as strange at the time?"

"No, nothing," Everleigh responded. "And

I'm always pretty observant of my surroundings. It's something my mother drilled into me."

"You can file an official report. We can assign an officer to watch your house. I'll arrange for campus security to walk you to and from your car."

Shaking her head, Everleigh said, "No, I'm not ready to do that. Declan, there's a chance that Wyle doesn't know where we are."

"I've had the letter dusted for prints," Declan said. "Hopefully, I'll hear something back soon."

Students began milling around outside her office.

"Why don't you come by my house this evening?" Everleigh suggested. "We can talk about this more in depth. If you don't have any plans, you're welcome to join us for dinner."

After agreeing to a time, Declan stood up. "I know you have to get ready for your class."

"I'll see you later."

She awarded him a smile. "Thanks for your help."

He smiled. "I'm happy to help."

As she prepared dinner, Everleigh recalled the many times she'd asked her mother about the identity of her father when she was growing up. All Deloris would ever tell her was that he'd died before she was born. She never pressed her mother for more information because it always seemed to upset her.

Two weeks before her death, Deloris had unburdened herself.

"Your father is James Ray Powell," she had revealed.

Everleigh swallowed hard, then asked in a disbelieving voice, "You're talking about the serial killer?"

Her mother gave a faint nod, which seemed to sap her strength.

Everleigh felt her knees go weak, like she was going to collapse. She practically fell into the chair by her mother's hospital bed.

"Did you love him?" she asked with a shaky voice.

"Love him? No... He raped me, Evvie... He would've killed me..." Her mother's voice warbled with emotion, the words taking most of her strength. "That night, all I could do was ask the Good Lord for help. I fought him with everything in me but he overpowered me. When it was over, I got to the gun my daddy gave me and started shooting... I don't know if I hit him. He ran off. Never knew his identity until I saw his picture on television after he was arrested sometime later. God protected me from a worse fate."

Deloris rested a moment before continuing. "It's not something I ever wanted to talk about or even tell you…" Her eyes watered.

"Evvie, I just couldn't take this to the grave. Had to clear my conscience. I want you to know that it doesn't matter who fathered you. I loved you from the moment I found out I was pregnant. When they placed you in my arms, my heart leaped with joy."

Then, Deloris had drifted off to sleep, the medication finally melting away her pain.

Everleigh didn't doubt her mother's love, and she hated that Deloris had been weighed down with this secret for so long. Her mother never intended to tell her about Powell, but for some reason, she'd changed her mind at the end.

Humming softly to soothe herself, Everleigh checked on the chicken breasts in the air fryer. It wouldn't be long before they were ready. She glanced at the clock on the wall. Declan was due to arrive within the next fifteen minutes.

"Mama, who's coming to eat with us?" Rae

asked when she strolled into the kitchen. "You put three placemats on the table."

"A friend from the university. His name is Professor Blanchet. He and I have some business to discuss afterward, so I need you to go on and get your bath out of the way. Pick out what you want to wear to school tomorrow."

"Mama, I wanna sleep in your room again."

"That's fine, sweetie," Everleigh said. The truth of it was that she would sleep better with her daughter right beside her.

She checked on Rae a few times as she prepared dinner and did a cursory sweep of her house. There wasn't a speck of dust to be seen; her home looked picture-perfect. She returned to the kitchen and wiped down the counter for the second time. Or was it the third? Cleaning often aided in calming her nerves.

This wasn't a social visit, Everleigh reminded herself. *I'm not looking to impress him.*

The doorbell sounded a couple of minutes after 7:00 p.m.

She walked briskly to the well-lit foyer, then peered through the peephole before opening the front door.

"Welcome to my home," Everleigh said, stepping aside to let Declan enter.

Her daughter joined them in the foyer, sparking a hint of amusement in his expression.

"This is Rae."

Declan smiled. "It's very nice to meet you. I'm—"

"*Perfessor* Blanchet," the little girl said, finishing for him. "You work with my mama."

"Beautiful and brilliant," he said.

"Yes," Rae responded with a grin.

Everleigh gestured for him to follow her into the living room. A charcuterie tray and plates were sitting on the coffee table. She placed some meat, cheese and a couple of crackers on a plate for Rae, who then sat quietly beside her.

Everleigh and Declan made small talk while nibbling on the appetizers. She forced her body to relax. It had been a while since she'd entertained such a handsome man. He didn't come off as flirty. Just professional.

He had changed into a pair of jeans and a black sweatshirt with the university logo emblazoned in red. She'd been given one just like it, only hers was in a vivid shade of red with the logo in black.

She stood up and said, "I need to check on dinner. I'll be back shortly."

Everleigh zipped into the kitchen, retrieved

the pan of yeast rolls from the oven and placed it on a warming rack. She swept crumbs from the counter into her hand to transport them to the sink.

Ten minutes later, they gathered around the dining room table.

Rae volunteered to bless the food.

"Amen. Great job," Everleigh said when she finished.

Her daughter kept the conversation lively while they ate.

"Do you like being a *perfessor*?"

"I do," Declan responded. "I enjoy teaching."

"My teacher is mean," Rae announced.

Everleigh chuckled. "No, she's not. Miss Davis is just a bit strict."

Shrugging, her daughter responded, "She don't know how to have fun. I miss my old teacher, Miss Pitts. She was funny and she liked to sing."

They chatted for a bit about Rae's school and her favorite songs. Then, taking a decisive bite, Declan said, "Dinner is delicious."

"Mama's a real good cook," Rae stated. "You have to eat her oatmeal-raisin cookies and her choc'late peanut-butter brownies. They're so-o-o good."

He grinned. "I'll have to remember that."

Everleigh kept her gaze on her plate, not wanting to become absorbed in Declan's attractive features. However, she took pride in her cooking skills and was glad he seemed to be enjoying his food.

When they finished eating, Everleigh and Declan carried the plates into the kitchen. She quickly rinsed them, then placed them into the dishwasher.

After sending her daughter upstairs, she said, "I never mentioned that you were also a police detective. I didn't want to confuse Rae."

"I figured as much," he responded while leaning against the island countertop. "Oh, there weren't any matches on the prints."

"Because that would be too easy," Everleigh muttered almost to herself.

They walked the short distance to the living room and sat down to finish their conversation.

"You may be right about the individual not knowing where you are. Right now, it seems you're safe."

"I hope it stays that way."

"Tell me everything you know about your mother's encounter with Powell," Declan said.

"I don't know very much," Everleigh responded. "He attacked her and if she hadn't been able to get to the gun she kept in her nightstand, Powell most likely would've killed her. Because she never pressed charges, the police didn't know that she was another victim who'd survived his death sentence." She looked Declan in the eye. "I really don't want this getting out to anyone. I especially don't want Powell learning that he has a daughter and granddaughter out here."

"I'll do what I can. But if we have to get the police more officially involved…the truth is going to come out, especially if arrests are made."

"I really don't want to think about that right now." Everleigh was mostly concerned about what this would do to her daughter. Families of violent criminals were often ill-prepared to deal with the complex set of emotions that come with being related to a murderer; and then there were accusations and threats by those seeking justice. People that would send letters like the one she received.

"I checked on Wyle Gaines. He left his job at around the same time you left Savannah."

A wave of anxiety washed over Everleigh. "Do you know where he is?"

"I don't, sorry."

"So what are you thinking, Declan?"

"At first, I liked Wyle for this. I'm not as sure now. I don't believe he had anything to do with the deaths of Powell's relatives, and that bothers me."

"Then you don't think they were random?" Everleigh asked.

"I don't," Declan said. "My gut is telling me there's something bigger at play here."

"So while it's possible that he could've sent the letter to me as an isolated incident, there actually *is* someone out there killing Powell's relatives?"

He nodded. "I believe there's a vigilante on the loose."

"It must be one of Powell's surviving victims," Everleigh replied. "Or a family member of a victim. Wyle is manipulative, a thief and a liar, but he isn't a killer. I still think he's capable of sending a threatening letter, however."

"I'm going to look into the family members of the victims."

She smoothed a hand over her hair. "Declan, I know we don't know each other well, but I really appreciate you helping me out like this. I didn't know who to ask, but I've heard nothing but good things about you around the campus. I really believe that you're the right person for this."

"I'm honored you feel comfortable enough to trust me with this."

"So what happens next?"

"I'll keep looking," Declan replied. "And if something's there, I will find it."

"I need to check on my daughter. I'll be right back."

He smiled and nodded.

Upstairs, she found Rae in bed playing on her tablet. "You're supposed to be sleeping," Everleigh said.

Rae looked up. "Can I play for a little longer please?"

"Okay. But when I come back up—it's lights out."

Rae sighed. "Okay Mama…"

Everleigh kissed her daughter on the forehead before returning downstairs.

"That little girl does not like going to bed before ten o'clock."

"I was just like that when I was a kid," Declan responded.

Thinking back to the reason for his being there, Everleigh said, "This probably sounds terrible but I was really hoping you'd find Wyle's prints on that letter. It's not that I want to... I'm not sure what I'm trying to say."

"You would rather it be him because the alternative is much worse."

"Yes. That's it exactly."

"Either way, you don't have to face this alone," Declan assured her.

She was comforted by his words, and their conversation turned to something more pleasant. The university. They talked about their experiences teaching, their students and classes. When Everleigh looked up at the clock, she was surprised to see the time ticking closer to eleven. She felt her cheeks grow hot with embarrassment for having monopolized his time for so long. "I didn't realize it was so late already."

He stood, too. "Yeah, I'd better get going. I know it was for a grim reason, but I enjoyed tonight. Thank you for a wonderful evening, Everleigh."

"I want you to know that you're my first dinner guest."

Declan broke into a grin. "Wow. You honor me once again."

Everleigh walked him to the door.

"Go through and make sure the windows and doors are locked securely," he said.

"I will," she responded. "That's my nightly routine. I'm also setting my alarm."

After Declan left, Everleigh made sure everything was secured before arming her security system.

Upstairs, she found Rae in the middle of her king-size bed fast asleep. Everleigh stood there watching her just like she had when she was a baby. Both then and now, her daughter's safety was her primary concern.

Everleigh took a quick shower, leaving the bathroom door wide open, then joined her daughter in bed.

She closed her eyes and tried to relax. A tremor exploded through Everleigh as thoughts about Declan flooded her mind. She was grateful that she didn't have to navigate this situation alone. Just before the winter break at the university, he'd been nothing more to her than a member of the faculty. But now, she was beginning to consider him a friend, a confidant.

Everleigh hoped Declan would be able to figure out everything without having to put on an official police-detective hat.

Chapter 3

Declan felt himself smile as he drove home from Everleigh's. He'd learned a lot about Dr. Taylor just from the decor. Large cranberry-hued curtain-framed windows welcomed in natural light. He'd read somewhere that individuals exposed to natural light on a daily basis experienced fewer headaches, and less eye strain and blurred vision. Her beige sofa was plush and comfortable with several throw pillows in neutral colors. An overstuffed matching chair with a rich cranberry-red throw folded over the arm sat near the cream-colored stone fireplace. He knew that neutral colors had a calming effect on a person. It was obvious that Everleigh relished a life that wasn't hectic or crowded. She used her environment to help usher in a sense of peace all around her.

On the drive back to Charleston, Declan recalled how much he'd really enjoyed spending time with the beautiful professor and her daughter. He found Rae delightful. But the evening also reminded him of what was missing in his life. He was forty years old. Declan wanted to start a family while he was still physically able to enjoy spending time with them.

It was clear that Everleigh and Rae lived alone. He'd heard that Everleigh was a widow, and he felt a touch of sadness when he thought of sweet little Rae growing up without her father. Declan vowed to protect them both to the best of his ability. However, he feared that meant he'd eventually have to make the investigation an official one. The only reason he hadn't thus far was because there was no obvious connection in the deaths to prove serial killings. Sure, the anchor point was that the victims were related to Powell, but there weren't any other letters like the one Everleigh received. Declan knew she didn't want people knowing about her relationship to Powell, and as much as he wanted to respect this decision, his priority was their safety.

An image of Everleigh formed in his mind. She had a really beautiful smile. It was funny that he'd never noticed it before, but then they hadn't had much interaction in the past. Declan especially enjoyed watching her with Rae. She seemed to be a very loving mother and he could see that they were close.

Dinner with them had offered him a preview of what life might look like if he got married. Declan had never been opposed to the idea—he just hadn't found the right woman. At one point, he'd thought he met her, but no... He'd never been more wrong. He'd ended up with a broken heart and had taken the past couple of years away from dating to heal.

Declan cautioned himself not to think about Everleigh in this manner. She was only interested in his help.

Not his heart.

Still, he found himself attracted to her courage and strength. Everleigh wasn't a wilting flower, shrinking in fear. Instead, she wanted to face this threat head-on. Declan was still smiling as she continued to dominate his thoughts. Her warm and friendly manner was contagious.

Declan could only describe the feeling he got when they were together earlier as *coming home*. He felt like a different person. He forced her out of his mind because he wasn't looking to get involved with her. He was committed to keeping Everleigh and her daughter safe.

★ ★ ★

The next morning, Everleigh dropped Rae at kindergarten, then headed back home since her first class wasn't until ten. Since she had some time on her hands, Everleigh searched her brain for a way to show gratitude for Declan's help.

She recalled his mentioning at a faculty brunch how much he loved the combination of chocolate and peanut butter. Rae had mentioned it as well when he had dinner with them. She decided that her chocolate peanut-butter brownies would be the perfect gift.

Humming softly, she walked into her kitchen and grabbed the ingredients, then set them on the island counter, where a rack of copper pots and pans dangled overhead.

Everleigh mixed ingredients in a purple ceramic bowl with a large wooden spoon. She found herself glancing around, eyeing the items she could use as weapons if necessary. Everleigh was determined that fear would not take control of her life. It was normal to feel afraid in the presence of real danger. But it would not overtake her.

Steam wafted from the coffee maker behind her.

Everleigh stopped long enough to pour her

second cup of coffee of the morning. She leaned back against the counter, savoring the French-vanilla flavor and admiring the new dishware arranged neatly on the open shelves. A clear stand held knives and shears with purple-and-chrome handles.

Bananas, apples and oranges intermingled with miniature boxes of raisins looked picture-perfect in the chrome wire-framed basket in the center of the island. A calendar marked up and color-coded with appointments, events, school holidays and special reminders popped up on the touch screen of her refrigerator.

If only I could check that letter off my list as solved. She'd like nothing better than to be on the other side of this situation, but until she was, Everleigh vowed to keep life normal for herself and Rae. She refused to be a victim.

She poured the batter into a baking dish and placed it in the oven. Everleigh set the timer, then rushed up the stairs to shower and dress for work.

The brownies were done shortly after she came back down, dressed in a black pencil skirt and matching jacket, a lavender silk blouse and a pair of black boots. She left the house twenty-five minutes later, heading for the university.

At the university, Everleigh waved at another faculty member on her way from the parking lot to her office. She stopped at the nameplate fastened to the wall with her name engraved on it. She unlocked the door, then opened it and entered.

A desk and rolling leather chair greeted her warmly. Everleigh loved teaching. She loved her job. In one corner of her office sat a box containing extra office supplies. The only things on her desk were a printer, calculator, phone and a couple photographs of Rae. Her laptop was in her tote—she carried it home with her every day.

Everleigh glanced out the window, watching students as they gathered in small groups to chat or made their way across campus to their next class.

A chill snaked down her spine when she spied a tall man in black hoodie and sweatpants beneath a nearby tree. He seemed to be watching the building. From a distance, he looked like Wyle.

Everleigh turned and strode toward the door. She rushed outside, only to find the man was gone.

Her eyes traveled the area, searching. She saw

several students dressed in dark hoodies. Her anxiety high, Everleigh forced herself to relax. She glanced around a second time.

No sign of Wyle.

She went back to her office.

Everleigh removed the container of brownies from her tote, then checked her watch. Declan's next class was in forty-five minutes. She wanted to catch him before it started.

Leaving her coat draped over the back of her chair, she started toward his office.

She almost turned around, worried he might misread her intentions. But, no, she was being ridiculous.

He's a smart man. Declan will know that this is just a token of my appreciation. He's not expecting anything more from me.

She paused outside of his office and took a deep, cleansing breath.

Declan was just finishing up with office hours. He'd walked one student through an extra credit assignment to help her make up for an exam she'd failed and shared tips on criminology careers with another. This student was a little older than the undergrads he'd met with so far, maybe in his thirties.

Of average height and build, he looked as if he took great care of his body. Athletic and possibly military judging from his cross-cropped haircut and posture.

"I just wanted to introduce myself, sir," the man said. He pushed back the hood of his thick gray sweatshirt. "I'm Aaron Edwards. I'll be starting here in January and I'm planning to take your class next semester. I just got out of the military a few months ago—military police."

"Thank you for your service to this country, Aaron. It's nice to meet you. You sound like a man who knows exactly what he wants."

"I've always wanted to be a criminologist."

"I look forward to having you in class," Declan responded.

He smiled. "Same here, Professor."

He walked the younger man to the door, intending to head out to teach his next class.

Everleigh was in the doorway. He broke into a grin.

She smiled at Aaron as he exited, then turned a bigger smile on him.

"I wanted to show my appreciation for your help, so I baked you some brownies." She held out the container to him.

"Chocolate and peanut butter?" Declan asked, sniffing.

"Yes," she responded. "I remembered you mentioning that you love chocolate and peanut butter during the brunch last month. Then when Rae mentioned my cookies the other night at dinner, you seemed to light up."

"That's because chocolate peanut butter anything are my favorites. Thank you," Declan said, smiling. "I'm not sure they're going to make it by the time I leave for the precinct after this class."

Everleigh chuckled. "As long as you enjoy them."

"How are you doing?" Declan asked. "Really?"

"It depends on the hour," she replied with a slight shrug. "For the most part, I find myself constantly looking over my shoulder. More than usual. Like, I was looking out my office window when I saw this guy in a black hoodie and sweatpants. Somehow, I thought it was Wyle. I went out to confront him and the guy was gone."

"You're going to find students in dark hoodies all over the campus."

"I know," Everleigh responded. "The only

reason he stood out was because he seemed to be watching the building."

"Are you sure it was Wyle?" He made a mental note to check to see if Wyle was still in Savannah. As long as he hadn't left town, Declan could rule him out as a suspect.

"I wish I could say that I am, but no. I'm not sure."

"I am going to do everything in my power to keep you and Rae safe."

Everleigh eyed him. "Thank you, Declan. I've been wondering if Wyle is planning to blackmail me with the information he has."

"I've been thinking about that myself and I checked on something. Powell has been incarcerated in a maximum-security prison outside of Reidsville, Georgia, for almost thirty-one years. He hasn't had any visitors in the past year. I don't think he and Wyle could have been in touch."

"I hope you're not thinking of going down there to talk to him," she uttered. "I don't want him knowing anything about me or my daughter, Declan."

"I understand, but you should be prepared in case the truth comes out."

Everleigh gave a slight wave of her hand in

dismissal. "I don't want to think about that right now." She folded her arms across her chest.

He nodded. "Gaines might have conducted a search on real estate. He could have found you that way. He might also have found you on the university's department page."

She sighed. "This is my first teaching job," Everleigh stated. "I worked as a psychologist for a counseling center in Savannah. I've done that since graduating from college. The minute I have an online presence, he found me.

That's one of the reasons why I'm not a fan of social media."

"It certainly works in your favor," Declan stated.

"Hopefully, all this might turn out to be nothing," she said. "That's my prayer."

"Mine, too. Thank you for these brownies."

Everleigh glanced up at the clock on the wall. "I guess I'd better get out of here. I need to get to my class before my students or I'll never hear the end of it." She slipped the tote on her shoulder. "Please let me know if you learn anything more."

"Will do," Declan agreed.

He sat the brownies down on his desk, then left his office. As much as he wanted to sample one, Declan decided to exercise self-control and wait.

When class ended, so did his self-control. Declan opened the Tupperware container and bit into a brownie. He closed his eyes, his tastebuds exploding with delight as he chewed. He quickly devoured a second one as he walked in quick strides toward the faculty parking lot. His entrance into the police precinct fifteen minutes later was met with friendly smiles and nods as he made his way to his office. He waved in passing to a sergeant as he strolled by his open door.

He'd come in an hour earlier to get a head start on his day. Declan wanted to make some calls regarding Powell. He needed to find out as much information about his victims and their families—all of them, including the ones who survived.

What stumped Declan most was how the connection to Everleigh was made. Especially since no one outside of her parents knew that Powell was her father. Her mother must have confided in Wyle. It was the only theory that made sense.

Chapter 4

Knowing that Declan was looking into the letter had placed Everleigh somewhat at ease. In the short amount of time that she's spent with him, she could tell he was definitely a "protector" type. Her late husband had been, too, which led to him becoming a firefighter—a job that cost him his life.

Declan was handsome—she'd always been attracted to men with bald heads, neatly trimmed beards and mustaches. She didn't *want* to like him in that manner, though. The last thing on Everleigh's mind was a relationship. Her focus was on keeping Rae safe while trying to find out who wanted to harm them, and then making sure they were comfortable in their new lives here. Because even under different circumstances, she wasn't interested in a relationship with someone with a high-risk job.

Everleigh ushered the last student in her class

to the door, then made her way back to her office. She slumped down into her office chair and dug into the insulated lunch bag she'd stashed under her desk that morning. Sighing softly, she put up her feet on the cushioned stool below her the desk as she ate her sandwich.

It had been a long morning. She'd finally convinced herself that she'd dreamed up the vision of Wyle on campus. From there, she'd gone from talking a student into believing that she could pass the upcoming final if she put more time in studying and taking good notes, to advising another that he needed to rewrite his final paper before the due date. Between classes and appointments, Everleigh managed to offer advice to a coworker who wanted to think that the assistant football coach half her age was sincere in his pursuits. She'd advised the woman to take things slow.

Excitement did not bubble in Everleigh's chest as she popped the lid off the container of raw carrots. She'd rather have had a large bag of potato chips to eat with the accompanying ranch dip, but she was trying to change her eating habits. Her recent birthday had her thinking seriously about the importance of a healthy lifestyle. Everleigh was satisfied with her weight—she had a high metabolism, which kept her looking trim, but there were some creases, wrinkles and folds that hadn't been there in her younger years.

She bit into the carrot stick, chewing thoughtfully as she took a moment to distance herself from the contents of the letter she'd received, to form an unbiased analysis.

Wyle Gaines wasn't the person who'd sent the letter. The sender was angry; the individual couldn't get to Powell because he was in a maximum-security facility, so they'd decided to take another route. Everleigh had recently lectured on displaced anger, which happened when someone directed their hostility away from its cause toward something or someone else.

She had explained to her students that the source of most displaced anger stemmed from adverse childhood events, which caused a disruption in a person's healthy emotional development and regulation. The sender could have experienced abuse or bullying. In some scenarios they might even have been a witness or victim of extreme violence.

As a therapist, Everleigh had dealt with clients experiencing displaced anger. They came to see her to learn how to manage their frustrations, to disengage from difficult situations. She knew how to handle a situation like that, but none of her clients were ever violent or threatening.

That wasn't to say she didn't know how to deal with scarier situations. Deloris had enrolled Everleigh in self-defense classes when she was younger. Deloris had insisted on her staying in karate all through her teen years. With her black belt, she could handle herself. She also had weapons, if need be. Everleigh possessed two bats and she was adept with a knife and Taser. She kept several Tasers hidden around her home for protection. She also had her mother's gun, but Everleigh wasn't a fan of firearms. Deloris's gun was packed away with some of her things in a local storage facility. She wasn't quite ready to get rid of her mother's stuff.

Everleigh glanced at the clock on her office wall, then dropped her feet to the floor. She had to meet with two more students and teach another class before she could leave campus for the day.

While her time was still her own, Everleigh left her office to visit the bookstore. There were a couple of orders waiting for pickup.

On the way back to the social-sciences building, Everleigh pulled out her ringing cell phone.

Without looking at the screen, she said, "Professor Taylor speaking…"

She heard heavy breathing on the other end.

"Wyle, this isn't funny."

Everleigh hung up. The number wasn't local, and the area code wasn't a Georgia one, but she was pretty sure it had to be him.

Frustrated, she dropped her purchases in her office before walking briskly to the classroom. Everleigh took several calming breaths while waiting for students to arrive.

She liked being punctual, so once everyone was seated, Everleigh dove right in. "Last week we discussed the seven approaches to the study of abnormal psychology—"

A shot rang out. Glass shattered and someone screamed. Everleigh shouted to her students, "Get down!"

They dropped to the ground, taking cover where they could. Anxiety fluttered in her chest and her heart jolted. "Remember the active-shooter protocol," she said. "Stay down and move toward the exit doors."

She was about to step out of her room when the building's security guard arrived, his face set with determination as he motioned for her to stay down and away from the door. Drawing his gun, he cautiously eased the double doors of her lecture room open.

The shooter fired a second shot.

"Someone is shooting into my class," Everleigh said.

The guard signaled for her and the students to stay low and get out. "Keep the students inside the building."

She did as instructed.

The exits had all been locked so no one could enter without a key.

Everleigh urged the students to find a safe place and stay there. Another faculty member directed them to the auditorium.

A third shot rang out...

Everleigh quickly ushered the frightened students to the auditorium, her voice trembling as another gunshot sounded.

Amidst the chaos, she heard a pounding on a door at the entrance. She saw a student with a cast on his foot outside, stark fear etched over his face. Adrenaline coursed through Everleigh's veins as she rushed forward to assist him into the building. She quickly slammed the door closed, locking it once more.

She waited for the ringing in her ears to stop, the light-headedness to pass and the knot in her stomach to ease. She stood trembling against the wall.

"Was anyone hurt?" someone in the vicinity asked.

"That last bullet hit one of the huge pots in the front," the young man wearing the cast responded shakily.

Thirty minutes passed without gunfire.

Everleigh ventured outside with a member of security, her gaze falling on the shattered remains of a terra-cotta pot that had been knocked off its perch by a bullet. Jagged shards of clay littered the sidewalk, while mangled leaves from the plant lay scattered around it like casualties of war. She wanted to close her eyes and pretend it was all a bad dream, but she couldn't.

Someone had just tried to kill her.

Where is Rae?

She had to get to her daughter. The college had activated their active-shooter safety protocols, but she had to find out if her daughter was safe. Security urged everyone to stay away from the doors and windows, so she crept carefully back to her office and called the school.

"Hey, this is Everleigh Taylor. I just wanted to check on Rae. Is she okay?"

"Oh, she's fine. Her class just came inside for snacks."

"That's great. I'll be there within the hour. I'm picking her up early today." Her appointments and class were canceled for the rest of the afternoon.

Everleigh hung up, then walked over to the campus police officer waiting to speak with her. She wanted to get this over with, so she could get to Rae. It wouldn't take long because there wasn't much she could tell them.

She wanted desperately to believe this was some random shooting, but Everleigh knew better. This, coupled with the sighting of Wyle on campus… The two had to be connected. Maybe he was willing to kill for her mother's house after all.

Declan received an alert about the shooting and was headed back to the campus. A black truck sped past him toward the university exit, but he wasn't able to catch a real glimpse at the Maryland license plate.

Students were running, panic and fear written all over their faces. Campus security was all over the grounds.

Declan released a sigh of relief when he found

Everleigh inside the building talking to a couple of campus police officers. He quickened his steps to join them.

"Are you okay?" he asked.

"I'm a bit shaken, but I'm fine."

"Was anyone hurt?"

"No, thank goodness," she responded. "Class had just started when two bullets came through the window. The third was fired at the front of the building. Officer Mack was just saying that it was most likely a random shooting." Her expression told him that she believed otherwise, but didn't want to say too much around the campus security officer.

When the officer walked away, Declan pulled her off to the side where they couldn't be overheard. "I think it's time we make this investigation official. Especially if someone just fired shots at you."

Swallowing hard, she gave a slight nod. "I know. I'm thinking Wyle is behind all this. I wasn't sure earlier if I'd really seen him, but now I'm convinced it was him. Probably wanting to scare me."

"Why don't I drive you home?" Declan suggested. "You can leave your car here." Everleigh was trying to display a calm he knew she didn't currently possess. She was playing with her wedding rings and her eyes darted from person to person.

"You don't have to do that," she said. "I have to pick up Rae from school. I can go to the precinct now if it's not going to take too long to file a report."

"It won't. I'll get you in and out as quickly as I can."

She gave him a tiny smile. "Let me check to see if I can leave."

Everleigh went to speak with the campus police before walking with Declan to the faculty parking area.

He followed her to the precinct and parked beside her.

"What if we're wrong about this?" she said as they approached the entrance. "Maybe the campus police were right. It could've been someone just firing a random shot. I'd rather not waste time filing a report."

"I only have to look in your eyes to know that you don't really believe what you just said. Everleigh, you're scared."

"I... You're right. I'm scared, Declan. But I'm not going to let anyone have that kind of power over me. I'm also angry."

"Would you consider teaching virtually? We can also arrange for police protection around the clock for the next forty-eight hours and re-evaluate the threat after that."

"I guess I don't have a choice," she responded. "I'd like to keep Rae in school, though. If I have to take her out— I can tell you that she's not going to be happy about this. My daughter's a social butterfly."

Declan smiled to reassure her. "I'm hopeful that it won't be for too long, but I think it's best she stay home with you."

"Okay. And I'd like to help," Everleigh stated. "I can't just sit and do nothing. I intend to find out everything I can about Powell and his victims—at least the ones we know about. I can't help but wonder if there are others who survived his attack but didn't report it."

"No other women came forward during his trial," Declan responded. "I checked."

Everleigh paced in the waiting area while he went to speak with one of his colleagues. Her eyes traveled to the American flag, Rotary Club plaques and framed map of Charleston County hanging behind the huge desk with a glass partition. Two officers, one male and the other female, were sitting at the desk and checking in visitors.

Public bathrooms and water fountains were situated to Everleigh's left. On her right, a door with a keypad and electronic lock led deeper into the precinct. It was the door Declan had disappeared behind.

Phones rang, the officers talked in quiet tones, keyboards clicked and the shuffling of paper echoed in the sparsely decorated waiting room. Her nostrils caught a whiff of sweat and body odor from a homeless man as he walked past her.

Everleigh glanced up at the clock on the wall, wishing Declan would suddenly reappear. Every time the electronic door clicked and opened; her hopes were dashed when it wasn't him.

Hip-hop music seeped out of the earbuds of a woman who was seated in front of her. Every now and then, Everleigh heard a police radio shrieking interlaced with a baby crying. A couple behind her were embroiled in a heated argument she hoped wouldn't soon get out of hand.

She'd begun to experience a jittery sensation and the hair at her nape stood at attention. Someone was watching her.

Everleigh's gaze slowly traveled her surroundings. Her body stiffened when she found the homeless man staring in her direction. He gave her a toothless grin.

She awarded him a small smile before looking away. She didn't want to provoke him if he was violent, or insult him if he was harmless.

As soon as Declan walked out, Everleigh jumped up and met him halfway. "I'm so glad to see you," she whispered. "That homeless man has been staring at me since he sat down."

"Did he say anything to you?"

"No, he just sat there looking. If I looked in his direction, he'd grin."

"That's Ralph. He's been here a few times," Declan said. "His things are always stolen whenever he stays at the mission. He comes to file a report."

"So he's more of a precinct regular," Everleigh responded. "Does he have any family?"

"He's in here at least once every other week. As for family, I don't think so. After his wife died, he just kind of lost himself."

"That's so sad," she murmured.

Keeping his voice low, Declan said, "I spoke to my supervisor, who contacted the chief on the island. There will be an officer parked outside your house while you're in what's considered a high-threat situation." He led her to a conference room. "I'll work on your report in here. I'll also email a copy to the precinct on the island."

"I really can't believe this is my life right now," Everleigh stated when Declan finished with the report. "My mom didn't like me working at the counseling center. She thought it was dangerous."

He got up, retrieved two bottles of water and handed one to her. "Is that why you decided to change careers?"

"Not at all," she answered. "After my mom died, I just felt like I needed to do a complete reset with my life. I wanted to start over fresh."

"I get that. I felt the same way but for different reasons. I wanted to find a way to help and educate people. I enjoyed mentoring young men, so teaching seemed the next step for me."

Declan filled out the report as they talked. When they were done, she asked, "Do you like being a criminal investigator?"

"I do. I love it," Declan replied. "I studied criminology because I love science, psychology and law—I'm able to combine all of them in my job.

I've always been interested in the causes of

crime and ways to prevent and control it—that's why I majored in criminology, and I also have a degree in criminal psychology."

"Where the focus is on studying the thoughts, feelings and behaviors of criminals," Everleigh responded. "There was a time when I was interested in forensic psychology, but as you can imagine, my mother was totally against it. Now that I know what happened to her, I can understand her reaction. I always thought she was being too overprotective…bordering on being a helicopter mom." She released a sigh. "I should've known it ran deeper than that. She was dealing with trauma."

"I hope you're not carrying any guilt over this. Because it's not your fault, Everleigh."

Looking up at him, she replied, "Maybe I could've helped her."

"She didn't want you to know."

Declan escorted Everleigh outside to her vehicle. "I'm gonna head over to the island to the station. I want to meet with the officers personally."

"Thank you for everything."

Everleigh left the parking lot. She noticed a

black SUV that pulled behind her, and admired the glossy richness of the color.

She picked up Rae twelve minutes later from school.

"Mama, can I play on your iPad?"

"Hello to you, too."

"Hey, Mama," Rae responded, a sheepish grin on her face. "Sorry."

"That's better," she said. "It's in my tote back there."

It wasn't until Everleigh took the exit toward the freeway that she spotted the same SUV behind her.

Are they following me?

She glanced into the rearview mirror, making sure Rae was secured in her seat. She then gave the command. "Call Declan."

When he answered, she asked, "Where are you?"

"I'm at the Angel Island precinct. Have you made it home yet?"

"There was a black SUV behind me when I left the precinct. It's still behind me," Everleigh said, keeping any emotion out of her voice. She didn't want to scare her daughter.

The SUV was now directly behind her.

She increased her speed.

"I'm about to cross the bridge."

"Come to the precinct," Declan instructed. "If they're still behind you, I can take it from there."

"Okay." She eyed Rae in the rearview mirror.

The little girl's attention was glued to her iPad game.

"I'm about to cross the bridge. I'll see you soon."

The SUV inched closer—too close for comfort.

Everleigh increased her speed, hoping to put some distance between herself and the SUV. She was relieved when another vehicle separated them. She sped up and went around a bus.

She took the exit to the precinct and didn't bother slowing down. The best thing that could happen in this moment was running into the police.

The SUV was back behind her.

Everleigh scanned the parking lot of the precinct when she arrived and quickly spotted Declan standing beside his car.

She hastily parked in the space next to him

and cast a furtive glance back, watching as the suspicious vehicle slowly drove past the entrance.

Declan got into his car, then called her cell.

All he said when she answered, "I'm following you home."

Everleigh took a deep breath and responded with a trembling wave of relief, "Glad to hear it."

"Mama, what are we doing here?" Rae asked, looking around. "We're at a police station."

"No reason. It's the wrong address," she responded. "We're heading home now."

"Good. I'm hungry."

Everleigh forced a smile at her daughter in the rearview mirror. "We'll be home soon."

As she steered them home, she noted that Declan was a car behind them, but she viewed every dark SUV as suspect. She conjured the image of the vehicle that had followed her. She was sure there had been a single person in the car, a man.

Wyle Gaines. It had to be him.

"Mr. Declan just pulled up behind us," Rae said. "I didn't know he was coming over. Do you have more business?"

"We do," Everleigh responded. "He's going

to have dinner with us, too. What do you think about pizza?"

"I want cheese pizza," she stated, sparking laughter.

"I already know that. I'll order a small one for you. I'm getting my usual veggie pizza."

Rae made a face. "Yucky."

Everleigh chuckled as she let her daughter out of the vehicle.

"Mr. Declan, I hope you like veggie pizza," Rae said when he entered the house behind them. "Mama does, but she's ordering me a cheese pizza."

"It doesn't matter to me," he replied with a smile. "I love any kind of pizza."

"Seriously, you can order whatever you like," Everleigh said.

"I'm good with the veggie pizza."

Rae entertained Declan by giving him the highlights of her day at school while they waited for the food to arrive.

"And Mandy...she was mean to me so I'm not her friend no more. I'm not gonna be mean back, but it makes me sad because God wants people to love each other."

"Yes, He does," he responded. "I know He's very proud of you, Rae."

"I'm proud of God, too." Rae got up and stalked into the kitchen. "Mama, if the food don't come soon, I'm gonna starve."

Everleigh glanced over at Declan, who was wearing a look of pure amusement on his face before he smiled down at her daughter. "Sweetie, it'll be here soon. There's a packet of sliced apples in the refrigerator. That should hold you over until the pizza comes."

"Thanks, Mama."

At the sound of the doorbell, Declan said, "Pizza's here." He gestured for Everleigh to let him get the food.

After they ate and Rae was settled for the evening, Everleigh and Declan spent most of the night searching for information on the victims and their families.

"James Ray Powell kidnapped, raped and murdered numerous young women during the 90s and possibly earlier," Everleigh stated. "After his arrest, he confessed to killing thirty women, but I'm sure the true number of his victims is higher."

"Lena Jones survived Powell. Back then, she was the only one willing to talk about her experience," Declan added from what he was reading. "She recounted how she woke up to find him standing over her. Lena stated that the only reason she was left alive was because of her roommate's boyfriend. They came home in the middle of the attack. He pulled Powell off Lena but wasn't able to stop him from escaping."

"I think you should talk to her."

"She's on my list," he responded. "She gave a couple interviews, then testified in court. After that, Lena requested that she be left alone. There are no photos of her on record to protect her identity. That was the only way she'd agree to testify."

"Her face was blurred on television," Everleigh said. "I can certainly understand why she'd want privacy."

"There's a chance that she may not want to relive that period of her life, if and when we're able to locate her."

Everleigh picked up one of the throw pillows, hugging it close to her body. "I know, and we'll have no choice but to respect her wishes."

"I asked you this before, but do you think Wyle would take things this far?" Declan asked.

"I didn't initially," she murmured. "But now... I don't know."

"Nothing in his background makes him good for this. But when someone is desperate..."

"I guess I want it to be him because if it's not, the alternative is just too scary to think about." She held back a shudder. "Did you find anything else?"

He nodded. "As far as we know, this is the first victim," Declan said, handing over a file. "Hazel Claire Baisden. She died thirty-eight years ago, leaving behind three children, now ages forty-two and forty. The oldest son died in a car accident last year. Another is a New York police officer and the daughter is a schoolteacher in Los Angeles. I looked them all up."

"What are your impressions of her children?" Everleigh asked.

He thought for a moment, then said, "If it's not Wyle, then we're looking for someone who hasn't been able to move on from the loss of their loved one. But in this case, I honestly don't think it's either of Baisden's two surviving offspring."

Everleigh agreed. "The individual is most likely consumed with anger, probably have been in trouble with the law... I believe this is something that he or she has been planning for a long time. I hate to say it, but none of this sounds like Wyle. If he's involved at all, we're actually dealing with two people."

"I agree. Our assailant is organized and determined." Declan met her gaze. "This person is not going to give up. The shooting on campus was just practice."

Everleigh felt a shakiness in her limbs, her heartbeat raced and her adrenaline spiked. She got up and began to pace. "We have to find Wyle and whoever else is after me."

"I'm going to do everything I can."

She nodded. "I know you are. I just don't like feeling like I'm trapped. I'm not sure whom to trust."

"You don't have to worry about any of your students. They don't fit the profile," Declan said.

Everleigh was surprised to hear this. "You've already checked? I have well over a hundred students."

He nodded. "None of them are connected to any of the victims."

"That gives me some relief." Frowning in confusion, she added, "I just can't figure out Wyle's connection to all this. If there isn't one, then how did they find me?"

"With technology, people can find pretty much everything about a person."

"Which is exactly why I'm not on social

media," Everleigh stated. "I find it too invasive. Still, I'm in no way connected to James Ray Powell."

"I can't figure that one out myself. Your mother must have told someone else outside of you and Wyle. Regardless of how they found out, they're a threat," Declan said. "That's why a cruiser will be parked out front throughout the night."

"Thank you for getting all that set up. I believe Rae and I will be fine, but having police parked outside the house makes me feel a bit more secure. However, my neighbors will most likely have some concerns."

"Who knows, they may feel more secure as well."

She grinned. "I hadn't thought about it that way. Our neighborhood's pretty quiet for the most part. Everyone parks in their garages— any cars in the driveway or parked out front belong to guests."

They stared at one another, and Everleigh felt her heart beating rapidly. She sat there trying to analyze what this was—a shared moment or just an awkward pause between them.

"I want you to know that you're not alone,

Everleigh. We can get through anything you're facing—we can do it together."

She watched him, studying his expression. It was almost as if Declan could read her mind; he somehow knew exactly what she was feeling in that moment.

Declan smiled then, stirring something within her.

They let the conversation drift back to lighter topics for a bit, then he stood up a few minutes later and said, "I guess I'd better get out of here."

Everleigh walked him to the front door. "I'm really glad I don't have to deal with this by myself."

"I'll see you tomorrow."

When Declan left, Everleigh prepared for bed.

Rae was asleep in the middle of Everleigh's bed, so she made herself comfortable on a chaise lounge near the bedroom window. She turned her attention to her laptop screen. What little information Everleigh was able to find on Powell's family wasn't very helpful. She sat back, feeling overwhelmed. It saddened her that innocent members of his family had possibly died simply because of their association to the serial killer.

She wondered if Powell knew about the letters. Or if he would even care about what was happening? Everleigh found a documentary on him that could be streamed online. She knew so little about this man, so she fetched her headphones and settled in to watch it.

Narcissistic rage was a dangerous trait. James Ray Powell had a distorted worldview, an enlarged sense of entitlement and, because of deep-seated issues of rejection, he wanted to make people pay.

Powell grew up in a middle-class home, wanting for nothing in terms of material possessions and opportunities. He was shy and socially awkward. After Powell was arrested, police found a 100,000-word manifesto on his computer, documenting various personal slights and instances of rejection. Some were small and simply a part of growing up.

Powell described feeling jealous whenever so-called friends didn't pay attention to him as much in a group, and documented his struggles with self-esteem. He also described in detail the moments where he was rejected romantically, and was bullied in school.

As Everleigh watched the documentary, she noted that Powell never saw a problem as his fault. There didn't seem to be any moments of introspection or self-awareness. Instead, any and all blame was placed on others—women in particular. It was their rejecting him that had fed his anger.

It sickened her that this man had fathered her. That she was conceived out of a such a heinous criminal act. Everleigh thought about a former client who became pregnant as a result of rape. The woman worried if she'd ever be able to love her child.

Everleigh had told her that God was able to take the worst this world had to offer and make hope and new life. She reminded her client that God was able to create resurrection out of a murder on a cross. She assured the woman that God could create a beautiful child out of the violence she'd suffered. In this very moment, Everleigh had to take her own words to heart, and allow them to soothe and comfort her.

Powell himself was interviewed for the documentary, and he stated that he did everything he could to get women to like him, that their negative response to his efforts led to the destruction of his life and that by denying him the affection he desperately craved, they'd created the monster he became.

Studying his actions and body language, Everleigh watched Powell's attempts to ingratiate himself with the interviewer. She struggled with separating the man from his crimes. More than that was the shocking realization that his eyes, nose and mouth were mirrored in her own. Her father, a serial killer, was looking at her each time she looked in a mirror.

When the documentary ended, Everleigh agreed with the diagnosis of narcissistic personality disorder. Powell displayed five of the nine established traits of narcissism. As for her, she felt nothing for him. No yearning to meet him. He was a dangerous man and not someone Everleigh wanted in her life or Rae's.

"Dear God, I know You and I haven't spent much time together since Britt died, but please don't let Powell find out about Rae and me," she whispered. "And keep us safe from whoever does know and wants to do us harm." Every time her husband had left for work, she'd prayed, asking God to keep him safe. She felt betrayed when Britt died saving a young boy. She'd been told that he was able to hand off the child, but found himself trapped.

Everleigh's eyes filled with tears as she thought of Britt alone in that burning house. She was proud of his heroic efforts, but there was a part of her that was angry that he hadn't thought of his own safety. Guilt seeped from her pores because of it.

She swiped at her eyes. "I just want all this to end. And everybody responsible—I want them found and locked up. We've been through enough, God."

Chapter 5

Declan decided not to leave Angel Island right away. Despite the cruiser outside the house, he felt the need to see for himself that Everleigh and Rae were safe, as he'd promised. He sat there for nearly two hours, but found nothing unusual and no one lurking around the neighborhood.

The island had always been a pretty little coastal town, and was growing in popularity. One of the main attractions was the low crime rate, along with the picturesque beaches, quaint neighborhoods and unique boutiques downtown. It was in close proximity to Hilton Head and Polk Island.

He paused to have a conversation with the police officer guarding the house before heading back to Charleston.

Once he was home, Declan checked on Everleigh and Rae via text.

Declan: Hey, it's me. How are things?

Everleigh: We're good. About to call it a night. Police are outside.

Declan: See you tomorrow.

Everleigh: Thx again.

Declan walked into his family room and sat down on the leather sofa. He eyed the jigsaw puzzle he'd started on a few days ago. He often turned to puzzles for stress relief.

He sat down and began putting the pieces together, but his mind wasn't on the puzzle—he was thinking of Everleigh.

There was an undeniable connection building between them, forcing him to concede the truth—he couldn't ignore the deep feelings he was developing for Everleigh. They weren't going away anytime soon.

Declan hadn't looked forward to their evening coming to an end. He'd enjoyed spending time with her and Rae. Everleigh possessed a warm, loving spirit and was always smiling. He loved her humor and the sense of freedom she seemed to have in her life, even in her current situation. But as strong as his attraction was to her, Declan would never act on those feelings.

With Everleigh at the forefront of his mind, he couldn't fully concentrate on the puzzle so he gave up for the night.

Declan made his way to the second level, where his bedroom was located.

He lay in bed thinking about Everleigh and the feelings she ignited in him. Although she was a widow, he could tell that in her heart, she was still very much a married woman. Declan was here to do a job, so he had no choice but to wrangle in his emotions.

"Somehow she knew she was being followed," he said. "Look, we're really gonna have be careful. She's talking to the cops."

"H-How do you kno…kn-know? The shots on campus could've come from a-anybody… and nobody was hit."

"She works with a detective or criminologist—the way I figure it, she must've told him about the letter. He followed her home tonight and then stayed for a while. I left when a cop arrived. Don't know if the dude left. He might still be there."

"Maybe they're d–dating," his brother said. "She's not a bad looker."

Shrugging in nonchalance, he uttered, "Don't matter to me. If he gets in the way, we'll just get rid of him, too."

"The daughter was in the car. I n–never agreed to anything about k-killing a child. That little g-girl is innocent."

Fury spread through him. "That girl has Powell's blood running through her veins. We said we were gonna take out the entire blood-line."

His words were met with silence. After a moment passed, he said, "Look, I don't like the idea of hurting a little kid, either, but she is his future."

"I don't like it," his brother responded.

"The decision's already been made. We're keeping to the plan."

"Whatever, man… I hate talking to you wh-when you're like this."

"I'm just following the plan," he repeated. "You should do the same."

Everleigh sat in her home office munching on a dill-pickle spear. As she chewed, her mind turned to her upcoming online lecture on borderline personality disorder, or BPD. In her career as a psychotherapist, she'd treated several people with BPD.

People suffering from the disorder experienced an intense fear of abandonment, instability, inappropriate anger, impulsiveness and frequent mood swings. There were several serial killers diagnosed with BPD. Powell was a narcissist. He didn't have this disorder.

Her doorbell camera app popped open on her screen.

It was Declan. He'd mentioned he might come by when they spoke earlier.

She walked up to the front door and opened it. "Hey...come on in."

"I sent you a text that I was on my way. I figured you were still in class."

She glanced up at Declan and smiled. "Done for the day. Are you hungry? I made a sandwich for Rae, but she wanted a hot dog."

"Sure," he responded, following her into the kitchen.

Everleigh retrieved the sandwich from the refrigerator and placed it on a plate with a pickle and some chips. "For some reason, I didn't think you had a class today."

She put it on the table in front of Declan.

"I don't, but I'm meeting with a student in an hour. I wanted to check on you and Rae first."

"We're fine," Everleigh responded, while trying to sound calmer than she actually felt. "Thankfully, everything has been quiet so far."

They settled in across the table from each other.

"I watched a documentary on Powell last night," she announced.

Declan eyed her. "Thoughts?"

"I'm glad he's in prison."

"He was given life without parole."

"He deserves it," she replied. "He's not repentant at all. He believes the victims got what *they* deserved. He actually said that women created the monster in him."

"People like him don't accept responsibility for their actions."

"You're right."

"Had you looked him up before now?" Declan asked.

"No, not until last night." She gave a slight shrug. "I don't know why I did it. It wasn't out of any special *feelings* toward him. That documentary confirmed one thing for me. I definitely don't want him in our lives. However, I really don't think it'll be much of a problem if he does find out. The one thing that came across the documentary and his interviews— James Ray Powell doesn't care about anyone other than himself."

Declan and Everleigh sat there talking for the next twenty minutes. He always enjoyed their conversations outside of the investigation.

"I'd love to hear your perspective on something," she said. "There's a scripture in Exodus about God punishing the children and their children for the sin of the parents to the third and fourth generations. Do you believe in intergenerational punishment for sin?"

He responded almost instantly, "Deuteronomy 24:16 says 'The fathers shall not be put to death for the children, neither shall the children put to death for the fathers: every man shall be put to death for his own sin.' Also, Ezekiel 18 is very clear on this. Guilt belongs to the person who sinned, not their family."

"Whoever is trying to kill me obviously believes otherwise," Everleigh said. "I know there's been trauma, but this is also misplaced anger."

"They're bound to make a mistake, and then we'll catch them."

She nodded in agreement. "That's what I keep telling myself. But then I think about the members of Powell's family—the ones who didn't deserve to die just because they were related to him. Whoever is doing this is no better than the man he despises."

Everleigh glanced down at her watch. "I guess I'd better get back to the computer. I have one more class."

"How's it going?"

"Teaching via video is a little weird, but my students are game for it and I don't mind too much. If you don't have anything else to do, feel free to hang out." Her smile was warm and inviting.

"Sure. I'd like that."

Everleigh appeared more relaxed around him than she had before. He hadn't expected to be awestruck by her beauty and warmth, which he found incredibly inviting. She had a way of looking elegant in everything she wore; from a suit, to a pair of jeans and a sweater. Declan liked to see her with her hair down, but whenever she was on campus, Everleigh kept her glossy tresses secured in a ponytail or bun. This awareness of her, even the unfamiliar urge Declan had to stare at her, was unlike him. It unsettled him whenever he was in her presence. He wasn't just attracted to her physical beauty; he was attracted to her mind. Declan was a man of faith and he liked that it was something they had in common.

At the end of her class, she rejoined him in the family room.

"Do you have any plans for the weekend after next?" he asked.

Everleigh shook her head. "What's up?"

"I'd like to take you and your daughter to the annual Christmas Festival on Polk Island. But only if there's no other incidents."

She grinned. "Sounds wonderful. Rae would love something like that, but I won't mention it until I know that we're going. Thank you for thinking of us, Declan. I've heard a lot about Polk Island but we haven't gone over there yet."

"You'd love it. It's a lot like Angel Island, but lots of tourists. However, it's very family-oriented."

"There will be rides, games and lots of other attractions."

"That's perfect. She doesn't care much for Ferris wheel-type rides, but if they have a merry-go-round, she'd be okay with that."

"There's a lot to see in Charleston, too," Declan said.

"Maybe you can show me around," Everleigh murmured.

"Definitely."

"This feels nice," she said after a moment. "This is the first time I've felt pretty normal since this whole nightmare started."

"I'm glad. Maybe after today, they might give up."

"That would be wonderful, Declan, but I'm sure you know better than that. They're too invested now."

Everleigh was right. He didn't believe the assailant had given up on killing her. That was why he wanted to keep her close by. Or so he told himself. That all of this was about keeping Everleigh and Rae safe from harm.

He and Everleigh had grown closer—things were good between them and Declan never wanted to tamper with that.

Chapter 6

Everleigh was up early the next morning because she hadn't slept well during the night. Every couple of hours or so, she'd ease out of bed to see if the police vehicle was still parked outside. She also checked for any unfamiliar cars in the neighborhood. Everything looked normal, but Everleigh couldn't afford to let down her guard.

She returned to bed and eased under the covers next to Rae, hoping to catch one more hour of sleep before starting her day.

An image of Declan's handsome face swam before her, along with the unexpected impact of his beautiful dark eyes.

Everleigh was a widow. She still mourned her husband. She definitely wasn't interested in dating, but she welcomed his friendship. She hadn't really made any friends locally, focusing instead on helping Rae settle in and excelling at her new job at the university.

Sleep continued to elude her so Everleigh gave up. She got out of bed and padded to the shower.

She dressed quickly without disturbing Rae and went downstairs to the kitchen.

Everleigh had just finished making breakfast when she received a text from another member of the psychology faculty. Robin Rutledge and her husband lived nearby. Everleigh didn't know her well, but she knew they were expecting their first child. She responded quickly and headed to the front of her house.

"I thought you might want to check out this new textbook on abnormal psychology," Robin said when she arrived. "Fall semester next year, I'll be teaching parapsychology. I saw that you'll be teaching Abnormal Psychology Two."

They taught classes on parapsychology here? That surprised her a bit. Everleigh had no desire to explore this area of psychology, which involved psychic phenomena such as telepathy and telekinesis. She accepted the book, then said, "Thanks."

"I noticed the police car out front. Everleigh, is someone really after you?"

After the shooting, Everleigh had had to explain to her department head what was going on. She'd asked that the word be spread quietly among other faculty members.

"We're thinking it might this guy that befriended my mom—he got very upset with me when I refused to sell him the house. I knew it the moment I met him that he was manipulating her."

"Is there anything I can do?" Robin asked.

"Just be on the lookout for strangers in the neighborhood."

"I'll let my husband know as well. He gets up all times of the night to walk the dog."

"Thank you, Robin."

Placing her hand on her swollen belly, the other woman added, "I'll be glad when this little one gets here."

"You don't have much longer."

"Six weeks."

There was a time when Everleigh thought she'd expand her family, but Britt's death changed that for her. She was grateful to have her daughter, but she'd never wished for Rae to grow up an only child. Perhaps the Lord had other plans.

After Robin left, Everleigh prepared a plate

and a large cup of coffee, then took it outside. The night before there had been a male officer.

"There must have been a shift change," she said. "I was expecting to see the officer that was here all night."

"Yes ma'am. I'll be here until three o'clock."

"Thank you for your service and especially for making sure my daughter and I are safe."

"It's my duty, ma'am." Accepting the food and coffee, she added, "Thank you for this. It smells delicious."

"Declan told me that there will be someone patrolling the area at night. I wasn't sure there would be anyone here during the day. I don't recall seeing anyone out here yesterday"

"There was a special duty officer here. They were in plain clothes and not in a cruiser."

She nodded in understanding. "I don't suppose there has been any movement in the investigation." It was a statement rather than a question.

"Well," Everleigh continued, "If you need anything, please just ring the doorbell."

The officer smiled. "Thank you, ma'am."

Back inside, Everleigh turned on the alarm. She loved the design of her house and the amazing view of the ocean from her kitchen, sunroom and patio. Everleigh had fallen in love with the home the first time the Realtor had brought her to see it.

She also had a view of the garden that they'd planted. The only thing missing out back on the sprawling deck was an outdoor kitchen. Everleigh wanted to have one built before the summer. She enjoyed grilling when the weather was warm.

Everleigh turned away from the window.

Her eyes traveled from the faux-finished stucco walls to the hand-painted breakfast table and chairs to the plush overstuffed sofa. She glanced down at the glossy hardwood flooring throughout the main level.

An hour later, Everleigh heard movement upstairs and searched out Rae. She found Rae in own bedroom with a book.

"Good morning, sweetie. What are you reading?" she whispered against her cheek.

"Umm… I'm just looking at the pictures. Will you read it to me?"

"How about you read it to me after breakfast?" she responded. "I made pancakes."

Nodding, Rae said, "Okay, but you have to help me."

"I'd be happy to, sweetie. You want to help me make the scrambled eggs?"

"I do. Yay!"

"Go wash your face and I'll get your apron," Everleigh said.

"I want my chief hat, too."

She laughed. "You mean your chef hat."

"I'm so happy," Rae announced when she walked into the kitchen.

Everleigh smiled. "So am I."

"Mama, why are you happy?"

Rae's question caught her off guard. She presented herself as if she didn't have a care in the world, when she was wavering somewhere between fear and anger. But somehow Rae was picking up on positivity Everleigh hadn't noticed in herself, too. "Because I have you," she responded. "Because I have my life, a job I really like… What about you? Why are you so happy?"

"Because you're my mama. And because my daddy and Grandma is watching over us in heaven."

"That's a great reason to be happy." Rae's happiness mattered to Everleigh.

"I'm also happy because it's gonna be Christmas."

She helped her daughter with her apron. "We can't forget that, huh?"

Rae shook her head. She planted herself on a stool. "Mama, it's gonna be a good one. You'll see."

"I know it will," Everleigh said. "Because I get to spend it with you."

She placed a plastic bowl in front of her daughter and handed her a whisk.

"Did you see the policeman outside our house?" Rae asked. "I saw him from the window upstairs. I think he was tired and he needed a nap."

She released the breath she'd been holding, grateful that her daughter didn't seem fazed by a police cruiser parked outside. "It's a woman officer." Everleigh retrieved the eggs and milk from the refrigerator.

"We should take her some food. She might be hungry."

"I already did."

"She might still want some pancakes," Rae said.

Smiling, Everleigh observed her daughter as she cracked three eggs into the bowl. Then she poured milk into a measuring cup and handed it to Rae. "You're so much like your daddy. He was always so thoughtful. He'd put the needs

of others before his own. He was a wonderful man."

"Grandma told me that Daddy will always
live in my heart."

"She was absolutely right about that," she responded. "And so will Grandma. She will live
in our hearts forever."

"Mama, I like Mr. Declan. Do *you* like him?"
Rae asked as she whisked the contents in the
bowl into a creamy mixture.

"Yes," she answered. "He's a really nice
man."

"A girl in my class has two daddies," her
daughter said. "Do you think one day I'll get
another one?"

Stunned by the question, Everleigh asked,
"How would you feel about that?"

Rae shrugged. "I don't know. I guess it'll be
good."

"Right now, we're just going to focus on
getting settled in this house," she said, pouring
the egg mixture into a frying pan. "It's almost
Christmas and we haven't put out any decorations yet." She thought it best to try to keep
things as normal as possible for Rae.

"Is that why I'm not going to school again?"

"No, that's not the reason. I spoke with your

teacher and we're going to try something new. You're going to be able to stay home but you'll be able to see everyone through the computer."

"Why?"

"We're trying it out. Remember, I'm even trying it with my class."

"But why?"

"It's a test run, Rae. That's all."

After breakfast, Everleigh set up her personal laptop. "See, there's your teacher..."

She waved, then said, "Everybody's at school but me."

"Okay, I need you to pay attention, sweetie."

This was the second day and she had already run out of excuses. Everleigh had no idea how much longer she would be able to keep Rae in the dark.

The weather became gloomy later that evening.

Thick, black clouds trundled in over the city. Lightning erupted as heavy layers of cold rain poured down, turning the sidewalks and streets to puddles. The temperature dropped as gusts of wind swept in, foreshadowing an early winter storm.

Everleigh turned away from the window. She

walked over to the sofa and sat down beside her daughter.

"I don't like when it rains. The thunder is scary," the little girl said.

She wrapped an arm around Rae. "I know, sweetie. But there's nothing for you to be afraid of—it's only rain."

Outside, the wind continued to shriek, and the rain poured down as if it had a point to make.

Truthfully, Everleigh didn't like bad weather, either, but she wasn't fearful of rainstorms.

"Why don't we get ready for bed?"

"Mama, come with me."

Together, they went through the house checking the windows and the doors. Everleigh was careful not to trigger the alarm. Then they retired to her bedroom.

She checked her messages while Rae took a bath. When the lights flickered, Everleigh pulled out a flashlight from a drawer in the nightstand. She also pulled out a couple of emergency candles and a lighter.

"Mama..."

"I'm coming, sweetie."

Everleigh crossed the room in quick strides.

She helped Rae dry off with a fluffy towel. "You smell like bubble gum."

Rae giggled. "*Strawberry* bubble gum."

After her daughter was settled in bed, Everleigh turned on the television. "The lightning and thunder have stopped, so we can watch a little TV."

"Yay!"

Her daughter fell asleep within the hour, leaving her to finish the animated movie they were watching alone. Everleigh went downstairs to get a bottle of water when it ended. Before going back to her bedroom, she stole a peek out the living room window.

A police cruiser slowed as it passed her house. The forty-eight-hour watch was over, so they were no longer camping outside the house but drove by several times throughout the night.

She suddenly had disturbing quakes in her body, but didn't fully understand why. Everleigh did one more walk-through for her own peace of mind.

There was a car parked at the corner, but other than that, she didn't notice anything or anyone. All the Tasers in her home were fully charged; there were items she could use to fend off an attacker hidden throughout and a very nice bat under the sofa and another one under her bed.

Everleigh had just slid under the covers when her phone started to vibrate.

It was Declan.

"Hey, did you get any rain in Charleston?" she asked when she answered, keeping her voice low so as to not disturb Rae.

"It was pouring down earlier. I think it's down to a drizzle now. Did I call at a bad time?"

She eased out of bed and made her way quietly over to the chaise. "No, your timing's perfect."

"I wanted to check in with you before calling it a night," Declan said. "Make sure everything is fine. I know the police are doing drive-bys every thirty minutes or so."

"All is well over here. Windows and doors are secured, the alarm is on..."

"Good."

"Don't you dare drive to the island to check on us," Everleigh said with a chuckle.

"Wow. You're getting to know me pretty well."

"Seriously, stay home. We're fine." She didn't want Declan going out of his way for them—he'd already done enough and she was grateful.

"I'm a phone call away," he said. "I don't care about the time. Seriously, call or text if you need me."

"I will, Declan."

"How is my little friend?"

"Sleeping soundly," Everleigh responded. "She doesn't like storms so she had a little anxiety earlier."

"I won't keep you."

"Thanks so much for calling."

"Do you mind if I come to the house tomorrow after work?" he asked.

"Rae and I would love to see you." Everleigh enjoyed Declan's company.

When they hung up, she glanced down at her wedding rings. "Britt, I miss you so much. Rae misses you, too." She paused a moment to gather her thoughts. "I really wish you were here. Someone wants to harm us... You'd know exactly what to do."

An image of Declan formed in her head.

"This guy...his name is Declan. He's been looking into this threat, so I don't have to deal with it alone."

Everleigh released a sigh. "Oh, Britt... I have to let you go."

She peeked out her window, then got up and

headed back to bed. She needed to get some sleep. Morning would come quickly.

He let out an impatient sigh. They had been parked on that corner for nearly an hour.

"Man, what's w-wrong witcha?" his brother asked. "You over there huffin' and puff...puffin' like you itching to blow s-something down."

"We could go in there and take care of them right now. What we out here waiting for?"

"W-We have to be careful, man."

"Ain't nobody watching the house anymore," he said.

"I don't g-guess you haven't noticed the cop that d-drives by every thirty minutes. She also upgraded her security system."

"How do you know?"

"When I came by here the other d-day, I saw the van pa...parked out front," his brother responded.

He laughed out loud. "That won't stop us."

Just then a police car turned on the street.

They ducked down in their seats.

"That's the second time that cop done come down this street. You see how he slows down when he gets to her house. Let's get out of here," he said when the cruiser disappeared.

"I don't have a good f-feelin' about this, man."

Muttering a string of profanity, he started the car. "I'ma listen to you this time. But as soon as I get the chance, I'm taking them out."

"I can't believe that you haven't eaten at Vanny's Place before," Declan said as they pored over a couple of menus, Everleigh had retrieved from a drawer in the kitchen. "It's an Angel Island staple."

"It was on my list to try," Everleigh responded. "We just hadn't gotten around to doing so."

"Do they have macaroni and cheese?" Rae asked from where she was seated on the couch in the family room.

"They do," he answered. "And it's delicious."

"I hope it's as good as Grandma's. She makes the best. Even better than Mama."

Declan swallowed his amusement. "Oh."

Everleigh laughed. "She's right. Mine doesn't compare to my mother's mac and cheese. She would never tell me her secret ingredient. One day Rae and I will figure it out, though."

She glanced down at the menu, then said, "So what do you recommend we try?"

"The rigatoni with shrimp, mushrooms and

peppers is one of my favorites," he said. "Another is the liver and onions."

"Do they have chicken?" Rae asked. "I like fried chicken."

Everleigh surveyed the menu. "They have it, sweetie. You can get a drumstick with mac and cheese and broccoli."

"Yay. That's what I want. And lemonade."

Declan tried not to stare at Everleigh while they waited for their food to be delivered. She was stunning. "Oh, I checked up on Gaines and looks like he moved out of his place. His neighbor said Wyle told him that he had to leave town and wasn't sure when he'd be back."

"I'd bet money that he's in Charleston," she responded.

Fifteen minutes later, the food had been delivered and they sat around the dining room table.

Everleigh blessed the food before they sampled their meals.

"Declan, everything smells delicious."

Fork in hand, he replied, "Wait until you taste it."

"Do you have any kids?" Rae asked.

"No, I haven't been blessed in finding a wife

yet," he responded. "But I hope to have some one day."

"Oh," the little girl murmured.

She sounded so disappointed, Declan thought to himself.

"She doesn't have a lot of friends," Everleigh explained.

"I'm not a kid, but I'd love to have you as a friend," he said. "You and your mom both."

Rae beamed. "Yay. I like friends."

Thank you, Everleigh mouthed to him.

"Did you move here because of the job?"

Nodding, she replied, "I'd made up my mind to relocate but I wasn't sure where. Then the offer came to teach…so here we are. What about you. Is Charleston where you grew up?"

"No, I'm originally from Columbia. I ended up here for the job, too."

"What do you do for fun?" she asked.

"I love spending time at the beach or a lake pretty much anywhere."

"You're a water baby…" Everleigh said. "That's what my mother used to call people who love being around water."

Declan chuckled. "Yeah that's me—a true water baby."

Pointing to the macaroni and cheese, Rae stated, "Mama, you gotta try it. It tastes almost like Grandma's."

Everleigh stuck a forkful into her mouth. "Oh, my goodness. This is delicious. You're right. It *does* taste like hers."

"Did your mom put cayenne pepper in hers?" Declan asked.

"That's it." She looked at him. "How did you know?"

"I asked the chef after the first time I had it. She told me that she uses Colby, cheddar, Monterey Jack cheese and cayenne pepper."

"We make ours with all those—I just never knew about the cayenne pepper. Mystery solved."

"We make a great team," he replied.

To Declan's delight, she agreed.

"Thank you both for having pity on me," he said after wiping his mouth on a paper napkin. "I didn't want to eat alone."

"Mr. Declan, you don't have to eat by yourself," Rae responded. "You can eat at our house all the time, can't he, Mama."

She smiled. "You heard my daughter. Feel free to join us when you can."

Breaking into a grin, he said, "Don't play...
I just might take you up on that."

"We welcome the company."

Her words touched Declan to the core.

Chapter 7

After dinner, Rae wrangled the adults into watching a Disney movie with her.

"You have gone above and beyond the call of duty, Declan," Everleigh said appreciatively. "And you've been such a good sport about it."

"I enjoy spending time with you and Rae. She reminds me so much of my great-niece Halle."

"As soon as I get Rae settled for the evening, we can discuss your findings if you don't mind sticking around," Everleigh whispered. She didn't want her daughter overhearing that part of their conversation.

"I'm good," Declan responded. "I don't have any other plans for the evening."

"You've been such a good friend to us. Rae's been through a lot to be so young. The loss of her father and then her grandmother..."

"She's not the only one. You also suffered those losses."

Everleigh nodded. "This is true. It's just that she's a little girl."

"Does Rae talk about her father much?" Declan asked.

"Yes, she does. When she brings him up, she talks about him being in Heaven with God. It's the same with my mom, too. Rae truly believes that her father and grandmother are with the Lord. It seems to give her a measure of peace."

"And you?"

"It's the same for me," Everleigh replied. "My husband loved God—so did my mother. I am confident that they will spend eternity with Him."

She allowed Rae to watch one of her favorite cartoons before announcing, "Time for bed. C'mon, let's go upstairs."

"Okay." She glanced over at Declan and smiled.

"G'night, little lady," he said to Rae.

Giggling, she replied, "Good night Mr. Declan. I hope you'll still be here when I wake up in the morning."

Everleigh hoped he didn't hear her sudden intake of breath. Her daughter had no idea the impact of her words. Rae liked Declan and it was possible that she'd begun to see him as a father figure.

She wasn't sure how she felt about this. Everleigh tabled the thought for now. They had more pressing matters to contend with, like finding Wyle. She hoped he was able to fill in some of the blanks.

Throughout the evening, Declan could hardly keep his eyes off Everleigh. He gave himself a mental shake and told himself that he needed to rein in his emotions.

From outward appearances, Everleigh looked fragile, but he knew she possessed a quiet strength—one of the many qualities that drew him to her, despite his resolve to keep their relationship platonic. She was the only woman Declan had felt connected to in a long time— she made him feel things that had been long forgotten.

"Baby girl is all settled in bed," Everleigh announced, walking briskly into the family room. She sat down on the sofa.

"I checked in with the police department on the island. There's been a car with Maryland tags in your neighborhood a few times. They could be visiting someone on your street."

"That's most likely the reason," Everleigh said. "If they were there for us, I'm sure we would've known by now. It's not Wyle. His drives a BMW and has Georgia tags."

"Well, tonight I'll probably drive around and do my own surveillance."

"Declan, you don't have to do that," she quickly interjected. "That's too much."

"I told you that nothing was going to happen to you and Rae on my watch. I meant that."

"My neighbors do have guests from time to time. I don't want to become paranoid. I refuse to live my life that way."

"I agree with you, but you have to remain vigilant. Don't let your guard down. If you feel like something's not right, we need to check it out."

"I just don't want you to start feeling as if you're chasing your tail."

"We've established that there is a valid threat against you and Rae," he responded. "The letter, the campus shooting and that SUV that followed you…"

"I guess I'm wavering in denial."

"I'm still looking for Lena Jones."

"She's most likely still in hiding," Everleigh said. "I don't blame her."

"At least there haven't been any more deaths in the Powell family," Declan stated. "At least none that we know about."

"And nothing to connect the three that were found."

He leaned forward, resting his elbows on his knees. "Tell me everything you know about Wyle and your mother's relationship."

"They worked together at the hospital—different departments," Everleigh said. "They would have lunch together and that soon progressed to dinners, the theater and even church."

"Was his interest in her romantic?"

"She said it wasn't—that they were just good friends. They used to talk on the phone for hours. They had similar interests. At least Wyle made her believe that they did. He knew about my mom's cancer before she told me. My suspicions grew when he began taking an interest in her finances."

"What exactly did he want to know?" Declan asked.

"She sought his advice about investments and stocks. I walked in one day while they were discussing it. My mom was about to hand over five thousand dollars for him to invest—I don't know in what, but I put a stop to it right then and there. I could tell Wyle wasn't pleased. I knew that he wasn't to be trusted."

"He's an amateur, so he's bound to make a mistake. I intend to be around when he does." Declan stood up. "I guess I'd better get out of here. I want to do a little surveillance of my own."

They bid each other good-night, and Declan whistled softly as he made his way to his car.

Forty-five minutes later, he was cruising past Everleigh's house with a coffee in a to-go cup. There were no cars on the street. No signs of anyone walking around.

He was grateful everything was quiet.

Declan liked that Everleigh wasn't the type to panic without reason, but he hoped she wouldn't be naive enough to think the danger had passed. There wasn't any record of violence in Wyle's background, but he had to consider that the man just hadn't gotten caught. Perhaps he was waiting for the perfect opportunity to make his move.

Everleigh woke with a start. She sat up, looking around in the dark and listening.

She picked up her tablet and checked the security cameras. Some of the tension in her shoulders melted away when she saw a police cruiser drive by.

Just as Everleigh was about to lie back down, the alarm began emitting the words, "Glass break."

"Mama," Rae shouted, startling awake.

"Honey, it's okay." She picked her up and said, "Barbie's in trouble." Rushing into Rae's room with her daughter in her arms, she asked, "You remember what you're supposed to do, right?"

The little girl nodded, hurried into the closet and hid inside the toy chest.

Everleigh armed herself with the Taser from her nightstand and waited a few minutes in the hallway before descending the stairs. Rae was supposed to call 911 and leave the phone on. There was an officer already in the neighborhood so it shouldn't be a long wait for help to arrive.

She didn't hear any movement—only deafening silence.

When she glimpsed an officer approaching the door, Everleigh rushed down the stairs to open it.

She sagged with relief. "My alarm just reported a glass break. I decided to wait for you before I investigate. I had my daughter hide. She's the one who called 911."

"That was a wise choice, ma'am," he said. "You stay in here and I'll check."

Everleigh nodded.

When the officer returned, he told her, "Someone threw a rock and it hit one of the windows in the back. It's gonna need replacing. Might've been some kids playing around. We try to keep them off the beach this late at night…"

"You didn't see anybody then?" she asked.

"No, ma'am."

"Thank you for checking—I'm relieved that it's nothing more," Everleigh said. "My little girl is hiding so I'd better go up and assure her that we're safe."

He smiled. "Yes, ma'am. I'll be right out front for the rest of the night. I'll keep checking the back of your house as well, but I suggest you get some motion lights."

"I agree."

After locking the door, she hurried up the stairs. "Rae, honey. Come on out. Everything is okay."

"Mama, did someone try to—"

"No," Everleigh interjected. "Some kids were throwing rocks and one hit our window. The police officer came and checked everything. He said he's going to keep watch for the rest of the night. There's nothing to worry about, sweetie."

"I did everything you told me to do."

"You did a great job. I'm so proud of you."

"Can we go back to bed now?" Rae asked.

Everleigh gave a nervous chuckle. "We sure can, sweetie."

The edges of night rolled back, giving the sun entrance. She lay in bed, still unable to fall asleep. Her daughter hadn't had a problem, however.

She eased out of bed and crept over to the window. The cruiser was outside.

Everleigh showered. She dressed in a pair of gray jeans and a thick burgundy sweater. She combed her hair, then pulled it into a messy bun.

Downstairs, she made herself a cup of tea, then sat down in the family room. Everleigh wrapped herself in the warmth of a throw.

She didn't realize that she'd fallen asleep until

she woke up to Rae cuddling beside her on the sofa.

"Sweetie, what are you doing up so early?"

"I woke up and you weren't there. I came looking for you."

Everleigh placed an arm around Rae. "You want to go back up to bed? I'll go with you."

"I wanna stay down here with you."

Her internal clock went off two hours later, waking Everleigh.

"It's time to get moving, Rae. I'll make breakfast while you get dressed."

"Okay, Mama," Rae murmured, rubbing her eyes and yawning. "Is the test over? Do I get to go to school today?"

"No, because it's Saturday, sweetie."

"I can't wait until Monday. Then I'll see my friends at school."

"Lord, please let this be over soon," Everleigh prayed, when Rae went upstairs to her room They would soon take a break for the holidays and it couldn't come quick enough for her.

Chapter 8

Everleigh took one look at Declan's face when he arrived Monday afternoon and asked, "What happened? I can tell by your expression that something's wrong."

"Powell's niece was found dead in Maryland on the same day someone shot at you. Around the same time, actually."

She considered his words. "So are you thinking that we were wrong? Or that this was a coordinated attack?"

"It's possible that Wyle was the shooter on campus, trying to scare you. But even if that's the case, there *is* an assailant targeting Powell's family," Declan responded. "I have to say that this investigation is becoming more convoluted by the minute."

Massaging her forehead, Everleigh said, "I don't know what to think right now."

"We have to seriously consider that if Wyle

Gaines is involved, he's somehow connected to another assailant."

"How was she killed? Powell's niece."

"She was shot twice. But no letter was found at the crime scene. The police are now looking to determine if all the murders are connected because of the victims' relationship to Powell. They're considering that there's a serial killer targeting the family but need some solid evidence."

"Declan, maybe we're overreacting about all of this," Everleigh said. "If someone other than Wyle was really after me, why haven't they made a move? They've had several opportunities to do so."

She didn't want to believe that a serial killer was targeting her and Rae.

"I don't think we're wrong," he answered. "Powell's relatives are not dying of natural causes. There is a real threat out there."

A chill snaked down her spine. "I knew you were going to say that."

"I pray I'm wrong, but I don't think that I am, Everleigh."

"In the meantime, I don't want to risk any of the students or other staff members getting harmed. There are only a couple days left before the holiday break. If this isn't resolved, I think it's best that I ask for a leave of absence until this is settled. Rae has another week but I'm keeping her home with me."

"I know you don't like it, but this is a really good idea," Declan responded.

She sat down to make the necessary phone calls. Declan leaned back in his chair and did some work on his phone.

Two calls later, she said, "They're emailing me the paperwork."

"That's good to hear."

"I already spoke to Rae's teacher, too. She won't be going back to school until I know that we're safe."

"I'm sorry, Everleigh."

"You don't have to apologize. It's not your fault. I just hope you find whoever is responsible. I don't want them controlling my life like this."

"I hope you know that I'm doing everything I can."

She smiled softly at him. "I don't doubt that. I don't guess you know about the little scare we had last night."

His expression quickly turned to one of concern. "What happened?"

"Someone was throwing rocks and one hit my window," she stated. "It set the alarm off. There was an officer in the neighborhood... I think his last name was Lee. He checked inside and around the back." Everleigh shrugged. "I don't think it was really anything, but I had Rae hide in her closet."

"Do you really believe that this was yet another random incident?" Declan asked.

She shook her head. "Robin's husband installed some motion lights in the back of the house this morning. The rock—that sounds more like Wyle. Psychological torture—I can see him doing something like this. He's more into the head games."

"I'd like to pin all this on Wyle, but we can't dismiss what's happening to the people related to Powell," he said. "We can't definitively prove that the deaths are all related yet, but my instincts tell me they are."

"I'd rather be cautious, trust me. I won't risk my daughter's safety. I hope you find Wyle soon. I'd like to know his connection in all this."

"The thing that bothers me most is that there haven't been any letters found with any of the victims. It doesn't make sense to only send a letter to you and not the others."

"It's possible they threw them away," she responded. "I almost threw mine away, but it felt real, so that's why I took it to you. They could've easily dismissed it."

"I thought about that, especially since they could've previously experienced harassment about because of their relationship to Powell. There was an interview with his sister. She received death threats for months right after he was arrested. She said her parents received them as well. Just so you know, I sent copies of the letter to all the investigators."

"I hope it helps them." Everleigh folded her arms across her chest. "Any updates on Wyle?"

"He's officially a person of interest now. If he's in Charleston, we will find out soon."

"Good," she replied. "It's time we get answers."

Everleigh turned off her computer monitor after her noon class ended. She didn't mind teaching virtually, though she'd enjoy it more under different circumstances. Part of it was having to deal with Rae.

"Mama, I'm bored," her daughter said from the doorway. "I wanna go outside."

"Honey, I'm sorry, but you can't. We need to stay inside the house."

"Why?"

"It's too cold outside."

"No, it's not."

"Rae, I'm not going to argue with you about this. I said no and I mean it."

Everleigh was a woman who loved the outdoors. She wasn't happy being a prisoner in her own home. Clearly, Rae wasn't happy with the changes, either.

"Why don't I make us some lunch," she offered, getting up from her desk.

In the kitchen, Everleigh made a peanut-butter-and-jelly sandwich for Rae and a salad for herself.

A few minutes later, she announced, "Your lunch is on the table."

"Yes, ma'am," Rae responded. "I'm still bored."

They sat down at the breakfast table to eat. "I know you are, but I have an idea. Why don't you work on your sight words?"

"You put them all over my room. It's crowded now."

She hid a smile. "I placed them there to help you recognize the words."

"I know, but my room is crowded."

Rae was irritable and her mood wasn't likely to improve until she got her way.

And that wasn't happening.

"Guess who's coming over for dinner?" Everleigh said, hoping this would cheer up Rae. They hadn't been able to find any common ground, so she was looking forward to having a conversation with no bickering.

"Mr. Declan?"

"Yes, and he's bringing dinner."

Her daughter's face lit up like a star on top of the tree. "Yay!"

Everleigh eyed Rae. Her attitude had completely shifted at the mention of Declan. It stayed that way for the rest of the afternoon. She didn't even have to ask her daughter more than once to clean up her toys.

It was a few minutes after six when Declan arrived. Everleigh was just as thrilled to see him as her daughter was.

"I brought dinner as promised," he said.

"Thank you," she responded. "You didn't have to do that, but it's much appreciated."

Afterward, he took them out for a drive. She'd told him earlier about Rae wanting to get out of the house.

She looked out the passenger side window

at the Christmas decorations highlighting each shop as they rode through the downtown area. The streetlights were decorated with holly, star-shaped lights and red velvet ribbons. In the middle of Center Square, a tall, beautifully decorated tree held court.

Declan parked the car and they got out for a closer look.

"Mama, look at the angel on top. She's so pretty."

"Yes, she is," Everleigh responded.

They stopped at a vendor selling roasted chestnuts.

"I haven't had these in a while," she said. "Now all I need is a cup of hot chocolate."

"They're selling some right over there," Declan replied. "We'll make that our next stop."

They sat down on a bench with Rae between them to finish eating.

Everleigh admired the red and while poinsettias in green pots that sat on the porch of the house on the corner.

An hour passed as they walked up and down the main street. Rae was so happy to be out of the house that she hopped, skipped and did a little dance.

"She's a ball of energy," Declan said.

"Yes, she is," Everleigh responded.

Rae wasn't a fan of the roasted chestnuts, so she stopped at the vendor selling gingerbread cookies.

They headed home shortly after that. Declan didn't want to keep them away from the house for too long.

After Rae went up to bed, Everleigh and Declan settled at the dining room table to discuss Powell's victims. It was becoming a routine, and though it was for a grim reason, she found she was starting to look forward to this part of her day.

She opened her padfolio and picked up her pen. "Where do we start?"

"It's an official investigation now."

She sighed. She'd known it was coming. "Okay, but I can't just sit here and do nothing. I've helped law enforcement in the past, consulting on several cases in Savannah. This concerns my daughter's safety. I can help."

"This goes against my better judgment, Everleigh."

"Don't make me beg."

After a moment, he said, "Lena Jones... I was finally able to locate her. She'd changed her name to Michelle. Unfortunately, she passed away a month ago. She had cancer."

"I'm sorry to hear that."

"I spoke with her husband," Declan stated. "According to him, she never wanted to talk about her past. He said that she was seeing a therapist until she got really sick. He didn't know anything about what had happened to her."

"Now what?"

"Let's look at the victims who had children at the time of their deaths," Declan suggested.

Everleigh checked her notes. "I think I've narrowed it down to eight…no, seven victims who had children."

Declan eyed her in surprise.

"I told you I could be useful," she said, grinning. "We already knew about the children of the first victim. You ruled them out."

"Yeah, we can move from the two surviving children."

Declan and Everleigh discussed what he'd found on two of the seven victims left on the list.

"Marcia Ricks had a daughter," he said while going through notes on his iPad. "That daughter is currently working as a guidance counselor at a high school in Loma Linda, California. She's married with three children."

She made notes, then looked back up at him to continue.

"Samara James was the mother of four," Declan stated. "One son is in prison. A daughter is a bible-study teacher—she's married to a pastor."

"And the other two?"

"Another daughter manages a fast-food restaurant. I haven't found anything on the last daughter as of yet. The next victim is Luanne Shelby."

"Do you know anything about her?"

"No. I'll run a check on her the first thing tomorrow. The same with the other three victims on our list."

"If this doesn't pan out, what do we do next?" Everleigh asked.

"I could go see Powell…"

"Why would you do that?" she blurted. "If you do that, Declan…you risk exposing me and Rae. That's the last thing I need to deal with—my serial-killer daddy. I don't want anything to do with that man."

"I don't have to mention you at all."

"You don't think he'd wonder why you're suddenly so interested in him?"

"I could just tell him that I study criminals, or that I'm looking into the deaths of his relatives, Everleigh."

"I'd rather you didn't talk to him at all," she said.

"Okay," Declan responded. "I won't."

"Unless it's *absolutely* necessary," Everleigh amended. "I want to find this person as much as you do. I just don't want more trouble in the process."

Declan drove around the block and parked a few houses away from Everleigh's home. He settled back in his seat, making himself comfortable.

His phone rang.

"Everything okay?" he asked.

Everleigh's voice came through the speaker. "You need to go home."

He laughed. "How did you know?"

"I'm learning how your mind works. We're fine, Declan," she said. "You don't have to sit in that car half the night. It's cold out there and besides, the police still drive by often."

"Then I'll leave after I speak to the officer on duty."

"Okay…thanks. Rae and I appreciate you."

They talked a few minutes more before hanging up.

A police cruiser rolled past the house.

Declan was about to leave when a dark sedan turned on her street. It drove slowly, and when it didn't stop, he breathed a sigh of relief. He watched until it turned the corner.

He was about to leave when the motion lights in Everleigh's backyard suddenly came on, lighting up that area. Declan jumped out of his car and took off running toward her house.

His hand on his holster, he crept around to the backyard.

"Declan, he's gone," Everleigh said from her patio. "When the lights came on, he ran off. I saw him from the window." She had a bat in her hand. "It was Wyle. I got a clear look at his face."

"What was he wearing?"

"A hoodie, a jacket—everything dark."

He glanced around. "No cameras back here?"

"I thought the motion detectors would be enough, but I'll be adding one first thing tomorrow." Shivering, Everleigh gestured to the door. "It's cold. Let's go inside. I'm sure Wyle's long gone by now."

They sat down in the family room.

"I guess it's a good thing you were still on the island after all," she said.

"What were you going to do with that?" he asked, pointing to the bat.

"Beat Wyle to a pulp, then use my Taser on him."

Declan bit back his laughter. "Okay."

"I was on the baseball team from middle school to college," Everleigh stated. "Trust me, I know how to swing a bat."

"And the Taser? Have you ever used one?"

"No, but I know how. I've taken several self-defense classes." She got up and looked out the window. "I'm also a black belt in karate. I can defend myself."

She certainly could.

Turning to face him, she said, "Now we know that Wyle is here and he's after me."

Declan nodded in agreement.

"So what do we do now?"

"I'll try to get you and Rae into a safe house. If you don't mind, I'll stay here tonight."

Her arms folded across her chest, Everleigh nodded. "That's perfectly fine. I'll feel better

with you being here, honestly. You can stay in
the guest room down here. I'll see you in the
morning."

"You okay?"

"I feel better knowing that I wasn't imagin-
ing Wyle being on campus that day."

Declan eyed her. "Did he see you?"

"He did," she responded. "He seemed star-
tled. For a second, I thought Wyle was going
to say something to me. He just took off running instead."

"Doesn't sound like he has the heart of a
killer."

"No, it doesn't," Everleigh said.

An hour later, Everleigh was still awake, so
she went downstairs to the kitchen.

She sliced several oranges into wedges, putting them into plastic snack bags. Next, she
chopped up an onion and green and red bell
peppers, placing each of them in separate con-
tainers.

When Declan entered the kitchen, she said,
"I'm sorry if I woke you. I was trying not to
make much noise."

"You didn't wake me." Pointing to the oranges, he commented, "Looks like you had some trouble going back to sleep, though."

"Whenever I can't sleep, I meal-prep. It relaxes me." She pointed to the teapot on the stove. "Would you like some tea? The water's already hot."

"Sure."

"Lemon and ginger, okay?"

"Yeah," Declan replied.

They made small talk while they sat at the breakfast table drinking their tea.

"This isn't how I envisioned Rae and I would be spending the holidays," Everleigh sighed. "I never thought we'd be running for our lives."

"I have an BOLO out on Wyle. He is to be taken to the precinct and I plan on interviewing him myself."

She took a sip of her tea. "I wish I could be there."

"I'll let you know what happens," Declan said. "I still don't think that he's our killer, but I'm hoping he can lead us to the perp."

"If these are two separate threats, then we'll be fighting blind." She shuddered at the thought.

When they finished, she bade him goodnight, then went up to her bedroom.

Rae was still sleeping soundly, without fear.

Although Everleigh had been trained in self-defense, she considered retrieving her mother's gun for protection but really didn't want one in the house with Rae. To ease her mind and the quakes in her serenity, she reread Psalm 91. It always gave her comfort and was a gentle reminder that God was the best security system in the world.

"Hey, why don't you and Rae come stay at my place for a few days?" Declan suggested the next morning. "It'll do you both some good to get away from the house. I have plenty of space and you won't have to worry about looking over your shoulder while you're there. Besides, I make an amazing chili. I top it with sour cream and green onions."

"We love chili," she responded. "How do you serve yours? With corn chips or corn bread? You can't go wrong either way."

"Corn bread."

"Sounds great," Everleigh murmured.

"So what do you say?"

"Sure. I think it'll do us both good to get out of here for a day or so."

"It's perfect," Declan responded. He was

going to enjoy entertaining them at his home. He would also rest better knowing they were safe and under his protection.

Everleigh headed to the staircase. "I'll pack really quick."

"Are we going somewhere?" Rae asked when she reached the second level.

"Little girls shouldn't listen to adult conversations."

"Are we?"

"Yes. We're going to stay with Mr. Declan for a couple of days."

"Yay!" Rae broke out into a little dance.

Everleigh couldn't help but chuckle. "Really? It's like that."

"Mama, we hardly ever go anywhere."

Rae was right. Even before this threat, they hadn't gone out much since moving to the island—the only time they really went anywhere was for work and school. Her daughter was lonely. And if she was honest, she'd admit that she was, too.

This would be good for them both.

"Come help me pack," Everleigh said.

Thirty minutes later, they were on their way.

When they turned into Declan's neighborhood twenty minutes later, she was a bit surprised that he didn't live in a condo or a town house. The brick home was a fairly large one, with three garages, and looked to be about three thousand square feet.

"Your house is pretty," Rae said.

Everleigh agreed.

"Thank you," he responded. "I've been in this house for two years now."

"It looks new. Did you have it built?"

"Yeah. I prefer custom-built homes."

That was a dream Everleigh had had at one point in her life. It was a dream she shared with Britt—a dream long gone.

Chapter 9

"Doggy," Rae gasped when they walked into Declan's house. She rushed to Everleigh's side and cowered. "Is he gonna bite me?"

"No, she's very friendly. You don't have to be afraid of her."

Peeking from behind her mother, Rae asked, "What's her name?"

"Billie," Declan responded. "Here, if you kneel down like this and hold your hand out, she'll come over and sniff you. That's how she says hello."

Rae came out from behind Everleigh and did as instructed. Sure enough, the Labrador retriever came up to her gently. As the dog sniffed her fingers, Everleigh ran her palm over Billie's glossy coat.

"She's beautiful," Everleigh murmured. She loved dogs but her late husband was allergic, so they'd never had one.

A few licks from Billie and Rae had changed her mind in favor of dogs, too. "You're a good doggy," she said. "So cute… I like you, Billie. You can be my friend."

Declan grabbed the suitcases out of his SUV and started back toward the house. Everleigh grabbed her leather tote and fell in beside him. Declan showed her to a bedroom upstairs with a small sitting area off to one side and a private bath.

"This is where you and Rae will be sleeping," he said.

A beautiful coverlet in teal and navy covered a king-size bed with a padded headboard.

Everleigh turned to him. "Is this your room?"

"No, my room is downstairs."

She relaxed. "Oh, good. I didn't want to put you out."

"Well, I'll leave you to it," Declan stated. "I'll head down to the kitchen to find something for us to eat."

The door closed, shutting out his tall frame.

"This room is so pretty," Rae said, sinking down on the bed.

"Yes, it is."

"We're gonna have so much fun here."

Everleigh smiled. "Starting right now…"

She glanced down at her wedding rings. After her husband's death, she had thrown herself into her work, her daughter and taking care of her mother, but it never occurred to Everleigh that she hadn't really moved on.

Until now.

She told herself that she didn't want to rush through her grief. That she had to make sure her daughter was okay. Everleigh didn't want to neglect Rae. She vowed to be there for her as much as was necessary. It wouldn't cushion the blow of her daughter's loss, but it would help her heal.

Everleigh remembered experiencing a wave of apprehension when her husband left for work that day. It was as if she knew deep down that something bad was going to happen. She'd spent most of the day in prayer, asking God to protect her husband; to bring him home safe.

That evening, there had been a knock on the door.

She knew before Britt's supervisor and a union official spoke a word. Her husband had died in the line of duty.

Everleigh felt in that moment that God hadn't heard her fervent prayers, or worse... He had chosen to ignore them. She remembered telling her mother that God had taken her husband from her.

Deloris had placed a gentle hand on Everleigh's shoulder and said, "I want you to try a different perspective. Consider that God welcomed Britt home."

It helped to look at his leaving through that lens, but it didn't stop her from missing him, or the heartache that his dying left behind.

After setting up a movie for Rae to watch, Declan said, "We can talk in my office."

Everleigh followed him down the hall into what looked like a library.

"You love books, I see," she observed. "From the looks of it, you're a mystery buff. You also like the classics and historical fiction, too."

"I checked out your books, too," he responded. "You like psychological thrillers and mysteries, romance and I glimpsed a few historical-fiction titles."

"We have that in common." She smiled when she glimpsed the framed degrees on the wall along with a beautiful display of abstract artwork. A jar filled with pencils, pens and highlighters sat to the left of the computer monitor. To the right was another jar filled with thumb drives. Everleigh noticed several colorful Post-it notes tacked to his monitor.

"Where you able to get any new information?" she asked, sitting down in the chair facing his desk.

"Not yet. I did request Olivia Ragland's file. She was Powell's last known victim. I'll let you know what I find out."

"Thank you. I just wish we could put a name and a face to whoever wrote that letter, if we're assuming it wasn't Wyle. It's not easy fighting the invisible man."

"He won't be able to remain invisible," Declan said. "Eventually, he's got to show himself."

He had grown tired of waiting around for orders. He waited until it was the black of night before making his move; the darkness was his protection. He'd convinced their *friend* to help him hack into her home security account and disable the alarm system. This time there wasn't anything standing between him and the entrance to Everleigh Taylor's house.

Her house had large arched windows in the front. He imagined that light from all four seasons poured through, gracing the air and illuminating the gray-stained wooden floor. The walls were light. It was too dark to see the true color, but even with the moonlight creeping through the windows, he saw that the baseboards were bold white.

The banister was made of oak, its grain flowing as water might, in waves of comforting brown hues. The living room was to the left. His eyes traveled over his surroundings. Nice, neat…everything in its place. It appeared to be a medley of memories, of photographs adorning the walls, all of them conjuring emotions of sweet moments—something he knew nothing about.

He and his brother had never grown up in a place like this, even when their mother was alive. But she kept their tiny apartment clean and neat. Their father cared more about getting high than he did a suitable place to raise a family. It was the reason why their mother left. She was determined to raise her boys by herself.

They'd been excited about the new apartment. She could only afford a one-bedroom, so she'd invested in a used sofa bed. Whenever they were home with her, she'd let him and his brother sleep in the bedroom while she took the sofa bed.

His mother was a good woman and she didn't deserve to die so young. She didn't deserve to be murdered.

Upon these walls were the pictures of the daughter, so obviously loved. His eyes traveled back to a photograph of Everleigh.

I want to hear her scream.

He silently made his way to the staircase, then growled when he found the bedrooms upstairs empty.

They were gone.

"You can't hide from me," he yelled. "I'll find you."

In his fury, he snatched a photo of Everleigh and her daughter off the wall and tossed it to the floor.

Chapter 10

Declan's wooded backyard was a sanctuary for nature and his place of serenity. It was fenced-in and private; safe and secure. Rae had spent the past hour outside with Billie, running back and forth. It thrilled Everleigh to see her little girl laughing without a care in the world. She wanted to keep it that way.

"She's having a ball," she said, watching from within the screened-in porch, Declan by her side.

"So is Billie," he responded. "She loves children."

"Obviously, you do, too."

"Guilty," Declan said with a tiny smile.

She sat down in one of the chairs. "This is just what we needed."

He sat down in the other chair. "Anytime you need to get away, you're welcome to come here."

"I can't get over how generous you are—first your time and now your home."

"I want to be a good friend," he told her. "I tend to treat people the way I'd want to be treated—it's what my parents taught me."

"They should be extremely proud of you, Declan."

"You certainly know how to make a man feel real proud, Everleigh."

"I'm only speaking the truth."

"What do you think about tacos for dinner tomorrow night?" he asked.

"Sounds great. Rae will love it. She's a huge fan of tacos."

He leaned toward her and whispered, "So am I. Beef, chicken, shrimp taco—love them all. It will be a create-your-own-taco night."

"Yum," Everleigh murmured. "Although it won't be taco Tuesday."

He chuckled. "No, it won't. We make our own rules in this house."

"Hey, I like the idea of taco Wednesdays."

"I ordered some stuff from the grocery store," Declan said as he stood up. "It should be here soon."

"Rae, it's time to come inside," Everleigh told her.

"Five more minutes, please."

"Okay, but that's it. I want you to clean up for lunch."

"Rae, how would you like to help me cook the meat for dinner tomorrow?" Declan asked. "We're having tacos."

"Yay," she squealed. "Mama likes shrimp on hers. I like beef and chicken."

Rae ran toward the porch with Billie on her heels. She stood there for a moment to catch her breath.

"Let's get you into a nice warm bath," Everleigh said.

"I have a virtual meeting with a student," Declan announced. "I'll be in my office if you need me."

Half an hour later, she was in the kitchen when he walked in with the groceries.

Everleigh pointed to the frying pan. "I was about to make some grilled-cheese sandwiches and tomato soup. Would you like some?"

Declan grinned. "You're taking me back to my college days. Those late-night grilled-cheese sandwiches used to get me through a lot of study sessions. I don't think I've had one since I left school."

She stood with her back at the counter while he put away packages of beef, shrimp, chicken breasts, cheese and other items inside the refrigerator.

"Really?"

"It's true."

"I'll have to change that right now," she said.

I can really get used to this.

Declan gave himself a mental shake. He couldn't afford to live in a fantasy world. He needed to stay focused on the reality of this situation.

After they finished eating, he decided to put some distance between himself and Everleigh.

"I'll be in my room working until it's time to cook dinner," Declan announced. "Do you need anything before I disappear?"

"No, we're good. I'll do my best to keep Rae from disturbing you."

"Let her enjoy herself." Declan wanted to say more, but thought better of it. "I'll see you in a few hours."

"Okay."

He walked away swiftly before his prized control faded and he kissed her. Everleigh trusted him and he didn't want to tamper with that trust. This was a safe space for her and Rae. He would never violate that.

Everleigh and Rae were in danger. His job was to protect them, keep them safe. Not pretend like they were a happy little family. Once they neutralized the threat, things between him and Everleigh would go back to the way they were before.

Well, maybe not exactly, he amended. They knew each other better now; perhaps they had laid the foundation of friendship. But that was about it. Declan shouldn't expect anything more to happen between them.

Declan sat down at the small desk in his bedroom. There were times when it was late at night or he just didn't feel like going to his home office, so he would work here instead. However, neither his mind nor his heart was focused on anything other than Everleigh. Already he missed the sound of her voice.

His pride would not let him venture back to the main level—it was too soon. He'd told Everleigh that he would be working most of the afternoon. He had to keep up the facade.

In that moment, Declan wished things could be different.

After spending the morning with Rae outside, they sat down to go through their notes while she was napping.

"You may have told me this already, but I don't recall," Declan said. "Where did your mom live when she was attacked by Powell?"

"She lived a block away from the college she attended."

"How was she able to get away?"

"My grandfather had given her a gun to protect herself. She was able to get off a shot, but I don't think she hit him. It scared him off, though."

"Someone would've heard the shot that night," he responded. "They might have called the police. Maybe they saw or heard something that night."

"You're right."

"If we go back to the estimated time of your conception, I might be able to isolate a time frame and we can check to see if someone reported shots fired."

Her eyes widened. "Do you really think we can do that, Declan?"

"We're certainly going to try."

"This other woman… Olivia Ragland," Everleigh said. "I saw that she lived in Atlanta at the time of her murder. Do you have her address?"

"I do," he responded.

She performed an online search. "Looks like she lived a block away from the college my mother attended. I wish I could remember my mom's old address. A cousin and I visited that area once. I bet Powell was hanging around the school and followed women home."

Declan nodded in agreement.

"It's entirely possible that he tried to talk to her and my mom rebuffed him," Everleigh said. "Her rejection would've set him off. He probably did the same thing with Olivia. I'm sure he was stalking them."

"I found out right before I came down that one of the women who survived, Kathy Kitt, was murdered a week before Powell was arrested," Declan said. "She was killed six months after he raped her. Another man is suspected of killing her."

"We know that Lena died recently, but is the other survivor still alive?" Everleigh asked.

He shook his head. "Not sure. Sarah Mason disappeared. Some believe she went into hiding, but her parents insist it was foul play. They say she wouldn't have left without a word to them. She's listed as missing. This was during the time Powell was roaming around free."

"Declan, do you think Powell returned to finish what he started?" she asked.

"I'm going to discuss these findings with my superiors. I'd like to read the investigation reports."

"Was the suspect ever arrested for Kathy's murder?"

He shook his head. "Her case is still open. But forensic evidence suggested Powell wasn't at the scene."

"A man like Powell…he'd want to silence the women," Everleigh mused. "He didn't like losing, so he'd never give up until he did just that. Silence them." She couldn't help but wonder if Powell had looked for her mother. If so, it must have frustrated him to find her gone. Suddenly, it dawned on Everleigh that her mother had also lived on Beech, the same street as Oliva Ragland.

The thought stayed with her all through the evening as she showered and prepared for bed. She decided to talk to Declan about it.

After checking on Rae, Everleigh brushed out her hair, and pulled on a soft fleece sweatsuit and wool socks. She headed down the hall to his office. There was no light beneath the door. He had probably gone to bed. She thought of the way her gaze kept drifting over his wide shoulders, muscular frame and long legs during the preparation of dinner. *Maybe I'd better not bother him. This can wait until morning.*

But, no, this was important. Renewing her resolve, Everleigh went downstairs and knocked on Declan's bedroom door. He abruptly pulled it open, causing her to stumble forward into his arms.

"Everleigh…" he said, helping her regain her balance. "Did you need something?"

"I've been thinking about that address in Atlanta where Olivia Ragland lived—I'd like to see how close it was to my mother's old apartment. She lived a block away from the college. When I saw that address, it nagged at me because I knew I'd heard of the street before. I'm pretty sure that she and my mom lived on the same street."

They went down the hall to his office.

"These are the only apartments on that street within five blocks of the college," Declan said.

"Then they must have lived in the same complex," she murmured. Everleigh looked up at him. "He attacked two women in the same area. I guess when my mom didn't report the attack, it bolstered his confidence."

"I agree," Declan said, "because that's the only time he ever struck twice in the same city."

Declan had felt a nearly magnetic charge in the air when he opened his bedroom door to find Everleigh standing there. His gaze had locked on hers and when she'd smiled, everything inside him tightened. It was getting harder and harder to keep his emotions under control.

When he left his bedroom shortly after seven, he was surprised to find Everleigh already up and in the kitchen. "I thought maybe you'd sleep in this morning," he said. "We were up until two thirty."

"Cooking calms me down," she responded. "I hope you don't mind that I took over your kitchen."

"I don't mind at all." He retrieved a mug from the cabinet and set it down on the counter. "I need a cup of coffee." Declan eyed the square baking pan covered with foil sitting on top of the stove. "What's that?"

"Biscuits. My mother's recipe. There's also bacon."

"I could sure use a couple slices."

"I can make scrambled eggs if you want."

"Biscuits and bacon will do."

Everleigh poured some freshly brewed coffee into his mug, which Declan carried over to the table. She took him some biscuits, butter and strawberry jam. She filled her own plate and mug, and then joined him at the table.

"I thought about what you said last night. I'm going to look deeper into Kathy Kitt's death." He took a sip from his mug.

"Good, because I really think Powell was responsible," Everleigh said. She cradled her mug between her palms, letting the heat seep into her skin. "Kathy could identify him, so he possibly shut her up permanently. The main reason my mom and Lena survived is most likely because they left town right after the attacks."

"You're probably right," he said. "Powell couldn't find them."

Declan took a sip of coffee. "I got Olivia Ragland's file and went through it from cover to cover. Her ex-husband and two young sons found her body."

She looked up at him. "Oh, how horrible for them. Very traumatic."

"Everleigh, do you have any of your mother's personal files?"

"Yes, I put all that stuff in a storage facility on the island. Why?"

"We need to go there—I want to check on something."

"What's on your mind?" she asked.

"Let's consider your theory on Kathy Kitt. Powell hunted her down and killed her. He doesn't like to lose."

"What are you getting at?" she asked.

"The apartments where Olivia Ragland lived—the ones we think your mom lived in, too."

"Yes?"

"What if they lived in the very same apartment? Olivia might have moved in after your mother fled."

"You think that Powell went back to finish what he started with my mother but found Olivia instead," Everleigh said. "If that's true… his rage would've escalated when he discovered that my mom escaped him a second time."

"That could be the reason why Olivia's death was more brutal than the others," Declan replied.

"If this is true, then…her sons—maybe it's one of them."

"It's certainly a possibility. I have my mother's possessions in storage. Maybe there's something there that can help us."

"It won't hurt to check it out."

Later, at the storage facility, they went through several boxes while Rae sat quietly in a corner with her tablet. She was sullen because Billie couldn't come with them.

After the third box turned up nothing, Everleigh said, "My mom kept practically everything, but I'm not sure she would've kept anything from her time in Atlanta."

"If we don't find anything here, we can always go to Atlanta and talk to the apartment manager," he suggested.

"Actually, I think we should do that," Everleigh responded. "We'd probably be more successful."

"Are you serious?"

"Yes, I am," she said. "We should go to Atlanta."

"We can leave first thing tomorrow morning."

After they left the storage unit, Declan said. "Why don't I drop y'all back at the house now to pack whatever you need? I need to run to the precinct, anyway, to talk to my supervisor. I shouldn't be gone too long. A couple of hours at the most. I really think I have something solid to present now."

"We've got everything we need with us. We can stay put while you go to the precinct," she assured him.

"Stay inside while I'm gone," he said, after letting them inside his house.

"That won't be a problem. I'll get dinner started."

"My kitchen is all yours," he responded with a smile, and headed out the door.

A few hours later, Everleigh was nowhere in sight, but the scent of seasoned beef waited for Declan when he got home. On the stovetop was a pan of taco shells.

He smiled. So this is what it felt like to come home to a family.

The feelings Everleigh evoked in him weren't easy to explain or articulate. Even when she wasn't around, his heart ached in his chest and Declan found himself hungering for her presence in his life. Whenever they weren't together, he felt a certain warmth as the pro-longed anticipation of seeing Everleigh almost seemed unbearable.

She strolled into the kitchen, surprising him. "Everything's ready for taco Wednesday."

"A man can get used to all of this really easy."

Everleigh smiled. "Enjoy it while you can."

Chapter 11

Everleigh took a deep breath. She was in way over her head with Declan Blanchet. She liked him way more than she could ever have anticipated. But then, she never thought that they would be spending so much time together.

Their Christmas break had started with her and Rae staying with him, and now they were on their way to Atlanta.

"Are we gonna have Christmas in Atlanta?" her daughter asked.

"No, sweetie. It's just a short visit. We might stop in to see some family. Cousin Bonnie lives there."

"Yay. I love her. She's so fun."

Everleigh chuckled and said to Declan, "My cousin is a big kid at heart. Whenever she came to visit, Bonnie would play with dolls, color—whatever Rae wanted to do. I'm going to give her a call to see if Rae can spend some time with her."

He nodded in understanding.

She and Declan could move about freely if Rae wasn't with them. Everleigh wanted to keep her daughter in the dark about everything that was going on around her, sparing her the trauma that came with victimization.

Everleigh thought of the trauma Olivia Ragland's sons must have endured when they found their mother's battered and mutilated body. She wouldn't be surprised if one or both of them were now focused on getting some type of justice. They had no evidence to support this theory, but her instincts told her they were getting closer to the truth.

They had just gotten back to their hotel from dinner. They had arrived in Atlanta before noon. Rae sat on the floor beside Billie, talking to her and rubbing her fur. One of her favorite movies was on the television.

Everleigh pulled a pack of playing cards out of her tote. "Do you remember how badly I beat you in Spades the other night?"

"You beat *me*?" Laughing, Declan shook his

head. "I don't think so. I have no memory of anything like that."

She grinned. "Well, why don't we play a quick game right now."

"I don't think you want to do that, Everleigh."

"Yes, I do," she responded while shuffling the deck of cards and placing them face down on the table.

Everleigh sank down to the floor.

Declan followed suit.

He drew the first card. "I have a ten."

Everleigh drew next. "You go first. I have a four."

She laughed at the expression on his face when he drew the next card. "What's wrong?"

"I'm fine. I got this."

She won the first round.

"Oaky. Okay," Declan said. "I'll give you that win."

"You're not giving me anything," she responded with a laugh. "I won that round on my own merit."

"Learning something new about you. You're very competitive." Declan hadn't had this much fun in a long time. He felt an eager affection coming from Everleigh. Every time her gaze met his, Declan felt his heart turn over in response.

"It's your turn," Everleigh said, bringing him out of his reverie.

He won the second round. "Okay, let's play one more game to decide the winner."

Everleigh nodded in agreement.

It was hard to keep his attention on the game. He was physically attracted to Everleigh, but he was also attracted to her mind.

"I guess you're the winner," Declan said a short while later.

He checked his watch, and then said, "I should probably go to my room. Rae looks like she's tired and sleepy."

He rose to his feet and then assisted Everleigh up.

They stood facing one another.

He hesitated a moment before walking to the door. Declan turned around to face Everleigh.

"Declan…"

He tingled as she said his name. He would've preferred to sweep her into his arms and hold her close to him for a long time. He wanted to kiss her.

His gaze traveled to her left hand.

"I'd better go," he whispered.

"I'll call you after Rae goes to sleep," she said.

"Talk to you then."

"Keep your head in the game," he whispered as he walked the short distance to the room next door.

Stunned, Everleigh sat down on the edge of the bed. She couldn't get past the look Declan had given her, or the way he'd stared at her lips. It was almost as if he wanted to kiss her.

She shook away the thought.

I'm misreading his intentions.

At least this was what she was telling herself. Everleigh wouldn't allow herself to believe that there was anything igniting between them.

Declan saw her as a woman in jeopardy. A woman he'd agreed to protect.

But what if she was right about what she saw in his expression. She hadn't imagined the warmth she'd glimpsed in the depths of his eyes.

Even so, he was too much of a gentleman to cross boundaries; Everleigh knew this much about him.

The deeper question was how she felt about all this. She wasn't sure.

Everleigh chocked it up to her emotions being all over the place due to the current stressors in her life, mixed with her grief. She was feeling a bit overwhelmed and unsettled, although she didn't want to show it. She was taking it day-by-day in an effort to keep calm so as not to upset Rae.

The little girl had no idea that her life was in danger.

She glanced over at her sleeping child, then joined her in the king-size bed.

Everleigh didn't fall asleep right away.

She lay there, staring up at the ceiling and wondering if she'd ever be able to feel safe again. Or if she could ever open her heart to someone new.

The next day, Declan and Everleigh headed out to drop Rae off with her cousin Bonnie.

He was still waiting to hear back from the apartment manager.

"What does your cousin do?" Declan asked as he followed his GPS to Bonnie's house.

"She's a nurse. She worked a double shift yesterday and didn't get off until seven this morning. She said she got a couple hours' sleep and is excited to spend time with Rae."

"How long has she lived in Atlanta?"

"All of her life, as far as I know," Everleigh responded as she stared out the passenger window.

"Was she close to your mom?" he asked.

"Her mom and my mom were close," she answered. "And Bonnie and I were close. Her mom died two years before mine."

"Is there anyone else you can think of in Atlanta who could shed some light on your mother's time here?"

"Nobody that I know," Everleigh stated. "Most of her family lived in the Savannah-Hinesville area. After what happened, my mom never wanted to come back here. Now I fully understand why. Atlanta held terrible memories for her."

Ten minutes later, they were on Bonnie's doorstep.

"Oh, my *goodness*! Look at my little Rae of sunshine," Bonnie gushed. "You've grown into a ball of more cuteness."

Ray broke into a big grin. "Hey, cousin Bonnie."

Everleigh introduced Declan.

"Very nice to meet you." He could see a family resemblance between the two women. The high cheekbones, the same complexion and warm brown eyes.

His phone rang.

"I need to take this," he said. "I'll wait for you outside."

Declan hoped to have some good news for Everleigh. He'd called the manager's office this morning and left a message.

They were just now returning the call and he hoped it was good news.

"Girl, that's one fine piece of chocolate," Bonnie whispered. "Are you sure y'all just friends?"

"I can't believe you just said that," she responded with a chuckle.

"He's gorgeous."

"Enough about Declan," Everleigh said. "Are you sure you're up to Rae spending the night with you?"

"Of course, I am," Bonnie replied. "We're going to have a good time together. You and Declan take care of your business."

She hugged her cousin. "Thank you."

When they drove away her cousin's house, Everleigh said, "I already miss my baby."

"Are you sure you want to leave Rae there?"

"I know she's safe with Bonnie. We just

haven't ever been apart. I told her to call me if Rae wants us to pick her up."

"Will you be upset if she doesn't?" Declan asked.

"I don't think so... I don't know." She glanced over at him. "I think I might."

"What do you tell your clients? Baby steps, right?"

Everleigh nodded. "Yes."

"We can always pick her up if it's necessary. And Bonnie doesn't live that far from the hotel."

"This is true... Okay, I'm focused now."

"Good. That was the current manager who called when we were at your cousin's house. She has only been with the company five years," Declan said. "Ezra Stone was the manager back when your mom lived there. He quit after Oliva Ragland died. Apparently, they have some new software they're using now. She said the old rental records were archived in a storage facility."

"Are we going to try to find this Ezra Stone?" she asked.

"Yeah. It shouldn't be too hard. We can see if he's on any social media."

They decided to have lunch at a local Italian restaurant.

On the way to their table, Declan told her a joke, he'd heard from one of his coworkers.

"You have an incredible sense of humor," Everleigh commented as she scanned her menu. She took a sip of her ice water. "I really like getting to know this side of you."

He laughed. "I'm assuming you originally thought I was pretty boring."

"Not really," she replied. "Well… I didn't really know what to think about you. You just seemed so serious all the time."

"You're not the first person to say that about me."

She met his gaze. "I hope that I didn't make you feel bad."

"You didn't." Declan reached across the table to hold her hand. "It's good to hear how you come across from other people."

He picked up his menu and began looking it over. "I think I'm having the chicken marsala," he said. "Do you know what you want?"

"I'm in the mood for fettuccine Alfredo with mushrooms."

They gave the server their orders when he returned to the table.

"Wyle Gaines is in the wind," Declan announced. "He may have already left Charleston."

"I can believe that," she responded. "He seemed so slippery to me when he was ingratiating himself to my mother. It doesn't surprise me that he'd be a coward now."

The waiter returned with their meals.

Declan blessed the food.

Everleigh sampled her fettuccine Alfredo. "This is delicious."

"Mine is really good, too," he responded.

Everleigh's eyes traveled the dining area. "It feels great being out like this among people again. It's nice not having to worry about someone trying to do me harm."

Declan wiped his mouth on the edge of his napkin. "I think we're getting close to finding out who's after you. Hopefully, Ezra Stone will be able to give us more information about the Ragland family. He probably won't be able to tell us much about the boys, Neil and Ellis— they were really young."

"You seem pretty positive that the person after me could be one or both of her sons without any real proof."

"I've never been one to believe in coincidences. It's been way too many since you got that letter, Everleigh."

"Oh, I agree. Too many."

"I'm not saying it's definitely them, but this gives us a place to start."

They left the restaurant and returned to the hotel.

Seated in Everleigh's room, they reviewed everything they'd learned about Olivia Ragland's death.

"Whatever happened to Olivia's husband?" she asked.

"I looked Ellison Ragland up. There isn't a current driving record, nothing about employment—he seemed to have just disappeared. Not even a death certificate."

"That's interesting…"

He nodded in agreement. "He's on my list of potential suspects, too. I want to be as sure as I can be about this," Declan said. "Now that we have his address, I'm hoping what we learn from Ezra Stone will give me some additional information that will connect all the pieces of this puzzle."

Chapter 12

"I guess you still ain't talkin' to me," he said.

"Wh-Why should I bother? It's not like you ever l-listen to me," his brother responded. "I t-told you not to go to her house. Not only did you go there, you broke in."

"Nothin' happened. I disabled her alarm. Besides she and the little girl weren't even home."

"Man, your rage is gonna end up gettin' you l-locked up."

"As long as she's dead... I don't care. Besides, you the one who told me I should hate Powell and his entire family. You told me that they have a sickness runnin' in that bloodline."

His brother uttered, "I hate being back in Georgia. I hate this p-place with a passion."

"We're staying in Temple for the night."

"I thought we was going to Villa Rica," his brother said, confusion coloring his tone.

"We are," he responded. "We just not staying

there. That town too small. Everybody knows everybody. I want to take care of business and get out."

"Man…" his brother said. "You know who you sound like right now… you need to chill."

"I'll chill when I'm dead."

Spending time with mother and child made Declan yearn for something he never really thought he'd have—a family. Past relationships had been ruined because of his chosen profession. Former girlfriends said they could handle his being in law enforcement, but in the end… they couldn't. The divorce rate was high in his field. He saw it happen within his own family. His sister's marriage ended because of her job with Homeland Security.

Declan was struggling to maintain control over his emotions and stay professional, but what he felt for Everleigh could no longer be denied. However, now wasn't the time to act on those feelings. He also knew as long as she wore her wedding rings, she wasn't ready to move forward in a relationship.

He strode out of his hotel room with purpose. It was time to meet Everleigh for breakfast.

She opened her door just as he walked up.

"Prompt as always," she said with a smile. "I like that about you."

"It's a quality I greatly appreciate as well."

They took the elevator downstairs.

"I called Rae. She told me she was having the best time with Bonnie. She asked if she could spend another night with her. I think I'm jealous."

"Your daughter adores you," Declan said.

"I know. I just miss my baby."

"So what did you tell her?"

"I told her that she could stay another night. She sounded so happy."

"I'll do my best to keep you entertained."

Everleigh eyed him. "I'm going to hold you to that."

After they'd shared breakfast at the hotel restaurant, they headed out to find Ezra Stone. Declan had secured his address the night before.

They walked up concrete steps to the raggedy wooden porch and knocked on the front door.

"What you want?" a man yelled from inside. "We ain't buying nothing."

"We're here to talk to Ezra Stone."

"What you want with my pops?" The door swung open wide, revealing a middle-aged man with a heavy scowl.

"We'd like to speak with him about an incident that happened when he managed the Catalina Apartments," Declan said.

"That ain't gonna happen, sir. My pops died seven months ago. He was murdered and the police ain't did nothing to find the person responsible."

"I'm very sorry for your loss," Everleigh stated. "I lost my mother six months ago. She used to live in the apartments during the time your father was the manager."

He eyed her. "How did she die? Your mama."

"She had cancer."

"What was her name?"

"Deloris Sanderson."

"*Wait a minute...* I remember her," he said, and his expression became animated. "She'd babysit me sometimes when she didn't have class. Deloris sure was a nice lady. I remember she was gonna be a doctor. She studied a lot."

Everleigh smiled. "That's right. She ended up being a nurse. Mama decided not to go to medical school."

He held the door open and stepped aside to let them enter.

"Sorry about earlier. I'm Jeremiah Stone."

Once they were seated in the living room, he

said, "I used to ask my dad about Deloris and why she moved away. He always said that it was probably best that she did. I didn't have a clue what that meant. Not back then."

"What do you mean?" Everleigh asked.

"I found out later that your mama was attacked and that's why she left the apartment without telling anyone. Then when that other lady moved into that same apartment and was murdered. Well, my dad...it did him in—he couldn't stay there after that. He was never the same. It ate at him all these years, so the police said his death was a suicide. But it wasn't. He would never kill himself. That wasn't him at all."

"Wait..." Everleigh said. "Are you talking about Olivia Ragland?"

"Yep, she be the one."

She frowned and said to Declan, "My mom must have told Ezra about what happened to her."

Jeremiah shook his head. "It was her daddy—your granddaddy—that told my pops. The way my pops told it, he came by maybe a week after she took off. Packed up her apartment. He let slip that something bad had happened to your mama. My pops, he felt horrible when he

heard that she'd been attacked. If he'd known…
I know that he would've tried to help your
mama."

"Did my grandfather say anything more?"

"I don't think so, but I really don't know."

"Was there ever a report about a gunshot?"
Declan asked. "You were probably too young
to remember."

"There was always gunshots. My pops would
make me hide under my bed or in the tub. I remember that. The neighborhood has changed
from the way it was back then. It's a much nicer
place to live now. I guess that's good because
it's so close to the college campus."

"I have one more question. Do you know
if your father was ever contacted by the other
victim's family?" Declan asked.

"Not that I know of," he responded. "My
pops had left the job after that Ragland lady
died. He never wanted to talk about it, but I
could just tell. He felt terrible. I think he even
felt like he was responsible for her—that he
failed to protect her."

"Jeremiah, why are you convinced that Ezra
was murdered?" Declan inquired.

"I know my dad. He wouldn't've killed hisself

like that. He hated guns. The one they found in the house wasn't his. He never owned one."

When they left the house, Everleigh asked, "Are you thinking that Ezra Stone was killed by the same person who wants to hurt me and Rae? You look like you believe Jeremiah."

"It's worth investigating," Declan said.

"My grandfather must have told him about me. That must be how these people found out about me. That's the only answer."

"I requested a copy of Ezra's file," he announced. "I'm picking it up in an hour."

"What a burden for him to feel responsible for what happened to my mom and Olivia. It wasn't his fault."

Declan nodded in agreement. "But I can understand why he'd feel that way."

"He was a protector," Everleigh said.

"There is the possibility that Jeremiah's right and he was murdered. If so, what was the motive?"

"One possible motive is because he couldn't save Olivia that night," she responded. "If we're right and one of her children is behind this... He rented her the apartment where the previous tenant was attacked. This is what you're thinking, right?"

"It's all speculation, but we might as well consider all possibilities," he replied.

"In the meantime, I plan to look into Olivia's sons. I want to know everything there is to know about them."

"If it's them, then we already know that they grew up to be very angry men with a lust for vengeance."

"And blood."

Everleigh had retired to her hotel room to rest after such a fraught morning. Declan went to his own room to read a copy of Ezra Stone's file. He spread the contents of the folder across the king-size bed.

There was a photo of Ezra slumped in a tattered, brown leather chair next to an equally worn couch, his legs thrust out in front of him, arms limp at his sides. His head drooped on his chest, blood leaking down the side of his face from a bullet hole in his left temple.

Declan looked at another photograph of the room that had been taken at a different angle.

"Did you find anything interesting?" Everleigh asked when she knocked on his door thirty minutes later.

"I'm not sure," he responded. "It certainly

looks like he died by suicide, from a gunshot to the temple."

"Looks can be deceiving," she murmured. "Could someone have set the scene up to look like that after they killed him?"

"It's possible," Declan mused. "From everything we've learned about him, like how he hated guns I don't believe he was suicidal, either. So do you still hold to your theory that Ezra may have been killed by one or both of the Ragland brothers because they blamed him for what happened to Olivia, or they thought he would have information about the previous occupant...my mother?"

"We've been assuming no one knew your mother had been attacked in the apartment because she didn't tell anyone. But Ezra found out from your grandfather."

She let out a frustrated sigh. "I wish we had solid proof. Right now, we're just pulling at loose threads. We may not have any real answers until it's too late."

"Powell lived in Villa Rica for a while," Declan said. "I saw somewhere that he lived there with a cousin. I think the name was Mattie Powell. If she's still around, maybe she'll be willing to talk to us."

Everleigh pulled out her iPad. "Let's see what we can find about her online."

She was determined to help him with this investigation. He'd allowed her to do so to keep Everleigh from going rogue on her own.

Declan finished off a bottle of water.

"I found her. According to this, she still lives in Villa Rica." Everleigh took a screenshot of the information. "Just texted it to you."

"I'll head out to see her tomorrow morning," he said.

Everleigh gave a slight nod. "Maybe she'll be able to tell you something useful."

"If she received a letter, that will certainly help," Declan responded. "We need more proof that a killer is targeting the Powell family."

"I'm going with you," Everleigh announced the next morning.

"Are you sure you want to do that?" Declan had been under the impression that she wasn't interested in meeting any members of Powell's family.

"Yes. Only, she doesn't have to know that I'm a relative."

"If you're sure," he said.

"I am," she responded.

"What about Rae?"

"Bonnie wants to take Rae to a birthday party this afternoon. She said she'd drop her off at the hotel afterward."

"Let's head out then," he said.

They got into the car and headed toward I-20 West.

Declan glanced over at her. She was twirling her rings around her finger. "Are you okay?"

Everleigh nodded. "I am. I don't know why I'm feeling so nervous."

"You're about to meet a member of your family on your father's side—only you don't want them to know it. I'm sure anyone would feel a certain amount of stress in that situation."

"I guess I'm curious," she said. "I think I need to see someone from that family who is not a killer. This probably doesn't make sense."

"Actually, it does," he responded. "I'd feel the same way. You need someone outside of Powell as a point of reference for your paternal side."

He parked on the street in front of a ranch-style brick home forty-five minutes later.

"You ready to do this?" Declan asked before getting out of the car.

"As ready as I'll ever be," she replied.

They got out and climbed the steps to the porch.

"The door isn't closed all the way," Everleigh said, touching his arm.

Declan examined it. "Looks like it was forced open. You stay out here."

"No," she responded. "I'm staying right behind you."

"Mattie Powell…" he called out.

There was no answer.

He stepped inside with Everleigh following closely behind.

"Stay here by the door," Declan instructed in a whisper. "I have a really bad feeling."

She nodded.

His weapon in his hand, Declan moved silently down the hallway. It was so quiet in the house that the only sounds he heard were the muffled thuds of his boots on the carpet and the ticking of a clock on a nightstand through an open bedroom door.

A woman was in bed, lying on her side.

"Mattie…"

She didn't move, but Declan didn't really expect she would. From where he stood at the door, he could tell she was dead.

"We have to call the police," he said, holstering his weapon as he returned to the front of the house. "Mattie's dead. She was shot in the

head. From the looks of it, she was sleeping—
she didn't see it coming."

"I guess that's a small blessing," Everleigh replied. She shuddered.

They waited outside on the porch.

"How long do you think she's been dead?"
Everleigh asked.

"At least twelve hours."

Everleigh suddenly looked fearful. "The
killer may still be in the area. I think we should
leave."

The whine of a siren sounded in the distance,
followed by the blare of a second vehicle. "Here
they come," Declan said, pulling out his credentials.

"That didn't take long at all," Everleigh responded. "What do we tell them?"

"That we came looking for information
about Powell."

Two patrol cars pulled up to the house.

An officer took their statement while the
other three entered the house.

"Did you know the victim?"

"No, we didn't," Declan replied.

"Then what were you doing here?" the officer asked.

"We wanted to talk to Mattie about her

cousin," Everleigh said. "I thought she might have some information about James Ray Powell."

"The medical examiner is on her way now," another officer said from the doorway.

Declan answered more of the officer's questions, and so did Everleigh.

When the homicide detective arrived, he and Declan walked off to the side to talk.

"Someone's threatened Mrs. Taylor and her child. We were in Atlanta to try to narrow down potential suspects. We drove out here to see Mattie Powell and found her body."

"How is your investigation connected to the victim?"

Declan looked back at Everleigh.

The resigned expression on her face told him that she knew what had to happen next. She walked over to where they were standing.

"The person who is after me believes that Powell is my father. I wanted to meet Mattie to find out more about him."

"Several of his family members have been killed," Declan said. "Two by gunshot and one was bludgeoned to death. I also believe there are two assailants."

"Any suspects?"

"Two brothers. Ellis and Neil Ragland. Their mother was Olivia Ragland, who was a victim of Powell's." He took out a business card and handed it to the police officer. "We're staying at the Peachtree Hotel downtown. You can have the detective contact me. I'm sure he or she will have some questions as well."

"How long will you be in town?"

"We plan to leave tomorrow afternoon."

"Someone will be in touch."

Declan placed his arm around Everleigh as they walked to the car.

"That poor woman. They're running around killing innocent people. They aren't any better than Powell." She looked up at him. "If they're here, do you think they've given up on me?"

"I wish I could say yeah, but the truth is that I don't think so, Everleigh. They may have moved on, but they'll be back. These people are bloodthirsty killers."

"I know you're right," she said. "As much as I don't want to believe it. What I want most is to find them before they find me. I'm sick of this cat-and-mouse game."

He hadn't heard her talk like this before. She wasn't anyone's victim. Everleigh was a fighter. A survivor.

"Why are you looking at me like that?"

Holding the passenger side door open for her, Declan said, "You're literally fighting mad right now. *I love it.*"

Everleigh laughed as she slid inside. "I guess I am. I'm more like my mother than I realized. She was a bear when it came to protecting me. Just the thought of two angry men wanting to harm my daughter—I want to put some serious hurt on them."

When he got in on the driver's side, he said, "Maybe I should worry about protecting Neil and Ellis from *you*."

"By locking them behind bars, I hope," she responded.

"Best place for them," Declan stated.

They started the drive back to the hotel.

En route he received a phone call.

"That was a Detective Bell. He and his partner are the lead investigators on Mattie Powell's case. They're coming to the hotel to talk to us."

"I'll order some food when we get there," Everleigh said. "I'm not hungry, but I know Rae will want something when Bonnie drops her off. I'll order enough for the detectives, too."

"He said they would be here in about an hour," Declan told her.

"I know I have to tell them the truth about my relationship to Powell. I just hope that they won't blab it to the world."

"We can ask that they keep it out of the reports," he said. "And hopefully, they will honor it."

"I guess there's nothing we can do about it if they don't," Everleigh responded.

He reached out and took her hand. "Everything is going to be okay."

She nodded in agreement. "I do believe that. I would just like to focus on making sure Rae enjoys the holidays. She's just a little girl."

Declan glanced over at her. "She's going to have that, Everleigh. I intend to make sure of it."

They made small talk during the rest of the drive.

After parking the car, Declan and Everleigh took the elevator up to her hotel room.

She ordered an assortment of sandwiches.

They sat down on the couch to wait for their food and the detectives to arrive.

"What if we were seen at Mattie's house?" Everleigh asked.

"By who?"

"By the person responsible for her death."

"The only other people who drove down that dirt road was the police. Her house is pretty secluded."

"You're right. I guess my mind is all over the place." She stood up and strode over to the only window in the room.

"Are you okay?" he asked.

She didn't answer right away, but instead turned to the window, her fingers tracing the contours of the curtains.

Mattie's death had affected Everleigh, despite her attempts to remain composed. She bit her lower lip and turned to face him, looking into his eyes. "I don't know what I would have done if I didn't have you to lean on."

He leaned down and kissed her gently, a moment of pause in their tumultuous lives that caught them both by surprise.

The kiss was broken by a knock on the door.

"They're here," Declan said softly.

Everleigh took a deep breath and murmured, "Let's get this over with."

Everleigh had no time to process what had just happened between her and Declan. The detectives were there to question them regarding Mattie Powell. There wasn't much they could tell him about her death specifically—only their suspicions.

Declan let the detectives inside the room. "We ordered some sandwiches," he said. "There's coffee and soft drinks."

The men exchanged glances. "It's been a long morning," said the one who introduced himself as Howard Bell. "I could use something to eat. But I'd prefer to take care of business first."

Everleigh sat down on the sofa beside Declan as the homicide detectives sat across from them in chairs.

"I understand you're a criminal investigator from Charleston. What was the reason for your visit to Mattie Powell?" Bell asked.

"Everleigh received a threatening letter dated six months ago and she came to me for help," Declan stated. "The person who sent it believes that she's Powell's daughter."

"*Are* you James Ray Powell's daughter?" Bell asked.

"Yes." It galled her to have to admit that horrible truth.

"She doesn't want anyone to know," Declan interjected. "So I'm hoping you will keep it away from the public."

Everleigh stood up when a knock sounded. "That must be room service."

"My mother was one of his victims," Everleigh clarified after signing the check and seeing the server to the door. "She never reported it. She didn't know his identity until months later after he was arrested."

Bell nodded in understanding. "We'll do our best to keep it out of the case, Mrs. Taylor."

"That's all I ask," she stated. "Thank you."

"I'm sure this is a stretch, but do you happen to have that letter with you?" Bell's partner, Detective Larry Rowe, inquired.

"I have a picture of it," Everleigh responded.

"She gave the original to me," Declan said. "I had it tested for prints but the results yielded nothing."

"There was a letter similar to this on her nightstand," Rowe announced.

Everleigh gasped. She glanced over at Declan, who looked just as surprised.

"Was it dated about six months ago?" he asked.

"Yes. We're not releasing that information to the public, so we ask that you keep it to yourself."

Declan gave a small nod. "Understood."

Everleigh pointed to the silver tray heaped with neatly halved sandwiches after the server delivered them to the room. "Please help yourselves. What would you like to drink? Water, coffee or soda?"

"I'll take water," said Bell.

"I'll have coffee," his partner responded.

Everyone helped themselves to the food, and they ate in silence for a while. When they were finished, the detectives rose.

"We have what we need," Rowe said.

Declan shook their hands. "I would really appreciate your keeping me informed about the investigation."

"We ask that you do the same," Bell replied.

"Are we free to leave Atlanta?" Everleigh asked.

"Yes, ma'am," Larry responded.

Everleigh looked over at Declan when the detectives left. "Do you think they'll keep their word?"

"I think they will do as they said—they will try to keep the information out of their investigation. It shouldn't be a problem because your being Powell's daughter shouldn't come into play. It has nothing to do with Mattie's murder."

"But when Ellis and Neil are caught, it will get out because it provides motive," Everleigh said. "I'll deal with it when the time comes."

Chapter 13

Everleigh played a reading game with her daughter that night while Declan made a visit to the Atlanta police precinct.

She'd already packed their bags since they were leaving first thing in the morning. She was actually looking forward to going home. Everleigh planned to tell Declan on the way back to Charleston that she and Rae were going back to their house. When Ellis and Neil came for her, she'd be ready.

"Mama, where's Mr. Declan?"

"He had to run an errand," Everleigh responded. "He should be back soon."

"I like him."

She smiled. "I know you do, sweetie. You know what? I like him, too."

"I miss Billie. I bet she misses me, too."

"Yes, she does."

They finished their game, so they moved on to a round of Go Fish.

Every time they heard a sound outside, they both stared at the door expectantly.

They were both looking forward to seeing Declan. Everleigh hoped he would be arriving any moment now. She didn't mind Rae's attachment to him, but she didn't want her to see Declan as a father figure—only as a friend.

Christmas was fast approaching and she still had a few things on her list she wanted to get for Rae. It was going to be the first one without her mom and the second without Britt.

Declan arrived a half hour later.

"We're so glad you're here," Rae declared. "Me and Mama missed you."

Everleigh averted her gaze. She didn't want him getting the wrong idea. She enjoyed his company—that was all it was.

Liar.

The truth was that she cared more for Declan than she ever cared to admit. He'd gotten under her skin and pierced her heart and soul.

"Everything go okay?" she asked.

He gave a slight nod.

Everleigh knew that he would share more once they were able to talk privately. Declan had gone there to see if there was any information on the Ragland brothers in the system. They wanted to know the type of people they were dealing with.

God, I just want to get back to my life. Is this Your way of getting my attention? If so, it worked.

She closed her eyes and sent up a quick prayer.

Declan smiled to himself as he watched Everleigh with Rae. They were laughing and talking about Christmas. The little girl was extremely excited about all the presents she was going to get.

Every now and then, a yawn interrupted Rae's chatter. She was sleepy but kept trying to fight it. Eventually, her exhaustion won out and she was fast asleep.

"She was trying her hardest to hang out with us," Everleigh said when she joined him on the sofa.

"She's adorable," Declan responded. "You're very blessed to have that little girl."

"I know. She's one of the reasons I smile every day." Changing the subject, Everleigh asked, "How did it go at the police station?"

"The Ragland brothers lived for a short time with their father after Olivia's death. He disappeared about a year after, and they were placed in a group home. As I thought, Ellis and Neil are no strangers to violence and criminal activities," Declan said. "The last known address is in Virginia. That was over three years ago, so they can be anywhere."

He handed her a couple of photos. "Neil is the one with the dreadlocks."

"I've never seen either of them before," Everleigh responded. "Ellis looks sinister with that scar on his forehead. I'm pretty sure they're heading back to Charleston."

"If you ever get tired of teaching, you should look into becoming a police detective. You've be good at it."

She laughed.

"I mean it. You have great instincts about people."

"I'll keep that in mind, Declan."

"You know, I sat in during one of your lectures," he said.

Her eyebrows rose in surprise. "When was this?"

"A couple of weeks after you started. It was on self-justification in everyday life. I loved what you said about us lying to ourselves daily.

We lie about how good or bad we are at the various things we do."

"It's true," Everleigh responded. "Our skewed beliefs infiltrate our day-to-day life so effectively that we rarely notice we're doing it. We can see fault so clearly in others but we're blissfully unaware of them when it comes to our own thoughts and behaviors."

"Why do you think that is?" Declan asked.

"Because facing the lie we tell ourselves would mean redefining how we see ourselves. If the Ragland brothers really are the killers—then they are a prime example of this," she explained. "They believe that they're justified in killing innocent people all because those people are related to James Ray Powell. They don't see themselves as killers. If Powell, Ellis and Neil were to face the truth, they would have to reevaluate themselves and it would be less than flattering. In their case, murderers. All of them. Most people would be unable to live with that label, so playing ostrich is much easier."

Declan could talk with Everleigh all night long, but they had to be up early in the morning. It was time to go home.

They had no idea where the Ragland brothers were, but at least now they knew whom they were dealing with.

"When we get back to Charleston, Rae and I are going back to our house," Everleigh announced the next morning. "I'm not going to stop living my life." One of the first things she planned to do was upgrade her security, this time installing cameras all around her house.

"I can't change your mind?" he asked.

"I've given it a lot of thought, Declan."

"I have to be honest. I'd feel better if you continue staying at my place until we have these guys in custody, but it's your decision. I'll make sure the island police keep an eye on your home."

"Thank you," she said. "I'm tired of hiding, but I don't want to put Rae at risk. However, this is the only way to catch them."

After they made it to Angel Island, Declan walked them to their front door. Everleigh took Declan's hand. "Come back this evening for dinner, please."

He smiled. "I'd love to join the two most beautiful girls on the island for dinner."

"Great. We'll see you then."

His words left her with a warm feeling in her belly.

When Declan drove away, Everleigh headed back inside and found her daughter in the hallway. "We've got a lot to do this afternoon. We're going to…" Her voice died at the sight of the broken picture frame on the floor.

"Mama, who broke the picture?" Rae asked.

"It must have fallen somehow," she said, but Everleigh knew better. Someone had been inside their home. The tiny hairs on the back of her neck stood to attention.

It had to be Wyle.

Everleigh opened up the app to her security system. She'd unarmed it when they first pulled up into the driveway. She was sure of it. After checking out Rae's room, she told her, "You stay in here. I'll come get you when I'm ready to get started. Okay?"

She locked the door when she left the room. Taser in hand, Everleigh went from room to room, checking closets, bathrooms—she checked the house from top to bottom.

Satisfied that no one was in the house, she opened her security app again and did a more thorough review. She felt a chill run through her when she saw that her system had been disarmed while she was at Declan's house. Wyle had a background in IT and Everleigh believed that he'd hacked her alarm.

She called her security company and changed the credentials. Next, she called Officer Lee and filed a report.

He came to the house almost immediately. She kept Rae busy while he did a walk-through, and she shared her suspicions about Wyle, how he'd been in her yard and how he had the means to disarm her security system.

When he left, Everleigh went online to purchase a second security system as a backup until she could change companies.

She took a moment to thank God that she and Rae had not been here at the time of the home invasion.

Everleigh briefly considered Declan's offer to stay with him. "No, I'm not doing that," she whispered. "I'm not going to let him run me out of my home."

"What you say, Mama?"

"Nothing, sweetie. I'm just rambling."

"Why?"

She chuckled. "I have no idea."

"Mama, you're so silly."

Everleigh embraced Rae. "I love you to pieces."

"I love you, too."

They spent the next couple of hours cooking together, and then they went upstairs to get ready for dinner.

Everleigh chose a sapphire-blue sweater dress and paired it with cognac-colored boots. Rae chose a navy dress to wear with her camel cowboy boots.

"Mama, wear your hair just like it is," Rae instructed.

Everleigh eyed her reflection in the mirror. Her hair was a mass of loose curls. She spritzed it with water and leave-in conditioner to tame the frizz.

Ten minutes later, Declan arrived.

She led him into the dining room.

He eyed the table, which she and Rae had decorated, and asked, "You did all this?"

Everleigh nodded. "Rae and I wanted to do something special for you."

"You succeeded."

Vibrant flames in red and gold flickered from the silver-colored candles, casting a soft glow on the succulent display of baked chicken, roasted potatoes, yeast rolls and steaming broccoli.

"Everything looks delicious," he said.

"Thank you," she murmured as she sat down in the chair he had pulled out for her. He did the same for Rae.

Declan walked around the table and eased into a chair facing her. "Did you cook all this?"

She nodded. "I did."

"And I *helped*," Rae interjected. "I made the *brock-li*."

Grinning, he said, "You did a great job, too."

"Me and Mama made brownies for dessert," Rae announced. "Chocolate peanut-butter."

Declan awarded them a smile. "I want you to know that this is much appreciated."

After dinner, Everleigh told Rae she could go watch television. With just the adults at the table, Declan said, "I've never met a woman like you. I haven't met anyone who would do something like this for a man they barely know."

Everleigh pushed away from the table. "I enjoy giving flowers to people while they can see and smell them, Declan. Life is too short—I don't take any day for granted."

He got up from the table and followed her into the kitchen.

Declan touched a finger to her chin. His eyes were bright with an emotion she couldn't identify.

His mouth curved up at the corners. His finger brushed against Everleigh's skin, moving back and forth, making it difficult for her to think.

He kissed her.

"I just don't think it's a good idea for us to get carried away," she murmured against his cheek before stepping back.

Their gazes locked and Everleigh moved forward again, letting him wrap his arms around her. He gazed into her eyes.

Everleigh drew his face to hers.

He kissed her again, lingering, savoring every moment.

Everleigh's emotions whirled. Blood pounded in her brain, leaped from her heart and made her knees tremble.

"Thank you," he whispered.

Puzzled, she asked, "For what?"

"For trusting me."

She smiled at him. "Thank you for being a friend to me, Declan. And for your protection."

"It's my honor, Everleigh."

"I thought we was watching a movie," Rae called from the family room.

"Here we come," she said, taking Declan's hand in her own.

When his gaze landed on the broken frame, Everleigh whispered, "It's nothing to worry about. I've already ordered a new one."

"What happened?"

"We found it on the floor broken when we came home earlier."

Declan's eyes didn't leave her face.

"I think Wyle... I know he was in our house while we were staying with you. But you don't have to worry. The security system have been changed and I've installed a backup security system—I have cameras everywhere now. Plus, a locksmith is on the way."

"Did you have a police officer come out?"

"I filed a report with Officer Lee. He came out and did a walk-through. Wyle came in through the back door."

"You should've called me," he said.

"You'd just gotten home. I knew that you were tired."

"I really don't like leaving you and Rae alone in this house."

"Declan, this is our home," Everleigh stated.

"I won't let some stranger run me away from it like Powell did my mother."

"Leaving is what saved her life."

He was right, of course.

Chapter 14

Declan was touched beyond measure by the lengths Everleigh went through to make the evening special for him. An invisible thread was pulling them closer and closer. But at the moment, he was still upset with her for not telling him immediately about the break-in.

Everleigh was trying to be brave, but it was also making her a bit reckless. How could he protect them if she didn't keep him informed of any threats? He considered staking out her house after he left for the evening, but he decided against it. He had to be at the precinct early, and Lee was parked outside the house. Declan would speak briefly with him before he left the island.

The next morning, he was at his desk at the precinct when his phone began vibrating, taking him out of his musings.

It was Detective Bell.

He pressed the button to answer. "Declan Blanchet speaking."

"I wanted to let you know that a vehicle belonging to Ellis Ragland received a ticket in Charleston two days ago."

Their hunch was right. The Ragland brothers were involved, and as he'd hoped, they'd made a mistake.

There wasn't anything new on Mattie's death. They talked a few minutes more before hanging up.

He let out a frustrated sigh, then called Everleigh. Declan hated having to give her this piece of news. They both knew this day would come…but he'd prayed for divine intervention in this situation.

There was no answer.

His muscles rigid and his jaw clenched, Declan left his desk and headed out. He was going to the house to make sure Everleigh and Rae were okay. He knew what the Ragland brothers were capable of and he didn't want to take any chances.

One of his coworkers approached him, but Declan responded in a rushed tone. He didn't have time to socialize. He was in a hurry to get to Angel Island.

It wasn't like Everleigh to not answer her phone.

He walked with haste out of the precinct and jumped into his car. He tried her again. "C'mon, Everleigh. Answer your phone."

No answer. A wave of apprehension snaked down his spine.

Declan rubbed the back of his neck while he drove, trying to stay mindful of the speed limit, praying for smooth traffic and the safety of Everleigh and Rae. Declan had promised to protect them and he didn't want to break his word.

"I can't fail them," he said to the empty car. "Lord, please keep them safe."

With hot coffee fresh from the pot, the latest edition of the *American Journal of Psychology* spread out on her kitchen island and pajamas still enrobing her fatigued body, Everleigh slowly devoured a spinach, mushroom and tomato omelet as she read an article without interruption.

After she finished off her omelet, she went upstairs to wake Rae.

"Hey, sweetie…it's time to get up."

"Mama, I'm hungry. I was dreaming about food all night."

"Oh, really? What kinds of food?"

"Choc'late cake, hot dogs, hamburgers and chicken."

"I see. Well, you can't have any of that for breakfast. So what do you think you'd like instead?"

"Choc'late-chip waffles, bacon and fruit."

"That's doable," Everleigh said. "C'mon, get up and head straight to the bathroom."

"It's almost Christmas, Mama."

She planted a kiss on her daughter's forehead. "I know...it's less than a week away."

Everleigh had breakfast waiting for Rae when she came downstairs. She cleaned the kitchen while her daughter ate, then Rae went up to her bedroom to play.

Everleigh saw the mail carrier turn onto her street from the window. She was expecting a package—a Christmas gift she'd ordered for Rae, which was due to arrive any day now. She opened the door while her daughter was upstairs, so that Rae wouldn't hear and come down to investigate.

Everleigh had taken only a few steps onto the porch when a tall, broad-shouldered man stepped out from behind the hedge. The look on his face was ominous, and the scar above his right eye made him look menacing.

He lunged toward her, grabbing her arm and dragging her onto the porch.

She had the presence of mind to swallow her scream. Everleigh didn't want to scare Rae. With her heart pounding, she struggled to break free.

Pain ripped down her arm as she wrenched it away from him. "Keep your hands off me."

Pointing a gun at her, he demanded lowly, "Don't make a scene. Just march into the house like you would any other day."

Lifting her chin in defiance, she uttered, "I wouldn't have a gun at my back if this were *any other day*."

"Shut up." His angry voice spiked the fear swirling around within her.

"I know who you are… Ellis Ragland. Listen, I don't have anything to do with James Ray Powell. I only found out a few months ago that he's my father. How did you find out?"

"You can thank your friend Wyle Gaines," he sneered. "We were at a bar minding our business when we happened to hear this guy complaining to anyone who would listen about the serial-killer spawn who cheated him out of a

fortune. It won't surprise you that I'm interested in serial killers, so I got to talking with
him. He told us everything about you—all we
had to do was get him drinking. Imagine our
surprise when it turned out which serial-killer
family did him wrong."

"Why are you doing this?" she asked.

"It's because of your mother that mine died."

Everleigh shook her head. "That's not true."

"Powell went to that apartment looking for
your mother," he said. "It's *her* fault."

"My mom died—there's nothing you can do
to her. I understand that you want to blame
someone, but that person is Powell and he's already behind bars."

"That's not enough payment for what I had
to go through," Ellis huffed.

"My mother was a victim. I'm not connected
to that serial killer and neither is my daughter.
I'm sure your mother wouldn't want you to do
this."

"I have to do it. There's a serial-killer gene,"
he said. "Did you know that? I expect you
should since you're a shrink. Once we heard
how you'd mistreated ol' Wyle, I looked up
your mama. That's how we found out about

the apartment. That's when we decided every-one with Powell's evil blood needed to die."

"Ellis, you need to know that there's no *se-rial-killer* gene," Everleigh stated.

"Sure there is. I've heard podcasts about it. Did you know that one of Powell's uncles was also a killer? The coward took his own life be-fore he could be apprehended."

"It's not true. However, there is a gene that can influence a person's level of aggression and emotional control."

"Don't try to trick me…"

"I'm not," she responded, her voice waver-ing. "I'm telling you the truth. That serial-killer theory was debunked—it's nothing more than a myth."

He shook his head. "Naw… I don't believe you."

She tried to keep from trembling as she spoke. "You can check on the internet," Ever-leigh stated. "I wouldn't lie to you."

"Get inside," he ordered, glancing around suspiciously.

Everleigh hesitated, fear and doubt mixing in her mind as she thought about protecting her daughter from him. "Ellis, you don't want to do this…"

He rounded on her with anger flashing in his eyes. "Stop trying to tell me what I want or don't want," he snapped.

"I'm sorry. I'm not trying to upset you. You have to understand that hurting me…hurting my daughter… I'm telling you that it won't matter to Powell. He doesn't even know we exist."

"You're his blood. I need to eliminate you."

"Look, there's a police cruiser about to turn on this street. He's going to stop here."

Ellis turned his head away from her.

Everleigh flexed her wrist and took a step toward him, aiming for his nose. She used the momentary distraction to her advantage and did a high kick, knocking the gun out of Ellis's hand.

He shoved her down in his effort to recover his weapon.

As she fell to the ground, she heard pounding footsteps.

Ellis tried to run away, but the yard was soon covered with police officers.

She heard Declan's voice, but didn't see him. All Everleigh wanted to do was get to Rae.

"His gun is over there," she told one of the officers.

"This isn't over," Ellis hissed at her.

"Please get him out of my yard. I don't want my daughter seeing this man."

Declan walked over to her. "Are you okay?"

Everleigh nodded. "I'm fine."

"Why didn't you answer your phone? I called you at least four times."

She looked down at her pajamas. "No pockets. I think my phone's in my bedroom." She looked up at Declan. "How did you know to come here?"

"Bell called and told me that Ellis got a ticket a couple days ago in Charleston. I was riding over here to tell you about that. But when you didn't answer, I got worried. I called the island precinct."

"I'm fine. I just want them to get him away from my house." Everleigh started shivering uncontrollably.

Declan gathered Everleigh into his arms, holding her close. He was relieved to find that she and Rae hadn't been harmed. He didn't want to think of the alternative.

She stirred slightly. "I'm so glad you got here when you did. And the police. Ellis was trying to force me inside the house. I guess he'd planned to kill us there."

"Where's Rae?" Declan inquired.

"She's in the house," she responded. "She was upstairs when I was on my way to check my mail. I really hope she didn't see any of this. I need to check on her."

"Try to keep her away from the windows."

Everleigh nodded.

When she returned a few minutes later, she said, "Thank goodness, Rae had gone back to sleep. Looks like she missed everything."

"I see you're very capable of handling yourself," Declan said, "But you shouldn't take any unnecessary risks. Ellis and his brother are *killers*."

"All that was on my mind is that I had to do whatever I could to protect my child," Everleigh responded. "Rae is who I was thinking about at the time." She paused a moment, then said, "Neil is still out there somewhere."

"We'll find him."

"What if he doesn't have anything to do with this?"

"Once we locate him, we'll know for sure," Declan said.

"I want to know everything there is about these men," Everleigh insisted.

"I do, too. In the meantime, I don't think it's safe for you to stay here."

He was relieved when she nodded in agreement. She said, "I was thinking the same thing. I guess I should find a hotel—"

"No, I have the perfect place. It's safe and away from Charleston. My sister is in Europe for a couple of months and her house in Columbia, South Carolina, is empty. I'd planned on spending the holidays there. You and Rae can join me."

"I've tried so hard to make this place a home for Rae and me. I hate to leave it, even for a little while." She bit her lip. "But we can be ready within the hour."

Neil watched the police take his brother away. He'd warned him against confronting Everleigh like this, but Ellis never listened to him.

He knew his brother would never give him up. Ellis would take it upon himself to spend time in prison alone rather than give Neil up. He'd always protected him, even when they were in that foster home. He nearly killed the man who'd been abusing him when he tried to touch Neil. They ran away and lived on the streets for months before they were picked up and taken to a group home.

Neil owed Ellis his life. He always willingly suffered the brunt of the abuse they endured. Whenever other kids used to tease him about his stutter, Ellis would step up and make them stop.

I won't abandon you now.

But he couldn't just show up at the precinct. Since the police had Ellis in custody, there was a chance that they also knew about him. If he wasn't careful, it would only be a matter of time before he was behind bars with his brother.

Neil was determined to find a way to get Ellis out. Once again, he'd have to put his dreams on hold.

I can do that for my brother. He needs me more.

A part of him wanted to stay to see what would happen next, but Neil changed his mind when two more cruisers pulled up to the house.

With so many police officers in the area, he decided to return to the motel in Charleston.

"Are we going on another trip?" Rae asked when Everleigh woke her. She sat up, rubbing her eyes. "I was still tired so I laid down."

"We're going away...yes." Everleigh's words

came out in a rush. "I've already packed your bag. Grab your hat and coat."

"Mama, where're we going?"

"Sweetie, just do as I asked. We need to hurry."

Declan appeared in the bedroom doorway. "Rae, why don't I help you with your backpack," he said. "Let's see if we can get to the car before your mom."

The little girl grinned. "Yeah. I'm real fast."

Everleigh gave him a grateful smile.

She went back to her room to see if she'd forgotten anything she might need while she was away. Everleigh made sure she had her cell phone, laptop and iPad, plus all her charging cords. She made a quick call to Robin to let her know that she was going to have deliveries routed to her house temporarily.

When she walked out of the house ten minutes later, she found Rae seated inside Declan's car, Declan standing beside the open trunk.

Everleigh glanced around before sliding into the front passenger seat. She didn't notice anything out of the ordinary. She released a soft sigh of relief that she and Rae were going away. It was clear that they were no longer safe.

During the drive, Declan asked Everleigh, "How you holding up?"

She glanced back at Rae, who was wearing a headset. She seemed engrossed in the movie she was watching on her tablet.

"He came to my house to kill me."

"I'm sorry," Declan responded.

Everleigh shivered at the very thought of Ellis being that close to her. She was always intentional about safety, but somehow, she'd missed him lurking nearby.

"Ellis is locked up now."

"True, but his brother is still out there. If Neil's involved, he won't be able to get to us right now, but we can't stay away forever. Declan, I'm not going to live my life on the run. I just wanted Rae to have her first Christmas here in our new house."

"I understand," he said. "I'm optimistic that Neil will be found soon—especially if he's in Charleston."

"I have confidence in you and the police department. I guess I shouldn't have waited this long to get them involved."

"You were trying to stay out of the spotlight and keep your daughter safe."

"I found out how Ellis and Neil found out

about me," Everleigh said. "Wyle Gaines. They overheard him talking about me in a bar, by complete coincidence." She shuddered. "He was supposed to be my mother's friend. I can't believe my mother would confide in him, but she did."

"Mama, I'm hungry."

Everleigh glanced back at Rae and smiled. "We're almost there. I put a sandwich and fruit in the bag beside you."

"Thank you."

"You're welcome, sweetie."

"Never in a million years did I think we'd be spending the holidays together," Declan said with a chuckle, steering the conversation to a lighter topic.

"I didn't see this coming, either."

"I'm glad to have this chance to get to know you, though."

She smiled. "Same here."

Everleigh was sincere about getting to know Declan. He had a great sense of humor and made her laugh. Something she hadn't really done in a while. He also made her feel emotions she thought had died with Britt. Emotions that betrayed her love for him. Everleigh knew that there was nothing wrong with moving on and finding love a second time, but she didn't want to chance it with Declan. She couldn't bear the loss. It would be too much.

It's not healthy to think this way. Everleigh wasn't a pessimist, but she preferred to face reality because it kept her from the hope of something more where Declan was concerned.

Chapter 15

Declan was dealing with his own feelings for Everleigh. She had an infectious laugh that he loved. She was intelligent, courageous and beautiful—not to mention a loving mother to Rae. But he couldn't forget that she still wore her wedding rings. A sure sign that she was still grieving the loss of her husband.

He drove around for a while to make sure they weren't being followed when they arrived in Columbia, South Carolina.

"Are you from Columbia?" Everleigh asked.

Declan nodded. "Born and raised. I attended college in Charleston. Fell in love with the city and decided to make it my home."

"This will be my first time here."

"It has kind of a small-town feel to it," Declan said. "But there are a lot of nice restaurants, culture and art."

"That's nice to know but I'm hoping we'll

only be here for a few days. You keep coming to my rescue. I honestly never thought things would get so crazy. Now you're mixed up in this."

"It's not a problem. I probably wouldn't have gotten to know you otherwise."

Everleigh eyed him. "Do you really believe that?"

Declan smiled. "Before this, I couldn't get anything out of you other than a hello."

"You must have thought I was unapproachable."

"Actually, I just assumed you were getting adjusted to the university. I never took it personally."

She smiled. "I'm really glad you didn't. I was focused on making sure Rae was okay and trying to process my grief."

"I understand."

Twenty minutes later, Declan turned on Lakeshore Drive.

"Oh, wow, this house is gorgeous," Everleigh murmured when he pulled into the circular driveway.

"This is the main house, where you'll be staying," he announced.

"Main house?"

"There's a one-bedroom apartment over the four-car garage. There's a guest residence on the property as well."

He led her up the steps to the main house.

"We're staying in here?" Everleigh asked. "Maybe you should put us in the apartment or the guest house?"

"I'll be staying in the apartment. My nephew currently lives in the guesthouse. In fact, he should be arriving shortly."

Chilly air kissed her skin as soon as she stepped inside. Everleigh pulled the folds of her coat together.

"I just turned on the heat," he said. "My sister's been away for a couple of weeks."

Her cold face warmed up at the sight of the gorgeous marble fireplace in the living room. This seemed like the perfect place to enjoy family gatherings or spend quiet evenings with a book.

All the rooms in the house were oversized. She fell in love instantly with the gourmet kitchen that was built to entertain. Nearly every room in the house seemed to offer generous views of the lake. The well-appointed great room also featured a wet bar and high ceilings.

Everleigh couldn't resist stepping out onto the

large covered porch that overlooked a saltwater pool, a cabana and the lake.

Rae joined her. "Mama, I like this house."

"So do I, sweetie. It's beautiful and very peaceful."

"Yeah."

Declan went to put his car in an empty space in the garage.

Upon his return, he said, "I put you and Rae in the bedroom down here. I figured you'd be more comfortable with having her in the same room."

"Thank you." Everleigh's gaze traveled her surroundings. "Is this the master bedroom?"

"It's one of two. There's another upstairs," Declan explained. "That's my sister's."

"I'm glad to hear that," Everleigh said. "Because I didn't want to invade her personal space."

A man who looked to be in his mid-twenties walked into the house.

"This is my nephew, Remy," Declan said.

"It's nice to meet you," Everleigh murmured, noting the police-academy hoodie he wore beneath his leather jacket.

"And you as well." He also shared the same eyes and full lips as Declan, and like his uncle, Remy sported a neatly trimmed mustache and beard.

Holding out her hand to him, Rae introduced herself.

He grinned. "It's nice to meet you, Rae. I have a little girl about your age. Her name is Halle. She's four years old."

"I'm five. Can I meet her?"

"You sure can. She's actually coming for a visit tomorrow. She'll be here until after the New Year." To Everleigh, he said, "My wife is finishing up school in North Carolina—graduating in May. After that, they'll be living here full-time."

"That's wonderful," Everleigh said.

"Did you notice anyone following us?" Declan asked.

"No, I was about three vehicles behind you once you entered the city," Remy responded. "I hung back to see if anyone followed you from the exit to the house."

"I didn't see anyone, either, but I didn't want to chance it without a set of second eyes."

Everleigh looked over at Declan. "You arranged all this?"

He nodded. "I promised to keep you safe."

"Did you show her the panic room?" Remy asked.

"Not yet."

Her eyes widened in surprise. "There's a panic room?"

"It's in the library, which is beside the room you and Rae will be staying in. I'll show it to you later. I'm pretty sure you won't be needing it because no one knows you're here. Plus, Remy and I will be around. You'll never be alone. One of us will always be close by."

Remy gave her an encouraging smile. "My mom said for you to make yourself comfortable and she looks forward to meeting you in the future."

Everleigh smiled back. "Please convey my gratitude to her."

Declan took them on a tour around the ten-acre property. "This land belonged to our grandparents," he said. "See that house over there?"

When Everleigh glanced in the direction of Declan's pointing finger and nodded, Declan continued, "That's where my grandparents lived. My dad was born in that house. When he got married, he built what we now call the guesthouse. Dad gave it to me when he and Mom bought a condo in Florida. I decided to renovate and update it. I plan to make it my home after I retire. In the meantime, Remy and his family are welcome to live there."

"That's very sweet." Everleigh admired the professionally landscaped grounds. There was a small garden, a fountain and a shaded pergola. She imagined herself strolling across the manicured lawn and sitting in one of the Adirondack chairs by the seawall while drinking a cup of coffee. "I could sit out here for hours just taking in the solitude."

"That's the idea," Declan responded. "This is where I come whenever I feel the need to clear my mind."

"I'm glad Rae will have someone to play with while we're here." Everleigh looked at him. "You've thought of everything, haven't you?"

"I tried."

"Declan, I want to apologize to you. I should have told you about the break-in as soon as I realized what had taken place. I think it was my pride. I didn't want to fall apart and become a victim. If I'd told you, maybe none of this would be happening right now."

"I have to be honest and say that I'm glad you and Rae are spending time with me," he admitted.

"You have such a way of putting my mind at ease."

Declan smiled. "There's no way Neil or Wyle can find you here. However, I would advise that you not use any credit cards—not even your debit card. If you need cash, I can give it to you."

"I keep cash for emergencies in a safe at home. I brought it with me, so I should be fine," Everleigh replied. She couldn't stop herself from yawning. She was suddenly feeling tired and sleepy.

"Why don't you take a nap?" Declan suggested when they were back inside the house. "Rae can keep me company while I make dinner."

"Are you sure?"

He nodded.

Everleigh walked down the hallway to the bedroom.

As soon as she climbed into the bed, her eyelids felt heavy. She'd been up since 5:00 a.m. and after her run-in with Ellis, Everleigh sought to escape the trauma if only for a short while.

"I can't wait for Halle to get here," Rae said as she ripped a slice of bread apart and tossed it into a bowl. "She's gonna be my friend." She sat at the counter while Declan stood on the other side facing her.

"I have a feeling the two of you are going to be great friends," he responded. Her curly ponytail bobbed up and down with Rae's every move.

"Mr. Declan, how is Santa gonna find me and Halle? We're not at home. He won't be able to find this house because there's no lights, no tree—there's nothing."

"Don't you worry. Remy and I will make sure Santa knows exactly where to find you two."

"I really don't wanna miss Christmas. It's Jesus's birthday."

"You won't," he promised.

"My daddy's in heaven. So is my grandma," Rae stated. "Maybe they'll tell God to make sure I don't miss it."

Declan chuckled. She was such a sweet and adorable little girl. If he was ever blessed with a daughter, he wanted her to be like Rae and Halle. They were both precious.

"The bread's all tore up."

"Good job." He then instructed her on what to do next.

Rae was a good listener and she followed his directions perfectly. "You're going to be a great cook when you grow up."

"I know," she responded. "'Cause Mama teaches me."

He smiled.

"Mr. Declan, I like it out here."

"I'm glad," he responded. "I want you and your mom to have a really nice time while you're here."

She scrunched up her face, then burst into giggles.

"What's that for?" Declan asked with a chuckle.

"I want to see Billie. I miss her. She's a cute doggy."

"I knew I had a surprise for you."

"What is it?"

"Billie will be here tomorrow," he confided. "She's coming with Sherri and Halle." Declan had been in a rush to get Everleigh and Rae out of town—he didn't want to delay the trip by going to get Billie, so he'd arranged for a friend to watch her until Sherri, Remy's wife, could get there. She was also going to pick up the packed duffel he kept in his coat closet for any last-minute trips.

"Yay."

Everleigh walked into the kitchen an hour later, and said, "Something smells delicious."

"Mama, Mr. Declan and I made meat loaf. I got to tear the bread and mix it up in the bowl. It got all squishy." Grinning, she added, "So much fun."

"Smells delicious. I can't wait to taste it."

"You and Rae have a seat," Declan said. "I'll bring everything out."

"Is your nephew joining us?" Everleigh asked.

"Yes. I texted him. He'll be here shortly."

"Declan, from the way all this looks…you're a good cook," Everleigh said.

"Not really. I've only prepared what I know how to make," he confessed.

"Don't let my uncle fool you. He is a great cook," Remy interjected as he took a seat at the table. "He just doesn't like doing it much."

"It's better cooking for others than just myself."

Smiling, Everleigh responded, "I get that. If I didn't have Rae, I'd probably never step into my kitchen. Actually, this isn't true. I enjoy cooking because it calms me."

"Well, I don't have that gift," Remy said. "When my mom is in town, she usually makes casseroles and meals for me to store in the freezer, but this time, she was too busy. I have to say that I'm glad my wife will be here tomorrow. I'm tired of eating fast food."

Declan nodded in agreement. "Sherri throws down in the kitchen. And she loves to cook. I also have to add that Everleigh knows her way around the kitchen."

He enjoyed watching her interact with his nephew. Every time she laughed; the sound was like music to his ears.

Remy cleaned the kitchen after they finished eating.

"I'm glad you were able to get some rest earlier," Declan said.

"I didn't realize until we got here that I was so tired. Now that I'm thinking about it, I don't think I've slept really well since getting that letter."

"I want you to know that you and Rae are safe. No one knows where you are. You can relax."

"How about a quiet stroll around the lake? Rae can come with us."

Everleigh met his gaze, then said, "Sure. It's a nice evening for it."

They slipped on coats and went outside.

"I'm trying to convince myself that I'm on vacation in this beautiful house on the lake," Everleigh said as they walked the grounds.

He smiled. "That's a great way to look at it."

"Who knew that we'd be spending the holidays together," Everleigh murmured, pulling the folds of her coat together.

"I didn't, but I'm actually looking forward to getting to know you better."

"I am, too. I'd like to have a friend."

"So, *friend*...what do you like to do for fun?" Declan asked. He was glad to hear that she considered him a friend, but he also felt slightly dejected.

"Fun? What's that?" Everleigh chuckled. "Seriously, I love all things basketball..."

He looked surprised. "Wha-a-at?"

"Don't act like you haven't seen me and Rae at the games. We sit two rows behind you."

"I thought you were just coming to support the team."

"No, we love it," she responded. "I also enjoy reading, love going to the movies and trying new things."

"Have you ever gone on a sunset sail?"

"I haven't."

"Okay, that's something we can do while

we're here. I'll take you on a tour around the lake," Declan said. "We can go tomorrow evening and take the girls. Rae and Halle will enjoy seeing all the Christmas decorations."

"Sounds like fun," Everleigh said. "I'm looking forward to that myself."

"Tell the truth…are you all hyped up for the holidays?"

She grinned. "I'm really grateful Rae and I don't have to spend it alone. I wasn't looking forward to that."

"Do you have any other family?" Declan inquired, then added, "On your mother's side."

"My mom was an only child. You met Bonnie—she was my mother's first cousin. I have distant cousins like her but they're spread out."

He took her hand in his. "I'm glad to have y'all here celebrating with us."

"'Jingle bells, jingle bells…'"

Declan and Everleigh stood there listening to Rae sing.

The little girl stopped in her tracks and looked at them. "Sing!"

"'Jingle bells…'" they all sang as they strolled back to the house.

Despite being in South Carolina, Everleigh knew the nightmare was far from over.

★ ★ ★

"Having you and Remy here makes me feel safe," Everleigh said after she put Rae to bed and joined Declan in the family room. "I see he's following in your footsteps."

"He's always wanted to be in law enforcement. My sister works for Homeland Security."

"Oh, wow," she murmured, impressed.

"My grandfather was an attorney. My father was a prosecutor, then a judge. I guess the law in one form or another is in our blood."

"I would agree."

"Remy's wife, Sherri…she's in school to become a registered nurse."

"That's wonderful," Everleigh responded. "My mother was a nurse."

"Her mother is moving in with them to help with their daughter. She's a retired teacher and she'll be homeschooling Halle."

"That's really nice that Halle will be surrounded by both grandmothers."

"My brother-in-law lives nearby. He and my sister divorced a couple years ago, but I have a feeling that they're going to reconcile. They're the best of friends. He never got comfortable with her working in Homeland Security."

"How often do you get to see your parents?"

"Two or three times a year," Declan responded. "They decided to spend Christmas on a cruise this year."

"I think it's wonderful that you still have your parents."

"I realize this more and more each day."

"Declan, I have to say that it amazes me some woman hasn't snatched you up. You're a good man."

He laughed. "Maybe I still need to work out some soul issues—at least that's what I tell myself. I don't just want to get married. I want to spend the rest of my life with the *right* woman."

"I get that," Everleigh said.

She wondered what type of woman Declan would choose to marry, then pushed the thought out of her mind. She had no right to think along those lines. She'd dismissed the first kiss as nerves in a tense situation. The second kiss… Everleigh wasn't quite sure what to think. Was there something more between them? She forced the thought away. She needed to focus on keeping Rae safe.

"Do you think Neil will try to finish what his brother started?" Everleigh asked. She couldn't help her thoughts turning back to the present danger.

"It's possible," he responded.

"I sent you a copy of the camera footage of Ellis. I guess he wasn't worried about the cameras outside the house."

"He's going to jail for sure."

"I'm glad to hear that," Everleigh said, folding her arms across her chest. "It's what he deserves. Same as Powell. He should be punished for his crimes."

Chapter 16

Everleigh woke to the smell of coffee floating down the hall from the kitchen. Declan must have come into the main house, she thought.

She took a deep breath before tossing back the covers and getting out of bed. She got dressed in a pair of jeans and a sweatshirt. Her hair flowed freely as she slipped on a pair of wool socks, then headed to the kitchen.

Steam wafted from the perking coffee maker with a pair of mugs waiting nearby. Her smile faded as she realized the machine was on auto.

Declan hadn't come down from the garage apartment yet. She didn't really like being in a stranger's house alone—it felt like she was invading the owner's privacy, even if it was with good reason.

Everleigh peered into the refrigerator.

"Mama…" Rae cried out when she walked into the kitchen. "I didn't know where you were."

She pulled her daughter into her arms. "I'd never leave without telling you, sweetie. And you know that I'd never leave you alone."

"Are you cooking breakfast?"

"I was thinking about it," Everleigh replied. "There's eggs, bacon, sausage…"

"Scrambled eggs, bacon…an-n-n-nd toast."

"Sounds good. I'll get right on it. You go brush your teeth and wash your face."

"Is Mr. Declan gonna eat with us?" Rae asked.

"I'm not sure," she responded. "I haven't talked to him yet."

"You should cook enough for him. He said he likes your cooking."

"Go brush your teeth, missy."

Laughing, Rae ran out of the kitchen.

Everleigh's gaze traveled the area. A shiny black-handled kettle in red sat on the stainless-steel stove. Black utensils were arranged in a red ceramic holder beside a matching set of canisters containing flour, sugar and coffee.

Near the window, wooden chairs were tucked neatly around a well-used granite-top table. In the center, a beautiful arrangement of silk roses in a red vase stood surrounded by miniature candles.

She could see a thin layer of dust on the window ledge.

Rae's return put an end to her musings.

Everleigh cooked bacon and scrambled eggs, as promised. She'd found a melon in the fridge and cut slices for her and Rae.

They sat down to eat as soon as the toast was ready.

"Are we gonna live here now?" Rae queried.

"No, we're not," she responded. "We're just staying here for a few days."

"Oh, it's a real nice house. How come we can't just let this be our new house? It has a huge playroom upstairs."

"Sweetie, this house belongs to Declan's sister. She's working out of town for a couple months. We're just here for the holidays."

Rae scooped up a forkful of eggs. "I hope we get to stay here for a long time."

Everleigh smiled. "You must really like it here."

"I do," she responded. "I like our house, too, Mama, even if this one is bigger."

"It's definitely larger than our home, but we don't really need anything this big. It's just you and me."

"Is Halle still coming today?"

"Yes. I know you can hardly wait to meet this little girl. I haven't seen you this excited in a long time."

"She gonna be my friend. Billie is coming, too."

"Really?"

Rae nodded. "Mr. Declan told me that she's coming with Halle." Taking Everleigh's hand in her small one, she continued, "Mama, I want a puppy."

"I know you do," she replied. Rae's opinion of dogs had changed drastically since she'd met Declan's Lab. "We need to get settled first, then we'll look for the perfect puppy for our home."

"Okay." Rae danced around the room.

Declan arrived halfway through the meal.

"You're just in time," Everleigh said. "There's more, but you'll have to heat it up."

"Not a problem. I'm starved."

"I feel terrible eating up your sister's food. I'm making a list so that I can replace what we've eaten."

"You don't have to worry about that," he responded. "I bought all this stuff and had it delivered here."

"Really?" Everleigh asked.

He smiled. "We have to eat."

"When is Halle coming?" Rae inquired.

"When I spoke to Remy, he said they were about an hour away."

The little girl's smile disappeared. "That's so long."

"She'll be here before you know it," he assured her.

Remy entered the kitchen. "I hope I didn't miss out on a hot breakfast. I'm tired of cereal."

"Help yourself," Everleigh said.

"Is Halle almost here?" Rae asked after they were finished with breakfast.

Remy grinned. "They should be arriving soon. She's excited about meeting you."

Everleigh's gaze drifted out the window. After a few moments, Declan touched her elbow.

"What are you thinking about?" he asked.

"I was thinking about Ellis and Neil," she responded. "I was angry initially, but the more I think about them... I feel bad."

He wore a look of confusion on his face. "Why?"

"Because I understand the root cause. Grief and anger. Their anger stems from a situation in which they tragically lost their mother. They can't strike out at James Ray Powell, so they're coming after his family...coming after me.

They don't realize that it's not going to bring them the results they desire, though."

"You're amazing, Everleigh. Ellis wanted to harm you and Rae. Yet, you're still compassionate toward him and his brother."

"No, I'm not. I just understand their reasons. I do pray for God to soften their hearts. Maybe Neil will leave us alone now that Ellis is in jail."

"I'll feel better when he's behind bars as well," Declan said.

"He's probably gone into hiding."

"Maybe, but at some point, he will be found."

"I hope so," Everleigh said.

She and Rae were taking a stroll around the lake when a car pulled up to the guesthouse.

"Mama, is that them?"

"I think so," Everleigh answered.

As soon as the door to the SUV opened, Billie rushed out as if happy to experience freedom.

Rae squealed with delight when the dog bounded for them.

A little girl with two fluffy ponytails came running behind her. "Billie... Billie..."

"It's *Halle*," her daughter said and took off running toward her.

She prayed Rae didn't scare the little girl off.

Everleigh's eyes filled with water at the sight of the two little girls hugging each other as if they were lifelong friends. Billie licked at their heels, wanting to get in on the action.

Declan walked out of garage and joined her. "Just looking at them, you wouldn't think Halle and Rae are just meeting for the first time."

She smiled. "I was just thinking that same thing. I think it's so beautiful."

They were joined by Remy and Sherri, and Declan made the introductions.

"Your little girl is so adorable," Sherri said. "She was grinning ear to ear when she ran up to Halle. Then she just hugged her."

"I was a bit worried she'd scare little Halle," Everleigh responded with a chuckle.

"Oh, no. Remy had already told her about Rae. She was just as excited about having someone to play with."

"Everleigh and I will keep an eye on the girls," Declan said. "I'm sure you and Sherri want to get the SUV unpacked."

"Thank you," Sherri responded. "It shouldn't take long."

Declan winked at his nephew. "No need to rush."

Grinning, Everleigh said, "I've learned something else about you."

"What's that?"

"You're a romantic. That was incredibly sweet of you to give them some time alone."

"I hope you don't mind that I recruited you to help me watch Halle."

"Not at all," she responded. "I think we should get them in the house. I can make lunch." She pointed toward the dock. "The boat out there…does it belong to your sister?"

"Actually, it's mine," Declan revealed.

"It's nice."

"That's the one we'll use for the sunset sail, if you're still interested. We can take the boat out this evening. People come from all over to see these houses decorated for Christmas."

"Sounds like fun. I can't wait."

Everleigh felt safe and secure, but she couldn't forget that this was temporary. After the holidays, she and Rae would be returning home. If Neil was still running free…

She shook away the thought. She wasn't going to worry about this now.

After dinner, Declan helped Halle and Rae into the boat after ensuring both girls were in life jackets.

Everleigh sat on the hard plastic seat wearing one as well.

He took his time motoring them around the lake.

"O-o-oh," Rae uttered. "Mama…the lights are so pretty."

"Yes, they are."

"Every house on the lake decorates for the holidays," Declan said.

"It's looks almost magical," Everleigh said.

When they returned, Declan secured the boat to the dock. Remy and Sherri were waiting for them on the dock. He helped the girls out first then assisted Everleigh.

"Sherri made hot chocolate and gingerbread cookies for y'all."

"Yay," Rae said.

Halle followed suit.

"Did you enjoy yourself?" Declan inquired.

"I did," Everleigh responded. "It's been a long time since I was on a boat. This was nice."

"Maybe you and Rae will come back when it's warmer—that's when I spend most of my time going up and down this lake."

"Sounds like fun."

"This is the way I like seeing you," he said. "You look really relaxed right now."

"Probably because I feel safe here."

Her words brought a smile to his lips. "That was the goal."

He placed an arm around Everleigh, wanting her to feel as if she was wrapped in an invisible warmth. He looked over at her, trying to assess her unreadable features.

She turned to face him. "What are you thinking about right now?" she asked.

Declan slowly looked down at her, his stomach dropping like a book tumbling off the top shelf as his gaze meshed with hers. Where their fingers touched, he felt a gentle warmth right to his core.

When Declan and Remy finished, the exterior windows were bejeweled with sparkling lights that glittered brightly.

"You and Remy did a great job," Everleigh said.

"We found some red and gold tinsel in a box in the garage," Declan responded. "There was a crate filled with ornaments right beside it. All we have to do is pick out a Christmas tree."

"When are you doing that?"

"Remy and Sherri are going this afternoon and they're taking Halle. I think Rae should go with them if that's okay with you."

"It's fine," she responded.

They left an hour later.

"I need to take care of some paperwork but it shouldn't take too long."

"It's fine. I need to get some air," Everleigh stated abruptly. She was beginning to feel like she couldn't breathe. She felt trapped.

"I'll go with you. I can—"

Shaking her head, she said, "If you don't mind... I just need some time alone, Declan."

He gave a slight nod. "Okay, but try to stay on this side of the lake."

Outside, she walked the trail, hoping the fresh air would help unsettle her troubled mind.

"Evvie..."

The hair on the back of her neck stood up. Everleigh turned around to face Wyle Gaines. "You don't have the right to call me that." She wasn't intimidated by his height towering over her. He kept his hands in the pockets of his dark sweatpants.

Staring her down, he responded, "Still so high and mighty."

"How did you find me?"

"I put a GPS tracker on your friend's car," he said with a nonchalant shrug. "There are some dangerous people after you. I guess you've figured that out already."

"You clearly couldn't keep your big mouth shut," Everleigh said. "I can't believe my mother trusted you with her secret."

"She didn't," Wyle answered. "Deloris never would've told me about your father. I could never get her to tell me anything about him."

Confusion colored Everleigh's expression. "Then how did you find out?"

"I overheard Deloris telling *you* that James Ray Powell was your father. After you refused to sell me the house… I got drunk at this bar and I guess I said too much. Those brothers…dangerous bunch. They bought me drink after drink and kept asking me about Deloris. I told them she'd died, then I told them about you."

"You're a horrible man."

"If I was really horrible, I'd tell them where you are. They asked me to find you."

"So they know I'm here in Columbia?" Everleigh asked, not quite sure if she could believe Wyle.

"No, and they won't know… I just need you to do something for me."

Folding her arms across her chest, she asked,

"What? Sell you my mother's house?" Everleigh hoped Declan would soon come looking for her.

"I'm thinking more like you sign it over to me. Your life and Rae's...that's worth much more than a little property, don't you think?"

"You're really a piece of work, Wyle." She didn't bother to hide her contempt. "I don't know how you were able to fool my mom, but I know you're nothing but a fraud."

"I can always hand you over to the brothers personally."

Wyle was talking as if he didn't know Ellis had been arrested. Everleigh decided not to mention it to him, either.

"I'd like to see you try that," she uttered, moving slowly toward him, hands balled into fists.

"Just give me the house and you'll never hear from me again."

"No."

Anger flashed in his hazel eyes. "These men won't hesitate to kill you. They are all filled with pure hate. I've seen it in them."

"So, you know they're murderers, huh?"

He seemed confused by her question. "Huh?

No. But they're violent. And they threatened to come after me if I didn't give them you."

Everleigh glimpsed Declan easing up behind Wyle, his hand on his gun.

"In case you don't know, the police are looking for you."

"Why? I haven't broken any laws," he snapped. "What did you tell them?"

"You hacked into my alarm system and broke into my house, Wyle."

"Look…" He looked as if he was about to take a step toward her. "You're not about to set me up. All I did was disable the alarm. Ellis made me do it. Evvie, I came here because I don't want to see any harm come to you and Rae. But I'm telling you…those dudes are cr—"

"Don't move," Declan ordered. "Put your hands on your head."

"You don't know what you're doing," Wyle said. "Everleigh, I can help you."

"No thanks," she responded.

Declan handcuffed him as sirens began to sound in the distance.

"Check your car," she said. "Wyle put a tracker on it."

The local police arrived.

"I'm the only one who can save you from the brothers," he said as they escorted him to the cruiser.

Everleigh embraced Declan. "He wanted me to sign my mom's house over to him in exchange for my life and Rae's."

"It wouldn't have stopped anything. Neil would still come after you," he said, "but he'd have the property free and clear."

"I was thinking the same thing."

"I'm going down to the precinct. Stay in the house. Remy should be back soon."

Everleigh nodded, rubbing her arms. "I'm going to make some tea to help steady my nerves."

"Maybe I shouldn't leave right now. If Wyle was able to track us...maybe he already told Neil how to find you."

"Wyle said he wouldn't give them my location if I signed over the house to him. That was the offer he made me. You go and I'll be fine. I think he was telling the truth about that."

Remy's SUV pulled into the driveway.

"Good, they're back," Declan said.

They had come home with a tall, full live tree.

"I can't wait to decorate it," Rae said when

they entered the house. "I like doing that. Me and Daddy used to decorate the tree while Mama baked cookies."

It made her feel good to see her daughter like this and know that she had good memories of Britt. Everleigh wasn't sure how resilient and well-adjusted Rae was after the loss of both her father and grandmother.

"Where did Mr. Declan go?"

"He had to run an errand," Everleigh answered. "He shouldn't be gone too long." Once again, she was grateful that Rae—and Halle—hadn't been around to see Wyle taken into custody.

When Declan returned, he complimented the girls and Sherri on the tree decorations.

"The Christmas tree was Rae and Britt's thing," Everleigh said. "We didn't have a tree last year."

"It will get easier with time," he responded. "Give yourself some grace."

"Some days I feel a bit overwhelmed."

"I think anyone would feel the same way in your shoes."

"But when I look at Rae, she just makes everything so much better for me. I'm not making any sense, am I?"

"You're making a lot of sense," he responded. "Children like Rae and Halle restore my hope for the future."

Chapter 17

Declan watched his nephew with Sherri and Halle and felt a thread of envy.

He yearned for a wife and family. It came as a bit of a surprise to him, because Declan hadn't thought much about it in recent years. He long accepted the fact that maybe he was destined to remain single. He had even found a measure of contentment in his bachelor lifestyle even though it wasn't his personal choice.

Spending the past few weeks with Everleigh and Rae brought those desires back to the surface. He wanted nothing more than to see them safe. It didn't seem fair that they had been targeted by two men hungry for vengeance and another out of pure greed. He took consolation that even in this situation, God was able to turn it into a blessing.

Everleigh was quiet through most of the evening. She chatted with Sherri and Remy, but other than that, she didn't say much until after everyone else had gone to bed.

"Declan, I don't know what I would've done without you today. Wyle was determined to force me to give him the property. Before I didn't really think he'd resort to violence...now I'm not so sure."

Her hand felt like silk in his. As he met Everleigh's warm gaze, affection for her jerked at his heart. Declan quickly pushed away his emotions. This wasn't the time or place to dwell on his feelings.

"I wasn't about to let anything happen." Declan reluctantly pulled away, then stood up and stretched. "I feel like some hot chocolate. What about you?"

"Sure," Everleigh replied smoothly.

He walked the short distance to the kitchen.

When he returned with two steaming mugs, Declan found her sleeping. She'd curled into a ball on the floor, a throw pillow cushioning her head.

He sat down and listened until Everleigh's breathing became steady and deep. She looked peaceful as she slept. Declan reached into a nearby basket and retrieved another blanket, placing it over his legs. He leaned back, using the couch as a backrest.

He'd been surprised by his reaction to her touch when she grabbed his hand. There had been times during his career when female victims grew attached to him. Often, they wanted to build something more, but he knew that most relationships born out of trauma failed.

The best thing for Declan was to keep things professional with Everleigh. Besides, she was still grieving the loss of her husband. His eyes strayed to the wedding rings on her left hand.

He turned his attention to the movie he and Everleigh had been waiting to come on. Declan didn't bother to wake her.

Fifteen minutes into the movie, he felt himself begin to nod off. Declan jerked awake. He was determined to watch until the end.

"Is today Christmas?" Rae asked.

"It's tomorrow, sweetie."

"Yay," Halle and Rae said in unison.

Everleigh broke into a smile. "Sherri, I'm so glad Halle is here. She's been able to keep my daughter entertained."

"I feel the same way about Rae," she responded. "Halle loves her grandparents, but she doesn't have anyone to play with whenever we're here."

"Declan tells me that you'll be living here soon."

Sherri nodded. "As soon as I graduate. It's been hard being away from Remy. When he applied to the police department here, we thought it would take a while. The process moved much quicker than we anticipated."

"I'd love to schedule some playdates if you and Remy ever come to Charleston."

"Of course. Remy and Declan are very close and they enjoy hanging out together. While they're out doing their thing, we can do something with the girls. And if you're interested... maybe squeeze in a girl's day or night out for us."

"I'd love that," Everleigh responded.

"Remy and Declan are going to take the girls to lunch and to do some Christmas shopping. While they're out, we can run some errands. I need to pick up some items for dinner tomorrow."

"Sherri, what can I do to help? I can cook for tonight and I'm happy to help with the Christmas meal. I make a pretty good macaroni and cheese, candied yams and dressing."

"Sounds good to me," she responded. "I'll focus on the chicken, mixed greens and sweet-potato pies. Declan always smokes the turkey and salmon. Remy…my poor hubby is in charge of putting the ice in the glasses and setting the table."

Everleigh laughed. "He said cooking wasn't his gift."

Laughing, Sherri said, "He was telling the whole truth of that. That man can barely boil a pot of water."

She enjoyed spending her afternoon with Sherri. They picked up some last-minutes gifts, then had a nice lunch at one of the restaurants in downtown Columbia. She was grateful not to have to constantly look over her shoulder.

"I'm glad you suggested we get these wrapped before going back to the house," Everleigh stated. "I don't know how I'd be able to get them past Rae. Oh, and thanks for the suggestion on what to get Declan." She'd wanted to have something under the tree for him, but was at a loss as to what would be appropriate.

"He's gonna love that wireless charging mat," Sherri said. "He's been wanting one since he saw mine."

Back at the house, Everleigh put her packages

in the bedroom, then headed to the kitchen to prepare dinner.

"I'm surprised Declan and Remy aren't back with the girls," Sherry said when she joined her.

"Declan just texted me. They took them to a festival for an hour, but are heading home now."

"They probably wanted to tire them out so they'd go to bed early."

Everleigh chuckled. "Rae's so excited about Christmas... I'm going to have a hard time getting her to go to sleep tonight."

"Halle will try to hang on, but one thing about her—when she's tired, she will go to bed."

"How long have you known Declan?"

"Not very long," she responded. "I started teaching in August. I met him that first week at a faculty meeting."

"He's a really nice man, Everleigh."

"Yes, he is," she said. "It surprises me he's still single."

"Declan's very particular," Sherri responded. "As he should be."

"I agree."

"He mentioned that your husband passed away. I'm very sorry for your loss. I can't imagine..."

"I wouldn't wish that on anybody, Sherri. My

husband was wonderful—and a great father. We just lost him much too soon."

"I see you still wear your wedding rings."

"I've thought about taking them off but… I'm not ready."

"Take as much time as you need, Everleigh. There isn't a set time limit when it comes to grief. It's different for everyone."

"A lot of people don't understand that."

"I lost my father three years ago," Sherri said. "I still grieve. My mother remarried last year and I was really upset with her at first. She explained to me that she and my dad truly loved each other—they had a loving and fulfilling marriage. She said that while she would never forget him, she was a woman who loved being married. She didn't just want companionship— she wanted a husband. She said she could move on without regrets or guilt because she'd been a good and faithful wife to my dad."

"How did you feel after that conversation?"

"Better. Much better. My mom is very happy. She would tell that she's been doubly blessed to have found love with two wonderful men in her lifetime."

Everleigh smiled. "I would have to agree with your mother. It is indeed a blessing."

"We're back," Declan said when he entered the house.

"Mama, I got you a present," Rae said, rushing into the kitchen. "I'ma put it under the tree after I wrap it."

"Thank you, sweetie," Everleigh replied as she leaned down to plant a kiss on her daughter's forehead.

Remy kissed his wife, then said, "We're taking the girls to the guesthouse so they can wrap their gifts."

"Dinner will be ready in about forty-five minutes," Everleigh announced.

"Don't worry," Declan responded. "We're not going to miss that."

Everleigh returned her attention to preparing dinner. She made meatballs from the ground-beef mixture. "Spaghetti is the perfect choice for tonight since we're having a feast tomorrow."

"Yeah, I figured we'd keep it simple. Besides, they all *love* spaghetti and meatballs."

"What's not to love?" she asked with a chuckle. "Rae and I can eat it all week long. We don't, but we could."

"We're the same way," Sherri stated while making a dinner salad. "Pasta is a staple in our house, too."

Sure enough, when Rae sat down at the dining room table, she exclaimed, "Spaghetti and meatballs...yay!"

"I love sp'ghetti," Halle agreed.

Everleigh listened to Rae and Declan interacting over their meal. Hearing them talk and laugh, she realized that he was bonding with her daughter in a special way. He would be a wonderful father one day, she thought to herself.

After her husband died, she'd put all her energy into her job and her daughter. There had been men who expressed interest in her, but she wasn't ready. Then her mother's cancer diagnosis came—Everleigh had no time for anything else outside her family.

Her hand curled into a fist under the table. Though she felt a growing affection for Declan, she didn't think she had the emotional capacity to open herself to heartache again. Losing Britt had almost killed her. It wasn't something she wanted to go through ever again.

Everleigh told herself that once the threat was over, she and Declan would remain friends. Nothing more. However, this declaration seemed to bring with it a certain sadness. She decided not to ponder on it any further. Instead, she opted to enjoy the food and the fellowship.

Sherri brought out dessert.

"My baby knows what I like," Remy declared with a grin. "She made her famous peppermint chocolate cake."

"I want cake," Rae said.

"Finish up your spaghetti first," Everleigh responded. "Then you can have dessert."

She bit back her laughter when Rae stuffed her mouth with a meatball.

"Finish up, but slow down, sweetie. The cake isn't going anywhere."

"I'll cut you a slice of it and put it aside until you're done," Declan said, picking up a small plate.

After swallowing, Rae responded, "Thank you, Mr. Declan."

When he cut a huge slice for himself, Everleigh asked, "Can I have a bite of yours? I don't want to overindulge."

"Sure."

Rae clapped her hands, then said, "Mr. Declan loves Mama."

Everleigh's fork fell to her plate. "Sweetie… we're *friends*. You shouldn't go around saying something like that."

She stole a peek at Declan, who looked like he'd been shocked speechless.

"But, Mama, you said that if a man shares his cake with you, he loves you."

"My mother told me the same thing," Sherri said. "Just saying…"

"Rae, I care about your mom and about you," Declan stated. "Friends can also share cake, too."

"I'm your friend," she responded. "So you have to share with me, too. You can't eat it all."

Remy burst into laughter. "Uncle, please tell me you saw that coming. She has her slice and some of yours, too."

Laughter rang out around the table.

Everleigh sent Remy a grateful smile for changing the flow of the conversation. When she glanced at Declan, he looked amused. He didn't look at all uncomfortable, which helped to ease her own stress.

Going forward, she would have to be careful with what she said around Rae, Everleigh decided. Her daughter was like a sponge, soaking up everything.

"Why don't you guys just stay here in the main house tonight," Declan suggested when they moved to the family room after dinner. "We can bring Christmas in together."

Sherri looked at Everleigh, then said, "I told you we should have gotten those pajamas…"

He glanced over at her. "You didn't want to do the whole matching-PJs thing? I thought you had real Christmas spirit."

"I didn't mind it—I wasn't sure how you or Remy might feel about it."

"Sherri knows I'm always down for the family."

"Rae and I…"

"Are still family," Remy said. "At least for the holidays."

Declan agreed. "Whenever you're with us, you become family."

Smiling, Everleigh responded, "I've learned something new about you."

"What's that?"

"You bring home strays. I bet you've always done that."

"She knows you, Declan," his nephew stated. "My mom used to get so mad with him when they were growing up. He was always bringing home animals. He didn't care what it was— dog, cat, bird… He even brought home a snake one time."

"That didn't go over well at all," Declan responded with a chuckle. "My sister was okay if it was a dog. Anything else had to go. She'd go running to our parents complaining."

"I can't say I wouldn't have done the same," Everleigh replied.

"Snakes are scary," Rae interjected. "I don't like snakes."

"Me, either," Sherri said.

"Okay…okay. I get it. I won't be picking up any stray snakes while we're here."

A collective sigh floated across the air.

Shortly after ten, Remy carried a sleeping Halle upstairs to bed.

"Mama, I'm getting tired, too."

Standing, Everleigh said, "I guess that's my cue. Rae and I are going to call it a night. We'll see y'all in the morning."

Declan eyed her. "G'night."

Everleigh took Rae to the bedroom.

"I'm gonna take this time to get some of the cooking out of the way," Sherri stated.

Remy looked over at Declan and said, "Uncle, you should've seen the look on your face earlier. You looked like you'd been caught with your hand in the cookie jar."

He laughed. "I froze. I didn't really know how to respond."

"Especially since you haven't fully accepted the truth of it yourself."

There was no point in lying, so Declan simply shrugged.

"Did you get any information out of Wyle Gaines?" Remy asked.

"He said that he'd promised Everleigh's mother that he would look out for her and Rae. Said that's all he was trying to do before he lawyered up."

"So he's actually denying everything he said to Everleigh?"

Declan nodded. "Said he didn't have any idea what she was talking about. Wyle even claimed that Everleigh's angry because he rebuffed her advances."

"Did you tell her any of this?"

"No, I didn't want to upset her. Besides, I'd take her word over Wyle's any day of the week."

"What *did* you tell Everleigh?" Remy inquired.

"Just that he lawyered up," Declan responded. "When I asked him about the tracker, he didn't confirm or deny. I thought for a minute Wyle was going to say that she put it on the car, but apparently, he thought better of it."

"What's his connection to the Ragland brothers?"

"Wyle told Everleigh that she met them in a bar. He had been drinking and was talking to anyone who'd listen that she was evil, like her serial-killer daddy. They became friendly with him and coaxed him to tell them more."

"I'm sure you asked Wyle for the missing brother's location."

"I did. He said he didn't know. That he hadn't talked to them since that night."

"Do you believe him?"

Declan rubbed his chin. "I'm not sure. I don't see them trusting a man like Wyle."

Remy nodded in agreement. "He sounds like a loose cannon."

"I was hoping to get a lead on Neil. He could be anywhere. I even considered that maybe they have been keeping tabs on Wyle. Maybe even followed him here." He looked into the blazing fire as flames licked at the wood. "I know she's ready for this to be over."

"It would've been a nice Christmas present," Remy said.

"I was thinking the same thing."

"At least you have Wyle and Ellis. Soon you'll have Neil in custody, too. You know I'll do what I can to help you with this, Uncle. I checked the camera footage and Wyle is the only person who set foot on the property."

"Neil will make a move—he has to."

"I agree, Remy. We just don't know when or where."

Chapter 18

Everleigh took in a deep breath.

Her stomach tightened as the memories of life with Britt washed over her. Sitting so close to Declan was having an effect on her. His body heat encircled her, making her dizzy. She'd felt a spark of something when he'd held her hand, too.

The attraction was not unexpected. Everleigh knew it was normal for an individual to be drawn to her protector, often after being thrown together through traumatic events or responding out of need. She'd seen this in the behavior of a few former clients. Still, Everleigh struggled in gauging her own feelings. She considered that possibly there was something more going on between them, but it was a passing thought. Not one she wanted to contemplate at the moment. She had more pressing matters to contend with.

Unable to sleep, she shifted her position in bed, turning to her left side.

It would be unfair to Declan to pursue a relationship she wasn't ready for. Everleigh didn't want to risk hurting him. He didn't deserve that. She also had to think of Rae and her attachment to Declan. She affirmed once more that it was best that they keep their relationship platonic.

The thought of Declan finding love with another woman didn't sit well with Everleigh, however.

I can't have it both ways.

The truth was that she didn't want to spend the rest of her life a widow. Everleigh could admit that she wanted to be married again; she wanted more children, too. *Give me the strength and the courage to move past my grief and my guilt*, she prayed. Everleigh didn't want to keep feeling as if she were betraying her husband with her feelings for Declan. Especially when she knew Britt didn't want her to stop living—he'd told her as much. He once told her that he hoped she'd find love and remarry quickly because he didn't want Everleigh and Rae to be alone. It was almost as if he'd known he would die a year later.

★ ★ ★

Rae woke up shortly after 6:00 a.m. "Merry Christmas, Mama."

"What are you doing up so early? I can barely wake you when you have to go to school."

"Can we get up now and open presents?"

"We're going to open gifts after everybody is up."

"That's gonna take a long time," Rae pouted.

"Maybe not." Everleigh slid out of bed. "C'mon, let's go wash our faces and brush our teeth. I'll check to see if anybody is up."

"They don't wanna sleep Christmas away," Rae said.

"I'm sure they don't, sweetie. I'll be back shortly."

The scent from the Christmas tree was strong, beckoning her into the family room. The sun sparkled bright through the huge windows, making the ornaments glisten. Holiday music suddenly poured out through the speakers embedded in the wall.

A smile trembled on her lips as Everleigh turned around.

"Merry Christmas." Declan stood there wearing a Santa hat with his arms filled with stockings. "I meant to hang these up last night but fell asleep."

"Let's do it now," she said, crossing the floor to relieve him of a couple.

They hung them across the fireplace. Billie ambled over to the tree and began sniffing at the wrapped gifts beneath.

They were soon joined by Remy.

"Merry Christmas, fam," he said. "Everything ready for the girls?"

"I believe so," Everleigh responded.

"Let the festivities began," Declan said. "I need to get my camera. It's in the apartment. Nobody touch a present until I get back."

"It's obvious he don't have children. They don't care about pictures."

Everleigh chuckled. "I guess I'll go get Rae. She's been up for almost an hour and I wouldn't let her leave the bedroom."

"Sherri and Halle should be down any minute."

Declan was back when she returned with Rae. The little girl ran over to Billie. "Merry Christmas, girl. I have a present for you."

"Marry Chrissmas," Halle said when she ran into the room. She embraced Rae and Billie. Not to be outdone, Billie licked them both.

"Billie! Stop that," Declan said. "She's just as excited as the girls."

"You should get a photo of the three of them," Everleigh suggested.

Sherri agreed.

They sat down to watch the girls open their gifts while Declan documented the day with his camera.

Everleigh blinked back tears of happiness. It was a delight to see Rae laughing and smiling after so much sadness. That first Christmas after Britt died, they had dinner with her mother, but the presents went unopened for two days. She and Rae were both in the thick of their grief, and her mother was sick. Everleigh was determined this year would be different.

When she'd woken up earlier, she'd felt a sadness because Deloris wasn't with them, but Rae cheered her up when she said, "Daddy and Grandma are having the best Christmas because they live in heaven now."

Everleigh carried the sentiment in her heart and it gave her joy. Deloris wasn't sick anymore and she was with family. In her mind, she could see her mother and husband together, their faces filled with smiles—smiles that radiated down to her.

Sherri sat down beside her. "Everleigh, I have to tell you how much I admire you. It takes a pretty strong woman to take care of a terminally ill mother in the midst of grieving the loss of your husband. Then moving to a new city and starting over. You're amazing."

"Thank you for saying that, Sherri. I have to confess I don't always feel so strong. In fact, there have been times when I've felt completely helpless. But then God brought Declan into my life."

"And now you have Remy and me. We've adopted you and Rae into our family. The girls get along so well, one would think they've known each other forever." Smiling, she added, "I feel the same way about you."

The two women embraced.

"I'm really glad to see Rae having such a good time. I think she needed this."

"How are you doing, really?"

"I'm fine until I think of having to go back home. Then I start to imagine the worst. But I rein in my thoughts." Her stomach knotted up and a sense of dread crept up her spine at the thought that Neil was somewhere out there.

"Declan is very good at his job and I know he'll find that guy."

"I trust him," she responded with a smile.

Billie trotted over, her toenails clicking on the hardwood, and prodded her furry head under Everleigh's hand, whining faintly. Automatically, she tugged the dog against her leg, rubbing her back. "Merry Christmas to you, too."

Chapter 19

"Sherri, you and Everleigh outdid yourselves in the kitchen. Dinner was fantastic," Declan said, rubbing his belly. "Now if you'll roll yourself into the family room, Remy and I will clean up."

"I don't mind helping," Everleigh said.

"You've done enough," Remy stated. "You two get a pass this year. Next year, y'all are in charge of clean-up."

She glanced at Declan, who stated, "I guess that means you and Rae have to join us next Christmas. I'm not doing it alone."

Tears welled in her eyes. Everleigh wiped them away. "I've been trying to hold them in all day. I am awestruck by the kindness and generosity shown to Rae and me. I was feeling so alone in the world after losing Britt and my mother." Her voice broke. "M-my heart rejoices because I see that God answered my prayers."

Declan took her hand in his own. "You and Rae mean a lot to me. You're not alone. When Wyle and the Ragland brothers are no longer a concern, I will still be around. Billie, too."

"I know that now."

He loved her—Declan knew this as sure as his own name. His feelings for any of the women in his past paled in comparison.

Everleigh turned and looked at him.

She held her arms out, low, palms facing him.

He blinked a couple times. Was she really offering him an embrace?

Declan didn't keep her waiting. He hugged her.

"There's so much I want to say to you," he whispered. "But now isn't the right time or place."

Everleigh gave a gentle nod.

His heart leaped with joy. This was the sign he'd been waiting for. Declan was more determined than ever to find Neil and put him in jail with his brother.

Everleigh snuggled under the blanket in front of the fireplace with Billie napping at her feet. Declan sat across from her with the girls. They had wrangled him into reading them a story.

Every now and then his eyes would venture to hers and he'd give her a secret smile, one filled with promise. Beneath the throw, Everleigh twisted the rings on her finger nervously. She'd almost taken them off earlier, but couldn't go through with it.

She told herself that she shouldn't rush this process. Everleigh was ready to move on, but she felt guilty for feeling this way. She considered the advice she'd give if a client came to her.

I'd tell the person that there isn't a time limit on grief, or when someone is ready for a new relationship. Some people are ready months after the death of their spouse, and for others, it may take years. Have I somehow placed an unrealistic expectation on myself of how long I should grieve?

Everleigh removed the rings and slipped them into the pocket of her jeans. There weren't any feelings of guilt, only peace.

Declan invited her to take a walk around the lake when the girls and Billie went upstairs to the playroom.

"It's so nice out here," Everleigh said. "The weather is perfect. Not too cold and not too hot. What's your favorite memory growing up here?"

"I'd have to say this Christmas," Declan responded. "Rae and Halle embody what it's like to see the world through the eyes of a child. In the job I do, I see a lot of the bad stuff going on in the world. Those two beautiful little girls have shown me the world in a different light. And then there's you, Everleigh. Just your presence has made this holiday special for me. I was given a preview of what life looks like when you've found the person who is a perfect fit for you." He met her gaze. "Do you understand what I'm trying to say?"

"I do," Everleigh responded. "And I feel the same way." She held up her left hand. "I'm ready to live again. I didn't really realize that I'd stopped living until the Ragland's forced their way into my life."

"I go back to work on New Year's Eve," Declan announced. "I'm putting all my focus on finding Neil Ragland. I'll come back to get you and Rae on the third."

They walked around the lake hand in hand as they laughed and talked. She and Declan paused to admire a huge oak tree.

"I love everything about this place," she said.

"Where we're standing right now is the land my parents gave to me. It's three acres. I've always planned to build a house here whenever I had a family. It's the perfect place to raise children."

"You're right," Everleigh said. "This place is perfect for a family."

Declan was tempted to say more, but instead asked, "Do you fish?"

Her smile disappeared. "Nope."

He gave a short laugh. "That's fine. Neither do I. We'll leave that to my sister."

Everleigh looped her arm through his. "Sounds great to me."

During their walk back to the house, she said, "I think we should set a trap for Neil."

"In what way?"

"He's probably been watching my house. I can go home and—"

Declan cut her off. "That's absolutely out of the question."

"Why? When I'm home, the island police will be close by. I'll be prepared."

"I won't have you putting yourself at risk. You have Rae to think about."

"As long as I'm away, Neil has no reason to make a move," Everleigh said. "We have to do something to draw him out."

"At some point he'll get impatient. He'll try to find a way to force you out of hiding."

"The only way I can imagine him doing that is if he came after Rae," she uttered. "I can't let that happen, Declan. We need to get to him first."

The days were flying by relentlessly. Already, it was the third day of the new year and soon enough, it would be gone. Everleigh remarked, "I wish Declan had been able to stay for New Year's."

"Me, too," Sherri said. "You two have gotten extremely close since Christmas, I see." She pointed to Everleigh's left hand. She was no longer wearing her rings.

"We have," she admitted. "But we're taking it really slow. I can't fully focus on anything else other than the safety of my child at the moment."

"I know all of this is going to work out," Sherri said. "No harm will come to you and Rae. God will protect you."

"I do believe that," Everleigh responded.

Rae walked out of the bedroom wearing a pair of jeans and her cowboy boots.

"Where's your coat?"

"Oh, I forgot." She ran back to the bedroom, returning minutes later with a dark brown coat.

Halle walked into the house with Remy.

"Did you find her boots?" Sherri asked.

"I did," he answered. "They were under her bed."

Picking up her purse, Sherri said, "I guess we're ready to go."

During the short drive to the restaurant, Everleigh recalled a conversation with Deloris a few days before she died.

Evvie, you weren't made to live alone, without being surrounded by family. Having the same blood don't make you related. You have to open your heart... Sure, the stakes are higher, but it's worth it in the end.

Everleigh thought it was a strange thing for Deloris to say at the time. But now it made sense to her.

An image of Declan formed in her mind.

He was definitely worth the risk, she thought as a smile danced on her lips.

Chapter 20

Declan drove to the university to pick up a textbook he'd left in his office.

When he left the building, there was a flurry of commotion around him, which prompted him to stop a security guard. "Hey, what's going on? Did something happen?"

"There's a gunman in the library. I heard there are five or six students inside."

"Are you sure about this?" Declan asked. "Did you get a look at the assailant?"

"He was tall—athletic build and long locks… He asked me for directions. He stuttered some. I never saw him before but I thought he was a student."

Neil Ragland.

Declan hated to call Everleigh with this news, but it would be better coming from him. Pretty soon, the campus would have media and police officers crawling all over it. While waiting for her to answer, an alert came across his phone. Everleigh would be receiving the same message.

As soon as she answered her phone, he said, "I wanted you to hear this from me. Neil's here on campus. He's in the library."

"I just got an alert about a gunman," Everleigh responded. "Do you know for sure that it's Neil?"

"According to the description I received from a security officer...it's him." Before she could reply, Declan said, "I have to go. I'll call you back."

He rushed over to where a crowd was slowly forming.

Thank God, most of the students were away for the holidays, he thought to himself. Declan was also relieved that Everleigh wasn't anywhere near the campus. At least she and Rae were safe.

"I need to get to the university," Everleigh told Sherri and Remy.

"We're two hours away."

"Then I need to leave right now. It's me he wants. I might be able to convince Neil to surrender." She looked at Sherri. "Are you fine with watching Rae while I'm gone?"

"Of course," she responded. "She'll stay in the guesthouse with us, but are you sure about this?"

"Declan will have a fit if I just let you go," Remy said. "Everleigh, you're putting yourself in danger."

"I want to make sure Neil doesn't hurt more innocent people, Remy."

"It's almost four. There's a flight leaving at five o'clock to Charleston. You'll get there much quicker. If you're ready, I can take you to the airport."

"Yes, I'm ready to leave. Remy, thank you," she responded. "And don't worry, I'll take care of your uncle."

Thirty minutes later, Everleigh was on the plane. She normally didn't like small planes but she didn't have any other choice.

It's time to put an end to this nightmare.

She prayed during the short flight to Charleston. Everleigh had texted Declan to let him know she was on her way to Charleston because she had to talk to Neil, try to reason with him.

Everleigh took an Uber to the university from the airport.

Faculty, staff and students had all undergone safety training for active-shooter and hostage situations. As soon as she arrived on campus, she saw that police officers surrounded the area.

She was approached by an officer.

"I work here," Everleigh said, showing her credentials. "Neil Ragland will want to speak with me."

She was led over to Declan.

"I wish you'd stayed in Columbia." he said when she joined them.

"I'm hoping I can talk Neil down. At least let me try."

"I'm not letting you go inside that library."

"We have to get those students out safely, Declan. Let me try to talk to him first."

He walked her over to the commander in charge. "This is Everleigh Taylor. She's the person he's after."

"I'd like to try to talk to Neil."

She whispered a silent prayer before picking up the phone.

"What?"

"Neil," Everleigh said calmly. "Please don't hurt the people inside. They don't have anything to do with this. I'm the person you want."

"Come join th-the p–party."

"Why don't you let the students leave first," she responded, ignoring the way Declan furiously shook his head.

"Neil, I understand the pain you're feeling."

"Your f-father is the c-cause of my pain."

"My mother was a victim, too. That's why she moved out of the apartment on Beech. She didn't know who he was at the time. My mother had no way of knowing that he would return and attack anyone else."

"Why did she l-leave then? She must've known he'd be back."

"She didn't, Neil."

"Powell has bad genes," he stated. "My brother said we have to r-remove the bloodline."

"I explained to Ellis that the serial-killer gene is a myth."

No response.

"Neil, I'm so sorry for the pain James Ray Powell caused your family," Everleigh stated. "You have to know that if you try to continue along this path, Powell continues to win. He thrived on taking power from the women he raped and he's doing the same with you and Ellis. *He wins every time you hurt an innocent person.*"

Out the corner of her eye, she saw police officers and the SWAT team take their positions.

"Do you really want to keep giving your power to the man who took your mother from you?"

Neil didn't respond right away, but when he did, he said, "My brother told me that if you don't wanna be a victim, y-you hit first. He says that people only respect strength. Besides, t-this world ain't nothing but a cruel place filled with people who are evil. Like your f-father."

"I'd like to help you…if you'd let me."

"I don't need your kinda help."

"Neil, I don't believe you're like Ellis. I haven't met you, but I'm pretty sure you really don't want to hurt anyone. I understand that you look up to your brother."

"He tried to protect me. I o-owe him my life."

Neil sounded calmer now. Everleigh noticed that he wasn't stuttering as much.

"There's already been too much death. Please let the students leave the library."

"It's too late for us now."

"If you release the students and turn yourself in, this doesn't have to end in tragedy," she said.

"You say that, but I can see the police," Neil responded. "They want me dead."

"We don't want that at all. None of us. I want you to know that it's never too late to do what's right." Everleigh paused a moment, then said, "You and Ellis were so young when your mother died and unfortunately two innocent boys ended up in foster care, your basic needs stripped away—love, identity and security. When something like that happens, it becomes easier to express anger and blame the closest target. Neil, I'm sure you don't want to become like the very person you hate."

She heard a click then silence.

Everleigh turned to Declan and collapsed in his arms. "I pray I was able to get through to him."

Declan held her close. "The ball is in his court now."

He continued to be amazed by Everleigh. Her tone was caring and soothing and free of judgment. He truly hoped that Neil would give himself up, but he wasn't sure how the man would respond. He and his brother were ruthless in their killing. Men like that rarely went down without a fight.

Declan was grateful that Everleigh was safe and he intended to keep her that way. There was no way he was going to let her walk into that library. Rae needed her mother. But she wasn't the only one. He needed her, too.

The negotiator called again, but Neil didn't answer.

"The library doors are opening," someone said over the two-way radio.

Everleigh's eyes grew wet with unshed tears when the six students rushed out. "Thank You, God," she whispered.

After they ran out, the SWAT team entered the building.

Declan embraced Everleigh.

"I hope he'll give up without a fight," she said. Deep down, she prayed she was able to get through to Neil.

"Look," Declan uttered.

Everleigh released a sigh of relief when Neil was escorted out in handcuffs.

She was about to walk toward him, but Declan held her back. "Don't get too close…"

Everleigh and Neil made eye contact for a moment before he was placed in a cruiser.

"I looked into his eyes," she said. "He doesn't have the soul of a killer."

Relieved, Declan embraced her. "It's over. The Ragland brothers are in jail, and so is Wyle Gaines."

She couldn't be happier. They could finally put this behind them and focus on a future together.

"I need to speak to the supervisor in charge for a second," he told her.

"I think I'll go to my office. Just come get me when you're done."

"I won't be long."

Everleigh smiled at him. "I'm not going anywhere, so take your time."

Chapter 21

Everleigh was about to enter through the doors of the social-sciences building when a tall figure of a man loomed in front of her, blocking her path. His face was partially shrouded by the black hoodie he was wearing. Something hit her, a memory of seeing someone in a hoodie watching her office... She'd thought it was Wyle. But...

"Where do you think you're going, Dr. Taylor?"

"Excuse me?"

Stunned, Everleigh glanced down at the gun in his hand. There were no other people around them. Everyone's attention was focused on the hostages and the police. "Who are you?"

"I'm Ellis and Neil's big brother."

She eyed him in confusion. "Olivia Ragland only had two sons."

"We have the same father. I was in a detention center when Olivia was murdered by your father. After that, I ended up in prison, so it took me years before I was able to find them after I got out. My brothers were abused physically and sexually by people who were supposed to be taking care of them."

"I'm really sorry that happened to them, but I'm not the one to blame—"

"Your parents *are*. Your mother's dead, and we can't get to your father." His face split into a grin. "But we have *you*."

Panic washed over Everleigh like a wave but she managed to keep her voice calm. *"Powell raped my mother."*

"I watched the way you handled Neil. I'm not lettin' you get inside my head, Dr. Taylor."

"Your brother was finally able to see the truth about this situation," she responded.

"He saw what you wanted him to see. Neil's always been the sensitive one. Afraid of his own shadow."

Everleigh tried to resist him as he practically dragged her toward a dark vehicle.

"You don't have to do this. You must know that the police will be looking for me."

"And they won't find you. Until it's too late."

She tried once again to pull her arm free.

He squeezed it tighter. "Don't try that again. I don't want to have to break that arm."

Everleigh could tell by the sinister expression on his face that he meant it.

At his SUV, he gave her a shove. *"Get in."*

She swung, clipping him in the chin.

He was quick in his reaction. "Feisty, I see. It won't bother me one bit to kill you right here." Pointing the gun at her head, he repeated his order. "I said, get inside."

He pulled a piece of wire from within the dash console and secured her hands together, then walked briskly around to the driver's side and got in.

Any hope of Declan coming to her rescue faded along with Everleigh's view of the campus as he drove them away.

Declan walked briskly toward the social-sciences building. He'd arranged to take tomorrow off because he was taking Everleigh back to Columbia. He knew she'd want to get back to Rae as quickly as she could.

"Professor Blanchet…"

"Hey—"

"Do you remember me? Aaron Edwards. Are you looking for your lady friend? Dr. Taylor?"

"I'm headed to her office right now."

"She's not there."

"What do you mean she's not there?" Declan demanded.

"I was in my car about to leave campus when I saw this guy forcing her into his SUV. It looked like he had a gun." He handed Declan a piece of paper. "Here's the license-plate number."

"How long ago?"

"About ten minutes ago. They were heading north."

"Thank you for this."

"Professor Blanchet, let me go with you," Aaron said. "I was military police and besides that, I can help you identify the SUV."

"C'mon."

They rushed to his car and drove in the direction the vehicle went. Declan hoped Everleigh's phone was still with her.

The most pressing question on his mind was who had kidnapped Everleigh. Both Ellis and Neil were in custody. So was Wyle Gaines.

Declan called a friend of his. "Hey, I need you to run a Maryland license plate for me."

When he got off the phone, he asked Aaron, "What brought you to campus tonight?"

"I came to talk to some students at the request of a friend," Aaron responded. "I've known her for almost ten years. Actually, she's the reason I chose to attend college in Charleston."

"I'm glad you were there."

His phone rang.

"The tags belong to a 2019 Honda Civic. They were reported stolen."

"What is the owner's name?"

"They belong to a Winston Powell."

One of the family members who had been murdered recently. "He's deceased. Whoever this perp is, he's connected to a string of murders."

"I hope you don't mind my asking, but what's going on?" Aaron asked. "I gathered that the guy arrested earlier was after Dr. Taylor. I heard something about a brother in jail."

"Yeah. The Ragland brothers blame Everleigh for their mother's death—something she had absolutely nothing to do with. There's a third man who's been stalking her, but he's in custody in South Carolina."

"And now there's a fourth player," Aaron said.

Declan nodded.

"How old were they when their mother died?"

"Young. Their father brought them home and they found her body."

"Where's Dad now?"

"No idea. He's been missing for a number of years."

"Maybe that's who this guy is," Aaron said. "The man I saw... He looked older, but I couldn't get a real good look at him because of his hoodie."

Declan stole a peek at him. "Hmm...it's worth investigating."

He called his friend back and said, "Hey, see if you can find any information on Ellison Ragland. Check all the databases. Send it to my phone."

"What is your name?" Everleigh asked.

"Romelle."

"Where are you taking me?" Everleigh asked.

"Somewhere where we can be alone."

"Why not just pull off to the side of the road and kill me now?"

He laughed. "You're still tryin' to get in my head. Ain't gonna happen, lady. You can relax because right now, you're worth more to me alive. If they want you back, they'll have to free my brothers."

"That's not going to happen. They won't release Ellis and Neil."

"It's either that or your little girl grows up without a mother. Think about everything that could happen to her without someone to protect her."

Everleigh raised her eyes upward and said a silent prayer. There was no one to help her. It was all up to God.

She refused to show him fear, so as calmly as she could manage, she said, "Romelle, you must know that this is not going to go the way you planned."

"Oh, it's gonna go exactly the way I want," he responded. "See, I ain't afraid of dying. But you—you have a daughter to think about. If you want her to stay safe, you will do exactly what I say." Romelle glanced over at her. "Folks like me and my brothers…we have to dispense our own justice. When Olivia died, you would've thought my pops would step up—he didn't. He ran away from his responsibility. When I got out of prison, I found him… He tried to tell me that they were better off without him. I shot him right then and there."

She gasped.

"Oh, he deserved it. He failed my little brothers. They don't know that I killed him. It's better for them to think that he's missing."

"It makes it easier for you to control them," she responded. "To get them to do what you want."

"This whole plan was my idea." He grinned at her, and the expression sickened her.

"But Wyle Gaines…" she began.

He laughed cruelly. "I heard from Olivia's landlord all about your mama. It's me who tracked her down. I was watching you for a while. I saw you turn Gaines down about the house. I got him talking about his troubles in that bar and then sent my little brothers over to hear all about it. I let Ellis and Neil think it was some kind of destiny, meeting Gaines. But it was my plan to take down Powell's family and end his bloodline. We even took out that pervert of a foster father. He died squealing like a pig…"

Everleigh prayed Declan was able to track her phone. But each mile marker they passed put more distance between them. She was going to have to do something.

Assessing her situation, she eyed the speedometer. They weren't wearing seat belts, and

Romelle was driving above the speed limit. It was much too risky for her to try and jump out of the SUV, especially with her hands tied.

Her eyes strayed to the steering wheel.

God, if I do this, I'm going to really need Your help. I don't want to lose my life—I just want to stop this vehicle and Romelle. A crash would draw the police.

Everleigh moved with purpose. She reached over, grabbing the wheel with her bound hands.

"Wha—"

The car veered off the road as they struggled in the front seat. Romelle punched her in the chest, and the force sent her backward, toward the passenger side door.

They were headed toward a thicket of trees.

Everleigh didn't know if her idea had been such a smart one, but it was the only thing she could think of doing at the time. Her chest throbbed as she braced herself for impact.

The SUV connected with a huge tree.

She heard the grinding of metal and the shattering of glass. Everleigh caught a glimpse of Romelle's body being hurled forward into the windshield before falling back into the driver seat. The impact was a hard one.

Glass cut into her flesh, pain slicing through her face and arms as the edges of darkness closed in around her. She prayed once more, begging God to spare her life.

Chapter 22

Everleigh opened her eyes with a start.

She was still inside the SUV.

Romelle wasn't moving. He looked unconscious.

Using her mouth, she worked to get the wire from around her hands. Once her left hand was free, her adrenaline kicked in; Everleigh slipped out of the vehicle and ran. She had no idea where she was or where she was going. She just knew she had to get away in case Romelle regained consciousness.

She took in a deep breath to clear her head as her anxiety level rose. Her face was on fire and she felt nauseous. Everleigh was so anxious to escape that she'd left her purse inside the vehicle. Her phone was inside.

"I'm not going back there," she whispered.

Everleigh took in her surroundings. The moon was out, but the sky was dark and ominous-looking. She swallowed her fear, trusting that God was true to His word. He was her protector and no harm would come to her.

Pain shot across her expression, compressing her features.

She saw the lights of a vehicle as it slowed and came to a stop. It wasn't the police. She feared that there could be others with Romelle. She didn't know how many people were helping Neil and Ellis, so she thought it best to remain out of sight.

Everleigh ran deeper into the wooded area.

In the distance, she saw two figures get out of the SUV and pressed herself against the tree. At one point, the SUV looked like Declan's, but he would've come alone. Tears filled her eyes in her disappointment.

Declan, where are you? I need you.

"That's the car over there," Aaron said.

Declan read the license tag, pulled off the road and parked his vehicle. He got out quickly. Panic rioted within his body as he prayed that Everleigh was fine. That she'd survived the accident.

I can't lose her now, Lord.

They cautiously approached the SUV. Declan had his gun drawn.

"There's someone inside," Aaron said.

Peering inside, he said, "It's the driver, but where's Everleigh?"

"Looks like she managed to get out of the vehicle. She's got to be somewhere in these woods."

"I need to find her quick," Declan said. "She could be injured. Stay with him."

He turned on his flashlight, searching the surroundings and calling out for her. "Everleigh!"

Nothing.

"It's me... Declan. If you can hear me, just follow my voice."

He walked deeper into the wooded area. "Everleigh, I'm here."

Declan heard a sound just ahead of him. He released the breath he'd been holding when the light from his flashlight landed on her.

His rushed to her side, embracing her. "She's alive," he yelled. "I found her."

"I was afraid I'd never see you and Rae again," Everleigh said before breaking down into sobs. "I was so scared."

Declan led her through the refuge of trees.

When they approached the SUV, Declan said, "This is Aaron. He'll walk you to the car. I want to make sure your kidnapper doesn't try to escape."

"No," Everleigh responded, tears running down her face. "We should go. Let's just get out of here," she pleaded. "Before he manages to wake up."

He walked back over to the wrecked SUV. "From the looks of it, he's not going anywhere. The police are on the way—I intend to make sure this guy goes from the hospital straight to the jail."

The blaring of police sirens broke up the silence.

Everleigh bent over as she tried to quiet her heavy breathing.

Declan wrapped his arm around her waist. "Are you okay? Are you in any pain?"

"Just got a little out of breath. I'll be fine."

A police car came into view.

"What is his connection to the brothers?" Declan asked.

"He's their half-brother," Everleigh responded. "His name is Romelle. Apparently, he was locked up when they were placed in a group home. How did you know where to find me? Were you able to track my phone?"

"Aaron happened to be sitting in his car and saw everything."

Everleigh turned toward him. "I'm so grateful you were there. Thank you for being so diligent."

"I'm glad I was able to help," Aaron replied. "I wanted to intervene when I first realized what was going on, but then I saw the gun."

"Wait… I've seen you before. On campus."

He nodded. "The day I met with Professor Blanchet. I was leaving his office and you were coming to see him."

"You have good instincts," Declan said. "I'm looking forward to having you in my class."

"I'm just glad we were able to get Professor Taylor back. It doesn't always turn out this way."

"I feel very fortunate," Everleigh responded. "Right now, all I want to do is see my daughter."

"After they check you out in the hospital, I'll take you to her," Declan said.

"I told you that I'm fine."

"It's dark but I can see that you have some bruising on your face as well as cuts. You're bleeding."

Declan, Everleigh and Aaron watched as Romelle was taken out of the SUV and loaded into an ambulance. A police officer walked over to speak with Everleigh.

When they were given the okay to leave, Declan said, "They're all in custody now."

"But it's not over yet," Everleigh responded. "What if Romelle manages to escape the hospital?"

"He won't," Declan assured her. "He's got some head trauma and might need surgery. But after he's out of the woods, he'll be handcuffed to the bed."

Declan held open the passenger-side door.

Everleigh slid inside. The only thing on her mind in this moment was seeing her daughter. She couldn't wait to hold Rae in her arms.

"Where are we heading?" she asked.

"The hospital."

"I don't want to do that."

"Everleigh, you need to be checked out," he said. "Then I'll take you to your daughter."

When they arrived to the emergency entrance, Aaron said, "My friend's coming to pick me up. I'll wait out here until she comes."

Declan shook his hand. "Thank you for everything."

"I'm glad it turned out this way."

After Everleigh was registered and given a room, Declan was allowed to join her.

"I just got off the phone with Sherri. She wants you to know that the girls are having a ball together. I told her we'd be there sometime tomorrow."

"Thanks, Declan," Everleigh responded. "I don't want her worrying about me." She shifted her position on the bed. "I really hope they don't try to keep me. I feel fine."

"You're lying," he said. "You have some cuts that need to be looked at, but not only that... you're grimacing every now and then. I can see that you're in pain."

Shortly, a doctor came in and examined her. "Mrs. Taylor, you've got glass in the cut on your forehead," the doctor said. "I'm going to remove it and put a bandage on you."

She turned her head to one side, eyes closed. "My head hurts and my chest. He punched me when I grabbed the steering wheel."

After an examination, the doctor didn't see any signs of external bleeding other than her head. He ordered a battery of tests to determine if she'd sustained any internal damage.

"Why is this taking so long," Everleigh complained.

Declan handed her his phone so that she

could call and talk to Rae. He hoped it would help to calm her some.

"Hey, sweetie."

"Mama, where are you?"

"I had to take care of something at the university. I had a little car accident. I'm fine, so there's no need to worry."

"Did you get hurt?"

"A few cuts and scratches," Everleigh responded. "But I should be there tomorrow. Okay? Mr. Declan is with me."

"Okay. I'll see you soon, Mama."

"That went much better than I thought it would," Everleigh said as she handed the phone back to Declan. "I don't know why, but I feel a little disappointed."

"I can assure you that little girl misses you."

A nurse walked into the room, putting a pause in their conversation.

When she left, Everleigh said, "Freedom first thing in the morning..."

He chuckled. "I'll be here early to pick you up."

Declan sent up a prayer of thanksgiving. The worst was over for now. When the Ragland brothers went to trial, Everleigh's secret would be exposed, but she wouldn't have to face it alone. He would stand beside her.

"I'm glad to finally leave this hospital," Everleigh said the next morning as they walked through the parking lot to the car. "I can't wait to put my arms around Rae. I wasn't sure I'd ever see her again."

"You risked your life trying to take the wheel like that," Declan said when they were on the road. "That accident could've ended up being much worse."

"I know, but I had to do something," she responded. "If I hadn't, there's no telling how this would've turned out."

"I'm glad I found you when I did."

"Me, too," she murmured. Staring out the passenger-side window, Everleigh asked, "Are we heading to Columbia?"

He nodded.

"Good."

"I had no idea there was another brother. We thought that maybe it was Ellison Ragland, their father, who kidnapped you."

"I can understand why," she murmured.

"Especially since Ellison has been missing for years."

Gently rubbing her temple with her right hand, she said, "We had no way of knowing there was a half-brother on their father's side. Romelle said that killing off Powell's bloodline was *his* idea. You should've heard him. He was proud of it. He said something else—he told me that he killed his father because he'd failed Neil and Ellis. That's why nothing's come up on Ellison."

"As soon as he recovers, the brothers will be reunited in jail," Declan stated. "Romelle can spend the rest of his life trying to protect them in prison."

"I got the distinct impression that Romelle was always the one in charge. Ellis had the most rage. Neil seemed on the fence, but he's loyal to his brothers."

"This explains why the victims were killed in different ways," Declan said. "I thought it was because the perp was deliberately trying to hide the connection between the crimes. I'm thinking now that Ellis was the one who bludgeoned his victims. Romelle had a gun so he probably shot his victims. I'm not sure Neil killed anyone. He was probably more of a witness than anything."

"Romelle intended to use me to try and get

his brothers out of jail," Everleigh said. "But he still intended to kill me. Just in the short time I was with him, I could tell he's a sociopath."

"While you were being examined, I found out that Romelle was arrested for killing another teen when he was fourteen," Declan said. "He's been in and out of trouble from the time he was eleven years old."

"Eleven? What on earth did he do at eleven?"

"He was killing animals."

Everleigh shook her head sadly. "Then he killed his own father and manipulated his half-brothers into murder. He created monsters."

The heaviness of sleep began to overtake her. "I'm going to take a quick nap for a half hour," she thought, succumbing to the need for rest.

When Everleigh woke up, Declan was turning on Lakeshore. She could hardly contain her joy. She couldn't wait to see her daughter.

When they walked into the house, Rae rushed to her side.

"Mama, you have a boo-boo on your head."

She wrapped her arms around her. "I'm fine. I promise."

"I was a good girl. Ask Miss Sherri."

"I'm so proud of you, sweetie."

"Were you brave at the hospital?" Rae asked.

Everleigh glanced over at Declan. "What would you say?"

"She was very brave," he replied.

"Mama, I'm proud of you," Rae said.

Everleigh spent the rest of her evening with her daughter until the little girl went to sleep.

She heard someone in the kitchen and went to investigate.

"I'm sorry. Did I wake you?" Declan asked. "I was in the mood for a piece of pie and some milk."

Everleigh sat down across from him at the table. "I wasn't sleeping. I thought you'd left already and I heard a noise."

Declan reached over and took her hand in his own. "How are you feeling?"

"A bit antsy," she responded. "Shaken...even a little bit scared... Okay, a lot scared, even though I know it's over."

He smiled. "That's normal."

"It's hard to stop thinking of what could've happened...you know, the worst-case scenarios."

Declan gave her a reassuring smile. "It may take a day or two but those feelings will go away." He pointed to the sweet-potato pie. "You should have a slice of this. It's delicious."

"It does look good."

Declan cut her a slice and placed it on a plate. "What would you like to drink?"

"Hot chocolate," Everleigh responded. "My mom used to make me a cup whenever I was down or felt afraid."

"Then I'll make you some."

"I don't know what I'd do without you, Declan," she said. "You've been a wonderful friend to me. You also kept your promise. You said you'd keep us safe and you did just that."

"Just so you know, I don't consider my job officially over until after Ellis, Neil and Romelle are tucked away in prison for good."

Everleigh took a sip of her hot chocolate. "What happens after that?" she asked. "We go back to a friendly wave and a nod."

"You can't get rid of me that easily," Declan responded with a chuckle. "I hope we will remain friends or something more…"

"I'd like that. I'd really like that. Since you're here, would you like to watch a movie or we could just talk," Everleigh said.

"If you're not too tired."

She finished off her pie. "Declan, can I ask you a very personal question?"

"Sure."

"Why haven't you gotten married?"

"I always thought I'd be married by now, but I guess it just wasn't meant to be," he responded. "What about you? Do you think you'll ever re-marry?"

"Just a few short weeks ago, I wasn't sure I ever would," Everleigh said. "But I really loved being married and I don't want Rae to grow up alone. I'd like to have more children."

"I'm happy to hear this because I'd love to take you on a real date. Whenever you're ready for something like that."

"I want to be honest with you, Declan. I'm very attracted to you, but the fact that you worked in law enforcement initially turned me off. My late husband was a firefighter. He died on the job. I didn't want to put Rae through another loss like that. Then I realized I was being irrational. I was angry with God because I wanted Him to protect Britt, and when he died, I felt that God failed me."

"Do you still feel that way?"

"I don't," Everleigh responded. "God has shown me in so many ways that He is who He says He is. He protected me when I was with Romelle. Crashing the car was risky and stupid, but God didn't let me die. I can't explain it—I just know He was with me. I was protected."

"It's funny you should bring my career up," he said, a crooked grin on his face. "I get so much out of teaching, and working with Aaron to get you home safely convinced me what I want to do. The faculty offered me a full-time teaching position and I've decided to take them up on it."

"You're leaving the police department?"

Declan nodded. "I'm really enjoying teaching. However, I'll still consult for them whenever needed."

Everleigh broke into a grin.

"Things just got interesting, don't you think?"

"Definitely," she responded.

Chapter 23

Everleigh sat on a bench outside of the social-services building, waiting for Declan's class to end. It felt good being on campus and teaching in-person. Most of her classes were in-person this semester, with one virtual class in the mix.

He strolled out of the building at twelve noon. Declan lowered himself carefully onto the bench beside her. "I like seeing your beautiful face back here on school grounds."

"I'm thrilled to be back, all things considered," she responded. "Rae's very happy being back at school with her kindergarten class."

"I was just about to ask about her."

"She's good. Oh, this is for you." Everleigh handed him a folded piece of paper. "Rae drew a picture for you."

"It's the three of us together."

She nodded. "Rae had a lot of fun at your sister's house. *With you.* She really likes you, Declan."

"I'm crazy about that little girl and her mother."

He planted a quick kiss on her lips, then said, "What do you think about dinner and a play?" he inquired. "This Saturday."

Excitement floated through her. "Are you talking about the new DeSantis play?"

"Yes," Declan responded.

"Oh, I'd love that," Everleigh exclaimed. "I've been wanting to see it, but I didn't relish going alone."

"I have tickets. I bought them with the intent to take my sister, but then her job sent her abroad."

"I'm excited."

"I can tell," Declan said with a chuckle.

"I don't know about you, but I'm hungry," she stated, holding up a lunch bag. "I made an extra sandwich."

Everleigh took a bite of her sandwich, but her eyes never left Declan's face as he swiped her pickle to add to his own sandwich.

"You love pickles, I see."

He grinned. "I do. I usually order extra pickles."

"I'll keep that in mind."

She retrieved a bag of potato chips. "I have another bag if you want it."

Declan gave a slight nod as he wiped his mouth on the paper napkin.

"I just got a news alert," Everleigh said while looking at her phone. "James Ray Powell is dead. Apparently, he had cancer."

Declan checked his phone. "I got a notification, too."

They sat in silence for a moment before Everleigh said, "I don't feel anything but relief. I'm not happy that he's dead or anything, but I can't deny that I'm relieved he won't ever know about me or Rae. I feel like I can finally close that door permanently."

"There's still four people out there who know about this."

"I'm not worried about Wyle Gaines. He has enough to deal with now that his past is catching up to him. And if he decides to tell anyone about me, he doesn't have any proof. As for the Ragland brothers—all three of them—they don't have any proof, either. There's nothing for them to gain in telling the world. Powell's dead. He was my biggest concern."

"They all have credibility issues for sure."

"I'm not worried," Everleigh said. "None of them have any power over me."

James Ray Powell was laid to rest in the prison cemetery two days later. Nobody had come forward to claim his remains. The world would breathe a collective sigh of relief now that he was gone, Everleigh included. For the first time since her nightmare started, the future looked promising once again.

Even if Powell hadn't died, she'd already refused to allow the sins of her father to weigh her down. There were still some emotions and processes she had to go through. She'd experienced a period of denial when her mother first told her about him, then rode the pendulum of shock and anger. But now she was in the acceptance phase. Powell's actions were not a reflection of herself or Rae.

Everleigh stood in front of the full-length mirror, checking her reflection. She'd chosen a velvet mid-length dress in burgundy with matching suede boots for her date with Declan.

Although the past two years had been filled with challenges, she was finally ready for her future.

Epilogue

One year later

"This place is uncomplicated living at its best," Everleigh said. "I almost hate going back to Charleston tomorrow."

Declan took her hand in his as they walked the trail around the lake. "So you really like it here in Columbia?"

She looked over at him. "I love it here."

"I guess we should get back to the house," he said. "I promised Rae I'd help her with reading."

"Don't let her manipulate you into reading to her when it's her turn to read out loud."

He grinned. "I won't."

As soon as they walked into the house, they were met by Rae, who said, "Mama, we found this while we were taking down the Christmas tree. It's for you." She held up a gift-wrapped box.

Everleigh took it from her. "Who is it from?"

"Oh, yeah... I forgot all about that one," Declan said.

"Open it, Mama."

"Okay," she murmured. Everleigh couldn't begin to guess what it could be—the box was rectangular in shape. It could be a shirt...anything.

She tore the wrapping away.

Inside that box was a beautiful hand-carved jewelry box—it was one she'd seen in a boutique downtown. Declan had pointed it out to her, but never indicated he'd purchased it.

His sister Marguerite, Remy, Sherri and the girls were gathered around her, admiring the gift.

Everleigh turned to thank Declan and found him on bended knee.

"That jewelry box is actually one of two gifts. Here is the second one," he said, opening the black velvet box to reveal a stunning engagement ring.

"Declan..."

"Will you do me the honor of becoming my wife?"

Tears of joy sprang in Everleigh's eyes. "Yes. Yes. *Yes*."

Rae clapped her hands in glee. "I'm getting another daddy."

Everleigh fell into Declan's embrace.

"Oh, my goodness," she murmured. "We're really doing this. We're getting married."

"Yeah, we are. I'm ready to spend the rest of my life with you."

She held her hand out, admiring the ring.

"Congratulations," Marguerite said. "I've always wanted a sister."

"Now you really are part of the family!" Sherri said.

Everleigh smiled. "Same here."

Remy brought out a bottle of non-alcoholic Champagne for the adults and apple juice for Rae and Halle. "It's time for a toast."

After each of them had a flute, Remy said, "Uncle, I'm so happy for you, Everleigh and Rae. From the moment Sherri and I saw the three of you together, we knew...we just sensed that your worlds would eventually become one. Cheers."

They took a sip.

She reached for Declan's hand, lacing her fingers with his. "I never really imagined that I'd feel this way again—truly excited about what the future holds. I know that there will always be challenges, but I'm glad I don't have to face them alone."

Declan looked down at their linked hands. "We will meet life head-on…together."

"Yay… Rae's my sister now," Halle said, sparking laughter from everyone in the room.

Declan flashed her a grin. "Let's just go with it for tonight."

Everleigh nodded in agreement. This was the start of a new life together.

★ ★ ★ ★ ★

The Marine's Deadly Reunion
Loretta Eidson

MILLS & BOON

Loretta Eidson is an award-winning author born and raised in the South. She lives in North Mississippi and enjoys family time with her four children and thirteen grandchildren. Her love of reading began at a young age when she discovered Phyllis A. Whitney's mystery novels. Loretta believes in the power of prayer and loves putting her characters in situations where they must trust God to pull them through tough situations. Visit Loretta on her website at lorettaeidson.com.

He that dwelleth in the secret place of the most High
shall abide under the shadow of the Almighty.
I will say of the Lord, He is my refuge and
my fortress: my God; in him will I trust.
—*Psalm* 91:1–2

DEDICATION

To my husband, who loved, supported and
cheered me on during his last days.

Kenneth, I'll love you forever. Rest in peace.

Thank you, God, for Your mercy and grace.

Chapter 1

Sergeant Daria Gordon cruised her hometown of Kimbleton, Missouri, one last time before she headed back to the police station to clock out. With temperatures dropping into the teens and the threat of a wintry mix, she could hardly wait to curl up by the fireplace in her new festive red pajamas. Just the thought of watching a Christmas movie and eating hot buttered popcorn made her mouth water.

The afternoon tourist traffic bottlenecked at the fork in the road in front of the Marketplace Grocery, which was nothing unusual for the Christmas season. A disturbance in the store's parking lot caught her attention. Two men scuffled between parked cars.

"Checking a fight between two male suspects in the Marketplace parking lot," Daria reported on the radio clipped to her uniform. She flipped on her flashing lights and siren, made a quick turn and pulled in behind a white SUV. Parking lots were private property, but she'd cruise by anyway to make sure no one got hurt.

A bearded man bolted and hopped into the passenger side of a waiting black Suburban. Tires squealed on the asphalt as they sped away. His opponent held a pistol, turned and stuck his head into the back seat of the white SUV. The one with the weapon was Daria's top priority. She must secure the threat.

She opened the door with her weapon drawn and eased from her squad car. "Police. Put your gun on the ground and place your hands on your head where I can see them." She readied herself for an abrupt reaction.

The suspect placed his pistol on the pavement and pushed it toward her with his foot. He lifted his hands in the air and stepped away from the SUV's back door, sporting a busted lip. The sleeves of his camouflage T-shirt bulged over his muscular biceps. She maintained a watchful eye and studied him. He looked familiar. That squared chin and those deep brown eyes reminded her of someone she used to know.

"I'm not the one you want." His warm breath fogged in the freezing temperatures. He glanced inside the vehicle and back at her. "You should've gone after those guys."

"I'll make that determination. You're the one I saw with a gun. Don't make any sudden moves." She adjusted her stance. "Back up." She eased forward and secured his weapon.

"That guy tried to take my baby. I had to protect her." He let out a huff. "I'm Jake Fisher. Want my ID?"

"Yes. Take it slow. Why would someone want to take your baby?" A slight lean, to glance inside the vehicle, confirmed a baby was inside. A little girl about eighteen months old stared at her with tear-streaked cheeks and a red nose that proved she'd been crying. The icy December wind didn't help matters. "Hello, little one." Daria smiled.

Poor baby. She must be freezing.

The child's eyebrows lowered. "No." Her lips pooched out.

She clutched a small rubber bunny in one hand and slapped the air toward Daria. Most children didn't like strangers getting too close, and her apprehension of Daria was a natural response.

"It was probably someone who works for whoever forced my sister's car off the road and killed her and my brother-in-law. You should go after them right now."

Daria reported the parking lot incident on the radio clipped to her shoulder. She gave a description of the black Suburban that had sped away. No license plate. Maybe the store's security camera captured the incident. She holstered her weapon as Jake handed over his driver's license, showing an out-of-town address.

"What's the nature of your visit to the Ozarks? Kimbleton, Missouri, is a long way from California." *Jake Fisher?* Could he be her scrawny best friend from middle school? If so, he'd grown some muscles. How many times had they talked about what they wanted to be when they grew up? He'd dreamed of becoming a professional football quarterback, and she'd thought about nursing. From the looks of his military attire, he'd changed his mind, as had she.

"I just returned from active duty after receiving word of my sister's death. She left me everything she owned." He pointed to the SUV. "She lived in the Ozark Mountains valley along the county line."

"Who was your sister?" Daria's curiosity stirred. Would he give the name she remembered?

"Amanda. Our family used to live here, but Dad moved us when he received a job transfer to California." He shuffled his feet and looked around before returning his attention to her.

It was him. The first guy she'd ever had a crush on. He'd matured well and was more handsome than ever. She'd gone out with several of the local guys through the years, but they weren't to her liking. Dating was the last thing on her agenda right now, although seeing Jake again might move it up the list. She couldn't give in to her attraction. He had a baby, which meant he was already taken.

"I remember Mandy. Jake, I'm Daria, in case you didn't recognize me." Her heart thundered.

"I thought you looked familiar." He rested his arm on the open car door. "Thought you wanted to be a nurse."

"Well, I thought you were going to play football."

With a mature and brawny Jake standing in front of her, memories of all the fun they'd had as kids resurfaced. Was he still the easygoing guy she remembered?

Didn't matter. She had to focus on proving herself an efficient, well-trained cop. Especially after her supervisor's warning to get control of her anger issues. That disruptive vacationer and his dad six months ago had gotten on her last nerve. Richard and Tony Schneider. She'd never forget their names. She'd scolded the belligerent son in front of a crowd. He became hostile, so she arrested him. His dad wasn't much better, but she'd let his angry remarks slide. She'd worked hard to get this job and didn't intend on losing it or being assigned to desk duty.

The child's cry drew her back to the present. What was she thinking?

Stay focused on the incident.

Daria relayed Jake's personal information to dispatch. "Officers are on the lookout for the vehicle," she told Jake, then waited while the department looked him up. Once they confirmed Jake had an unblemished record, she handed his pistol back to him.

She'd been so focused on Jake that she hadn't noticed Christmas music playing through the speakers of the shopping center across the street.

A gust of wind cut through her clothes and sent chills to her toes. She zipped up her police-issued jacket. The child had to be freezing, too. With sleet and snow in the forecast, the roads were sure to be treacherous after nightfall. How could he stand there in the cold wearing that short-sleeved T-shirt? And where was the baby's mother?

"You might want to turn some heat on in your car. I'm sure your little girl is cold." Daria observed his gentleness toward the child as he tightened a pink blanket around her legs, then started the vehicle, adjusted the temperature setting and turned the fan on high.

"Should've thought of that myself. Thanks." He straightened and faced Daria, holding the door ajar. "No disrespect, but if you'd left me alone, I could've caught up with that car and taken care of the situation." His lips tightened. "I was a sergeant in the Marine Corps, so I've had plenty of experience with enemy tactics."

A woman wearing her heavy coat and carrying a bag of groceries hurried by them toward her car. She stared at them in passing. Daria nodded at her. "Hello, Caroline. I hope you and Mr. Hall are doing well."

The lady wasn't the social type and didn't respond, but since she was the bank president's wife, Daria wanted to acknowledge her presence. Caroline slid into her car and drove away.

Daria looked back at Jake.

"Excuse me? I'm glad you're back in Kimbleton, and I appreciate your service to our country, but you're not in Afghanistan anymore. I'm the authority in this town, and this is my jurisdiction. You cannot take the law into your own hands, regardless of your experience." She stared into his determined eyes and bit back the agitation rising inside her. "Besides, if you had chased after them with this child in the car, I could charge you with endangerment to a minor."

"Didn't mean it like that, and you're right. I've got to protect Emma." His fingers swiped over his military haircut. "Someone is following us, and I wondered if he was the same person who murdered my sister and ransacked her house."

"Murdered? I heard of an Amanda killed in an accident, but the last name wasn't familiar. I never associated her with your family until now. I'm sorry for your loss, but there's been no report of foul play."

"Police report said they lost control of their pickup and crashed. They claimed it was an accident, but Amanda had been saying someone was after her. She was a cautious driver. I know my sister, and that wreck was not an accident." He rubbed his arms and pulled a jacket out of the car. "It was murder."

"You can't go claiming murder unless you have proof." He sounded so certain. The Jake she remembered never exaggerated; well, maybe when they were kids and he pretended to be a quarterback.

"I intend to prove someone killed her." Jake's jaw tightened.

She'd have to do some digging on her own to verify his story. "I'll see what I can find out. In the meantime—"

Tires squealed. The Suburban was back, and it raced up the parking lot an aisle over from where they stood. The passenger window rolled down and the barrel of a shotgun stuck out.

Daria dived for Jake and slammed into his chest, which was like hitting a brick wall. His thick arms swung her around and they fell into the back seat, protecting Emma. Bullets thudded into the surrounding vehicles. Daria shot a quick glance at Emma and shimmied out of the car with her pistol in hand. How the two of them fell in through that door at the same time, she didn't know.

She radioed for backup. "Shots fired. I repeat. Shots fired." She located the black Suburban in the distance as it exited the large parking lot and disappeared down the street. "Black Sub-urban. No plates."

Daria backed up closer to Jake. As an author-ity figure, she'd tried to protect both of them, but his strength had overpowered hers, land-ing them in the car. Should she be mad at Jake or thankful?

"Emma." Jake pulled the screaming baby from her car seat and stepped out of the car. He held her firm against his chest. Her shrill cry made Daria want to hold and comfort her. He dangled Emma out in front of him. Daria checked her body and clothes for blood. "Are you hurt, baby?"

"Ma-ma." Her fingers went to her mouth. Jake wrapped his arms around her again.

"She looks okay. The blast of the gun must have scared her." Daria scanned the area for the car's return. Sirens sounded. Help was on the way.

Emma reached for Daria. Surprised at the child's interest in her after her earlier response, Daria holstered her weapon, took the baby and wrapped her arms around the trembling bundle. Her heart squeezed. It had been a while since she'd held a baby, and it felt good.

Jake tucked a pink fuzzy blanket around his

baby's body. She laid her head on Daria's shoulder. Her cries grew silent. Daria didn't need any more convincing. Someone was out to get Jake.

Or was it Emma they wanted?

Jake stood close to Emma while Daria held her. "Am I free to go? I've got to get her out of the elements and out of danger. They could come back with more weapons."

He could still hear the fear in his sister's voice over the phone as she begged him to take good care of her baby mere days before her death. She said if anything happened, he had sole custody of Emma, his niece. Two weeks later, they summoned him home. Police located his brother-in-law's pickup bottom side up off the mountain road. Both were deceased at the scene.

Whoever killed them would pay. Seeing death in a war zone was one thing, but losing family cut deep, and it put him on edge and on high alert.

He chewed his lip as uncertainty boiled inside him. Wars he could handle—shooting guns, maneuvering stealthily and securing the enemy—but he knew nothing about taking care of a baby. His aging parents weren't physically able to care for her on a day-to-day basis. Even though he was thankful Emma was with them when his sister's accident happened.

Asking for help from his ex-fiancée wasn't an option. The Dear John letter she'd sent him while he was deployed said it all loud and clear. How could she ditch him like that? He was on his own.

"Jake, are you listening?" Daria's hand squeezed his forearm. His muscle tensed. "I said you're free to go, but I'll escort you and Emma home." She handed the child back to him and walked toward her car.

"You don't have to do that. I'm good. I know how to handle these guys." Jake buckled Emma in her car seat. Those little fingers still gripped the small rubber bunny. Perfect size for her hands.

"I'm right behind you." She got in her car and waited.

He started the car and headed home.

A huff escaped his lips. His rearview mirror revealed Daria's squad car following close behind. He could defend himself. She'd been kind to him and looked all official in her uniform, but she was a cop, and the police didn't help Amanda when she filed a report about the threats. No one took her seriously. Was Daria one of the guilty parties? Who could he trust? No one.

Trust was a rare commodity and an endangered trait. Jake had trusted too much, especially on the battlefield, and it got his buddy Nolan killed. Nolan had insisted he could crawl unnoticed from the bunker and throw a grenade across the enemy line because he was smaller in stature than Jake was.

"Trust me. I've got this," he'd said. Jake had prayed for whatever good it did. The enemy shot him as he lifted his torso from the ground and threw the grenade. Successful throw, but seconds too late.

Jake wiped his hand across his mouth. Would he ever overcome the guilt of his friend's death? He glanced back at Emma. She'd thrown diapers, clothes and more little rubber animals out of the diaper bag and found her pink-and-white cup. Smart and self-sufficient. They just might get along.

"You found your cup, didn't you?" He smiled at her through the rearview mirror.

"Yes." She shook her head up and down, making her short black curls dance. "Cup." Her dark onyx eyes latched on to his eyes in the mirror and melted his heart.

There was no way around it. He had to take care of this tiny human and carry out his sister's wishes. Failure wasn't in his vocabulary. Somehow, he'd figure it out.

The shooter was another story. He preferred investigating on his own. Once he had proof, he'd present the evidence to the authorities. He'd begin by questioning Amanda's coworkers at the bank.

Jake turned into the driveway and pressed the remote. The garage door opened. Daria parked midway on the drive. He pulled the car into the garage and closed the door. His thoughts drifted back to the disarray of the house when he'd first arrived this morning. He'd considered calling the police and reporting the incident, but what would they do? They didn't protect his sister. At least he took pictures as proof the intruder had been there. Had he found what he was looking for? Jake didn't know, but he was certain he and Emma were now in their crosshairs.

Jake rolled his shoulders and popped his neck before he got out of the car and opened the back door to get Emma. He scooped up the tossed contents of the diaper bag and stuffed them back inside the bag. With her cup in one hand, hanging by the handle, and the white rubber bunny in the other, Emma's arms stretched out to him.

"Want you." Her legs kicked as he picked her up and her dainty arms wrapped around his neck.

So, this is what the love of a child feels like.

"You're the only one who does, kiddo." He patted her back, went inside and set her down. "Guess I need to open the front door. It would be rude to leave Daria sitting outside in the cold." He liked her, but he didn't want her telling him what to do and how to do it. He had his own way of tracking down the enemy.

"Door." Emma ran to the door and tapped it with one finger.

"Yep. You talk pretty good for one who's so little." He scooped her up with one arm, opened the wood door with the free hand and unlocked the security door. "Come on in."

"Thanks." Daria stepped inside, holding an iPad. "Brrr, it's getting colder. No doubt bad weather will set in later. I hear we have a chance for sleet and snow tonight."

"Don't plan on getting out." He fought the resentment welling up. If she'd gone after the guy who sped away when she'd first spotted him, there wouldn't have been a shooting, and this whole mess could be over and done with.

"Nice house. But what happened in here?" She walked into the living room, obviously looking the place over. "From what I remember, Amanda loved to decorate. Didn't matter what it was but this wasn't her style."

"I told you it got ransacked. Like I said, she left me everything. She'd always kept a clean house and fussed at me if I put my feet on her coffee table." Jake pointed to the navy leather couch. "Have a seat if you can find a spot. I still have cleaning to do after the intruders tossed everything."

"Ma-ma." Emma toddled down the hall, pointing to the master bedroom. "Ma-ma. Bed."

"Funny how the kid recognizes names." He watched Emma waddle up and down the hallway, then into the living room. She set her cup on the leather ottoman and pounded the rubber bunny next to it. The chair and ottoman were navy, too, and everything matched.

"She's so cute. I adore her dark hair and eyes." Daria turned and looked at him. "I'd like to meet your wife. Is she here? She doesn't need to be afraid. I'll have a police presence outside your home for a while."

Jake bit his tongue. He didn't want to be rude to his childhood friend and cause more friction between them. "Let me reiterate. I am a marine. I understand the dangers of the enemy. No disrespect to you or your occupation, but your department didn't help my sister, so I have a hard time trusting they will help me now. And for the record, I am not married, and I don't have a girlfriend."

Daria's eyebrows lifted. "Oh. I just assumed." She pointed to Emma.

"When I told you Amanda left me everything, she left me her only daughter, too. Emma is my niece."

"I see." Daria walked over to the fireplace and picked up a family photo from the mantel. "I'm still trying to figure out how I didn't know Amanda lived in Kimbleton. I should have figured it out. Better yet, I should have seen her around town." She put the photo back in place.

"You know, it shouldn't matter who calls for help, whether the person is a friend or an unknown. They should follow up on every death threat." Jake's comment came out a little more cynical than he intended.

She spun and propped her hands at her waist. "We take our jobs seriously. You, of all people, should know that and understand the law of the land and police jurisdictions. You have protocol in the military, and you had to abide by them. Now that you are home, you must consider who will care for Emma if you take the law into your own hands and kill someone or get yourself killed. I really am sorry for your loss, but let the police handle it."

Jake held back a smile. "You've gotten pretty feisty through the years."

"Stop. I'm serious." She shook her head.

"Why didn't you go to nursing school like you'd dreamed?" Jake studied Daria. It was nice to have an old friend still in his hometown, even if she was a little bossy.

"You're changing the subject." Daria closed her iPad. "I almost finished my nursing degree, but once I started clinicals and saw the number of people wounded from fights, gunshots, knives, overdoses, etc., I opted for the police department in hopes I could help stop some of these needless crimes. Why didn't you pursue football and become the quarterback you talked about? You were always good at sports."

"Somehow, after the war broke out, playing

football seemed irrelevant. The desire to join the military and serve my country took priority. Guess God didn't want me to be involved with sports. Maybe I needed the discipline. I don't know." Jake pulled out his phone. "What's your number? I'll send you the pictures I took of the mess the intruders left. I've cleaned some of it up."

"You shouldn't have touched anything and called us immediately. Now you've contaminated the crime scene." She gave him her number and lifted her cell. "I'll take a few more pictures to add to the report."

"Go ahead." He scooped Emma into his arms and followed Daria through the house as she took pictures of the disarray in each room. "By the way, it's nice to see you again." He let his squirming niece slide from his arms to the floor.

"You, too, Jake." Daria returned to the living room. "I'll go finish my report in the car before I head back. If you need anything, you've got my number. I'm just a phone call away."

"Thanks, I appreciate it." Jake walked Daria toward the front door.

Bullets shattered the living room window. Emma screamed. Jake dived for Emma, pulled his weapon and covered her with his body. He held her like a football and inched back for better cover. "Are you okay?" he asked Daria.

She held her pistol in one hand and the radio clipped to her shoulder in the other as she rolled across the floor toward them. "Shots fired. Need backup."

Chapter 2

Daria shielded Jake and Emma as more bullets pelted through the window. Glass from framed pictures on the opposite wall shot like daggers across the room with each hit. She inched her way to the side of a window and fired back.

Emma's cries filled the air. Poor baby. Daria prayed for the first time since her friend's death four years ago.

Dear Lord, I know I haven't reached out to You in a while, but please, help keep baby Emma safe.

It couldn't hurt to try, although Daria had a hard time trusting Him after her prayers had gone unanswered when Joni had her heart attack.

Jake rushed toward her. What was he doing?

"Stop. Get down." Daria threw her hand out toward him.

"You watch Emma while I go out the back door and scout out the shooters." Jake pushed

Emma into her arms, then retrieved his pistol from his shoulder holster.

"Oh, no you don't. You stay put." Emma latched on to Daria and laid her head on her shoulder. "We're going to have to agree to disagree and work together. You be the trained marine, and I'll be the experienced police officer. Put our wisdom together and we might survive this attack. Help is on the way. It may take them a few minutes, considering how far out of town we are."

"I can get to them. Don't patronize me." His eyebrows lowered.

"I'm not, Jake. I'm trying to get you to work with me and not against me. Here in the States, it's my responsibility to protect you and Emma. I realize you are a well-trained soldier with many hidden talents. I don't doubt your abilities. Trust me and let me do my job."

"People earn trust, and I'm still assessing you." He eyed her and then backed off. A smile emerged as he lifted his eyebrows up and down. A gesture he did back in their school days when she was upset. "I remember you always babysitting and carrying a kid around in the neighborhood. You're good with babies.

That's why you're the only one I trust to be near her right now."

"You are impossible." She held back her frustration at his bantering. "This is serious business. There's a shooter out there determined to take us out. It's nothing to joke and laugh about." Unbeknownst to him, she was still assessing him, too. He seemed innocent enough, but his resistance to her authority would have to stop.

"You're right." He leaned close to the window and pushed the curtain aside. "I still could creep up on them."

Daria rolled her eyes. She raised up just enough to peer out of the broken window and not expose Emma. "There are two people over there, running through the woods. Did you see movement in those bushes? Not sure if it's another shooter or an animal."

"Car doors slammed." Jake pointed. "There, in the distance. Do you see that black car? I can't figure out the make or model through all the foliage. Over there, a third shooter running to the car."

Tires squealed as the car sped away. Daria radioed the update.

She leaned against the wall with Emma still

hanging on and sucking on two of her fingers. Emma held her other hand out to Jake. He took her and held her against his chest.

"Everything's going to be okay. Uncle Jake won't let anything happen to you." He kissed the top of her head and smoothed her hair.

Who knew this tough military man could be so gentle? Those biceps bulged, and Emma rested securely in his arms between his broad shoulders. The transformation in Jake's demeanor warmed Daria's heart.

"What exactly did Amanda and your brother-in-law do for a living? Any idea who has a vendetta against you?"

"No clue." Jake paced, holding a sleepy baby. "Tom was an attorney in Los Angeles. He transferred to Kimbleton and set up a virtual office so Amanda could be closer to Dad and Mom after they retired and moved back. Amanda worked at the Crow's Ridge Bank across the county line for a couple of years. She advanced from teller to auditor in a short time."

"Do you think the threats came from someone at work?" Daria made notes on her iPad.

"Last time we talked, she didn't mention the bank. Said she was looking for a more reputable job. I couldn't help but question her word choice. Reputable. Wouldn't her position at the bank meet that criterion?" He placed the sleeping Emma on the couch and put pillows around her.

"One would think so." Daria followed him and gazed down at Emma's innocence. Who would want to hurt either of them? He hadn't been in town long, and someone was already gunning for him.

Her eyes shifted to Jake. "I'm here to help. I'll do what I can to find out what happened to Amanda and Tom, and who is behind these shootings. I'll locate your sister's file and figure out where the investigation trail stopped."

"You're not doing this alone. These people don't care who they eliminate as long as they get what they want." He stepped back over to the window and looked out. "The cops are here." He looked back at Daria. "*More* cops are here."

"My coworkers can help figure this out." She approached the front door and opened it at their knock, then introduced everyone. "Cramer, McDaniel, this is Jake Fisher, a friend from the past. The sleeping beauty on the couch is Emma, Jake's niece." She explained the situation.

"She's eighteen months old and shouldn't be

in the middle of this mess." Jake shook hands with them. "Any idea if the shooters were caught?"

"Officers are involved in a chase as we speak. We will keep you updated. Anyone hurt?" Cramer made notes on a little spiral notepad he pulled from his shirt pocket.

"The shattering glass and loud shooting frightened Emma, but there are no injuries. Jake calmed Emma's cries, and she finally drifted off to sleep."

The officers walked around in the living room inspecting the damage. They paused in front of Emma. McDaniel tightened his jaw, while Cramer pressed his lips together. After working with them for several years, Daria recognized the anger stirring inside them over a baby being amid the danger or possibly being a target. An even more unreasonable thought.

"Did you see the shooter?" Cramer walked over to the broken window. "How many were there?"

"Best we could—"

"Three," Jake interrupted and squared his shoulders. "They had a black car waiting on the road over there." He pointed.

Heat rose in Daria's cheeks. He'd cut her off

while she was giving the report to her coworkers. *Control your temper. Breathe.*

"The forest was too thick to get a description of the shooters." Daria stared at Jake. Was she being unreasonable, or was he being disrespectful? She'd let it go this time.

"They did a number on the windows and walls," McDaniel said. "This is now a crime scene." He turned and faced Daria. "They will have to stay somewhere else for a few days."

"This is my property and we're not leaving. I'll board up the windows and clean up the glass. Emma needs to be in her familiar surroundings. I've got this covered." Jake pushed his shoulders back with his legs slightly apart and his hands behind his back like the military "at ease" stance.

Daria noted his body language and his readiness to argue. "Jake, you should know a crime scene is off-limits to everyone except authorized personnel. I understand your position and your ability to face these shooters, but the thing you must consider is Emma's safety and her vulnerability for emotional trauma should anything else happen. You have a baby to consider now."

The hardness in his face relaxed. "I guess you're right. My thinking is still in military mode. This was my sister's house, and I don't want any more destruction to happen to it."

"After you replenish Emma's diaper bag, I'll take it with me to the car while you get a few necessities, then we'll go to the station. Maybe we can figure things out from there." Daria pointed to Jake. "I'll pull my squad car close to the garage door in case someone's still lurking."

"We will set up the crime scene tape," McDaniel said. "Two squad cars will escort you to the station."

"Perfect. Thanks." Daria turned to Jake. "Grab some more diapers, changes of clothes and a couple of blankets. Be sure to bring some snacks and whatever else she needs."

Good thing she'd had experience babysitting. She dreamed of having a family of her own one day and becoming a stay-at-home mom.

She spun and ran into Jake. He grabbed her shoulders and kept her from falling. A tingling shot across her shoulders at his touch—a warm sensation she'd never experienced.

"Are you okay?" Jake's dark eyes bore into hers.

His firm grip made her feel safe. Wasn't that backward? She was the authority figure. She was supposed to keep him safe. Who was protecting whom here?

"Yes. Did you get the food items and some things for yourself?" She pulled away from his hold and walked past him. "I'm going to the car. Don't linger when you come out. I don't want anyone's crosshairs on you or Emma."

"Got it." His expression grew solemn. "We'll be waiting."

Daria grabbed the diaper bag. She spotted the tiny rubber bunny still on the ottoman beside Emma's cup. She tossed them both into the bag. Cramer and McDaniel stepped inside.

"Time to go," McDaniel said.

"I moved the baby's car seat to your vehicle." Cramer straightened his uniform shirt.

"Thanks. I hadn't thought about that. Grab those two backpacks for me. Jake doesn't need to be bogged down with baggage getting in the car. He needs to focus on Emma." Daria rushed out the front door to her car. She popped the trunk and her coworkers placed the rest of the baggage inside, then slammed it closed.

She rolled forward and the car hobbled badly. She got out and checked her tires. Sure enough, her back tires were flat. She ran back inside.

"What is it?" McDaniel met her at the entrance.

"Looks like someone slashed my back tires." Goose bumps rushed over her arms, and it wasn't the chilly winter wind. Had the shooters cut them before they showered them with bullets and then ran or were there more gunmen hiding in the forest, waiting for their next move?

Jake appeared from the kitchen, holding a sleepy Emma. "We can take my car. It's in the garage where we're better protected loading up. I spotted an extra car seat over in the far corner if you want to grab that one."

"Perfect. Cramer, can you grab the diaper bag from my back floorboard? McDaniel, do you mind getting the backpacks from my trunk? I don't have a good feeling about this. Stay alert." Daria rushed into the garage and located the car seat. She secured it in place, since the other one was now in her disabled vehicle.

Cramer and McDaniel entered through the front door and met her in the closed garage. Daria took the diaper bag and placed it on the floor of the back seat.

Jake came out carrying his niece. His size made her look so tiny. He buckled her in. She whined. He gave her the rubber rabbit and her cup. She gripped the bunny and tucked it up under her chin like she was hugging it and drifted off to sleep.

"I'll drive," she said and held her hand out for the keys.

"I don't think so." Jake hopped into the driver's seat. "Besides, should anything happen, you need to be free to focus."

"I'm not arguing. Let's get out of here, quick." Daria sat on the passenger side and buckled up. She radioed the waiting squad cars and updated them on the vehicle switch.

The garage door opened. Jake backed out and drove around Daria's squad car faster than she expected. The waiting squad cars were in position. One at the end of the driveway and one behind them.

"How fast do you want me to drive?" Jake's eyes cut over to her eyes.

"How important is Emma's and your life? We don't know if there's another shooter hiding in the forest. Stay on the tail of the lead squad car."

Jake rode the bumper of the car in front of them, as Daria instructed. He checked his rear-view mirror and passing vehicles for suspicious activity. All seemed clear. His muscles tensed at the attempts on his and Emma's lives since he'd arrived home. He mulled over the sequence of events. Amanda must have hit a nerve with someone, but she'd never been a troublemaker. She was the introvert in the family. Quiet and meek. Everyone loved her. At least, he thought so.

Who knew Daria would still be in Kimbleton, and had become a law enforcement officer rather than a nurse? It looked like she'd done well for herself as a cop and was insistent on maintaining the law in the area. A sparkle had shone in her eyes when he'd smiled and made his eyebrows dance. Timing was off, but after all these years, he could still read her mood by making eye contact. She was none too happy with him for interrupting her in front of her coworkers. He'd have to tone down his extrovert outbursts.

"Are you cold?" Jake noted Daria with her arms crossed. "The sun's going down, and the temperature is dropping."

"I'm not worried about me. It could be a little cool for Emma, though." She reached over and tucked the soft blanket around the baby's sleeping body. "There. That's better."

Jake turned up the heat and adjusted the air vents to blow more toward the back. Daria turned the vent by the window toward herself. Just as he thought, she was cold, too. She never was one to complain. Guess that's why they got along so well when they were kids. Now she'd become outspoken and authoritative. Nice change.

He glanced back at Emma. His heart hitched at her innocence. She had his sister's features and some of her personality. Could he care for her like Amanda did? Probably not. He wasn't the mom. One thing he could do was protect and love her. He would tell her stories of her parents, so she'd never forget them. Amanda would like that.

They pulled into the police station just as a police officer hung a Christmas wreath on the double glass doors. He parked and got out of the car.

"I'll get Emma." He looked at Daria over the top of the car. "Will you grab the diaper bag?"

Daria didn't waste any time getting the bag and meeting him on the driver's side. He lifted the lightweight child into his arms. Her head popped up. Eyes wide. Daria raised the hood of Emma's coat over her head to keep the chilly wind off her face. Emma tossed it off with her hand.

"Let's get inside." Daria pointed to the doors.

The officers who'd escorted them on the road entered behind them. A fresh scent of pine hit Jake's nostrils and sent him searching for the source. There it was. A live Christmas tree in the corner of the entry, decorated for the season. The smell reminded him of the times he went hunting with his dad and they walked through patches of pine trees.

Daria sniffed the air and smiled. "Mmm, what smells so good in here?" Daria glanced over at the tree and smiled. "With everything we see in this line of work, it's nice to have a little festivity. I hope we can solve this case soon so you and Emma can try to have a normal holiday."

"Yeah, best I remember, you always thought everyone should enjoy the holidays as much as you." Jake followed her down the long hallway. "It's too much work putting a tree up, decorating, then having to take it all down and pack it up, all within a month. Don't get me wrong. I'm all about the food and desserts at this time of year." He patted his stomach with his free hand. "I'll think about the tree. Too much going on right now. She won't know the difference."

"You used to put away a lot of food in that

hollow leg. As far as a tree, she may not be old enough to understand Christmas, but she'd be captivated by all the twinkling lights. Making memories is super special. She'll love you even more for taking pictures. Right now, we have more important matters to take care of." She opened a door and showed Jake inside.

"Nice big room." He pulled out a rolling leather chair and sat down, placing Emma on his knee. "That's a huge picture window. You could sit in the warmth and watch the city from here."

"I'll be right back." Daria closed the door behind her.

Emma straightened her legs and scooted off his lap, then took off running around the table. She stopped at a cabinet set up as a coffee station with a water dispenser.

"Bite." She pointed to the sugar canister. "Cup." She toddled to the picture window. The cold weather fogged the lower portion as darkness descended over the town. Emma pressed her hand on the glass while her nose and forehead butted against it. Everywhere she touched left its mark. She slapped at the foggy places and giggled.

"Wish I had all that energy." Jake admired

her cuteness. So many of her mannerisms reminded him of his sister. His heart sank. If only Amanda were here. "I'll find the ones responsible for your death if it's the last thing I do."

"What's the last thing you'll do?" Daria had returned to the room with a laptop in her hand.

"I was thinking out loud." He turned his swivel chair to face the oval-shaped wood table. "I'll find the killer with your help, of course."

Daria's eyes latched on to his eyes for a moment. He could tell she was evaluating his statement. She walked over, pulled the floor-length gray curtains across the large window, returned and sat in the chair next to him. "I need your full report on everything. When you arrived, when things started happening, the break-ins, the shooting, etc., etc. Had you received threatening calls or suspicious mail?"

"None of that. Only the break-in." The interview was short since there wasn't much to report. Daria's fingers slid across the keyboard as she typed. No wedding band, not even an indent of a ring ever being on her finger.

"Here it is. Took me a minute, but I found it." She clicked on the icon and the document opened. "Looks like someone placed it in the wrong electronic folder."

"On purpose?" Jake's pulse increased.

"No, not at all. I suppose it was just a clerical error." She cleared her throat. "I'll let you read your sister's comments."

Jake leaned toward the small screen and read out loud, "'I've received a couple of death threats in my personal email, and I believe I'm being followed. My family and I need protection. There are questionable things going on, but I cannot give names because I don't know who to trust. They know what I've done.'"

"What did she do?" Daria sat back in her chair.

Emma slapped at one of the other leather chairs. It turned. Her smiles and jabbers touched Jake's heart. She gripped the chair and turned it in circles until she tripped over her own foot. She pushed up and toddled over to her diaper bag sitting on the floor, then plopped down beside it. Jake monitored her while she tossed diapers out of the bag and pulled out several rubber animals from the bottom. She still held the little bunny but lined up the rest of the rubber farm animals with her other hand, then knocked them over and giggled.

"I have no clue what Amanda meant. I'm almost certain it's something to do with her bank job. Why else would she look for another job?" Jake rubbed his chin. "Why didn't the police take her seriously?"

"It says they sent an officer out to her house and looked around." Daria squinted at the report and looked at him. "It also says that there wasn't enough information to go on, and they couldn't do anything unless something else happened."

"Like death? That's some protection." Jake stood so fast his chair almost fell over. "So, Amanda and Tom are dead because 'something' had to happen. That's hogwash." Heat pulsated in his face, and he bit back his emotions. He paced. Emma ran over and grabbed his leg.

He looked down at her, stopped and picked her up, burying his face in her little neck.

Daria walked over to him and placed her hand on his arm. "I'm sorry."

"Don't even go there." His voice rose louder than he meant. He blew out several huffs. "The police got what they wanted and then ruled it an 'accident.' Did anyone investigate or did they assume?"

"I'm sure they did a thorough investigation. I was on vacation when it happened. That's why I didn't know anything about it. I will check into it and see what their findings were." She patted his arm gently, then smoothed her finger across Emma's cheek. "I'll go to the bank tomorrow and question the employees."

"I'm going with you." Jake tightened his lips. He wanted to see these people face-to-face and look them in the eyes.

Chapter 3

Daria wasn't about to tell Jake he couldn't go to the bank with her. The hurt on his face pricked her heart. Investigating with a baby in tow wasn't the best idea, but Jake wasn't about to let her out of his sight. She'd have to give it some serious thought.

"We can't stay at the station all night. Emma needs a comfortable, warm place to sleep. Is that big hotel I remember still at the foothills of the Ozark National Forest?" He held Emma like a football again while he picked up the diapers and toys and stuffed them back into the diaper bag.

"It's still there. They've done some remodeling in the past ten years. It's nice." Daria breathed a sigh of relief. At least he didn't ask to be taken home. "I'll get your car and pull up at the back door. When you walk out of the conference room, turn right, then left in the first hallway. The exit is straight ahead. I'll meet you there."

"Got it." Jake adjusted his hold on Emma, handed the keys over to Daria and tossed the diaper bag over his opposite shoulder.

Daria eyed him before she left the room. She compared him to a gorilla carrying a baby chick. His height and strong build, holding a petite baby, looked awkward, but he managed just fine. Once he got used to caring for her, he'd be a great substitute dad.

She stepped out into the cold and reported their destination to Lieutenant Jeffers. Sleet bounced off her face and her breath fogged. It was going to be a cold, treacherous night for anyone on the streets. She slid into Jake's car and eased to the back door of the station. Jake stepped out and covered Emma's head until he reached the car. She clung to him and didn't want in her car seat. He talked in a smooth tone and got her buckled in.

Good job.

"Remind me of how far that hotel is from here." He rubbed his hands together. "What is the temperature?"

"Not sure exactly, but I think it's somewhere around nineteen degrees." She pulled onto the street.

Thank You, God. Traffic has thinned to minimal cars. Did I just whisper a prayer?

Vacationers had already retreated to their hotels and condominiums. Who would want to walk the town in the sleet and snow?

"Oh, the hotel is about twenty minutes from here. It's about five minutes from the Marketplace Grocery where the road forks and narrows from four lanes to two." She rolled to a stop at a red light. "By the way, this is a nice SUV."

"Not my choice of vehicles, but I can't complain. Amanda had her own taste in things." His tone was solemn. "I'd get a Mustang or a motorcycle."

"I can see you with one of those. Of course, I've known some girls who like motorcycles too." She rolled through the green light and watched the rearview mirror. The headlights of the cars behind them were a distance away. Safe so far.

"What about you? What's your preference?" Jake shifted his body and faced her.

His gaze made her cheeks warm. Was she blushing? Glad it was dark outside.

"I have a Jeep. Its off-road capabilities are excellent for the area." She smiled, proud to announce her choice of vehicles in the Ozarks.

"Not too bad. I figured you would drive a midsize car or even a Volkswagen."

"Are you serious?" She snickered. "I like those, too, but I still like the Jeep best. The hotel is just ahead."

His laughter took her back to when they were kids. They'd rolled down grassy hills every chance they had. Only, one hill they'd selected dropped them about three feet, and they'd bumped into each other. They'd howled out belly laughs until their sides hurt. The only difference now was his masculine build and his deep voice.

Bright lights lit up the portico. Fake snow framed each glass door and window to the entrance. An extra-large Christmas welcome mat lay in front of the double glass doors.

She pulled up and unbuckled her seatbelt. "Stay here. I'll get the room."

The registration desk looked cheerful with all the festive decor. She took in a deep sniff of the pine aroma from the live Christmas tree. A small gold bell sat on the counter. Daria rang it twice.

Her young friend Shelby, whom she'd been

mentoring and had helped financially a few times, stepped out of the office behind the desk wearing sunglasses.

"Daria, uh, it's good to see you." She picked up a pen and tapped the counter nervously. "How can I help you?"

"Are you okay? You're red around your eyebrow."

"Another migraine. I've been rubbing my forehead and eyebrows because the light hurts my eyes." Shelby tapped on the computer. "What can I do for you?"

"I'm sorry you're not feeling well. I need a room for a friend and his baby." Daria looked around. Something seemed off. "Are you sure you're okay? You looked stressed."

Shelby smirked. "Oh, you know me. I'm always stressed. No worries, though." She clicked on the computer. "How about the fourth floor? It's nice and spacious. I can give you the police discount."

"Perfect." Daria still wasn't sure about Shelby's headache. It must be so hard to work with the constant pounding. Bless her heart, she'd had a rough time since her parents' accidental death a few years back. "It's Christmas. Time to de-stress and have fun." Daria backed away and headed outside.

She walked out of the automatic doors, happy she'd secured a room on the highest floor possible. She opened the back door of the car and reached in for Emma. Jake stepped out and grabbed the diaper bag.

"Want to get the bags from the trunk?" Daria shuffled Emma in her arms and opened the trunk. Jake tossed the handles of his bags over his shoulder. A big yawn covered Emma's face. Poor baby. She didn't deserve to be in this situation.

Jake took a sniff as they walked through the entry. "Smells like the forest."

They stepped into the elevator. Jake's expression changed.

"What's wrong? I got you a room on the top floor with a beautiful view." She studied him. "No one can reach you easily up there."

"I'm not comfortable on the top floor. There are limited escape routes this high up." His irritated tone punched her in the gut.

"Jake, you're on US soil, not in Afghanistan. You're not being reasonable." She focused on her tone and kept her temper in check. If he kept pushing her buttons, she'd have to walk away rather than lose it.

"I'm just saying. You haven't been where I have, so your perception is going to differ from mine." He took Emma and patted her on the back. The bags dropped from his shoulder and hung on his arm. "I'll stay this time, but I'd like to be moved to the bottom floor tomorrow."

"Okay. I had good intentions, but you're right. My thoughts are not your thoughts."

Hmm, did I just quote the Bible?

Daria's spirits dropped as disappointment set in. She thought she'd done well, maybe even impressed him, considering the season and all the tourists piling in for the Christmas holidays. She admired his tenacity. His take-charge demeanor and determination were commendable, but she placed the responsibility on herself to protect them regardless of his attitude or difference of opinion.

She slid the room key into the slot and the door opened. Daria took the diaper bag from Jake and set it and the two backpacks on the floor, while Jake put sleepy Emma on the bed in the second bedroom. A whimper came from the room but quickly grew silent.

"I'm not sure if she'll go back to sleep, but for

now, I've got pillows around her. She's got her sippy cup and that silly rubber toy." Jake took off his jacket and rubbed the top of his head. "I appreciate all of your help. You've been tremendous in seeing to our safety and needs. I can take it from here. You should go home and get some rest, so you'll be ready for work tomorrow."

"In case you don't remember how things work here in the US, I *am* at work. Protecting you and Emma is my job right now." She expected a rebuttal, but he walked away.

His body language told her he wasn't happy. She'd already figured out that he resented her thinking she had to protect him. She got it. Really. He stood tall, in fact, a little more than a head taller than her. His driver's license stated his height was six foot two. He was broad shouldered, stout and, according to him, well educated in his military field. Best she remembered, he'd made honor roll throughout school, so he was very intelligent. His giving in to her was probably a little demeaning to his ego.

He placed the diaper bag on the table, unpacked it and rearranged its contents, including the little rubber toys. He tapped the bottom of the bag. "This is a quality, well-made bag. The bottom of it is solid. My sister probably paid a high price for it. Leave it to her to get the best for her baby."

"That's nice." Daria wanted to smooth things over with Jake before she left. She approached the opposite side of the table from where he stood.

"I never asked how your parents are doing. I know you said earlier they'd retired and moved back to Kimbleton, but physically could not keep Emma." She stuck her hands in her jacket pockets.

He placed two small cans of apple juice in a side pocket of the diaper bag, then put an empty sippy cup and the remaining diapers inside the bag. "They are up in years. Dad uses a walker and Mom thinks she's steady enough to use a cane. Honestly, they need to be in a nursing home, but neither will even consider it. Can't say that I blame them. I wouldn't want to lose my independence, either. Now that I'm home, I'll have to keep an eye on them."

"That's an enormous responsibility. My parents are still active and doing well. I don't know what I'll do when they need 24-7 care."

He stopped busying himself and looked at her with a serious but soft expression.

"You've really changed, for the better, I mean. You're authoritative, fearless and good at your job." He adjusted his stance. "I'm proud of you for outgrowing your shyness and squeamish personality that I remember from school."

She held his gaze while her insides did flips. Fearless would not be how she'd describe herself, because right then she was terrified of his sincere compliments. How long had it been since someone complimented her so deeply? She tried not to swallow hard. He would notice. Good thing her hands were in her pockets. She could feel the sweat in her palms.

"Thank you, Jake. I don't know what to say. I'm glad you're back in Kimbleton. Just sorry for the reason that brought you here. I don't doubt for one minute you can't take care of yourself and Emma. I see you as strong and fully capable. The only drawback is my boss assigned me to watch after your safety. It's not a matter of your weakness. You're not weak by any means. It's my job and I must follow through, and, I might add, I'm glad he assigned me. We understand each other." She turned. "I should go and let you get some rest. I've said too much."

She placed her hand on the doorknob. His long arm reached ahead of her and pulled the door open. For a millisecond, his warm breath hit her neck. She bit her lip and stepped into the hallway.

I can't let him get to me. We're friends. That's it. Friends.

She cleared her throat. "You can never be too safe. Please lock and deadbolt your door. I don't trust anyone right now."

She had to get away before gushy words started spilling from her lips. Had Jake sensed the same connection she had? Her heart fluttered every time his deep brown eyes zeroed in on her. She shook it off. Mixing police work with personal feelings wasn't allowed in the department.

Jake leaned on the doorjamb and watched Daria walk away. He'd stared into her brown eyes, and her light brown hair glistened in the hall light. His breath hitched. For an instant, he'd wanted to kiss her. Where had that come from? What was he thinking? They'd only re-connected a few hours ago.

She stopped at the elevator and pushed the button.

"Good night. See you in the morning." Jake nodded.

The elevator door opened. "Rest well." She stepped in and the door closed.

He stared down the hall. What just happened? He wasn't looking for a relationship, even if they were old friends. She was a cop. There was someone after him and Emma. He stepped inside the room and locked the door.

He rubbed both hands over his face, then made his way to the brown couch. His weary body sank into the fabric's softness. Nothing like the beds he'd slept on overseas. It had been a long day escaping the mysterious US enemy. Daria, the one girl he'd always cared for and thought about, was back in his life. He'd have to keep her at arm's length and not get involved with her. He had Emma to focus on and caring for her would be a full-time job.

Jake huffed. He needed to check on Emma, change her diaper and put her warm, footed pajamas on her before he relaxed too much and fell asleep. He pushed to his feet and eased into the room where she slept. She'd rolled over and her little rear stuck in the air.

He slowly took her coat off, something he should have done earlier before he laid her down, carefully placed her onto her back and proceeded to change her diaper and clothes. She whimpered. He gave her the sippy cup and covered her up with a fluffy pink blanket. One of her hands held the cup handle and the other hand lightly patted her head and twirled hair between her fingers. She turned on her side and her eyes closed.

He yawned and stretched his arms into the air before going to the master bedroom. A hot shower sounded good. Fancy hotels always had nice decor, but this one had an enormous bathroom with white robes hanging on the back of the door, monogrammed hand soap, even a television on the wall opposite the tub. Who wanted to spend that much time in the bathroom?

A slight thump caught his attention. Had Emma fallen off the bed? His first thought was to rush into the room, but instinct said to wait. He listened. She wasn't crying. Something felt off. He stepped out of the shower and wrapped a towel around his lower body. Steam from his hot shower fogged up the mirror.

His pistol lay on the chest. He grabbed it and plastered himself against the bedroom wall by the door and eased around enough to see into the living room. No movement. His eyes squinted as he studied every item in the room. Wait. The diaper bag had fallen off the table, and Emma's extra sippy cup was under the chair.

He straightened, moved quietly to Emma's room and glanced inside. She looked undisturbed and peaceful. Jake breathed a satisfied breath, even though his heart pounded from the adrenaline rush. He returned to the dining area, retrieved the diaper bag and cup and placed them in the chair. Then he returned to his room, redressed and repacked his bag. With uncertainty hanging in the air, he'd sleep fully clothed as he'd done in Afghanistan, ready to bolt if necessary. His pistol remained in his holster as he mounted it around his shoulder.

The bright-colored geometric bedspread wasn't his style, but who cared? It was a bed. He laid across the firm mattress and stared at the ceiling. He reminisced about fun times with his sister and going deer hunting with Tom. He was a great brother-in-law, and he made Amanda happy. They'd been so excited about her pregnancy. Jake had spoken to her many times over the phone and could hear the joy in her voice. He wiped the wetness from his eyes, thankful no one was there to see a marine crying.

"Maa...ma, Maa...ma." Emma's crying shot him to his feet.

He ran to her room. She sat in the middle of the bed, rubbing her closed eyes. Jake picked her up, along with her cup and rabbit, and went into the kitchen. He couldn't decide what to give her. Milk or apple juice? Since he wasn't a fan of milk, he filled the cup with the juice. She reached for it before he'd secured the lid. When he pulled it away to pop the lid on, she screamed loudly.

"Whoa, I'm sorry, but I had to put the lid on good or we'd both have apple juice all over us. Here. You're okay." He handed her the cup, patted her back and paced with her. Her crying finally stopped. "Who knew you could turn a cup upside down and it wouldn't drip? What will they think of next?"

Jake thought he heard a faint noise but after listening for a few seconds and hearing only silence, he shook his head and went back into the living room. "I'm a little jumpy tonight, but we are in a hotel. Maybe we can relax a bit. What do you think, little girl?" He laid his head gently against his niece's soft curls. "You sleep, short ribs. I've got you."

She drank from the dripless cup with her eyes closed. He slumped on the couch, holding her against his chest. Her breathing grew deeper, with the cup curled in her hand against her side. He admired her tiny features before he closed his eyes. A dull headache emerged and sleep failed him.

His marine security thinking shifted to planning an escape route should he need it. Top floors of hotels are normally nice with an incredible view, as Daria had pointed out. Why was he so uptight about it? Too many places during the war blew up, leaving people trapped under all the debris. Daria only wanted them to have the best care possible. Had he been too hard on her?

He looked around the semidark room. A dim nightlight from the kitchen cast a haze across the ceiling. Jake blinked. He must be more exhausted than he thought. Were his eyes blurry?

Funny, he hadn't noticed the growing fog a little while ago. Had the temperature dropped so much outside that he didn't have the heat turned up enough? What sense did that make?

"What's going on?" He grew suspicious.

The room was a comfortable temperature, but curiosity got the best of him. He slid Emma onto the couch and scooted off. She wiggled for a second but settled down. Jake stood and listened. What was that light hissing sound and that slight chemical odor? He went into the kitchen and turned on the range hood light.

"Where is this haze coming from?" The hair on his neck bristled and investigative mode kicked in. He pulled out his phone, turned on the flashlight app to keep from waking Emma, and walked into the living room. The small light confirmed his suspicions. A thin cloud had formed across the ceiling and more of the substance stirred with his movement. The odor grew stronger as the cloud began filling the room.

His eyes landed on the pilot light of the gas fireplace. A sudden surge of adrenaline shot through him. He coughed. The thump he'd heard earlier wasn't the diaper bag at all. Their location had been compromised. He scooped Emma up, still wrapped in her blanket, grabbed their coats and his bags and rushed out into the hall, which was free of the cloudy haze. More confirmation something was amiss.

No way would he use the elevator. He wasn't about to get trapped between floors. A lighted sign hung above a door at the end of the hall. Stairs. He ran and thrust the door open. Cold, fresh air hit him in the face. Ordinarily, he'd take three steps at a time or even jump from level to level, but with Emma in his arms, he'd best be sure-footed.

His feet moved almost at lightning speed. Thankfully, the staircase was lit with security lights. "Third floor. Two more."

"Second floor, finally first floor." He bolted through the door and rushed down the hall toward the check-in desk. He paused, but no one was there. He exited through the automatic doors. This time frigid air blasted him, and a chill rushed over him like a splash of icy water. He hadn't taken the time to put on a coat, and he'd failed to put Emma's coat on her.

"Lord, which way do we go?" He paused and studied the cars in the parking lot. "Is that my car? Did Daria not leave, or did someone give her a ride?"

Jake checked for ice on the asphalt before picking up the pace. He headed for his car, noting a squad car had parked beside it. Daria jumped out of the squad car.

"What are you doing out here in the middle of the night? It's freezing." She opened the back door for him to buckle Emma into the car seat. Emma rubbed her eyes and whimpered until her cup met her lips.

"Watch her while I go back to find the hotel staff so they can warn others to evacuate. There's a gas leak in my room and everyone needs to get out before it explodes." Jake turned to run back inside. "I paused to report the leak to the person at the front desk but no one was there and I didn't see a fire alarm pull station anywhere."

"No, don't," Daria said as she grabbed his arm. "Shelby should have been in there. I'll call for backup." She released her hold on him and notified the authorities on her shoulder radio. "What happened?"

"Get in and I'll explain." Jake opened his passenger door and got in. He shivered and placed his hands in front of the heat vents. Daria slid behind the steering wheel and gave him a questioning look.

Boom.

Flames burst through a top-floor window

and glass rained down into the parking lot. He shot a look at Daria, and her widened eyes said it all. The blast wasn't an accident.

"They found us." He leaned forward and stared at the red, orange, and blue flames curling out of the window.

"How?" Daria called 911, then turned toward him. "Tell me what happened."

"I noticed a haze in the living room, so I got up to check it out. The air had a faint smell of insecticide. I started coughing and felt like I was suffocating. My head pounded. Emma was just below the fog, but her little body couldn't have handled much of it." He took in a deep breath, realizing he was talking fast. "That's when I grabbed her and our bags and ran down the stairs."

"I don't get it." Daria looked back at Emma. "No one knew where you were staying except my lieutenant and my friend Shelby. Come to think of it, she acted nervous while I made your reservation."

"She could have been threatened." Jake was certain that's what happened. His stalker had probably hid in her office.

A fire truck and ambulance pulled into the parking lot. Daria stepped out of Jake's car and approached the paramedics. She pointed at him, sitting in the car. They got their gear and walked toward him.

Firefighters jumped from the trucks, pulled hoses and hooked up to the water hydrant, while others grabbed their tools and ran toward the building. Huge streams of water shot through the air to the windows of the blazing room.

Daria moved around, meeting up with the squad cars as they pulled into the parking lot.

Other hotel patrons were escorted out of the blazing hotel wrapped in bed linens and blankets. Some were barefooted and shivering. Firefighters ushered them a safe distance away from danger. In a moment's time, a yellow school bus rolled onto the parking lot. Police officers sent the people to the bus to get out of the cold.

Thoughtful move.

A paramedic opened Jake's car door. "Sir, are you okay? The officer said you'd breathed some fumes. Tell me what happened."

Jake coughed, then cut his eyes to Daria out in the parking lot. She looked back at him. He was fine. Still coughing some, but okay. He explained the situation again. "Check my eighteen-month-old niece first. She's in the back."

"Yes, sir." He yelled at another medic as he opened the back door. "Grab me a child's mask."

The paramedic ran toward them with a small plastic bag containing a mask. The guy ripped it open and hooked it up before placing the mask over Emma's nose and mouth. She slapped at it, shook her head then started screaming. Her small hands tried to get it off, but the medic held it in place.

"Should I hold her to keep her from screaming?" Jake couldn't stand hearing her crying so hard.

"With her screaming like this, she's taking in more of the oxygen with every deep breath, which is good. Give her a couple of minutes and she should be fine."

The second medic placed a mask over Jake's mouth and nose. "Breathe in this oxygen for a few minutes. You probably breathed in more of the gas than the baby."

Jake coughed a few times. The cough urges grew farther apart until they finally stopped. He took off the mask and handed it back. "I think I'm good now. Thanks."

The paramedic let Emma pull off her mask. She threw it on the floor. Her red eyes and snotty nose were proof she didn't approve of them. She reached for Jake. He hopped out and pulled her from the car. Her coat lay on the floor along with her diaper bag.

Jake sat on the edge of the back seat with the door open. He put Emma's coat on her and re-wrapped her with the blanket. A funny-shaped cloth hung halfway out of the bag. Jake wiped her face and nose. She screamed again, pushed his hand away and laid her head on his shoulder.

Such dainty arms wrapped around his neck calmed his jittery nerves. Protective mode for his sister's baby, now his baby, intensified. Such innocence, totally dependent on him, became a reality.

Jake shivered in the cold. His coat lay on the back floorboard, too, but he hadn't had time to put it on. Temperatures were much colder than earlier and small snowflakes hit his face. Emma had to be cold, too. He held her close, stepped inside the front seat and turned up the heat. She dropped her cup and put two fingers in her mouth, then stilled. He caught the cup before it landed in his lap.

Daria walked across the parking lot toward the car. Her breath fogged in the snowy night air. She'd worn her coat and gloves. Her nose was red. Just the sight of her returning to them set him at ease. The calming effect of her presence frustrated him. He couldn't get involved, even though his feelings for his childhood friend grew stronger. He had a kid to raise.

Smoke boiled into the night sky while firefighters fought the inferno. If he'd hesitated a minute longer, he and Emma wouldn't have made it. If he'd slowed his pace and walked down those stairs, they wouldn't have made it.

God, only You could have timed our escape that perfectly and saved us. I don't know why You didn't save Amanda and Tom, but please save anyone who is still in that hotel.

Daria hopped in the driver's side and shut the door. "Oh, it's nice and toasty in here." She took her gloves off and sat back. Her glance toward the squad car parked beside them and her solemn expression told him something was up.

"What's going on? You look upset." He shifted in the seat, still holding Emma.

"Personal stuff." She pushed a loose strand of hair out of her face. "I don't know how they knew where you were. I spotted a man sneaking around, a man who looked kind of sketchy. He stood at the corner of the hotel. I monitored him while talking to my lieutenant, Nolan Jeffers, but when you came out, the man ran into the forest. If I had questioned him when he appeared, maybe I could have gathered information and prevented the fire."

"You don't know he was involved." Jake reached over and took her hand. "Besides, at that point, there was nothing you could have done to stop the explosion. It's not your fault. Somehow, they knew our location and which room we were in."

Chapter 4

Daria gasped and her heart rate increased at the thought of her young friend who worked inside the hotel. She jerked her hand from Jake's hold. "Did you say you didn't see Shelby on your way out? She works the registration desk."

"No. Since no one was there, I kept running."

An uneasiness settled in her gut. Shelby should have been among the crowd or in the bus. Daria slid her gloves back on. "I'll be back."

She rushed through the crowd and checked the bus. No sign of her friend. Daria ran carefully on the icy parking lot toward the hotel.

A firefighter stopped her in the parking lot. "Officer, you can't go inside. It's not safe."

"I understand, but I need to check on the girl who runs the front desk. Her name is Shelby. She was there a little while ago." Daria pointed to the hotel. "Would you, please, have someone check the registration desk?"

He turned toward the fire truck. "Rogers, Middleton, check the registration desk. See if you find anyone."

Two firefighters rushed inside. Daria tapped her foot. She expected them to escort Shelby out at any moment. Instead, next to her, the radio clipped to the firefighter's shoulder crackled to life. "Lieutenant, you need to see this."

"Stay here." He left her standing in the freezing parking lot and ran inside.

Tears threatened her police composure. "Please be okay." Daria bit her lip and waited for their return. She glanced back and spotted Jake motioning for her. He held a serious look, with his lips drawn tight, and sat with that staunch marine posture. Her gaze returned to the hotel entrance before she met him at the car's passenger window. She placed her hand on the edge of the glass.

"What's going on?" Jake rested his hand on hers, and the gentleness of his touch sent warmth through her. She stepped out of his reach and sensed him eyeing her. He pulled his hand back inside the car. "You were right about the weather. I would come help, but I've got a tiny bundle in the back and I can't leave her alone."

"No worries. I've got this. You're doing the right thing protecting her." Daria lowered her eyebrows at him. "They're checking to see if they can find Shelby."

"Is she related to you?"

"No. She's single, working her way through nursing school. I've helped her out a few times since her parents died in a boating accident several years back."

"That's humanitarian of you." Jake broke eye contact with her. "I think I see movement inside."

Daria pointed to Jake's car. "Stay with Emma. I'll let you know what happens."

His body language said he wanted to be among the action. But he'd confirmed taking care of a baby was his priority. She returned to the middle of the parking lot and waited for the firefighters to exit.

She glanced back at Lieutenant Jeffers, who approached and stood by her. "What's the update?" He rubbed his hands together in the cold.

Daria explained about her friend working at the front desk. The lieutenant had given her a hard time for months since she'd messed up and lost her temper a while back. Now that she'd completed anger management classes and had an important case, she wished he'd show her more respect. She'd done as he asked.

He coughed and spat on the frozen ground. "Remember to maintain a professional relationship with your victim. Any signs otherwise, and I'll pull you from the case."

She bit her lip. Just because she knew Jake from their school days didn't automatically put them in a relationship. She was only there to protect him and his niece from whoever had targeted them. Who knew she'd be involved in a murder case and be assigned to watch over the two of them? If she solved the crime, it could give her a chance to prove herself with her fellow officers and make her lieutenant proud.

The hotel doors pushed open, and two firefighters carried someone out. A lump formed in her throat. *Please don't let her be dead.*

Paramedics met the firefighters just outside the door with a gurney.

Daria rushed over. "Is she okay?"

Shelby's hand reached out to her. Daria took her hand and looked down at the badly bruised face of her friend. "Shelby, who did this to you?"

One of the medics stepped in the way, causing her to drop Shelby's hand. "You can question her once we check her out. She's received several blows to the face, and she has a large hematoma on the back of her head."

"Did you fall and hit your head?" the other paramedic asked.

"No." A whisper slipped from Shelby's lips.

"We're going to transport you to the hospital."

Daria slipped around the paramedic. "Just give me a minute." She turned to Shelby. "Can you talk? What happened?"

"A man came into the hotel right before you did, asking for an area map. We usually have them available for tourists." Shelby winced and reached for her bruised forehead. "When I turned back around, he punched me in the eye. That's why I had my sunglasses on. He hid in my office with a gun. But once you'd checked in and left, he returned and used my face as a punching bag and I must have passed out. He threatened my life if I mentioned he'd been there. He knew you were bringing someone to the hotel, and forced me to give him a specific room number. He took my master key."

Heat rose to Daria's cheeks. How did he know they were coming to the hotel? Daria maintained control of her anger. She smoothed her finger across Shelby's hand. "These paramedics will take care of you. Can you describe the man who assaulted you?"

"Not really. With the drop in temperatures, it was understandable that he'd wear a sock cap and a bulky black coat. I won't forget his beady green eyes, though."

Daria's skin crawled. She'd just described the attire of the man who stood in the shadows at the corner of the hotel, except she hadn't seen his eyes. Guilt gripped her for the second time. It was all her fault. She'd put Jake and Emma in danger, and now Shelby. How could she prove herself a good cop if she kept messing up?

"We need to get her to the hospital," the paramedic said. He and his partner rolled the gurney to the ambulance.

"I'll check on you later." Daria walked over and updated her lieutenant and coworkers before joining Jake and Emma in the car.

"Is she okay?" Jake adjusted the heat vent.

"Yes. I think so. Someone punched her in the face and hit her over the head. They're taking her to the hospital. Have you spotted anyone acting suspicious?"

Daria placed her gloved hands on the steering wheel and studied all the activity going on in the parking lot. The ambulance drove away, and firefighters sprayed water that froze as drops landed on the pavement. Police officers taped off the entrance to the parking lot and blocked bundled-up passersby as they crowded around to watch the action. Who would want to stand in the snowy, freezing temperatures at two fifteen in the morning? Was the person responsible for the fire among them, fuming over his failure to eliminate Jake and Emma?

"Not yet, but that doesn't mean—"

Daria jumped from the car and took off running toward the crowd. Her feet skidded on the slick parking lot. She managed to stay upright. The hooded figure she'd seen earlier at the corner of the hotel stood at the back of the crowd.

He bolted, ran across the street and down an alley that split and led behind the town's businesses. She pushed through the crowd. He disappeared before she could continue the chase.

She radioed her fellow officers. Several arrived and began searching the back doors of businesses and parked cars. A light snow carpeted the alley. His footprints disappeared in a freezing pool of water leaking from a faucet. It was useless to track him in the dark with the frigid weather. She must get Jake and Emma to a safe place.

Daria made her way back to the car. She pulled her gloves off and held her hands over the heat vents. "I missed him."

"Missed who? What happened?" He faced her.

"I spotted the guy who'd been standing at the corner of the hotel. I lost him, though."

Jake opened his car door and stepped out. "Tell me where you last saw him, and I'll track him."

"No. You're staying put." She sensed tension rising.

He got back in the car and shut the door. His narrowed eyes confirmed his frustration. She touched his arm. "I'm here to protect you and Emma. Whoever set up that explosion knew what they were doing to target your specific room. The fire chief will do his investigation and let us know."

Emma threw her cup on the floor. "Bite." She reached her hand out and wiggled her fingers. "Bite."

"When was the last time you fed her?" Daria reached for the diaper bag. "Aren't there snacks in here?"

"I gave her juice and some of those puffy cheese sticks." Jake helped remove items from the bag. "I'll see if there's something else I can give her."

"I'm talking about an actual meal. And have you changed her diaper?" Daria eyed Jake.

Jake wiped his face with his hand. "I changed her before she went to bed. That's why she has her pajamas on. The attempted abduction and the shooting earlier messed with our routine. I've only given her snacks. She's a good baby. But in answer to your question, no she hasn't had a, quote, unquote, proper meal since breakfast. I'm surprised she hasn't screamed."

"Babies require a meal just like we do. We get hungry, Emma gets hungry, and sometimes more often. They enjoy snacks, but a healthy meal is better and lasts longer."

"I get it." He located the cheese puffs and handed Emma one. "Where can we get something to eat at three in the morning?"

Daria buckled her seat belt. "I know just the place. Buckle up." She pulled up close to Jeffers for permission to leave the scene. He waved her on.

She exited the parking lot, thankful for minimal traffic on the slick street. In about three more hours, the town would come alive with more vacationers, where accidents were likely to happen.

Jake turned back around, facing the front of the vehicle, and propped his elbow on the edge of the car's window. "In the war, we went long hours before stopping to eat or drink. I've got to think about Emma's needs above my own."

"You'll get used to it. She will let you know when she's hungry. Just like now. Besides, you know you can trust me. I'm here for you." She bit her lip. Investigating Jake's case could make or break her career, and dissolve or resolve a new friendship with him. A man she'd always cared about.

I need Your wisdom, Lord.

Her cell rang. Why was Officer Cramer calling her this late? She opted not to put it on speaker.

"Officer Gordon here."

"Daria, I received a call from an anonymous lady who insisted on having a confidential meeting with you," Cramer said.

"Kind of late or early to be getting calls, isn't it?" Daria's inquisitive radar went up. "Could be a setup. When did she want to meet?"

"Right away." Cramer's words fell flat.

"Said this couldn't wait. She'll meet you at the twenty-four-hour café."

Daria didn't have to guess which café. The town only had one that stayed open all night.

"Did she say what was so important that it required an immediate meeting at this time of the morning?" Daria hadn't wanted to encounter anyone else tonight, but if it helped the case, she'd take a moment.

Cramer cleared his throat. "Only that it was a matter of life or death."

"What was that all about?" Jake evaluated Daria's body language. Something had shifted her thoughts. Her eyebrows lowered, and she'd pursed her lips.

Her eyes cut toward him as though she debated answering his question. "A woman wants to meet me at the restaurant."

"This late? Someone you know?" He looked out of the rear window to see if someone was following them. Not a vehicle in sight, only their tire marks in the light snow. "What about? If you don't mind me asking?"

"Didn't say other than it's a life-or-death situation." Daria slid her hands around the steering wheel of Jake's car, then gripped it again at the three and nine position. Her knuckles whitened slightly with her grip.

"Is it about our case?" A renewed burst of energy rushed over him at the thought of more evidence that could help solve the murder of his sister and brother-in-law.

"Our case? Jake, this investigation is in the hands of the department. There's no 'ours' about it. You need to focus on Emma and let us do our job."

Jake swallowed his pride. Well, partly. He'd still like to get his hands on the person responsible for almost killing an innocent baby. He valued his own life, but he'd give it for Emma's safety, or Daria's. Part of that safety was caring for Emma's needs. After all, she was a little human who had the same basic needs he did. Only in smaller portions. Something he'd have to keep in mind.

Daria held firm to her status as a police officer, and he admired her tenacity despite his constantly overstepping the boundaries. Everything inside him wanted to go into stealth mode and seek the enemy. He could sneak around better alone, but what would he do with Emma? There was another dilemma he'd have to figure out. Was Emma supposed to go with him everywhere now? Could he handle someone tied to his side for the rest of his life? He rubbed his forehead. What was he thinking? Yes, he could and would adapt to having Emma in his life forever.

"I assume we are going to meet this anonymous person right now?" He handed Emma another cheese puff. "Come to think of it, I haven't eaten, either. Just hasn't been a priority." He rested his arm on the passenger door's armrest.

"I know it's late, but we all have to eat." Daria kept her eyes on the road as she drove and talked. "It's like adding fuel to the car. Food adds strength to our bodies. But you already knew that."

Jake weighed Daria's comment. Of course, he knew the necessity of keeping the body nourished. His thoughts flashed back to active duty, hiding in the bunker with everyone ready for battle, and how he reminded everyone to drink plenty of water and eat, to stay alert and watch for the enemy.

"Yeah, I'm aware of keeping the body fueled." His tone came out a little sharper than he'd intended. Plans for his future took a U-turn in a moment's time with one phone call announcing his sister's death and then becoming a substitute dad. Uh, and mom. So much for becoming a career marine. To be so smart and concerned for the safety of his men, he now had to turn that focus on the needs of his niece. He must pull himself together and focus better.

Daria's silence had him wondering if he'd upset her. He had to stifle his need to be in control and work alongside her. They were great friends years ago. Could they slide back into that same status now, or possibly shift to dating and see where it would lead? Her shoulder-length brown hair complemented her unblemished complexion, and her uniform only enhanced her good looks. She was intelligent, determined and protective. And she loved babies. Traits he appreciated.

She slammed on the brakes. "Look out."

He grabbed the dash with one hand and stretched his other arm out toward Emma, mere seconds before a car ran a stop sign. It slid on the icy street, turned around, then headed straight toward them. Daria pressed the accelerator, but the tires spun. She inched forward and slowly picked up speed, but not fast enough.

They were going to crash.

Jake dove over the front seat and covered

Emma with his body. His long legs landed on the dash and kicked the ceiling of the car. A hard hit shoved his car sideways and through the intersection. Emma let out a scream. Her deep brown eyes widened, and her lower lip quivered. He kissed her forehead, smoothed her curls and quickly grabbed the other sippy cup that had fallen out of the diaper bag.

Emma took the cup with one hand and patted Jake's cheek with the other. She put the cup to her lips.

"It's okay. Uncle Jake won't let anything happen to you." One hard shove and he was back in the front seat. "Daria, are you hurt? Did you get a good look at the driver? He clipped the back fender and sped away." He placed his hand on her shoulder.

She clipped her dangling police radio mic back on her shoulder. "I'm fine, just furious I couldn't maintain better control. How about you and Emma?"

"We're good, but if my car is still drivable, we might need to get moving before he returns and rams us again." Jake buckled himself in while Daria reported the incident.

"We can't leave the scene, Jake. There might be evidence on the road that will direct us to whoever did this." She opened the driver's door. "And, no, I didn't get a good look at the driver. The tinted windows made sure of that."

A blast of frigid air swept through the car as she stepped out. Sirens blared from the distance. Jake opened his passenger door and eased from the front seat, then opened the back door. He wrapped the blanket snugly around Emma and scooped her into his arms. Sleet mixed with snow hit his face. He made sure the blanket covered Emma's head.

Daria turned in circles, studying the area. She turned to Jake and patted Emma on the back. "Why don't you take her over to that store's covered awning and get her out of the snow? Hold her close. It will help keep her warm. It's not safe to stay in the street by the car right now."

"What about you?" Jake wasn't used to leaving a lady alone in a dangerous situation, and it didn't feel right even if she was a cop.

"I'll stay here and explain what happened. Now, go. Take care of Emma." Her words held authority and concern. "When a squad car arrives, the two of you can get in the back so you can stay warm."

Jake did as he was told. He made it under the

awning and stepped close to the store's door to avoid the wind. He readjusted his hold on Emma. She bent her knees and scrunched in the blanket. She was cold. His heart went out to this small bundle. He shivered too. The squad car couldn't get there fast enough.

Daria, the scrawny little girl he used to know, stood tall in the middle of the street, with her hands at her waist. She was still turning in circles keeping watch. He reveled in the difference a few years had made in her. She could be on his team any day with her tough yet sensitive and fearless demeanor.

Three police cars with sirens blaring and lights flashing pulled onto the scene. Emma's head swung around. She pulled her arm out of the blanket and pointed.

"See." She looked him in the eyes. A couple of tears slipped down her cheeks.

"I see. Do you like the flashing lights?" He wiped her tears, patted her back and tried to cover her.

Daria motioned them to the squad car. He didn't hesitate. With ice steadily forming on the road, he'd have to be sure-footed. He recognized two of the officers as Cramer and McDaniel. They walked over and joined another officer while Daria met him at the car and held the back door open for them. Jake wasn't used to anyone holding the door for him or trying to take care of him. Kind of nice. The warm car thawed his almost frozen fingers. He'd never complain about how cold he was, though. He was a marine.

The quiet of the night suddenly came to life. A car with a loud motor slid around the corner of the intersection and started shooting as it sped away. The officers fired back. Daria dove into the back across Jake's legs, covering them with her body.

McDaniel rushed back to them. Cramer and the other officer hopped in their cars and chased after the speeding vehicle. Daria pushed against the floorboard to get out. Jake placed Emma in the seat and helped Daria get up. For a moment, they were face-to-face, staring into each other's eyes. Amid the danger, he had an overwhelming urge to kiss her, which caught him off guard.

Chapter 5

Daria stretched her arm out of the car to Officer McDaniel, who took her hand and pulled her to her feet. She dared not look back at Jake. What had just happened? Was he still looking at her? His expressive eyes pierced hers in a way she'd never experienced. Kind of like... he wanted to kiss her. She scolded herself for thinking that way. Certainly she'd misread him. It wasn't the time, nor the place, to entertain personal thoughts. Besides, Lieutenant Jeffers wouldn't approve.

"Looks like they shot randomly into the air." McDaniel shook his head. "Good way to get yourself killed."

"A warning, you suppose? The whole incident looks suspicious." She pushed the fallen strands of hair back behind her ears. "I'm glad no one was hurt."

"Where were you going at this hour?" Mc-Daniel shoved his hands into his pockets.

"The twenty-four-hour restaurant. We haven't had dinner. It's about breakfast time now." A shiver crawled over her body. "That's the vehicle his deceased sister left him. I need to get the baby's car seat."

"I'll get it. You stay with Jake and Emma." McDaniel walked toward Jake's vehicle in time to meet with the approaching wrecker.

The driver hopped out of his truck and rubbed his hands together, then got to work loading the SUV. By the time he finished, the sleet and snow had stopped. Temperatures still hung in the twenties with frigid gusts of wind.

She turned and stared at the squad car where Jake and Emma were, out of the cold. She could tell Jake itched to help, but he continued showing his love for Emma by staying with her and protecting her. He might be a tough marine, but he had a heart of compassion.

She returned to the squad car and found Emma sleeping soundly, holding her cup in one hand and her little bunny in the other. She looked content and comfortable. A sigh slipped from her lips.

A hand gripped her arm through the car window. She spun.

"Are you okay?" Jake squeezed her arm.

"I'm thankful no one was hurt. Yes, I'm okay. Please stay here while I assist McDaniel so we can get out of here." Daria picked up a couple of car parts she could handle and dropped them together at the curb. Icicles had formed on the cold metal and sparkled with the reflection of the only streetlight around the area.

Cramer and the other officer returned to the scene and helped the wrecker finish clearing debris from the street.

"I'll drive you back to the station where you can file your report and get one of the impounded cars off the back lot." McDaniel said. "We're not allowed to ride civilians around in police cruisers unless it's a special case. I suppose this one qualifies as special."

"Thanks." *So much for meeting with the anonymous person.* They may have missed out on meeting the lady. If it was that important, maybe she'd call again. Her stomach told her they still needed to eat. A hot meal would be nice.

The station was a welcomed sight and a warm place to file her report. She grabbed her iPad and showed Jake where to get them a cup of coffee. They returned to the same conference room they'd been in earlier. Daria had placed the couch cushion on the floor and put a tablecloth from the credenza over it. Jake placed sleeping Emma on the cushion, took her coat off and covered her with her blanket.

Daria sat at the table and began her report. In a few minutes, Jake returned with two cups of steaming caffeine. He set one in front of her and moved to the opposite side of the table with his cup. Her report took longer than normal because of all the details she had to remember. Jake tapped the table. She sensed him staring at her.

"Why aren't you married by now?" Jake's inquisitive look and off-the-wall question took her by surprise.

She leaned back in her chair and twisted the stylus between her fingers. "I thought I answered your question earlier. I'm busy with my job, and no one around here is my type."

Jake's eyebrows lifted and a smirky grin rolled across his face. "What exactly is your type?"

Wish he wouldn't do that. He is already handsome enough.

She grinned. "Well, I suppose a tall, broad-shouldered, burly, strong and intelligent man that resembles a marine, maybe."

He pointed to himself. "Are you calling me burly?" He flexed his biceps.

"Who said I was talking about you?" Her insides warmed. At first, she was joking, but it hit her that having him around all the time wasn't a bad thought.

"Oh, pardon me. I can tell there's a line of marines at the door waiting for your approval." The sparkle in his eyes lightened the moment.

"They must call for an appointment to meet with me. It's imperative I interview them before making a decision." She burst out laughing. "You are impossible. Let me go get that car. We still need to eat and feed the little darling."

His stomach growled. He slapped his hand over his belly. "Guess that says it all. Let's go."

She paused at the door and pointed to the drawn curtains. "In case you haven't noticed, the sun's coming up. It's actually time for breakfast."

Daria closed the door behind her and pulled on her police-issued coat. The back lot had a few icy places, but for the most part it was clear. Maybe the town's streets would be in the same condition or clearer.

A black midsized car lit up when she clicked the key fob. She unlocked it and got inside. The cold leather sent chills down her legs.

Brrr. Warm this thing up.

The motor started on cue. She pulled around to the back door and put Emma's car seat in the back. Jake stepped out with Emma and buckled her in.

Emma whined and stretched out her arm, opening and closing her hand. "Bunny. Bunny."

"Where's her little rabbit, Jake? Check in the conference room."

In a matter of seconds, Jake returned and handed her the small rubber bunny. She settled back and leaned her head against the car seat's headrest, bouncing the white rabbit on her leg. "It was in the hallway. She'd dropped it."

"It's strange how children get so attached to things. Usually, it's a blanket or stuffed animal, but a small rubber rabbit?" Daria pulled into the early morning traffic. A few cars were on the street and a couple of people wrapped up in coats walked along the sidewalk.

"You've got me. I've been overseas on active duty." He pulled the visor down. "That sun's bright. Anyway, I guess Amanda bought them for her. There's a complete set of little rubber animals in the bottom of her diaper bag. A kid thing, I suppose."

Daria turned into the parking lot of the twenty-four-hour restaurant and parked. The red Open Twenty-Four Hours sign blinked like lights on a Christmas tree against the window. Visitors couldn't miss the building with its yellow painted wood structure. "I suppose my mystery person gave up a long time ago. If it's important, she'll reschedule."

"I hope she's still here. I'm curious about what she wants," Jake said. "I can smell bacon frying." He unbuckled Emma and pulled her out. "Do you smell bacon, Emma? It's delicious. You might have to try it." He kissed her cheek.

They reached the restaurant's clear glass door. Daria opened it for him.

"No, I've got the door. You go," Jake said.

"Just go." Daria nodded.

"Nope. Ladies first." He held the door open as they had a standoff.

"Fine." She went inside first. The sign read Seat Yourself. "Any preferences?"

"Booth in the back, by the emergency exit door. I like to see what's going on." He walked that way.

Daria stopped off and picked up a high chair.

She recognized the senior man sitting on a stool at the breakfast bar. "Mr. Treadway, you're up early. Are you still staying busy at the Oakland Grill?"

"Busier than I'd like, but it keeps me going." He took a drink of his coffee and set it down as he turned and looked at her. "Well, I do say you are out mighty early, too. I see you have company." He smiled and winked.

"Yep, something like that. You enjoy your coffee and stay warm."

"Hey, I need to talk to you." He pointed to Daria.

"Can it wait? I'm pretty busy right now." Daria patted him on the back.

"Sure, sure. I don't want to interfere." He nodded.

Daria returned to their table and placed the high chair at the end. Jake sat Emma down and scooted the chair closer. She rubbed her eyes, then pounded the bunny on the table.

"That was Mr. Treadway. He refuses to retire, so he helps at a restaurant in the middle of town. He said he wanted to talk to me."

"About what?" Jake caught Emma's toy before it fell off the table. "Working will keep him young."

"Bite, phees." Her hand opened and closed. "Mama, bye-bye." She kicked her legs. "Bite. Bite."

A gray-haired server carrying a tray approached their table with two coffees and a child's cup of apple juice and fries. "Here you go. You two looked like you need a kick start this morning, and this little doll has been here before. Her mom always ordered her apple juice and french fries." She placed a small box of dry cereal in front of Daria. "Her mom always packed one of these in the side pocket of her diaper bag. Thought you might want an extra."

"Thank you," Jake said. "Good to know." He unzipped the empty pocket and stuffed it inside.

Emma dropped the rabbit and clutched the cup with both hands, then put one hand down and picked up a fry.

Daria lifted her eyebrows. "You knew her mother?"

The server threw her hand in the air joyfully. "My, yes. Amanda was in here every week, like clockwork. She and Emma always sat at the table by the window. She and Tom came in here without Emma the morning of their tragic accident."

"Do you know of anyone who was upset

with Amanda?" Daria hoped the server had more information.

"Heavens, no. Everyone loved her and her husband." The server pulled out her order pad. "What would you like to eat this morning?"

They placed their order and sipped on the hot coffee. A woman on the opposite side of the restaurant wearing sunglasses and a scarf wrapped around her head and across her nose and face moved from one table to another until she was close to where they sat. Daria tensed and patted her side where she'd holstered her weapon. Could this be the woman who wanted to meet with her?

"I'll be back in a minute." Daria slipped from the booth and approached the woman. "Did you make an appointment to meet someone?"

"Yes." She looked around nervously. "I've been waiting all night."

"Who did you have an appointment with?" It didn't hurt to double-check.

"You." She ducked her head and looked up again.

Daria sat down and waited for the lady's explanation. She spotted Mr. Treadway leaving the restaurant. She'd find him later.

"The baby over there is Emma, right? That's

Amanda and Tom's daughter. Am I correct?"
She bit her lip.

"First, what's your name and your connection with this family?" Daria sized the lady up. She looked nervous and even frightened.

"I'm Liz Colton. I worked at the bank with Amanda. I'd seen pictures of her baby on her desk, then after the accident, I saw the child's picture with her parents in the paper."

"Ms. Colton—Liz. Why did you want to meet with me, and why don't you take those sunglasses off and uncover your face so I can see you?"

"Can't do that. Someone might recognize me. I had to tell you I believe they murdered Amanda because she discovered something illegal going on at the bank and downloaded documents on toy flash drives."

Chills raced down Daria's spine, and it wasn't the cold air. "Toy flash drives?"

"Yes." Liz pointed at Emma playing with the bunny. "You might check what she has in her hand."

Seriously?

Was it possible the little bunny Emma held on to so tightly held incriminating evidence?

She could hardly hold herself in her seat, but she had to hear Liz out.

"What else can you tell me?" Daria tried not to sound aggressive with her questioning. Finally, some concrete evidence, maybe.

"Our manager came in and didn't shut his door all the way. I overheard him talking on the phone. No idea who he was talking to, but he stated his hidden camera caught Amanda downloading private files that could cause his empire to crumble. He said if that flash drive landed in the wrong hands, it might implicate him and upper management in embezzlement. If they could crack the codes. Then he laughed."

"What did Amanda do when she realized they suspected her?"

"She fought tears and wondered what they'd do to her. She started receiving death threats if she didn't return the private documents. Amanda was a go-getter. She'd gone this far, so she had to have the rest of the files. I told her to go to the police. She went to the station and filed a report, but they didn't take her seriously. Her last words to me were if anything happened to her, to make sure her family knew how much Emma loved her little rubber toys. Amanda told me to find you and tell you what happened." Liz picked up her purse and pushed it up on her shoulder.

"Why me? Can you come down to the station and give your statement?" Daria scooted to the edge of her seat. Liz was about to bolt. "How can I get in touch with you?"

"She knew you from childhood and trusted you. I've stayed too long. Don't try to contact me. They'll kill me, too, if they find out I know stuff. I'm sorry for Jake's loss, but I've got to go." She stood, straightened her coat and rushed out into the cold.

Jake tapped his foot on the tile floor. What was going on between that lady and Daria? He scooted to the edge of the red fake leather seat with intentions of finding out, but the woman darted outside. Daria returned to the table.

"What happened? Fear was in that woman's eyes." Jake leaned in toward Daria and lowered his voice. "What did she say? Was it about Amanda?"

"Yes." Daria blew out a breath. "But let's check on something first." She picked up the little rubber bunny that Emma had let go of to eat her fries. "Watch this." She pulled the top from the bottom and a flash drive appeared.

Jake sucked in a breath. "Is it real?"

"As real as they come, just in novelty form. Who would suspect something that looks like a child's toy?" Daria snapped the two pieces back together and placed it back on Emma's tray.

Jake reached into the diaper bag and pulled out the collection of rubber toys. Daria and he pulled apart each little farm animal, and sure enough, they were all flash drives. He dropped his hands on the table. "I cannot believe we've had the evidence with us all along. What did she tell you?"

Daria explained what Liz had to say. She had confirmed his suspicions that his sister's death wasn't an accident. She'd been murdered. They put the toys back together and tucked them into the firm bottom of the diaper bag, where Amanda had hid them.

"Finish eating. We've got work to do." Daria bit into her breakfast sandwich and stuffed a tater tot into her mouth. "We need our energy."

Normally he could down a big cheeseburger in two bites, but Daria's news stole his appetite. She was right. They needed food for strength. He conceded and did his best to shove down some of his breakfast.

Emma hummed and mashed french fries on

the high chair tray as she ate. It was a relief to see her satisfied and playful. Oh, how Amanda and Tom must have adored her. He did, too. His heart broke all over again for his loss. He sucked it up and pulled himself together. Like Daria said, they had work to do.

As soon as they finished eating, they walked toward their vehicle. Clouds had moved in, and large snowflakes hit him in the face. The brisk wind whipped around his ears and sent a shiver across his shoulders. Emma's little eyes blinked fast as snow landed on her nose.

"It's cold out here, Emma. Do you like the snow?" He patted her back and wrapped the blanket tighter. She pushed her arm out into the cold air and slapped at the fluffy flakes.

He paused and squinted at what appeared to be writing on the back of their car. The words were almost covered with snow. He deciphered *Hot Head*, evidently written with shaving cream. He shot a glance at Daria. Her face turned as red as the flashing Open sign in the restaurant's window.

"Is this some kind of joke? Was it intended for you?" He put Emma in the car seat and stepped back.

"It's nothing. Let's go." Daria hopped in the

car and turned on the windshield wipers, pushing the newly fallen snow to small piles at the sides of the glass.

Officer McDaniel pulled in beside their vehicle, studied the almost hidden white writing fading quick, and rolled his window down. He chuckled. "Some of the guys are hazing you. Don't pay any attention to it. A quick wash at the drive-through will erase it or it could freeze in these temperatures." He rolled his window up and got out. "Have a good one. I'm going for my coffee and gravy and biscuits."

McDaniel walked away. Jake placed his hand on Daria's shoulder.

"Is there a story behind this hazing thing?" He spoke as softly as he could. Obviously, the message hurt her feelings. If someone was willing to do that, who knew what else they might do.

"Yes. It's embarrassing and partially true." She propped her arms across the steering wheel. "Last year, we had a lot of tourists. Most of them were pleasant and enjoyed themselves. There was one guy and his dad who'd had too much to drink. The son became a menace to others. His disrespectful behavior, name-calling and aggression grew worse. He refused to settle down after I warned him several times. I lost my temper and arrested him for disturbing the peace. Now some of my coworkers think I have a short fuse and I don't have what it takes to be a cop. I plan to prove them wrong."

Jake rubbed his hands together, then wiped one hand down his face. Harassment was wrong. He didn't appreciate the judgment passed on her and their public display of humiliation.

"Who are these guys?" Names would help him confront the right people.

"I'll not disclose their names. I have my suspicions about who instigated the whole thing." She sat back and started the car. "Let's get to the station and see what's on Emma's drives."

Snow packed fast on her windshield and the wipers fought to clear the glass. Her phone rang. She answered and put it on speaker.

"Officer Daria Gordon."

"Daria, this is Allan Simmons, Kimbleton's fire marshal. The report came back on the hotel fire. It's been confirmed the fire started after someone placed two bug bombs on the mantel of the gas fireplace. Once the fumes built up and reached the pilot light, it exploded. I'm glad Jake ran when he did, or this wouldn't have ended well."

"So it wasn't a bomb." Daria's eyebrows lowered. "Please let me know if anything else comes up."

"Yes, ma'am. Give me a call if you have any more questions."

"Thank you for the update." She disconnected the call. Her eyes met with Jake's. "You were right. The perpetrator purposely planned your demise. Emma's too."

He and Emma were the targets. Not that he needed any more confirmation. Someone had already proven Emma and he were in their crosshairs. His fingernails dug into his palms the tighter he squeezed his fists. The stakes were high and deadly.

He looked over his shoulder at Emma. Her head rested against the side of the car seat, and she held the little rubber bunny up against her neck as her eyes had grown heavy. She'd be asleep soon. He couldn't let anything happen to her.

The windshield fogged up. Daria turned the defroster on high.

Jake retrieved a cloth bib from Emma's diaper bag and wiped the inside of the windshield. Heat from the defroster cleared their view and began melting most of the flakes. Last night's light dusting had turned into a heavy snow-storm. He shifted his eyes to the almost covered side mirror. A dark green truck followed close behind them.

"That truck has been behind us for a while now." He turned and looked out of the rear window. Lines from the rear defrost slowly melted the ice, but still hindered his view.

"It pulled in behind us as soon as we left the restaurant. Why?"

"Looks like we're being followed." He stared at Daria before looking in the side mirror again. His pulse gained speed.

"It's not a tail, if that's what you're thinking." Daria's eyes sparkled and her lips smoothed upward. His stomach flipped. That was the look she gave him multiple times when they were younger. Best friends forever, they'd say, until he'd moved away and lost touch.

She continued, "It's a plainclothes cop escorting us to the station. I should have told you he'd be following us. Relax. You're jumpy."

"No, I'm not." He straightened. "I'm alert and cautious."

"Is that so?" She laughed. "Then how come it took you five minutes to notice?"

"I spotted it right off but was keeping an eye

on it. Besides, Emma distracted me for a minute." He grinned, finding humor in his poor excuse.

"Ohhh, so now you're going to blame a defenseless child."

"You still laugh the same." He put his hand on her shoulder and grew serious. "I've missed that sound." An old memory popped into his head of them, running and jumping in a pile of leaves as kids, then rolling down the hill, laughing until their stomachs hurt. He was too grown up now to do such childish things. Maybe Emma would enjoy the fun when she got older.

Daria's expression grew serious. He hadn't meant to kill the joking between them.

"I often wondered what happened to you. I even watched football for several years, expecting the announcer to scream 'and there goes Jake Fisher, quarterback for the Eagles executing a perfect throw.'" She slowed and turned the corner. "It's nice to see you again."

"Yes, it's great to reconnect. Having a trustworthy friend in town makes life a little easier." He'd purposely shut down any discussion about relationships or dating. Not that he was totally against it; he just didn't think he was ready now that he had Emma. That was a lot to swallow.

Jake checked his side mirror again and noted smoke inside the cab of the green truck. The cop's vision had been obscured and he swerved and stopped. "The inside of our escort's truck is smoking. He isn't behind us anymore."

"What do you mean? Is it on fire?" He noted her eyes went to the rearview mirror.

Jake tensed. "No. Something isn't right. I can feel it."

Daria called the station and reported the green truck might be on fire. "We're almost there, Jake. Hang on. Maybe they can tell us what's happening."

Crash!

Emma screamed.

Someone rammed them. In broad daylight. Their car thrust forward.

"Where did that come from?" Daria worked the steering wheel and kept them on the slick road. "Who knew we're driving this car?"

"It's a black truck. It's coming at us fast." Jake reached back and pressed the blanket to Emma's chest. Somehow, he needed to get her out of harm's way. "Watch out. He's about to hit us again."

Chapter 6

Daria gripped the steering wheel tighter. Her pulse went into overdrive. Her protective radar skyrocketed. "Maybe he'll back off when we reach the station. Is it the same black vehicle you spotted through the forest after the shooting at your house?"

"Could be, but I can't make a positive ID," Jake said.

She pressed the accelerator to go faster than she preferred in the winter conditions, with two civilians in the car. There was nothing she could do. The station was within view. She radioed for help moments before she had to turn.

Wham!

The truck shoved her vehicle past the station's driveway. Daria slid sideways, then straightened. "He's got nerve chasing us right here. I have no choice but to keep going. Maybe I can lose him on Chisel Road."

"Want you," Emma cried out.

"Give her the cup, Jake, and pray that settles her for a bit." Daria bit her lip. She'd asked Jake to pray, as if she thought it would help. Maybe it would. "We can't take her out of the car seat."

Jake reached into the back and handed her the cup. Daria glanced in the rearview mirror. Emma sniffled as she drank.

"Isn't Chisel Road that winding road where we used to get carsick?" Jake eyed Emma, concerned for her safety. "In this weather, I'm not sure I'd risk it. Why not circle back toward the station?"

"Can you get a make on the truck?" Heat rushed to Daria's face. She had to change the subject.

Why did he keep questioning her decisions as a police officer? She never left town like he had. She knew these roads well and understood it wasn't the best choice, but it might deter the tail and cause him to retreat.

"Looks like an old Durango. I haven't seen one of those in a while."

She made a quick turn onto the curvy road and fishtailed. The truck slid sideways and almost ran off the road. She gained ground, leaving her pursuer behind.

"Whoa." Jake grabbed the dash. "I hope you know what you're doing."

"Stop doubting me." She fumed. "Keep an eye on the truck." Truth was, she now doubted herself. The narrow, snow-covered road made it difficult to keep good traction. Another sharp curve lay ahead. She slowed enough to maintain control.

"Gun," Jake said.

Bullets blew out her back tire the moment she started into the curve.

"Hold on. I can't keep it straight. We're going to crash."

Jake flew into the back seat. The car sailed off the road and banged against trees as it plummeted into a ravine. Air bags deployed, smacking Daria in the face. Emma's screams pierced her ears.

An abrupt halt whipped Daria's neck and slammed her deeper into the air bag. Why hadn't she heard from Jake? Her shoulder hurt and her face stung. She pushed at the air bag and forced her body to turn enough to see Emma. Something covered the child's head.

She reached back as best as she could and tugged at the blanket-wrapped diaper bag Jake must have stuffed in the front of Emma. How had he had the wits or time to do that before the crash? Quick thinking on his part. He probably saved Emma from whiplash or serious injury. He was more of a father figure than he'd given himself credit for.

Jake's legs were across the floor, but she couldn't turn enough to see his face. Emma needed consoling. How could Daria get out of the car?

"Jake." She reached back and touched his leg. "Jake. Answer me. Are you okay?" What kind of question was that when he wasn't moving or speaking?

God, we need Your help.

Icy water rushed over her feet.

"Oh, no, Emma. We're at the edge of the river. I've got to get us out of here."

Daria reached for her radio. Static. Her hands fumbled around the seat until she located her phone wedged between the seat and the console. She punched in 911.

"911. What's your emergency?"

"This is Sergeant Daria Gordon of the Kimbleton Police Department with two civilians in the car. We've been chased down and run off the road at the second curve on Chisel Road.

Shots fired. We need backup immediately and medical help."

Her hands shook. She managed to put her phone in her front shirt pocket. Heavy footsteps crunched under the snow and twigs snapped. She sucked in a breath. Whoever was out there was getting closer, and she couldn't reposition her body to see who it was.

Please be here, God. Give me wisdom.

No time to waste. She squeezed through the broken window. Pain shot through her left shoulder. Weakness washed over her. Black dots invaded her eyesight as heat covered her like an electric blanket. She couldn't pass out. Emma and Jake needed her.

Arctic wind hit her face about the same time her feet sank ankle deep in the icy water. Shock from the cold helped pull her from the darkness that tried to consume her. She glanced over the top of the car. Two men had descended into the ravine and were coming toward her with their guns in a ready position.

A surge of energy infiltrated every muscle in her body. She tugged at the back door of the vehicle until it released from the large dent in its side. Metal scraping metal interrupted what silence she'd tried to keep. Jake lay on the floor and wasn't moving. Emma's cries spilled out into the forest for all to hear. She shook Jake. No response. Her heart thrashed against her chest.

Voices grew closer. Those men were about to eliminate them.

"Thought you could get rid of us, didn't you?" a gruff voice said. "You still have something we need."

God, we need Your protection.

This could go one of two ways. She could step from behind the car with her weapon drawn and face her pursuers, identifying them and hopefully subduing them. Or she could step from behind the car and give them a direct shot to take her out.

Her heart pounded hard. She pressed her lips together, firmed her grip on her Glock and stepped through the water into the open. The two men shot almost simultaneously, followed by two answering shots from close by before Daria had a chance to shoot. One man's gun flew out of his hand. He turned and ran. The other man's shot hit the tree close to Daria's head. He dropped to the ground, yelling. Where did those shots come from? Sirens roared.

Daria spun and spotted Jake hanging out of

the broken window on the opposite side of the car, holding his weapon. He nodded and gave her a thumbs-up before he worked his way out of the demolished vehicle with Emma and her blanket in his arms and wrapped her in his coat. He turned a circle before facing her again.

"What is it, Jake?" She spun and searched behind them.

"Checking to see if there's a third shooter hiding out."

"I only saw two." Had she missed something, or was he being extra cautious? She scanned the area. Nothing suspicious. "Did you see more of them?"

"No." He rubbed at his dark, stubby hair. "One can never be too careful. The sounds of the rushing water might make it difficult to hear another shooter lurking nearby."

Sirens grew closer. Blue lights flashed on the road above them. Officers emerged and flooded the area. She'd never been so happy to see blue uniforms against the brilliant sparkling snow. Two officers secured the man shot in the shoulder.

In the distance, three officers walked toward them with the second shooter. The men were read their Miranda rights, then escorted to an ambulance. They'd receive medical treatment before going to jail. Daria could hardly wait to get Jake and Emma settled so she could question the prisoners.

"That was some gutsy move back there. You could have gotten yourself killed." Jake stepped up, holding Emma in one arm. He put the other arm around Daria's shoulders.

"All part of the job. I couldn't let anything happen to you and Emma. If it meant risking my life, then so be it." She ducked away from his arm. Pressure from his hand on her shoulder ached somewhat. Nothing a couple of over-the-counter pain relievers couldn't handle. "Thank you for assisting."

"Instinct." His eyes narrowed. "I'm still uncertain about another shooter out there."

Emma leaned from Jake's hold toward Daria with her arms stretched out. How could these two get to her emotions in such a short time? She loved babies. Even more when they wanted her to hold them. Emma had captured her heart from the beginning.

"Come here, baby. Let's get you warmed up." She took the petite eighteen-month-old and readjusted her blanket. Emma instantly wrapped her arms around Daria's neck, squeezed and laid her head on Daria's sore shoulder. Maybe it was just jammed or strained, and not a torn muscle. At least, she hoped not. The pain wasn't as intense as it had been right after the crash.

Three paramedics came toward them with their backpacks.

"You shouldn't be moving around until we get you checked out." The gray-haired paramedic dropped his gear in the snow and moved toward her.

"Hey, Steve. Glad you guys are here. Check Jake and Emma first." She pointed to Jake. "He was unconscious for a couple of minutes."

"No, I'm good." Jake pointed back at her. "She hit her shoulder and Emma was in her car seat. I shoved the diaper bag in front of her to help cushion the blow. Speaking of diaper bag, I need to get it."

"I got it." One of the firefighters handed it to him. "Fast thinking. You probably saved her from popping her little neck or from whiplash."

"There are enough of us to check all of you." Steve moved toward Daria and Emma. He put the stethoscope to Emma's back while the other paramedics checked Jake. Emma pushed his hands away. "Need to put a pediatric cervical collar around her neck, but she's not going to like it. Little ones rarely do. They'll remove it after a CT scan. Same with you two. These collars are for your protection."

Emma fought with Steve. She pulled at the device, screamed and cried until Jake took her from Daria and walked a distance away from Steve.

"She's been through a lot in the past couple of days." Daria blew her warm breath on her hands. "I pray she doesn't have nightmares."

"Which shoulder hurts?" Steve listened to Daria's heart rate.

"My left shoulder. It's nothing."

Arctic wind stirred the frozen leaves and whisked them around like sleet. "Since everyone is mobile, let's get them out of the cold for triages," Steve said. "We're all freezing, and the baby shouldn't be out in this wind."

"Come on, we're moving to the ambulances," Daria said.

Steve scooped up his gear, as did the other paramedics.

They waited for Jake, Emma and her to move uphill before them. Daria walked beside Jake and Emma. He carried the baby and diaper bag on one side, and she moved to his opposite side. Her foot slipped on the frozen forest floor.

Jake's big hand caught her by the left arm up close to her armpit. Intense pain shot through her shoulder.

She screamed and her ears started ringing. Black dots invaded her eyesight, and her knees buckled. Everything went dark.

Two paramedics dropped their gear and caught Daria before she hit the ground. Firefighters from the top of the ravine slid down the hill to help. Jake had the powerful urge to pick her up and carry her, but with a clinging baby in his arms, he couldn't react as fast as he'd wanted.

"Here." Jake held Emma out to one firefighter. She screamed, turned a circle in his arms and grabbed him tight around the neck. "I can carry Daria up to the top."

"No need. A litter is on the way down," the stocky man said. "Besides, that little one needs you right now."

He could carry both. Their weight couldn't compare to the dead weight he'd carried after some of his buddies were wounded or killed in battle. He sensed the need to hold and protect Daria and Emma. Was his hard-core marine status going soft on him already?

"What, what are you doing?" Daria pulled at the belts on the litter. "I'm fine. Let me up."

"They'll let you up once they get you to the top." Jake high-stepped it and caught up with her, holding both arms around Emma. "You passed out."

"Seriously? Well, I'm okay now. I can walk." Daria grimaced.

"I saw that." Jake stared down at her. Her shoulder-length brown hair had fallen from the knot on her head and laced her shoulders. There she was. A more mature Daria. Trustworthy and beautiful. True to her job, willing to sacrifice her life for Emma and him. Such admirable traits in his friend. "You're in pain. Let them check you out. Then we'll be on our way."

Daria's actions reminded him of the story he'd heard from his marine buddy about God. Only God sacrificed His Son's life for everyone in the world. "Trust in Him," his fallen buddy had repeated to the guys in his squad more times than he could count. The realization of Daria's actions stirred his emotions and made him realize the deep truth of his comrade's words. God's Son died for him. Jake swallowed the knot forming in his throat.

One firefighter's foot slipped, causing one

end of the litter to tilt sideways. Daria's hand flew into the air. Jake grabbed her hand while the firefighter regained control. Emma curled her arms up against his chest and pulled her knees up. She was cold. He was, too. He let go of Daria's hand and secured his hold on Emma, tucking her blanket snug around her again.

Jake glanced up into the trees and whispered his buddy's brief prayer.

Forgive my hardheadedness, God, and forgive me of my past actions that weren't pleasing to You.

Small snowflakes tapped against his cheeks. The wall of rejection and lack of trust he'd formed after receiving the Dear John letter from his ex-fiancée crumbled the moment his gaze fell on Daria and her willingness to die for him. Even though he'd protected her, too, by disabling the shooters. She was an outstanding cop and a beautiful lady and didn't know it.

His chest swelled. He'd reconnected with his best friend. Could he see her as more than a friend? Better yet, could she see *him* as more than a friend? He chewed the side of his lip.

At the top of the ravine, authorities escorted them to different ambulances. Daria's voice carried over to where Jake sat. "I've got to keep an eye on my victims. They're in danger." He shook his head. She still wanted to protect them, even though she had a hurt shoulder. Eventually, she'd have to come to grips with the fact that he really was a trained marine. His skills were at a different scale than her policing skills. He could take care of himself and keep her and Emma safe.

"You'll go to the hospital and get checked. Same with the others," Jeffers told Daria.

"Yes, sir. What happened to my escort?"

I'd like to know that, too.

"Someone tossed a smoke bomb through his window." Jeffers joined the other officers nearby.

Jake leaned over and looked around the door of the ambulance. Daria lay back on the gurney. She didn't look happy. He sat back and studied his sleepy niece. One of her hands still held on to the neck brace, but her deep breathing showed she was relaxing.

A firefighter approached the ambulance. "We'll get the car out of the ravine and tow it in."

"Thanks, but you might relay that information to Daria." He took the rubber bunny from Emma's grip and replaced it with her cup. She whimpered, but curled her cup against her chest. He dropped the bunny in the diaper bag and pointed to Daria, then paused. "Could you deliver this diaper bag to her, as well? She's in the other ambulance. It's important."

"You've got it." The firefighter strode over to Daria. Jake watched as he handed the bag to her. She looked in his direction, gave him a thumbs-up, then called Lieutenant Jeffers to come back.

Jake could have handed the little rubber toys over, but it was Daria's case. She deserved to do the honors. Her lieutenant's eyebrows lowered as he listened to Daria. Then his eyes widened as she extracted the small rubber animal flash drives and explained the value of them. He motioned for Cramer to bring an evidence bag. Daria dropped the evidence in and dated it according to protocol. Jeffers took the bag to his car and drove away.

Daria's smile said it all. It was her case, as she'd reminded him numerous times, to turn in the suspected evidence that could prove his sister's and brother-in-law's deaths were murder and put the killers behind bars. Jake wouldn't have trusted many people with his sister's case, but Daria was different.

"I need to buckle the child in the car seat.

It's built into the captain's chair. You can sit on the bench seat over there and buckle up." The paramedic's voice jolted Jake's attention back to his ambulance. He climbed in, locked the gurney in place and sat beside them while the driver closed the door.

Emma's sleepy eyes opened slightly. She gripped the paramedic's jacket. He took her hands, eased them away and placed them in her lap before buckling her in. Jake settled back and buckled up, keeping his attention on the little figure in the big seat.

The rough ride to the hospital reminded him of riding in a jeep over rocky roads to base camp. Why couldn't the designers of vehicles make them absorb all the bumps for a smoother transfer? Especially for the wounded. Emma succumbed to sleep. Her little head bobbed with each bump in the road.

The ambulance brakes squealed as it came to a stop. They'd arrived at the hospital's emergency entrance. Jake unbuckled Emma, waking her, and stepped out of the vehicle. Once inside, he spotted Daria still lying on a gurney. She insisted she had to guard him and Emma. He couldn't help but smile at her persistence to follow through with her job despite her injury.

She rolled her head sideways and his eyes met with her eyes. She lifted her head from the pillow.

"How is Emma? Are you okay? What did the doctor say?" Daria asked.

"We're fine. We just arrived like you." Jake patted Emma's back. "Let the doc check your shoulder. I'll find you when we're done."

Paramedics wheeled Daria's gurney down the hall to a room. Emma and he followed the nurse to another room, where a cartoon jungle scene decorated the walls. A small basket of rubber toys in individual packages sat on the counter. Perfect for Emma. Her head popped up off his shoulder. Her eyes widened when she spotted all the bright colors. He admired her uncombed dark curls and how she resembled his sister.

"See." She pointed to the wall with a brightly colored toucan sitting on a brown tree limb with green leaves.

"I see." Jake let her touch the bird on the wall.

A nurse entered and held the basket of toys in front of Emma. "Hello, cutie. Do you want a toy?"

Emma reached over and pulled out a rubber

giraffe. A perfect fit for her small hands and a relief to Jake, since she no longer had her little rubber rabbit. He unwrapped it for her. Little girl's giggles and gibberish filled the room and warmed his heart.

After CT scans and a thorough check, the doctor removed their neck braces. He put Emma's coat on her, then he made his way to Daria's room. She sat on the edge of the bed with a sling on her arm and a frustrated look on her face. They'd removed her neck brace, too.

"Knock, knock. Is it okay to come in?" Jake stepped inside at her nod, with his and Emma's discharge papers rolled up like a scroll. "What's the diagnosis?"

Emma pointed at Daria, leaned away from Jake and reached for her with the toy in her hand.

"Oh, you have a new toy. I like your giraffe." She eyed Jake. "Just a bruised muscle." Daria took Emma in her one good arm and kissed her cheek. "The doctor said it would be sore for a few days, but I'll be fine. It won't stop me from doing my job. What about you?"

"Emma had a tiny cut on her arm. They cleaned it and put a Band-Aid on it. My CT

scan went well. I've always been a hardhead."
He chuckled.

"That's not funny. We could have all been seriously hurt or killed." Emma squirmed out of Daria's lap. Jake helped her crawl onto the bed and sit up.

A nurse came in with Daria's discharge papers and read her the suggested instructions for healing. "Rest your shoulder as much as possible for forty-eight hours. Use a cold pack every twenty minutes for pain or swelling. If you have any problems, return to the ER."

"I'll make sure she takes it easy," Jake said.

The nurse turned to him with wide eyes.

Oh, no.

She pointed her finger at him. "You need to follow doctor's orders, too, mister. A mild concussion isn't anything to ignore. Marine or not, you've still got to heal." The nurse walked out of the room, leaving the door open.

"What?" Daria's face reddened as she tossed the sling aside and pulled on her coat. "You said you were fine."

"Well, I didn't say those exact words. I just didn't expound on it."

"You are impossible." Her glare had a touch of anger and frustration.

Jake turned his focus on Emma to avoid more eye contact with Daria. Her response had more of an impact on him than he thought it would. Amid her tight lips and glaring eyes, that she cared touched him.

He grabbed the diaper bag he'd spotted on the floor beside the counter and followed Daria to the waiting room, where Jeffers, Cramer and McDaniel sat waiting for them. Her phone beeped. She stopped and pulled out her cell. Jake stood right behind her and couldn't help but see the anonymous message she'd received.

It's not over.

She looked up at him.

He turned and scanned the room for anyone who looked suspicious.

Chapter 7

Daria shifted her eyes around the hospital's waiting room. Couldn't be one of her coworkers, could it? No. Where was her trust? She searched for movement outside the big hospital window. No one as far as she could see. Maybe someone watched her from the distant thickness of buildings and trees across the street.

She struggled with whether she should tell Jeffers about the text. In one way, she didn't want him to know because he might insist on pulling her off the case or putting Jake, Emma and her in a safe house. However, if she didn't tell, and he found out later, he could suspend her for withholding information, which wouldn't be good for her already shaky record.

She'd faced death with this case too many times already, along with Jake. Emma didn't deserve to be involved. One attack after another and the child still found peace in Jake's arms. Daria paused and closed her eyes for a second.

Lord, thank You for answering my prayer. You spared our lives. Forgive me for not trusting in You and for going my own way. I need You in my life. Every minute of every day. Help me make better decisions that will protect Jake and Emma.

"Are you dizzy or something?" Jake's whisper interrupted her silent prayer. She opened her eyes.

"No. I'm good. Just needed a moment to gather my thoughts and thank the Lord for protecting us." She proceeded across the room toward Jeffers.

He stood as she approached. "Daria, Jake, I'm glad everyone is okay, and especially glad this little one wasn't hurt." He fluffed Emma's curls and shook Jake's hand before facing her. "We've glanced at the flash drives. Every one of them has Excel files loaded with codes instead of names, password-protected charts and money laundering locations. We will need to look deeper into them and see if we can crack the codes. Well done, Daria."

"Wasn't me, sir. Amanda, Jake's sister, risked her life downloading the information." She placed her hand on Jake's arm. "Further investigation should prove her and her husband's crash wasn't an accident. Someone ran them off the road on purpose."

"I commend her for risking everything to stop this crime and bring justice to this city. Thanks to her, we now have evidence to warrant a search." Jeffers pushed his arms through his heavy coat and walked toward the door. "I'm sorry for your loss, Jake."

"Thank you," Jake said.

"Before you go, there's something you need to see." Daria lifted her cell for him to read the threatening message. She could almost read his expression, and it wasn't to her liking.

His eyes narrowed. "I'm placing the three of you in protective custody until we resolve this case."

Daria gasped.

No.

She bit her tongue and calmed herself. "I'd rather you didn't do that. Jake and I are on the verge of busting this case open."

Jeffers straightened his shoulders. "You and Jake? Since when did he join the police department?"

"I didn't mean it like that." She shifted her stance. Wrong choice of words. "I am handling the case according to protocol. And I'd appreciate your allowing me to carry it through."

Jeffers rubbed his chin. His expressive eyes narrowed again. She stood tall with her head held high. Maybe he'd notice she wasn't cowering.

He cleared his throat. "Cramer, you and McDaniel escort the three of them to the safe house."

His comment dropped like a boulder on her confidence. Heat rushed to her cheeks. Jeffers didn't think she could do it, and Jake would witness for himself the distrust of her lieutenant. Embarrassed and humiliated, Daria bit her lip to keep from saying something she shouldn't, which would prove she still had a temper.

Jake stepped forward and was about to speak, but she held her hand up. Thankfully, he backed away. An argument would only make things worse and could cause her to be suspended.

Jeffers's stern gaze turned to her. "Daria, you go with Jake and the baby to the safe house and keep a watch on them. Should a breach take place, they are in your hands."

Adrenaline shot to her toes so fast, she almost jumped up and down. Not an appropriate response for an officer of the law being given an assignment. She held back a relieved smile.

"Yes, sir." Her position, and his belief in her, had been restored, or so she hoped. "Before we go, is it possible for me to question the shooters?"

"Which is it you want, Daria? Bodyguard for the victims or to interrogate the prisoners?" His gruff tone didn't sway her.

"Both, sir." She stood her ground again and glanced at Jake. His slight nod meant he approved.

"Fine. Let's do this." Jeffers let out a huff. "McDaniel, you take them to the station, and Cramer will follow. When she's done, have another seized car ready for her. Then you and McDaniel escort them on to the safe house in unmarked cars."

"You've got it." McDaniel put his coat on, as did Cramer.

Jake pulled the hood of Emma's coat over her head and tightened the blanket around her body. "Now we're talking."

Daria zipped her coat all the way up to her neck. The blustery wind sent chills through to her bones, or so it seemed. Snow covered the ground and made walking a little treacherous.

She'd experienced winters like this before and knew the roads would be slick. She paused at the squad car and opened the door.

"Hurry, get Emma out of this wind." Daria placed her hand on Jake's back as he bent and slid into the car.

Another squad car pulled up beside them and the officer jumped out and opened his trunk. What was he doing? He opened their back door and put a child's car seat in. "Roads are too risky to not buckle her in properly," he said.

"Thank you. Remind me to buy you coffee at the doughnut shop sometime." Daria gave the officer a thumbs-up.

"I will. Chocolate glazed is my favorite with black coffee." He backed out of the car. "Drive safe." The door slammed, and he drove away.

"Your lieutenant thought of everything." Jake put Emma in the seat and buckled her in.

"Actually, I knew he had a baby's car seat in his trunk. He always carries one just in case. I sent him a text and asked him to deliver it to us," McDaniel said.

"Good thinking." Daria looked back at a happy Emma playing with her giraffe.

The drive to the station wasn't as bad as she expected. Jake, Emma and she rushed from the squad car into the station. McDaniel drove away. Probably to switch out cars as instructed. The aroma of fresh coffee captured her senses. She turned to Jake, and Emma leaned into Daria's arms. Her shoulder ached, but she'd pop a couple of over-the-counter pain relievers as soon as she put Emma down.

"I smell coffee." Jake darted toward the coffeepot in plain view. "I'll get us some."

"Thanks. I could use a hot cup right now." Daria entered the familiar conference room where Emma and Jake had been before. She set Emma down on the floor and took off her little pink coat. Daria removed her coat, too, and draped it over the back of a chair. Emma's wouldn't hang so she placed it on the table.

Jake entered with their hot beverages. The aroma permeated the room. It smelled so good.

"Here you go." He handed her one and placed sugar and creamer on the table. "I wasn't sure what you wanted in yours. I like mine black. The stronger, the better."

Her hand touched his as she took her coffee. Bigger, stronger hands than she remembered from years earlier. Was her crush from long ago reshaping itself and growing stronger? He must have noticed her pause.

"Your hands are like ice. Hold this cup a minute and you'll warm up." His serious expression didn't match his comment. Had he sensed their connection?

She quickly blew on her hot coffee, took a sip, then walked toward the window. The conference room door opened.

"You ready?" Lieutenant Jeffers stood in the doorway.

"Yes." Daria picked up her pace toward the door. She stopped and looked back. "I might be a while. You and Emma make yourselves at home. You know where the coffee is, and there are snacks in that credenza along the wall. Oh, and be sure to feed Emma that jar of baby food in her diaper bag. She has snacks and juice in there, too."

"Don't worry about us." Jake retrieved Emma's sippy cup from the diaper bag. "I'm learning how to be an uncle."

Daria darted to the front desk where the clerk kept over-the-counter pain meds. She tossed two in her mouth and swallowed them with a sip of her coffee. She rushed down the hallway, down the stairs and into the first interrogation room. After a couple of hours, she'd gathered information, but not everything she needed. Names. She needed names.

Jeffers directed her to move on to the second interrogation room where the other shooter waited. By the time she arrived, the guy was more than ready to talk. He and the other man claimed innocence, but that was expected in most any case.

"Tell us who is behind these attacks. Who killed Amanda and her husband?" Daria leaned forward at the table where the shooter sat on the opposite side.

"I had nothing to do with it. Gregory Hall, the bank president, the vice-president and his assistant manager are all involved in money laundering and embezzlement. Don't know who put the hit out on that Amanda girl," the man said.

"Why did they want her dead?" Daria sat back and crossed her arms.

He picked at his fingers. Daria slapped the table. He jerked back.

"I asked why they killed her."

"Because she was a threat to their operation. She had to be eliminated. The boss caught her on his hidden camera, downloading stuff on some type of kid's flash drive. Couldn't let her get away with all that information."

Daria stood and paced the room. "What else can you tell me?"

"I'm a dead man already. They'll kill me if I walk out of here." He straightened in his chair. "I told you who all was involved. I think there's one more person, but I wasn't privy to his name."

Her muscles tightened. Someone still lurked, waiting for the right opportunity to make his move. Could he or this other person have messaged her from a burner phone? She walked out of the room and leaned against the wall. Jeffers stepped out behind her.

"I'll send officers out to pick up each member of the bank's management team and bring them in for questioning. Murder, mishandling of funds, money laundering and embezzlement. Strong charges if we can get the proof. We need to crack those codes."

She pushed from the wall. "I'll go check on Jake and Emma. I'm sure they're ready to get out of here."

"Head straight for the safe house. You know which one?" Jeffers asked.

"Yes. Four miles outside of town."

"Correct."

The day had flown by with all the trauma they'd encountered, and the questioning took longer than she'd planned. Daria returned to the conference room where Emma had fallen asleep in Jake's arms and Jake's head lay on top of Emma's. He'd fallen asleep, too. An empty baby food jar lay on the table with drops of pureed carrots decorating it. Emma's lips still had proof of orange leftovers. They had emptied the diaper bag onto the floor, and a wet diaper hung halfway out of the trash can. She suspected he'd tossed it.

She couldn't help but smile. There was enough proof tossed around the room that he had tried to take care of Emma and evidently succeeded.

Daria tapped lightly on Jake's shoulder. His eyes popped open, and he looked up at her. There for a moment, she wanted to lean down and kiss him. She stepped back.

"It's time for us to go to the safe house. McDaniel has a car warming in the back." She smiled at him. "From the looks of this room, you two had a good time. I'll gather everything and help you get her coat on."

"Did you find out anything? What did they say?" Jake sat up.

"We don't have names, but besides the accusations against bank management being involved, there's someone out there still calling the shots."

Jake shuffled Emma in his arms while Daria gently slid the sleeping baby's arms through her coat. He handed her to Daria while he put his coat on. His insides churned. He hadn't been in town long enough to make enemies and yet here he was, still feeling like he was in the war zone.

"Are you ready?" Daria asked. "The safe house is waiting."

"Why not just go back to the hotel? If they're still coming after us, let's face them head-on." Jake exited the building into the cold and slid into the back. He buckled Emma into her car seat and covered her with her blanket. She still gripped the little giraffe.

He hopped out and got in the front with Daria. His fingers were already half-frozen from the short time he'd been exposed to the elements. He rubbed his hands together in front of the air vent, blowing hot air.

"I shouldn't have to answer that question, Jake. You're smart enough to figure it out. Besides, I've been assigned to protect you and Emma, so I must keep my guard up." Daria drove slowly out of the parking lot. "Of course, I've already been keeping a watch on our surroundings since the moment I saw you in the parking lot holding a gun. We've encountered a lot of near-death experiences. I take my job seriously."

"And I listen to my instincts." Jake sat back. "I've already told you I have special training."

"Let's not revisit that conversation." Daria glanced at him. "We've both had training. Now we utilize that knowledge to stay out of the killer's crosshairs. Agreed?"

Jake understood her position, but he sure wanted to leave Emma with Daria while he did his own scouting. She'd made it clear she was the authority. He must abide by the rules, well, unless he saw fit to make some adjustments.

"Agreed." Staying out of sight of the enemy was his goal. Keeping Emma and Daria safe was his priority. He kind of enjoyed having Daria around, even if she was a little bossy. "Why don't we drop Emma off at my parents' house, where she'll be safe?" He tapped the door's arm-rest with his fingers.

"And put them in danger, too? If only we could place Emma in safe hands, but right now, your hands are the safest. Whoever is watching us may know every move we make. If we leave Emma somewhere, they will think we've left vital information in the same place. We can't risk it."

Jake stared at the car in the distance in front of them. Daria was right. He'd only put others in danger. He tightened his fists and loosened them. The minute Daria had explained the shooters had given up information, he'd sensed the whole takedown was too easy.

"Yeah, bad idea. But you'd think since police have the flash drives, they'd retreat and run." Jake glanced back at Emma. Sound asleep. He stared out of the rear window. "I see your friends are escorting us to our destination. Isn't that a telltale sign to anyone watching that something's going on with three cars caravanning down the street?"

"They are a suitable distance away and the vehicles are different models. It's not like we're chained together. If they were closer, I'd have to agree." Daria turned into a dark driveway, drove around to the back of the house hidden by the forest and stopped.

From the looks of the place, there was no electricity, no streetlight and it was hidden by the trees. How were they supposed to stay warm in a place like this, especially if they were stuck here for a while.

"I know you think that's logical, and this is a small town, but I don't see it in the same way." He turned and faced the front. "Look, one car stops half a block from the house, we turn in and disappear in the forest, while the other car turns in behind us. Tell me that doesn't draw attention."

"Are you insinuating we don't know what we're doing?" Daria's voice rose an octave.

He threw up his hands. "I'm not challenging the police department's procedures. It just seems odd to me. If I were watching for a target overseas, I'd become suspicious if three unknown vehicles approached at the same time." He dropped his hands. "I'm just saying."

Daria rubbed her forehead. "This is what we've always done, and everything turned out fine."

"Okay. I surrender." Jake unbuckled his seat belt. Maybe he was too exhausted to think clearly. Wouldn't be the first time, but he'd never admit it. "What are we waiting for?"

"McDaniel is checking the house out to make sure it's all clear."

Jake would argue the point again. Things didn't feel right, but who was he to push his way of thinking on Daria? Shouldn't the house have been cleared before they got there?

"For your information, there are two officers already inside the house. Smothers and Evans. Cramer will drive away as soon as he gets the all clear from McDaniel."

She appeared confident in their system, so he let it go. Daria's phone lit up with a text.

"It's clear. Let's go." She stepped out of the car. "I'll get the diaper bag. You get Emma."

Jake moved as stealthily as possible and prayed Emma wouldn't cry. Daria met him at the front of the car. They made their way in the dark to the back door. An officer he hadn't met held the door open for them. They entered and stopped in a dark room while the officer closed the back door and locked it behind them, then another officer opened the mudroom door.

Light flooded the place and warmth hit him in the face. "Impressive."

"Jake," Daria said. "This is Officer Smothers and Officer Evans. They will stand watch tonight."

Jake shook their hands, then evaluated the interior of the house. Blackout curtains everywhere. From the outside, it looked like an abandoned house. Who knew it would be cozy and welcoming?

A gas fireplace warmed the living room. Carpet covered the floor, he assumed to keep down the sound of movement inside the house. Oddly, the dragonfly decor wasn't what he'd expected. In the mountains, people normally decorated with deer or bear themes and built log furniture. Not so in here. He liked it.

Daria stood with her hands at her waist. "Do you approve, Mr. Skeptic?"

"Okay, I deserve that." He patted Emma's back. "Where should I lay her down?"

"In here." Daria turned and walked into a small bedroom. "You can put her in here in this porta crib. We'll be able to hear her if she wakes up."

Jake leaned over, placed her on top of a fuzzy, soft yellow blanket and eased her coat off. She rolled over, still asleep. A night-light cast star shadows on the ceiling. *Nice.*

They returned to the living room, and he sat on the sofa in front of the fireplace. For the first time in two days, he relaxed. Daria picked up a tote bag and disappeared into another room. He'd given her a hard time, but she stood her ground and didn't get angry. She'd shown no signs of an anger problem. Raised her voice a time or two, but that's not full-fledged anger. He looked around for the officers. Where'd they go?

Daria entered the room again, only this time wearing a navy police sweatshirt with the side tucked above her weapon, blue jeans, and her feet decked with warm-looking boots. She had let her hair down, and it danced on her shoulders every time she turned her head. Jake caught himself staring.

"What are you looking at?" Daria paused with her eyebrows lifted.

"My best friend from middle school." Jake smiled. "She looks nice."

Daria snickered. "Thanks, but you should meet *my* friend from middle school. He is easy on the eyes." She walked past him to the open kitchen and pulled out two disposable coffee cups. "Can I interest you in a fresh cup?"

"Sure, but I didn't see you bring a bag inside. Did you have clothes already here?"

"No. We keep a change of clothes handy for situations such as this. Evans brought my bag in when he arrived."

"Good thinking." Jake eased from his seat

and joined her in the kitchen. He had an urge to wrap his arms around her but backed off. She must have sensed something because she had a questioning look on her face. He reached for the empty cup about the time she dropped a coffee pod into the coffee maker. Their hands touched. Their eyes met.

Jake set his cup down. "Excuse me. I'm getting in the way." He pointed to the small kitchen table. Why was he suddenly nervous? "I… I'll just sit over here and wait."

"It only takes a minute. These instant coffee makers are the greatest thing since microwaves." Her voice sounded a little shaken.

Awkward. We'd been the best of friends. Why am I so uncomfortable?

Best change the subject. "Where are your friends? I haven't seen them."

"Evans is keeping an eye out from the back entrance where it's dark. Smothers will roam from room to room to monitor the windows and listen for unusual noises." She placed two cups of hot coffee on the table and sat down.

Jake took a quick sip from his cup. "What's the plan?" He tapped the table with his finger and tried to focus on the situation at hand and not on his beautiful, brown-eyed bodyguard or partner or whatever she was. He must reel in his admiration of her. She was a smart lady. She'd figure it out if she hadn't already.

She held her coffee with both hands and placed her elbows on the table. "As long as we have an uneventful night, I'm working on a safe and more comfortable place for you and Emma to stay until this case is resolved and your house is repaired."

"And where might that be?" Jake studied her. Where would be safer than the safe house? "This place is nice enough."

"I know. We've worked hard to keep it a secret, but one never knows—"

A loud noise sounded at the back door.

Jake darted out of the chair and faced the door. Daria jumped to her feet with her weapon drawn, and Smothers stood in the middle of the room in a ready stance with his weapon in hand.

Chapter 8

Daria edged to the mudroom door. Her hand slowly turned the knob to the small entrance door where Evans held up. The uncertain sound of scuffling had her ready for the intruder. Smothers moved closer and tried to get Jake to back off. Jake backed to the opposite side from her, took her hand from the doorknob and motioned he would open the door on the count of three. She and Smothers could surprise whoever had overtaken the officer. Her rapid pulse sent adrenaline racing through her body.

She exchanged glances with her coworker and nodded her head in agreement. Jake held up three fingers, then counted down. Three, two, one. He jerked the door open. Daria aimed her weapon, lowered it and burst out laughing. Smothers relaxed his stance and laughed. Daria turned her focus on Jake, laughing. His laughter hadn't changed. She liked the sound of it.

Evans, who was supposed to watch the rear entrance, had knocked over a box of cleaning supplies and a mixture of cleaning liquids had spilled on the floor, making the floor slippery. His foot slipped every time he moved, and it sounded like a fight going on.

"Now that I've entertained everyone, somebody help me up," Evans said. "I don't think anyone will come through here tonight."

Jake reached his muscular arm out and, with one quick tug, Evans almost flew through the kitchen. He kicked off his shoes and turned to Jake.

"Remind me not to make you angry." Evans brushed at his soaked pants. "At least it smells good."

Daria sat back down in her chair, still chuckling, and picked up her coffee. "I've got to hand it to you, Evans. You sure know how to entertain."

"I'd say he successfully tested our reflexes." Jake scooted his chair back in place and slurped his coffee.

"Good thing he'd brought a change of clothes." Daria shook her head and held back more laughter. Of all the unexpected occurrences during a serious situation, this one ranked at the top. Evans picked up a small bag from the corner of the room and disappeared into the bathroom.

Smothers grabbed himself a cup of coffee and returned to his post roaming the house, keeping watch. Evans emerged from the bathroom in a slightly wrinkled uniform. He tossed a few towels on the mudroom floor from the entrance to the kitchen doorway. He picked up the strewn bottles and glass cleaners, then threw another towel down and closed the door.

"That was one of the funniest bloopers I've ever seen a police officer do." Jake's smile covered his face. A real smile, like old times.

"I'm sure he's embarrassed. He's not one who goofs around." Daria yawned. "Want to move to the living room and enjoy the fireplace?"

"Thought you'd never ask." Jake took his coffee with him. "I've been eyeing the recliner since we walked in the door."

Daria curled her legs up under her on the sofa. Its softness consoled her weary body. "So, why didn't you write me or call after your family moved away?"

Jake's jaw dropped. "Did you seriously expect a middle schooler to communicate? I never liked reading until I was in high school, and my writing wasn't legible. Still isn't."

"I guess not." She pulled the gray blanket off the back of the sofa and covered her legs. "I thought about you a lot after you left. I wrote to you, but I'm not sure I had the correct address. Do you plan to stay in Kimbleton, or will you sell your sister's house and move away?"

Jake pulled the footrest up on the recliner and leaned back almost flat. "Kimbleton is home to Emma and me. Besides, my parents are here. I want to be close to my family."

"Good. I'm glad you're back." She turned sideways on the sofa, still sitting up, and rested her head on the soft fabric. "Maybe we can walk the mountain trails together once this case is closed."

A snore met her ears. He hadn't heard her. Just as well. She tossed the blanket off and went to check on Emma. Amazingly, she'd slept through all the commotion. She'd rolled over onto her tummy and pulled her arms and legs up under her. Poor baby. She needed a good night's sleep. Daria readjusted her blanket and tucked it snug around her little body. She'd always loved children, but Emma held a special place in her heart.

Daria tiptoed around the house to check in with Smothers and Evans before she returned to the sofa. She spotted Evans on his phone.

"Love you, too." Evans slid his cell into his pocket. "Had to check on Karla, you know, my wife. She hasn't been feeling well. A bug, I guess."

"I hope she gets to feeling better. Is everything okay back here?"

"Quiet for now." Evans turned back and checked the window.

Daria returned to the living room where light snores continued at a steady pace from her tough marine. Her marine? She liked the sound of calling him hers.

"You need to quit roaming and get some rest while you can. That shoulder of yours needs a break." Jake's unexpected comment caused her to jump.

"I thought you were asleep. You were snoring." She settled back into her relaxed position.

"It's a gift, I guess, after being on active duty." Jake never opened his eyes. "I sleep, but I'm aware of what's going on around me. Thanks for checking in on Emma."

Daria stared at Jake lying there relaxed and half asleep. It was a blessing that he knew her whereabouts, but a little strange. She yawned and laid her head back.

"You're welcome." Her words slid out in a whisper. She closed her eyes, allowing herself to sink into the soft cushion and sleep.

A shot fired. Jake and Daria jumped to their feet. Smothers ran into the living room from one direction with his weapon still holstered and Evans ran in from the back with his weapon drawn.

"It's okay. Some guy just shot a deer. I saw him in his orange vest and rifle in the distance." Smothers backed away. "Get some more rest if you can. The sun is just on the horizon."

Emma whined.

"She's probably wet and hungry." Daria pulled out a diaper from Emma's bag. "We're going to have to get more diapers soon. There are only two more. She needs milk, too, not just juice." Daria held the fresh diaper in the air. "Do you want to do the honors, or do you want me to?"

Jake's grin said it all. "I'll let you do it. I know you like babies." He sat back down in the recliner.

"I figured you'd say that." She grabbed Emma a change of clothes, too.

Emma sat up in the porta crib, rubbing her eyes. She stretched her arms out to Daria. *Precious*. Most babies just waking up are ready to be cuddled. She'd soaked through her clothes. Daria placed her on the nearby bed and handed her the nearly empty sippy cup until she could get her changed.

She pooched her lips out and shook her empty cup. Full-blown cries filled the house. Jake appeared at the bedroom door in a flash. Daria picked her up and handed her to Jake.

"What's wrong with her?" Jake's wide eyes and confused look tickled her as he followed her through the house. "What do I do? I haven't heard her cry like this before."

"And it won't be the last time." Daria went into the kitchen in search of some milk. "She's hungry and her cup is empty."

"Oh, is that all?" He sat at the table, holding Emma. She screamed louder and stiffened. "Are you sure she's not hurting?"

Daria searched for milk but couldn't find anything except for the coffee creamer. "Looks like she'll have to have this coffee creamer. We don't have milk. Good thing you like your coffee black."

She poured the creamer into the sippy cup,

all the while Emma fought with Jake, reaching her hands out for her cup. Daria tightened the lid and handed the cup to her. She leaned back on Jake's chest, satisfied.

Jake's eyebrows lifted. "I don't act like that when I'm hungry."

"I sure hope not." Daria grinned and shook her head. Jake had a lot to learn about taking care of a baby. However, she admired how gentle this tough marine was with Emma. It only showed he had a soft side to his rough exterior.

Evans and Smothers entered the kitchen.

"Looks like a hunters club has arrived. They've gathered in the woods behind the house," Evans said. "At least, I hope that's where they're from. But I don't like it. There's too many to monitor."

Smothers spoke up. "Same here. I saw them walking around to the back of the house. Could be harmless, but I'd suggest we pack up and leave for safety's sake."

"I don't have anything to pack up except for a diaper bag." Jake held Emma close. "Well, maybe putting on her coat and wrapping her in the blanket."

"You take care of her." Daria went toward the bedroom. "I'll get her things and grab my bag."

An unsettled feeling knotted in Daria's stomach. Were they hunters or did they have a part in the illegal activity in town? Would they surround the house? Surely, they wouldn't harm Emma.

She stuffed everything in the diaper bag, including the little giraffe. Daria paused in the living room and put on her coat before helping Jake put Emma's coat on her. Emma wouldn't let go of her cup. Jake pulled it from her hand, and she let out a squeal. He handed it back after getting her coat on. He handed her off to Daria and put his coat on, then took her back into his arms.

"Is it always like this when she's hungry?" Jake wrapped the blanket around her.

"Not always. But you must realize, she's only had one decent meal. Didn't you put a small box of dry cereal in that zipped side pocket yesterday? Give that to her. Maybe it will suffice for a bit. She was definitely hungry. Enough so that she didn't balk over coffee creamer."

Smothers paused at the mudroom door. "Are you ready? Let's make this quick. Evans will go out before you. Cramer and McDaniel are at the edge of the woods to help cover you in case something goes wrong."

The old racing pulse hit Daria instantly. Why were these hunters right here, right now?

Jake and Daria didn't waste any time getting into their car. Daria started the car and backed out as fast as she could, planning on a fast getaway. Four hunters aimed their rifles toward her vehicle.

Smothers, Cramer and McDaniel engaged in gunfire, turning the men's attention to them so Daria could get away. A bullet pinged her door before she could drive off.

Her car slid on the ice.

"Go, go…" Jake sat sideways with one hand on the dash and one hand on the back of the seat. Emma wasn't bothered by the shots. Her cereal and sippy cup had her occupied.

"I've got it." Daria straightened and maintained control of the vehicle.

An unmarked car pulled beside them, blocking them from the shooters. Evans threw up his hand and pointed forward. Wherever he'd parked, he'd shielded them in record time. Jake decided Evans had redeemed himself from his slippery fall in the entryway.

Daria slowed when she reached the main part of town. She merged into the morning tourist traffic. Lines of cars overflowed into the street as people waited their turn in the diner's drive-through.

Jake took in a deep sniff. "Mmm, gotta love the smell of bacon."

"It's coming from the mom-and-pop place on the left." She pulled into the other lane and passed a slow driver. "We can't risk it."

"Don't tell me," Jake said. "Are we going back to the station where it's *safe*?" He made quotation marks with his fingers. "We could go back to my house. I know how to barricade us in and watch for the enemy."

Daria huffed. "Jake…"

"I know, I know. I'm not in Afghanistan anymore. But it would work. Prepare and draw them in." He found himself amused at harassing her with his antics about the war. He liked the way her nose curled up at his humorous thoughts.

"I'm meeting with Jeffers to discuss an alternative plan. Julia, our administrative assistant, has already called for a full breakfast delivery to the station." Daria stopped at a red light.

"Now, that's what I'm talking about. Prompt service." Jake tapped the armrest with his fingers. He tensed, sitting in the heavy traffic with unknowns all around them.

He zeroed in on different cars and studied their behavior. Emma sat glassy-eyed with her head leaned against the headrest of her car seat, her hand still looped around the handle of her sippy cup, remnants of cereal sprinkled on her coat and a streak of escaped coffee creamer at the side of her mouth. If only Amanda could see her now. If only he could see his sister right now.

Daria turned on a side road and then into the back parking lot of the department. She glanced over and smiled at him.

"In case you haven't figured it out, we will change vehicles again when we leave." She stopped at the back entrance. "Let's go inside. One of the guys will change out the cars and install her car seat."

Jake stepped out and made sure his feet wouldn't slip on the frozen pavement before he unbuckled Emma. She came to life and started kicking, reaching her arms out to him. Amazing the rush of warmth that overtook him, knowing Emma wanted him. He pulled her out and held her close. Her arms wrapped around his neck with her sippy cup dangling by two fingers.

"Bite," she said.

"In a minute. Food is waiting for us." Jake spoke into her ear. Her little curls tickled his nose. "You just had cereal. Are you still hungry?"

Once again, the well-heated station was a pleasant relief from the freezing temperatures outside. Since he'd been there several times, he knew the way to the conference room, so he didn't wait for Daria to give him instructions.

"Where are you going?" Daria shut the door and made sure the automatic lock clicked closed.

"To the conference room. Where else?"

She pointed to a different hallway. "We're going this way where there are no windows."

"Because?"

"To cut down on visibility and glass."

"And random shootings. Got it." Jake lifted his eyebrows and stepped into a smaller room with a table and four chairs. Nothing like the well-decorated conference room. The aroma of bacon hit his nostrils. He smiled and winked at Daria. "Somebody knows how to order a breakfast." A small coffee maker with different flavors of coffee pods sat on a built-in shelf.

Emma's plate was obvious by its flower shape and divided compartments. It looked rather festive with all the food placed in sections. It contained a cup of strawberries, small pieces of toast, pieces of cheese and more dry cereal. He spotted two half-pints of milk nearby.

The three of them enjoyed their bountiful breakfast and had a moment to relax after their harrowing morning. Jake sighed. Everyone was alive and well, and that's what counted.

"I'll be back in a few minutes." Daria opened the door and paused. "I've got to meet with Jeffers." She spun and closed the door behind her.

Jake picked at the remains of breakfast. He could've devoured a whole pound of crispy bacon, but the four pieces he'd had served their purpose and were delicious. Emma took bites of her strawberries. She played with some and smeared them on the table like painting a picture.

He recounted all the near-death misses he'd encountered since arriving in town. None of his marine buddies would believe he was battling an enemy in the US. He couldn't believe it himself. All he wanted was a quiet life with his little niece and maybe Daria if she'd have him.

Emma pointed to a group picture of police officers on the wall. "Da-da."

"I don't think that's your daddy." He studied the picture and noted Daria standing in the middle. She'd made a name for herself, and he was certain this case would earn her the respect she was due.

Daria stepped back into the room. She popped another pod into the coffee maker. "I met with Jeffers. He said officers caught Gregory Hall trying to leave town." Her coffee finished, she pulled out the chair and sat down. "First, Gregory said he was going on a trip for the holidays. Then, he changed his story and said his life was in danger."

Jake joined her with a fresh cup of the hot brew. "Sounds like he's hiding something. Why would anyone want him dead if he's calling the shots? All the coded records were on his computer."

"That's just it. He insisted we don't know who we're dealing with." She took a drink. "Honestly, that's the truth. We *don't* know who we're dealing with. If it's not bank staff, what are we missing?"

His gut churned. Who was playing games with them? Taunting them everywhere they went. Could it be an inside job? He'd only just arrived in town a couple of days ago.

Daria reached over and lightly squeezed Jake's arm. "I've lined up a place for you and Emma to stay. It's the safest place I know outside of the police station."

Jake lifted his eyes to her. "And where might that be since nowhere else seems to fit the bill?"

She smiled that familiar caring smile. "My brother's house. Robert is an investigator with the department now. I'm sure you remember him. He has a garage apartment that he rents out to vacationers, and right now there's no one staying there. You and Emma are welcome to stay as long as you like. He's looking forward to catching up on old times."

"What if trouble finds us? Won't we be putting him in danger?" Jake hesitated. He didn't want to involve anyone else and risk someone dying in his place.

"No. Trust me. He's already making plans for your arrival."

"Who am I to argue? Emma and I will do as you say." *As long as I agree.* Jake pushed to his feet. "Let's go. I'm ready to see another one of my old friends."

"Okay, give me a minute. I've got to make

sure the car is ready and we're clear to leave." Daria took the last drink of her coffee and dropped the disposable cup in the trash. She left the room again.

Jake gathered the trash from their breakfast delivery and tossed most of it in the small trash can. He found a napkin and wiped Emma's hands and mouth. "A wet rag would be better, but this will have to do."

He set her on the floor and watched her toddle around the room. She slapped the chair's cushion and jabbered indecipherable words. So strange for him to tower over this little human and for her to walk with such short legs. Jake admired her cuteness. She made her way around the table and back to him. Her arms draped around his leg. He reached down, picked her up and kissed her rosy cheeks, then ruffled her hair.

"You are too cute for your own good. But you probably know that. My guess is your mama told you multiple times a day." He glanced at the clock, then back at Emma. "If Daria doesn't return soon, it will be time to eat again."

The door flew open. "Okay, we're all set." She put her coat on.

Jake did the same and bundled Emma up.

"Hold on." He filled both of her sippy cups with the half-pints of milk. "Should've done that before now, but she had her juice." He smiled at Daria and walked out with Emma in his arms.

It hadn't warmed up much during their breakfast, but with the bright sun beaming down, Jake knew some of the ice would melt on the roads, especially with the added tourist traffic. The drive to her brother's house wouldn't be so treacherous. They got into the car and drove away.

"Is your brother married?" Jake enjoyed the drive through his old mountain home place. People were out hanging tinsel and Christmas decor along the main part of town.

"Yes. He married Gina, but you may not know her. She moved into town the same summer you moved away. They have two children. A boy, Isaac, eight years old, and a girl, Alexa, six."

Her cheerful tone had him almost forgetting they were still on the hit list from an unknown enemy. His nerves were a bit on edge. He must keep his eyes open, his marine intelligence intact and be ready for anything.

Chapter 9

Daria relaxed the moment she pulled into Robert and Gina's driveway. Home away from home and filled with love. The moment they stepped out of the car, Alexa and Isaac met them. They'd been sliding in the snow and had already heard a baby was moving into the garage apartment. They were excited to see her, especially Alexa. She jumped up and down and clapped her gloved hands.

Robert opened the front door and greeted Jake with a handshake. "Hey, man, it's great to see you after all these years. Come on in. Gina has lunch ready. She even had me get the high chair out of the attic for Emma."

Daria made her way into the kitchen where Gina was pouring fresh glasses of iced tea. "We're here. I have someone I want you to meet. Well, two someones." She laughed. "This is the Jake Fisher you've already heard about. And this little doll is Emma."

Gina held her hands out to Emma. She willingly fell into Gina's arms, who turned and put her in the high chair with all kinds of snacks on the tray. Emma squealed and picked at her food.

Everyone sat at the table and talked about old times over a delicious pot roast lunch with all the fixings. Despite all the noise and conversation going on between Jake and Robert, Emma fell asleep. Daria's eyes rolled as weariness caught up with her.

Gina placed her hand on Daria's arm. "These guys can talk for hours. You look exhausted. Why don't you go catch a nap on the couch? I'll take care of Emma."

Daria excused herself and moved to the living room. Her body seemed to understand it was going to rest in a safe place. The minute her head touched the cushion, everything went silent.

Laughter from the distance bolted her to her feet. She'd slept too long. The setting sun made the twinkling lights on Robert's Christmas tree dance brighter, and the fragrance of his fresh tree reminded her it was the season she loved so much.

Daria followed the voices to the dim sun-room. Emma sat content in Jake's lap. Robert and Gina sat on the sofa facing a foot of freshly fallen snow. The entire scene was a peaceful, heartwarming sight.

"I didn't mean to sleep this late. My apologies." Daria entered the room. "Have you shown Jake the garage apartment?"

"No. Thought we'd let you do the honors," Robert said. "By the way, Jake, I figured you'd be about my size, so I set out some clean clothes for you. Hope they fit."

Jake stood, holding Emma. "I've enjoyed catching up, and I appreciate having a place to stay." He faced Daria. "Okay, show me my quarters." He placed his hand on her back.

She drew in a breath at his touch. "Sure, but everyone still needs to put on their coats."

In a matter of minutes, Daria unlocked the garage apartment. He roamed around, checking things out. Daria went into the spare room and turned down the cover on the toddler bed. She took drowsy Emma from Jake, changed her clothes and laid her in bed with a soft stuffed teddy bear and her sippy cup, then covered her up.

Emma shuffled her legs but didn't offer to get

up. Daria turned to leave the room. Jake stood in the doorway, watching her. He walked over and kissed Emma's head. Little hands lifted and touched his cheeks, and she lifted her head and kissed him on the nose.

Daria's heart melted at the precious moment she'd just witnessed. She backed away and waited for Jake in the living room. He stepped out and pulled Emma's door almost closed.

"She kissed me. Can you believe it?" Jake's eyes widened. "I hope to make my sister proud."

"You are already. Now you need to get some rest. I'll see you in the morning." She zipped her coat. "Jeffers told me to take a few days off to let my shoulder heal. Maybe we can all get some much-needed rest."

She walked to the front door and reached for the doorknob, then turned back. "Good night, Jake." His eyes captured hers. Was she reading his expression correctly?

He stepped closer. "Do you think we can renew our friendship?"

"I think after the past couple of days, we already have." Was he thinking what she was thinking? She needed to hear him say it.

"What I mean is, can we renew our friendship and see where it leads?" He shuffled his stance. "I realize we've only just reconnected, but it seems like yesterday we were racing across the playground toward the swings."

Robert stepped out on the side porch. The door slammed behind him and the noise disturbed their conversation. Robert walked over to his truck.

Daria looked back at Jake. "Get some rest, Jake. Robert will stand guard tonight. We'll talk tomorrow." She walked away before she made a hasty decision. He needed to sleep on it and see if he still felt the same in the morning. She didn't want the turbulence of their day and the emotions involved to sway his thinking or hers. But they were both protectors and made a great team in her eyes.

She got in her car and waved as she drove away. Home was calling her name. Robert and Gina wanted her to stay the night, but she longed for the comforts of home. Her whole routine had turned into a nightmare. The sun had set and the evening hours dropped the temperature below freezing. The slick roads made travel treacherous, but she made it home.

In a matter of minutes, she'd prepared for bed, then crawled in and pulled the covers to her chin. Thoughts of the past two days rolled through her head. Relieved Jake and Emma were safe at her brother's, she could get some undisturbed rest and continue her investigation tomorrow. If only her mind would shut down.

Had the threatening text she'd received come from the unknown ringleader? The bank president seemed to fit the position, but evidently there was someone higher pulling the strings.

Every time she closed her eyes, Jake's dark brown eyes stared back at her. The seriousness of his gaze mesmerized her. Made her feel like a kid again. Concern about the case had her stumped.

A creak in her kitchen popped her eyes wide open. She slid out of bed, paused and listened. Someone was in her house. She secured her weapon and eased out of her bedroom and into the hallway. The intruder's steps drew closer while the lights of her Christmas tree in the living room formed a silhouette on the wall of a person inching her way. She readied her stance with weapon in hand and flipped the light switch on. Nothing happened.

God, help me.

The figure moved closer. She sensed him close but couldn't see in the darkness. A hard object hit her head. She dropped to the floor, lying partly on her weapon. Her ears rang relentlessly. Pain shot through her sore shoulder and head. Footsteps, two sets, scrambled around her. One of the intruders flipped her over on top of her weapon. They must not have seen it. Would they finish her? She barely opened her eyes and struggled not to grimace as the ache in her shoulder intensified. From what she could tell in the dark, they both wore ski masks.

"We proved our point," a deep voice said. "Should we take her out?"

"No. We were instructed to scare her. Probably knocked her out. Next time she dies," the other man said. The smooth tone in his voice sounded familiar.

They rushed away. The front door slammed shut.

Were they gone or were they coming back? *Who were they?*

She fumbled under her hip for her pistol, then pushed to her feet, falling against the wall. Her staggering feet made it difficult to move fast. She made it back to her bedroom, grabbed her cell and fell across her bed as she punched in 911. All went silent.

The distant sound of voices invaded the ringing in her ears and caused her to stir. Someone called her name. Help had arrived.

"Daria, where are you?" Footsteps rushed through her house and into her bedroom, with flashlights searching the room. "Here she is."

Her head throbbed. The police had arrived, and she was safe. Tears escaped.

McDaniel leaned over her. "Are you okay? Who did this?" He turned away. "Get the paramedic in here, stat."

She moaned, then pushed slowly to a sitting position and thought her head would explode. Two paramedics came in with their equipment and a gurney. They had her lie back. She swayed. Strong hands helped her lie down.

"Evans, call her brother, Robert. You've got his number, don't you?" McDaniel said.

"Got it." Evans's voice faded as he left the room.

Daria squinted at everyone surrounding her, holding flashlights. Were there really that many people in front of her, or was she seeing double? She was coherent, but everyone seemed far away. "I… I'm gonna be sick." The room spun.

"Here, take this." A paramedic handed her a bag, just in case.

More strong arms picked her up and placed

her on the gurney, covering her with a blanket. Cold air hit her face, increasing the strength of the headache. They loaded her into the ambulance. Once at the hospital, another familiar face looked down at her. The same doctor she'd seen earlier. He checked her eyes and felt around on her head, then ordered a CT scan.

"Can you tell me what happened?" the doctor asked.

McDaniel stood at the corner of the room with his lips drawn tight.

She explained the shadow she'd seen before the lights went out. She'd only seen one shadow but heard two sets of feet shuffle around her. They wore ski masks. There was no way to make a positive ID.

The technician came in and wheeled her to radiology, then returned her to her room in the emergency department. It didn't surprise Daria when he told her she had a concussion and needed to rest for a few days, and she still needed to take it easy on that shoulder. She'd already planned on resting, but not under doctor's orders after being assaulted in her own home.

The door to her ER room opened and Robert ran in, glanced at her and turned to Mc-

Daniel. "What happened? I got here as soon as I could."

Jake stepped past Robert. She reached her hand out to him. He rushed to her side and took her hand, then put his other hand tenderly against her cheek. "I'm so glad you're okay. We'll find out who did this."

It was all Jake could do to maintain control of his anger. If anyone had an anger problem, it was him. And if he could get his hands on whoever attacked her, well, it wouldn't be nice. Standing there looking at her, he realized his feelings were more than friendship. If anything had happened to her, it would have devastated him.

After the doctor discharged her from the hospital, Robert and Jake helped her into Robert's truck. Jake put his arm around her so she could lean on him. Why was someone after her? Was it to keep her from protecting him and Emma? The flash drives were in police hands, as were the two shooters. Whoever broke into her home must know that by now. So, was there something else these intruders were looking for?

They pulled into Robert's driveway. Gina

flipped the front porch light on and opened the door.

"Is she okay? I've got the guest room ready for her." Gina stepped out into the cold and held the door open for them.

Jake picked Daria up. She wrapped her arms around his neck and leaned her head against his chest. His emotions soared. He placed her on the bed in the guest room. Gina stepped beside him, as did Robert.

Daria blinked and looked up at them. "Hey, I'm okay. Just have a monster headache. Thank you for everything."

"The doctor said you need to rest and limit activities for a few days." Jake searched her face. She'd been through a traumatic ordeal.

"I'll be okay. You guys don't need to look so worried." She placed her hand over her eyes. "Could you turn the light off? It hurts my eyes."

"Okay." Jake kissed her hand. "If you need anything, just say so." He stepped back while Gina covered her up.

Everyone left the room. Jake paused in the doorway. Should he sit in the corner chair in case she needed something during the night? Was it safe to leave her there alone?

"Jake," Robert called out to him. "Come on, man. She'll be okay and she's safe here, as are you and Emma."

Jake closed her door and had to pull himself away. Out of all the situations he'd been through overseas and in the US, he felt the tug, like a magnet, to protect her. He went into the kitchen, where it seemed everyone always gathered. Robert sat at the table with a glass of water.

"It's after 1:00 a.m. We all need to go to bed and get some rest." Robert took a gulp of his drink. "I want to talk to Daria and see what she remembers, but I'll wait until morning." He downed the rest of his water and stood. "I'm calling it a night. We will find who did this."

"Good night." Jake pondered his next move. Should he go to his garage apartment or sit in the hall at Daria's door? Emma slept soundly in Robert and Gina's master bedroom, so he didn't have to worry about her.

The house fell quiet while Jake struggled with leaving the house. He went into the living room and sat on the sofa. Sleep evaded him. His brain wouldn't shut down after almost losing Daria. He sat there for what seemed like hours before easing down the hallway and sitting on the floor by her door. He laid his head back against the wall and relaxed. That was it. He needed to be closer to her.

He'd only just closed his eyes when a nudge from a boot moved his leg. Jake jumped to his feet. "What's wrong?" He blinked to clear his vision after being in a deep sleep.

"Nothing's wrong," Robert said. "Half the morning's gone. Thought you might want some coffee to get you going."

Jake looked back at Daria's door, then joined Robert in the kitchen where Emma sat in the high chair with milk around her mouth and her hands in oatmeal. Gina stood over the stove frying bacon. It smelled wonderful. He spotted their two children out in the backyard building a snowman.

"Why didn't you wake me sooner?" Jake rubbed his eyes.

"You were out of it, and you needed the rest or whatever rest you get by sitting on the floor," Robert chuckled. "We understood, though. It's no secret how you feel about her. We've noticed the way you two look at each other."

A noise down the hall caught Jake's attention. He almost knocked the chair over, jumping up to check on Daria. She'd emerged from her room. He eased up, kissed her on the forehead and wrapped his arms around her. He could hold her forever.

She reciprocated his hug, then pushed away. "Where is everyone?" Her soft tone alerted him that her head still hurt.

"In the kitchen. I don't have to tell you Gina's cooking bacon. You can smell it all over the house." He took her hand and walked with her down the hall. "How are you this morning?"

"My head still hurts, but I'm okay. The ache in my shoulder has subsided." Her slow movement showed differently. She dropped his hand as they joined her family at the table.

Gina rushed to her side and hugged her. "Good morning. I fixed your coffee. I'm so sorry about last night. So horrifying."

Robert sat back in his chair, eyeing her. Jake could tell the wheels were turning in Robert's mind and he was giving Daria time to wake up. Gina set some biscuits on the table.

"Eat up, everyone. I've already fed the kids and sent them out to play to keep the noise down for Daria." Gina joined them at the table. She bowed her head. "Dear God, thank You for this food we are about to receive. Continue to heal Daria and keep everyone safe. Amen."

Robert cleared his throat. Jake wondered when he'd chime in and start questioning Daria. "Sis, do you remember any other details about last night's intruders?"

"There were no real details." Daria straightened her shoulders. "There was a noise in the kitchen, the Christmas lights were on, a single silhouette cast on the wall, but for only a second before the house went dark. I eased down my hall and someone knocked me over the head. I wasn't unconscious, but they thought I was. He rolled me over, and suddenly I was aware of two people stomping through my house, then out the front door. That's it."

"Have you had any encounters with anyone lately that would cause them to come after you?" Robert took a quick slurp of his coffee and set the cup down.

Jake spoke up. "Since I arrived in town, there's been nothing but attacks on Emma, Daria and me. Mainly me. I suppose they are after Daria now, since she's been assigned protective duty over us."

"None that I'm aware of, Robert." Daria bit off a piece of bacon, irritated with the way Jake answered for her. "Some of the guys at the station have been giving me a hard time over that arrest I did a while back. They all call me a hothead, but they wouldn't do anything this drastic."

"So there's no one who stands out as particularly suspicious?" Robert continued. "I know your head hurts, but I need you to think."

Jake sat at the edge of his seat over Robert's questioning. If he had something to say, Jake wanted to hear it. "What is it you're getting at, Robert? Spit it out."

Daria placed her fork on the table and turned her eyes on her brother. "What are you trying to tell us?"

Robert leaned back, looked around and drew in a deep breath. His hesitance to speak increased the tension in the room. Jake shifted his eyes from Daria, to Robert, to Gina, and back to Robert.

"I've been an investigator for the department for eight years now, and I've never encountered a situation like we have now. Regarding your case with the embezzlement and the flash drives, I'm highly suspicious we have a leak in the department. Apparently, all these continuous attacks are because of another piece of evidence that came up missing from the bank, specifically Gregory Hall's office."

Robert placed his hand on Daria's shoulder. She winced. "You guys need to watch your backs and be cautious."

Daria shrugged her shoulder out from under Robert's hand. She placed her elbows on the table and leaned her head in her hands. "I don't get it. We turned in all the flash drives." She turned her head toward Jake. Her weak eyes stared into his eyes. "What piece of evidence are we missing? Another flash drive? What?"

Jake lifted his hands and shook his head. "I have no clue. I've been gone for years. I don't know what belongs to Tom and Amanda and what doesn't. We can search the house again if you want."

"Yes. We need to do that." Daria scooted from the table.

Gina touched her arm. "Honey, you've been through enough. You need to rest like the doctor ordered."

"Killers don't rest, Gina." Daria stood. "They won't stop until they've completed their job. I'll be fine after I take a couple of those over-the-counter pain relievers."

"First things first. Daria, I know how determined you are. If you insist on pressing forward in your condition, Jake will have to watch after you." Robert tossed his truck keys on the table. "Jake, you can drive my truck and take Daria to the station so she can file her report. Gina said she'd be happy to watch Emma while you're gone."

Jake picked up the keys and stood. "I've learned in the past few days that when she sets her mind on something, there's no changing it."

"You learn fast." Robert slapped Jake on the back.

"I'm going to the apartment to clean up while Daria gets ready. Thank you for a delicious breakfast and for all of your hospitality." He exited the house and went to his temporary quarters.

Had Amanda hidden more evidence? Was it even her at all? Had someone else caught on to what his sister had involved herself in and become greedy, trying to blackmail bank staff? Would he know the item if he saw it?

Chapter 10

Daria made her way to the shower after Gina gave her two pain relievers. She closed her eyes while the hot water beat against her shoulders. A flash of a man's dress shoe near her head popped up so vividly she let out a quick scream. She couldn't tell what color the shoe was, but the shape of it she'd seen before, somewhere.

Her headache calmed down some. She finished her shower and dressed, then went to go talk to Robert. He was her brother, after all, and they worked for the same police department. Gina pointed her toward his home office. Daria knocked as she entered.

"Hey, do you have a minute?" She sat in the chair in front of his desk.

"Sure. What's up?" He leaned back in his leather desk chair and crossed his legs. "Did you remember something?"

"How'd you know?"

"It's not unusual for victims to remember more details after a few hours or even a few days." He smiled at her. "What have you got?"

She explained being in the shower and the flash popping into her head. "I've seen that style of shoe before, but I can't remember who wears them."

"That's good. While you're out today, not following doctor's orders, pay attention to people's shoes. Especially people you know. Maybe something will click."

She stood and walked to his doorway. "I will. See you soon."

"Take care of my truck." Robert's voice echoed down the hall.

Jake met her in the living room, tossing the keys in the air and catching them. He looked handsome in Robert's black jeans and blue pullover sweater.

"I'm ready." She patted her side. Her pistol sat housed in her holster.

Jake walked her to the passenger side of the truck and opened her door. His hand touched the small of her back, steadying her as she stepped in and buckled up.

"Thanks." Daria rubbed her forehead.

God, thank You for sparing my life.

Jake slid into the driver's side and gripped the steering wheel, obviously admiring Robert's truck. "Now, this is what I'm talking about. A real truck."

They backed out of the driveway and eased down the partially thawed road. The sun had melted spots here and there. Jake appeared in deep thought.

"Something on your mind?" She put on sunglasses. The bright sun bouncing off the crystalline snow felt like a spotlight in her eyes, increasing the dull headache.

"When I heard someone assaulted you, my heart stopped. I had to get to you and make sure you were okay. I haven't had the best attitude since we reconnected. It's not you. It's me and it's not a cop-out. I've blamed myself for my comrade's death. I was supposed to throw that grenade. My commanding officer approved the change and allowed my friend to toss it instead. He became a casualty of war while I lived to be here today." Jake turned the corner and pulled down his visor. "After all that's happened, I prayed and surrendered those hurts to God. I finally realized the guilt over his death wasn't mine to carry. My friend volunteered and knew the risks. He was a great guy. He gave his all for our country."

"Jake, I don't know what to say other than I'm sorry you and your buddies had to go through that battle and lose friends in the process. God is faithful to take over and help us find peace." She laid her head back on the headrest. "Since this is confession time, I must admit that I could have handled my actions toward that disorderly vacationer differently. My duty was to protect other tourists from his unacceptable behavior in public. Maybe my arrest was a little hasty, but he had become more disruptive and obnoxious."

She stared out of the passenger side window and sighed. "My goal is to prove myself a good cop in control of her temper, find the ones responsible for killing Amanda and Tom and be the best friend a friend can have." Her eyes shifted to Jake.

She may have been off kilter last night after going to the hospital, but she remembered his gentle embrace. "I'm glad to know you surrendered to God because I rededicated my life to Him last night. He's given me a whole new outlook on life, and I don't have to answer to anyone but Him."

Jake stopped at the red light. His silence told her he was deep in thought. Maybe all this confession was too much, but since they'd started, she wanted to finish and be clearheaded.

"Another thing." She rubbed her forehead and placed her hand on the seat beside her. Jake's warm hand covered hers and squeezed lightly, then let go.

"What's that?" His compassionate eyes hit her like an arrow of love to the heart. The light changed again, and they continued their journey down the road and through the last leg of the forest toward the station.

"My career is no longer my passion. I'm looking for something more out of life." Her pulse increased as she held her breath for his response.

He slowed with the traffic, stopped at the light and stared straight ahead. Was he going to respond? Had she put him on the spot? She'd wanted to unload everything while she had the chance.

He shifted and faced her. "I meant what I said in the early hours this morning before the assault. As a scrawny kid, years ago I thought you were the best friend ever. It wasn't until seeing you again that I realized my best friend could be my soulmate." He held her hand in both of his.

Tears escaped, her head pounded and her lip quivered. "I prayed before going to bed last night that you meant what you said. As a kid, I understood the feeling of friendship. Maybe that's why I could date no one around town. No one compared to you."

Jake leaned across the seat and kissed her lightly. She returned the kiss but pushed away and sat back.

"When you moved away, my world caved. I thought I'd lost you forever. Maybe God's working His plan for us now, but I don't want to move too fast. A lot of things have happened through the years, and now you have Emma. You might need—"

"Is Emma a problem?" Jake's lips tightened.

"No, that's not what I meant."

Now what have I done?

Jake continued driving. He turned on the narrow road by the tree-filled park that led to the back of the station. The snow-covered ground was beautiful and could be a romantic drive, but after their serious conversation, he thought Emma was a problem for her. Tension filled the air.

"Jake, let me explain. I was only trying to say…"
Crash!

Daria screamed. Their truck skidded across the icy road. Jake straightened and kept control of the vehicle. "What happened?"

"Someone just rammed into us. Daria, hold on. A gray pickup is gaining speed and headed straight for us." Jake swerved and skidded. The man's pickup slid off the road and hit a dumpster.

Daria pulled her weapon from her holster and hopped out into the snow. Her head spun. She held on to the car door. A man barreled from the driver's side and ran across the street toward the park. Jake took off after him. Daria steadied herself and jogged in the same direction.

The frozen undergrowth cracked with their footsteps. Snow fell in chunks from playground equipment and the icy tree limbs, making the chase more of an obstacle course. Jake tackled the man and they rolled in the snow. Thankful no children were around, she continued her chase and caught up with them about the time Jake flipped him over and pinned him down.

Daria tugged the ski cap off the man's head, revealing his face.

She gasped. "You."

"Do you know him?" Jake looked up at her, then back at the guy.

"Yes. Richard Schneider. He's the vacationer I arrested. The one I told you about." She stepped closer to him. "What are you doing here? You could have killed us."

"That was the goal." He sneered.

"Are you retaliating against me, or are you taking orders from someone?" She clenched her fists.

The nerve of this guy.

He snickered. "You have no clue who you're dealing with."

No, I don't.

"Drop your weapons." A raspy, angry voice sounded behind them.

Daria's muscles knotted. She regretfully dropped her weapon in the snow.

I know that voice. Jeffers? Whatever's going on, God, please protect us.

Jake kept a straight face. He dropped his weapon.

Richard jumped to his feet and grinned. "They hired me to help get rid of you. Looks like I've almost completed my job."

Daria turned around. Her jaw dropped. Just as she thought. "Lieutenant Jeffers, what are you doing here? What's going on?"

"You refused to be removed from this case. So, now you'll be killed in the line of duty," Jeffers said.

The look on his face and the weapon pointed at her didn't make sense. Was he there to help her, or had he really hired Richard to eliminate her? Daria couldn't wrap her mind around what was happening.

He tossed Richard a rope. "Tie them up. Can't use cuffs or authorities might link their disappearance to someone on the force."

More police officers appeared in the distance and crept up behind Jeffers. She chewed her lip. *Don't flinch or this might not end well.*

Jake looked at her. She lightly nodded.

"Don't try anything," Jeffers said. "You forget I know body language, too."

McDaniel's voice shouted from behind the lieutenant. "Jeffers, drop your weapon."

He ignored McDaniel's orders.

"Don't make us take you down." Cramer lifted his weapon at Jeffers.

Daria blinked. Was she dreaming this nightmare? Jeffers, whom she thought was a faithful boss, had betrayed the department and the trust of the town. Had she been both a pawn and a menace in her lieutenant's illegal scheme? She couldn't believe her eyes, and she couldn't get past the regretful look in his eyes.

McDaniel, Evans, Cramer and Smothers, plus several other cops, stood with their weapons in a ready position pointed at their lieutenant.

"Don't make me say it again, Jeffers," McDaniel said. "Drop your weapon."

He dropped his gun and raised his hands in the air. He turned his focus on Jake. "You were supposed to die in that hotel fire."

Jake's face turned red. His knuckles whitened with his clenched fists. Daria gripped his arm to keep him from punching the lieutenant.

Cramer and Evans ran over and grabbed Jeffers. Cramer scooped the pistol up off the ground. Smothers handcuffed Richard and read him his Miranda rights.

McDaniel stepped up beside Daria and handed her a pair of handcuffs. "You can do the honors. Handcuff Jeffers and read him his Miranda rights. The department has been monitoring him for months."

"Why was I not informed of this situation? You mean my life has been in danger and no one thought to warn me?" Heat rose to Daria's cheeks.

"We have evidence that will put him away

for years." McDaniel squared his shoulders and looked her in the eyes. "We've been watching Jeffers since you arrested Richard. His demeaning attitude toward you was unwarranted. We began noticing some inconsistencies in his work ethics, but we couldn't figure out what was going on. Things didn't add up, so we watched and waited. Good thing we were still tracking him, or today could have turned out a lot worse."

"But why not inform me? I thought we were all on the same side." Daria rubbed her temples.

"We are on the same team, but he was on your case too much. Then Jake arrives with information about his sister and the supposedly misfiled complaint of death threats which led to her death. You were too close to Jeffers, and you were feeding him information on your investigation." McDaniels stepped back. "Who do you think alerted your stalker to which hotel you took Jake and Emma to?"

A sense of betrayal washed over Daria. Was she used as a decoy to prove Jeffers a rogue officer? He never seemed the type to betray anyone.

McDaniel pointed to the cuffs in her hand. "Cuff him, unless you want me to. It would save a long court hearing time if we could find that last bit of evidence."

Daria snapped the cuffs closed and shook her head. "What evidence? You have the flash drives."

Cramer and Evans took the lieutenant from Daria and put him in the back of the squad car. A place she figured he'd never been. Anger and confusion fumed within her.

Evans tapped Daria on the shoulder. "For the record, we had suspicions about Jeffers's illegal activity, so we had to play along. And I'm sorry to say part of that playing along meant harassing you about your temper and trying to humiliate you into quitting your job. He knew you were a good cop, and you'd stop at nothing to uncover his wrongdoing if you caught wind of it. You didn't deserve the hazing the department gave you at his orders."

"He was responsible? This boggles my mind. I can't wrap my head around what just happened. What evidence do you have on him?" Daria fought tears at this new revelation.

"We found an unusually large sum of money in his bank account. He insisted it wasn't his, but we both know people don't just drop money in private accounts." Evans let out a huff. "I'd like to believe him, but you know as well as I do that we have to follow protocol. Arresting him is part of it. Besides, he just assaulted you and Jake and was about to eliminate both of you."

"Thank you for clarifying." Daria turned to Jake, who stood beside her. "Now I have a double report to complete, and I'm not sure how to answer all the questions."

He put his arm around her shoulders and walked her back to the truck. Her sore shoulder still ached a little, but not as bad as her concussion.

McDaniel ran toward her. She paused, questioning the serious look on his face.

Something isn't right.

"Daria, I just received word from my confidential informant that this case isn't over. Now that Jeffers is in custody, there's an additional threat stirring. And they're after the rest of the evidence."

Chills raced down her spine. "I still don't know what evidence they mean. And how many people are tied to this crime? I thought we had everyone."

Jake rushed Daria back to the truck, where she'd have a bit of shelter if a shooter was still close by. He slid on the icy road trying to clear the area. Had the person hired a sniper or a stalker? He couldn't take any chances. Daria's safety was of utmost importance.

Daria's nostrils flared. He'd seen that look before. Either she was furious or engulfed in fear. Her fist hit the seat. She was angry.

Jake drove as fast as he could on the slick roads. His tires slipped a few times. He'd get her out of the public eye as soon as possible. The station first, to fill out her report before any detail faded, then to the safety of her brother's home.

She rubbed her forehead.

It had been a while since she'd taken anything for her head. He'd find the medication she needed once they reached their destination. All the movement she'd encountered this morning was not what the doctor ordered.

"Almost there," Jake said. "Need to move quick and get inside."

"In case you've forgotten, I don't move quick right now, but I'll do the best I can." Daria unbuckled her seat belt.

"No worries." Jake's insides went into stealth mode. Get her out of the danger zone, should someone be gunning for her, or for him. "I'll help you."

He rushed to the other side of the truck and helped her steady herself from the fast motion. "Come on. I've got you."

"Let's go to the small conference room where we had breakfast yesterday. I prefer the security it provides." She held her head high. "I'm not going to fall over. It's this relentless throbbing in my head. Makes my stomach queasy."

He walked her inside and sat her in a chair. "Where do I find medicine for your head?"

"Jake, I can get it. I'm not an invalid." She pushed to get up.

He stopped her. "You rest, please. Just tell me where to find it."

"Cramer keeps a bottle of over-the-counter pain reliever on his desk. It's down the hall toward the front of the building. You can't miss it. He likes to fish. You'll see a largemouth bass mounted on the wall of his office."

"Be back in a sec." Jake's pulse worked double time. He walked at a steady but fast pace. His marine training kicked in. Hostiles could be anywhere, and he trusted no one. Especially since Jeffers was involved. How many other officers had gone rogue?

He passed several cubicles where officers sat working. A mounted fish caught his attention off to the side in an actual office.

Cramer must carry clout to have an office like this.

There on the desk was the large bottle Daria described. He scooped up the bottle.

Jake made a loop around all the cubicles and found a kitchen. He looked around, then stepped inside. The refrigerator held soft drinks and the coffeepot sat half-full. He felt the pot. Barely warm. He slipped a couple of soft drinks into his pockets and picked up two bags of potato chips from a large bowl containing multiple single-size snack bags.

Back in the room, Daria sat with her head in her hands. He placed the bottle of pain relievers on the table in front of her.

"Oh, you found it." She poured two tablets into her palm. "Thank you."

"You're welcome." He tossed the chips on the table, retrieved the canned drinks and popped open both cans. "I raided the kitchen. Coffee was cold."

"Thanks. Something salty looks good right now. Maybe it will help calm my stomach, too." Daria placed the two pills in her mouth and took a drink of her soda. "Jake, I need to finish what I was saying before the crash. I love Emma so very much. I'd love to hold her and steal kisses from her every day. I only thought you might want more one-on-one time with her before I enter the picture."

Jake looked up at her. "Don't you get it? You're already in the picture."

Daria sat back, staring at him. "I didn't look at it in that way." She smiled.

He reached over, put his finger under her chin and planted a brief kiss on her lips. "It's all good." He ripped the chips open and handed her the bag. "Where do I find the papers or the report you need to fill out?"

Daria looked up at him and rolled her eyes. "I should have told you when you went to get meds. I can go."

"Humor me. Let me get what you need. You should be at your brother's house resting." He placed his hand on the doorknob. "Now, tell me what to look for?"

She let out a huff and dropped her shoulders. "Fine. My cubicle is straight across from Cramer's office. Grab my iPad off the top of my desk. That's what I use to complete reports."

"You're right, I could've gotten everything

in one fell swoop." He stepped out and closed the door. She was so independent.

I'm the same way, maybe even more so. Determined. The Marine Corps made sure of that.

Her iPad was right where she said it would be. He retrieved it and the power cord.

He spun and turned the corner out of the cubicle. He stopped abruptly. What was that on the floor in Cramer's office? Jake stood tall and checked across the room. No one appeared interested in his presence and no one peeked over the top of their cubicle walls.

He backed up and walked around Cramer's desk. His heart skipped a beat and heat rose into his face. Two of the rubber flash drive toys lay by one of the wheels of his rolling office chair. A small drawer to the left wasn't shut all the way. He pulled it open with his little finger. The entire collection of Emma's flash drives had been tossed inside.

Jake reasoned that he'd been so focused on the pain reliever bottle he hadn't paid attention to what was on the floor.

Best he could tell, it appeared Cramer must have been in a hurry to leave, so he'd tossed them in, two fell out without him knowing, and he'd failed to close the drawer completely.

Was Cramer involved? Why weren't the flash drives in a more secure place?

Jake fumed. He scooped them all up and dropped the two-inch drives in both of his pants pockets, then casually walked back to the small conference room.

Daria's tired eyes searched him as he walked in. "What took so long?"

Jake placed her iPad and cord on the table, then emptied his pockets. The rubber toys toppled onto the table in front of her. "This."

Her jaw dropped. "Jake, where did you get these? They are supposed to be locked away in the evidence room. You can't just take things."

"Cramer's office."

Her eyes widened. Instant tears rolled down her cheeks. "Oh, no. Is he involved, too? He's such a nice guy and a longtime friend. Is he our threat now? Jake, this is too much. Who else is involved?"

"I don't know, but we're getting out of here." Jake stuffed the toys back into his pockets and took her hand. "Let's go."

She picked up her iPad and shoved the cord in her coat pocket. "Get your soda and chips. We don't want to leave evidence that we were here. I know you've been all over the building, but half the time we don't pay attention to who is walking around. At least, not in our small town, where we rarely have trouble."

"Got it." Jake opened the door and escorted Daria to the truck. He hopped in the driver's seat and eased the truck back onto the town's main street. He wasn't naive enough to believe no one saw them, but he didn't have to make it look like they took off in a hurry, or were guilty, per se.

Daria's straight posture let Jake know her thoughts were reeling in what had just happened and probably theorizing the situation. He had to remain alert and watch for hostiles.

"Thoughts?" Jake considered holding her hand, but he didn't want to overwhelm her.

"Cramer is a 'by the book' type of cop." She was silent for a moment. "Doesn't make sense for him to be so careless or sloppy with valuable evidence. I may be wrong, but my gut tells me someone is trying to set him up."

"Makes sense after seeing the toys scattered like that. We still need to be cautious around him until we know for sure." Jake gave in and squeezed her hand, then let go. "But if someone is setting him up, who could it be? Any idea?"

She rubbed her forehead again. "Not at the

moment. I'm thankful the meds are finally kicking in."

"You might process things better if we turned into a drive-through and got something to eat. These chips aren't going to hold us long." His stomach growled.

Daria lifted her eyebrows.

He laughed. "I'm hungry. What do you say?"

"Sure. I wouldn't want a tough marine to go without a meal."

Her playful humor lightened the mood. She felt better.

He drove into the burger joint's parking lot and sat in the drive-through line with other cars. "What would you like?"

"Whatever you're getting."

"Really? Two cheeseburgers with all the fix-ings, fries and a chocolate milkshake?"

"What?" Her head spun. "No. You must be starving. Just get me the junior burger and fries. I have a soda already."

They placed their order and approached the window for their food. Two cars passed by them and parked side by side. One backed in and one pulled in, aligning the driver's windows. Daria's hand slammed against his arm, almost making him drop his shake.

"Look." She slid down in her seat.

Jake placed his shake in the cup holder. He pressed his head back in the headrest's leather and tried to avoid being seen. Cramer and someone wearing a hat and scarf covering half their face. From the distance, it looked as though Cramer's face reddened. Cramer shook his head "no" and pulled away.

Had either of them spotted Daria and him? The other car backed out and drove the wrong way out of the parking lot.

Jake reached over to the serving window and got their food. "What was that all about?"

Chapter 11

Daria's stomach twisted, and it wasn't her concussion causing the discomfort. Why had Cramer met with an unidentified person in a busy place? Maybe he thought the busier the better, and no one would notice. If the situation were different, she may not have given him a second look, but there was too much going on. She and Jake had to keep their eyes open.

"I don't know what's going on. I thought Jeffers was calling the shots, but evidently there's someone else picking up where he left off, unless he wasn't the head of the operation." She bit into her burger and stuffed a fry in her mouth.

"We can eat on the way, but I'm thinking we need to have a serious discussion with your brother. Maybe he has some insight or suspicions, so we can formulate a plan." Jake slurped his milkshake.

"I agree." Daria didn't want to think too

hard. It increased the pounding in her head, which was more due to stress than concussion at this point. "Let's go find Robert. We have his truck, so we know he's working from home today."

Silence ruled inside the vehicle as they finished their fast food. The temperature outside had warmed a little, but Gina had mentioned another cold front coming through later in the day with another foot of snow. Daria couldn't control the weather, but maybe, with the help of Jake and Robert, she could figure things out.

She glanced at Jake. Her heart beat faster. Not only was he handsome, but inside that marine-tough exterior, he was still the guy who loved to have fun, and she had fallen in love with him already. She could hardly wait to be free of this deadly case and see where life with him and Emma would lead.

They turned into her brother's driveway. Undisturbed snow always looked like a fluffy blanket until children scurried around the lawn and built a snowman. One arm was a small stick, the other a branch. She couldn't help but chuckle.

"I'm ready to see Emma, then we'll find my brother." Daria picked up her iPad and opened her door before Jake could make it around the truck. Isaac and Alexa ran out of the front door, excited to show off their snow creation. Gina stood at the glass door, holding Emma.

"Look what we did," Alexa said as she jumped up and down and clapped her glove-covered hands.

"It's beautiful." Daria kissed her cheek.

"I helped do most of it." Isaac stuffed his hands in his coat pockets. "She's not very good at building a snowman."

"I am too." Alexa huffed and propped her hands on her waist.

Daria pulled them close and gave them a big hug. "Both of you did a splendid job of making that snowman look real. Just like Frosty."

"We're going to build another one." Isaac took off running, with Alexa trailing behind.

Daria admired both of the kids' enthusiasm. She stepped onto the porch and went inside while Jake held the door open for her. She leaned toward Gina and kissed Emma on the cheek. Warmth inside the house felt like someone had wrapped her in an electric blanket. She sniffed the air. "Is that spiced cider I smell?"

Gina tilted her head and smiled. "Yes. I remembered how you raved about it the last time

I made it. Thought you might like some after all you've been through."

"You are so thoughtful."

Jake had already tossed his coat aside and taken Emma into his arms. Such a sweet sight. He kissed Emma's neck, and she giggled. His face brightened as admiration and love for her revealed itself. He fluffed her curls. She ducked from under his hand.

He kissed her neck again and faced Daria. "Sorry, I had to get some Uncle Jake lovin' from my girl."

"Don't let me stop you." Daria slid her coat off and placed it on the coatrack by the door. She picked up Jake's coat and hung it up, too. Seeing this tall, muscular marine cuddling with his dainty niece was a postcard-perfect picture. "She missed you."

Gina returned to the living room with two cups of her homemade spiced cider. Emma kicked her legs to get down. Jake placed her on the floor. She toddled over to the security door and slapped the glass, leaving tiny handprints. She giggled and danced in place, watching Isaac and Alexa playing in the snow.

"Thank you." Daria took the cups and handed Jake one. "The best hot cider anytime of the year, but especially on a wintry day." She sniffed and blew at the steaming beverage. "Smells fabulous." She sipped the drink. "Perfect."

Jake followed suit. He smacked his lips and smiled. "Very good. Thank you."

"You're both welcome." Gina motioned to the sofa. "Have a seat and enjoy or join us in the kitchen. Robert is working on his laptop."

"Oh, good." Daria motioned to Jake, who had already relaxed in the living room. "We needed to discuss some business stuff with him. Some crazy things are happening, and we're hoping he can give us insight or direction."

"Well, go right in." Gina wiped her hands on a paper towel. "I need to fold clothes, and I'll let Emma help me. She loves to empty the basket and fill it back up."

"Thank you, again, Gina. You are so thoughtful." Daria walked into the kitchen. "Good afternoon. What are you focused on?" She set her cup on the table and pulled out a chair.

"Hey, man, hope we're not interrupting." Jake sat in the chair beside her.

Robert closed his laptop, leaned back in his

chair and took a drink from his cup. "How are you feeling today after that nasty concussion?"

"The headache has been on and off. Jake has kept me on a pain reliever schedule." She patted Jake's arm. "The department has a problem. I don't know if you've heard about it yet."

Robert's eyebrows lowered and wrinkles appeared on his forehead. "Um, no. I've been working on an Excel spreadsheet all day." He sat up straight. "What's up?"

"First off," Daria said. "Did you know that Lieutenant Jeffers was under surveillance?"

Robert wiped his hand across his mouth. "Why do you ask?"

"Because they arrested him today after holding Jake and me at gunpoint. McDaniel, Evans, Cramer and Smothers, plus a handful of other cops, came up from behind and arrested him. That young vacationer, Richard Schneider, that I arrested a while back was involved with Jeffers. He's in custody, too." Daria opened her iPad. "What can you tell me? Obviously, you know something or your reaction to my question would have been different."

"I'm an investigator with the department, Daria, and there are some things I am not at liberty to share, even with family." Robert sat back and crossed one leg over the other. "I knew there were suspicions of his hands being dirty, but we hadn't gathered enough evidence to make an arrest."

"You could've warned me or told me to watch my back or something." Daria closed her eyes and took in a deep breath. "I worked with him every day. He could have killed me at any time. Honestly, I still can't bring myself to believe he is guilty." She couldn't blame her brother for doing his job. If only she'd had an inkling that Jeffers may have gone rogue.

Jake spoke up. "Kind of like the old saying of being between a rock and a hard place. I've been in those situations while on active duty. Not necessarily by my peers or my comrades, but in some tough places. I get it."

"Now that we know you know about the be-hind-the-scenes stuff," Daria continued, "Jake found those toy flash drives in Cramer's office."

Robert dropped his leg and sat up again. "Cramer? What does he have to do with the case?"

"You tell us." Daria stood and walked to the kitchen window.

"We returned to the station after someone rammed your truck from behind and the whole takedown took place." Jake scooted to the edge of his seat.

"Wait, somebody hit my truck?" Robert jumped to his feet. "How bad is it, and why were you in Cramer's office?"

"Sorry, but yes. The damage isn't too bad. Just a dent in the fender. I went to Cramer's office and got Daria his bottle of over-the-counter pain meds." Jake continued explaining how things went and how he found the toy flash drives.

"Cramer isn't that sloppy. He'd never remove incriminating evidence and toss it around carelessly. Sounds like a setup." Robert plopped down in his chair and crossed his arms.

"That's what we thought. Maybe even Jeffers." Daria chewed on her lip. "On top of that, we pulled through the town's burger joint, and while we were waiting in line at the drive-through, who do you think we spotted?" She went through the whole scenario with Cramer and an unidentified person.

"We eased away, unnoticed, I hope." Jake gulped his drink.

Robert tapped a finger on his lips. "Cramer has an impeccable record. He's by far one of the best cops we've had in years, outside of you, sister." He winked at her.

Daria shook her head. "Don't go there. I know I've messed up plenty of times. You're right, Cramer is trustworthy and an outstanding officer."

"Any idea who the person in the other car was? Male? Female?" Robert asked.

"They made great efforts to conceal their identity." Jake walked over to the stove where the pot of hot cider sat. "Mind if I have another cup?"

"Help yourself." Gina walked in with a stack of kitchen towels and put them in a drawer. "If you need anything, just give me a shout. I'll be in the other room."

Emma toddled behind her. "Ma, ma, ma, ma." Her eyes lit up when she saw Jake. She ran to him with her arms lifted, holding her rubber giraffe.

"She's gotten comfortable with you." Daria reached over and smoothed her fingers across the top of Emma's soft hand. She pulled her chair out and sat back down.

Emma straightened her legs and wanted down again. Jake let her slide off his lap. She went back into the living room with Gina.

"Anything else?" Robert's eyes shifted from Daria to Jake, then back to Daria.

Jake cleared his throat.

"Yes. One minor detail." Daria paused. "Mc-Daniel said a trusted source heard we are still in danger because evidently there is a missing piece of evidence this unknown person wants." She lifted her hands and dropped them to her lap. "What are we overlooking, Robert? Any clue what evidence they want?"

Jake stood and paced. What he thought would be a quiet return to civilization had turned into another fight for his life that involved two innocents. He'd never known his old hometown to have this much mystery behind it.

Daria's cell rang. He spun and faced her. Her phone hadn't rung in two days.

"Hello?" Her eyes went from him to her brother, then back to him. "No way." Her hand covered her eyes and her voice cracked. "How did it happen? Okay. Thanks for calling." She sat staring at her cup.

"Spit it out, Daria." Robert leaned forward.

Jake returned to his seat and took her hand. "What happened?"

"Smothers was just found dead in his car a

few minutes ago." Daria covered her face with both hands. "Gunshot to the head."

Heat rushed to Jake's face. He clenched his fists. "This has gotten out of hand. We've got to stop this senseless violence before someone else dies."

If he could encourage Daria to rest, he could slip away and do some investigating. He stood and put his hands on both of her shoulders, remembering one was still sore. "This has been an unusually long, stressful day. Why don't you go rest a little while?"

She spun and glared up at him. "Jake Fisher, I know what you're thinking, and you aren't going scouting without me."

Jake dropped his jaw.

Busted.

Robert pushed to his feet. "And neither of you are going anywhere without me. Besides, it's my truck."

"You've got a point there." Jake shoved his hands into his pockets and shrugged. "That settles it. Where do we begin?"

They all marched into the living room and grabbed their coats. Robert tossed Jake a pair of gloves. Jake helped Daria with her coat.

She borrowed a scarf from Gina's coatrack and wrapped it around her neck.

"Weapons?" Robert asked as he checked his and clipped it to his waistband.

Jake lifted his jacket, shirt and all, exposing his shoulder holster. "Got mine."

Daria patted her side. "Mine, too."

Gina stood with her hands propped at her waist. "Do I need one, too?"

Jake watched as Robert walked over and kissed his wife. "You know where yours is if you need it. Someone killed Smothers. We've got to go."

"Oh, dear, that poor man." Gina covered her mouth, then leaned over and picked up Emma, who rubbed her eyes. "Let me know if I can do anything. Please be careful."

The worried look on Gina's face tugged at Jake's heart. This family, this town, shouldn't be going through such a dangerous time. It was almost Christmas. Everyone should be happy. He had to help them get this beautiful tourist town safe again.

Robert's kids ran circles out in the front yard, throwing snowballs at each other. A flash of Amanda and him, throwing snowballs as kids, then tackling their snowman and knocking him over, swirled through his memory. The pain of loss pierced his heart. His brave sister, Amanda, exposed this huge crime.

Jake hopped in the passenger side of the king cab truck beside Daria, with Robert at the wheel. He enjoyed sitting close to her, but he would have liked it better if she had stayed at the house with Gina and the kids.

"You could've gotten in the back, Daria. You would have had a lot more room." Robert backed out of the driveway and pulled out onto the road.

"Are you kidding? I'm right between you two men. Now I'll hear every detail of your conversations," she said.

Jake took her hand in his. He cared for her deeply. She had clarified her comment about Emma. He loved her and knew she loved Emma. Thoughts of moving forward with their relationship felt right.

"Don't you two get serious about each other and think you're going to hang around all the time." Robert grinned. He reached the end of the road and pulled out onto the main highway.

"We make a great team." Jake squeezed her hand. "What's the plan, and where do we begin at four in the afternoon?"

"I figure we should get to the station before shift change and question everyone there. Then, question the second shift personnel as they clock in. After that, we will walk the streets and question town citizens without alarming the tourists. Somebody knows something," Robert said.

"Exactly," Jake chimed in. They were going to be great friends. Robert and he thought alike. He might even become his brother-in-law one day if it worked out with Daria.

Jake's insides jumped backflips. Finally, they were doing the chasing instead of the running and hiding. His type of tactics. There'd been so much uncertainty earlier, he didn't want to put Daria in harm's way. Maybe he'd been too overprotective. She was a cop. Injured or not, she was determined to see the case through. He couldn't blame her.

"Whoever is looking for us will be surprised with us out in public asking questions," Daria said. "May even force them into making a move."

"It's a risk we have to take, like bombarding the enemy lines." Jake placed his arm on the door's armrest. "A risk we have to take if we want to conquer the enemy."

They arrived at the station and went inside.

Robert stood at the front desk and announced that no one was to leave until each person answered a few questions.

Jake enjoyed the interviews and studied each person's body language. Everyone took part even though they grieved the loss of Smothers and the shocking news of Jeffers's arrest. After all the officers from the day shift had been questioned, Jake roamed the department to see if they'd missed anyone.

Daria caught up with him in the kitchen and got a bottled water from the refrigerator. Jake poured himself a cup of fresh coffee.

"This shift was in the clear. Now we wait for the next." He lifted his cup to his lips. "That's hot."

Daria backed up and stared at him.

"What?" Jake took another sip.

"You realize this is where I work. You don't. You're a civilian and you're sure making yourself at home." A grin slid across her face.

"Of course, but my girl and her brother work here, so I figure it gives me a little clout." He moved to the kitchen doorway. "Looks like shift change to me."

"You are impossible." Daria worked her way around him. "Maybe you should get a job here."

Jake caught up with her. "You know, that's not a bad idea. I'll think about it." He looked across the room at the officers coming and going. He wouldn't mind working here. He figured since he was physically fit, a sharpshooter, had experience reading body language and all those other things an officer should be able to accomplish, he'd fit the position.

Another round of questioning went as well as could be expected once word spread of their fallen officer and the possible betrayal of their lieutenant. Only one person remembered seeing Jeffers rush into Cramer's office earlier in the day, which could explain the unethical placement of the toy flash drives. But no one knew anything about additional evidence.

Jake followed Daria and Robert to the front of the station. He stared across the street to all the patrons walking the sidewalks and going in and out of souvenir shops. Christmas tinsel and fake snow decorated shop windows. One shop even had a small flashing train circling a miniature decorated tree.

The snow made the town look even more festive, but it meant they had a cold investigative outing ahead of them.

"Jake. Are you listening?"

Daria's voice brought him back from admiring the town. "What? Yep."

"What did we just say?"

Busted again.

Daria reached up and turned his head in her direction. "You and I will stroll along casually and talk to people. Robert will do his own window shopping and see what he can find out."

"Sounds like a plan to me." Jake took Daria's hand. "Which side do you prefer walking on so you can get to your gun if needed?"

"Switch sides." Daria held her hand out. "Robert, are you ready?"

Robert turned his coat collar up and stuck his hands in his pockets. "Ready."

Jake paused. "Wait. Where do we want to meet up and what time?"

"It's 8:00 p.m. now. Let's meet at the Oakland Grill at 10:00 p.m. By then we'll be icicles and ready for something hot to drink."

"I agree." Jake rolled his neck until it popped. Adrenaline had his body feeling like a jet revving up to get going. "Let's go."

He and Daria held hands and strolled up the town's main street, greeting passersby. It dawned on Jake that he couldn't tell tourists from townspeople. He leaned closer to Daria's ear.

"I have to go with your lead. I don't know who is vacationing and who lives here. Everyone looks the same. I'm probably the one who sticks out like a drop of strawberry ice cream in a bowl of vanilla."

She laughed. "No worries. I'll introduce you to the locals as long as I can remember their names."

Jake shivered with a gust of wind. The temperatures had dropped since they'd arrived earlier. Small snowflakes peppered down. Light Christmas music filtered down the street and shoppers were dressed in their winter coats and hats. No one had a clue there was a killer on the loose.

Chapter 12

Daria squeezed Jake's hand every time they met a local. Most of them were harmless, out doing their Christmas shopping. A few homeless people hung around a fire in a fifty-five-gallon drum at the entrance of an alley at the north end of town.

"Who would be crazy enough to stalk someone in this freezing weather?" Jake wrapped his arm around Daria's shoulders.

She leaned her head toward him. "An actual stalker or criminal watching for the right moment to strike. You should know that, Mr. Marine. Let's talk to these guys."

Some men moved away as she approached. She'd seen them before, and they knew she was a cop.

Jake tossed a hand up. "Hey, guys, hope you're staying warm by that fire."

A couple of them grumbled.

"Good evening," Daria said. "How's everyone hanging tonight? Hey, Monti, Greg, Trevor, and is that Randall over there? We're not here to bother you guys. It's much too cold. Did any of you hear about Officer Smothers being shot today?"

"Nope. Too bad, though. I liked the guy." Trevor held his hands over the fire. His fingerless gloves didn't do much to keep his hands warm.

"Yeah, I heard." Randall stepped out of the shadows. "Makes us kinda nervous. We don't know who done it."

"Who would kill a cop in our quiet town?" Monti coughed and spat in the fire.

"I don't know, guys, but if you hear anything, would you let me know? We want to make sure everyone stays safe and has a nice Christmas." Daria stepped back. "Stay warm."

Jake lightly bumped against her shoulder. "You handled that like a pro."

"Thanks. I've had a little experience, and most of those men know me." Her foot slipped on an icy patch, and Jake caught her before she hit the ground.

"That was close." He helped her stand upright but held her next to him.

Her heart fluttered with expectation.

Jake glanced around, then back at her. "Since Jeffers isn't here and you're not specifically on duty, may I have permission to kiss you?"

"A quick kiss. I don't want to draw too much attention." She prepared herself. Anticipation increased.

He settled her on her feet, took her into his arms and planted a kiss on her lips. He moved back slowly and smoothed the back of his hand across her cheek.

"Was that quick enough?" He grinned.

Warmth rose to her cheeks. Had her face turned red? "That wasn't quick and unnoticeable, but it was really nice."

"Want me to try again?" Jake's childish grin made her laugh.

"Maybe later." Daria straightened her coat and shivered. "The Oakland Grill is down the street, three blocks away. I don't know about you, but my feet and hands are almost frozen, and the snowflakes are getting bigger. I'm sure Robert is already there warming up and drinking coffee."

She tried not to show her ecstatic feelings as she held her hand out to him. He didn't hesitate. His big, gloved hand wrapped around hers. "Let's go find your brother."

Shoppers dwindled, and the once-crowded walkways grew scarce. Even the locals knew when to call it a night. Jake was right again. The likelihood of locating anyone who knew anything about Smothers's death in the freezing temperatures was zilch to none.

They trekked down the street at a decent pace, watching for ice along the way. Mostly snow crunched under their feet. A few more steps past the alley and they'd be in the restaurant's warmth.

"Psst."

Daria stopped and looked across the street.

"What are you doing?" Jake asked.

"I heard something."

"Psst."

She spun and faced the alley, surprised to see Mr. Treadway, her elderly friend who helped at the restaurant. He stood in the shadows of the streetlight. She dropped Jake's hand and entered the alley, noting Jake towering over her. He was in protection mode, and she appreciated it. Not that she didn't trust Mr. Treadway, but she didn't trust the killers wouldn't see him talking to her and threaten him.

"Mr. Treadway, what are you doing out here without your coat? May I help you back inside?" Daria touched his thin arm.

"Shhhh." He put a bony finger to his lips. "I wanted to talk to you, but you were busy. I heard somebody talking on their cell about some kind of toy flash drives you found. He stood right by the kitchen door within earshot of me. Said that information was useless to the police unless they found the little black code-book that had all the names in it." He shivered. "I gotta get back inside but figured that's what you and your brother were looking for. Mind you, don't tell nobody you talked to me. I'm just an old man minding my business." He turned and hobbled to the side door of the restaurant.

"You're amazing, Mr. Treadway. Did you get a look at the person?"

"Nope. And I couldn't tell if it was a man or a woman. The voice was muffled. But I'm guessing a man." He stepped inside and closed the door.

Jake opened the main entrance door for her to enter the restaurant. "There had to be at least two of them talking."

"That's true. And that still means at least two more people are involved." Daria pulled off her gloves. "There's Robert at that back table. He has a thing about sitting with his back to the wall."

"I get it." Jake walked behind her and pulled her chair out when they reached the table. No sooner had they sat down than the server walked up for their order.

"I'll have hot tea." She picked up a menu. "Hot vegetable soup with cornbread sounds good, too."

"Coffee, black." Jake took his coat off and hung it over the back of his chair. "I need to look at the menu."

Robert cupped his hands around his coffee mug. "No leads on my end of the street. What about the two of you?"

The server returned to the table with their hot beverages and took Jake's order.

Jake leaned close to the table. "I'll let Daria tell you what she found out."

Daria looked around to make sure no one was listening. "You know Mr. Treadway, right?"

"Yes. He works here in the kitchen," Robert said. "An older gentleman."

"Right." Daria leaned toward her brother. "He stopped us in the alley right beside the restaurant." She explained what she'd learned. "Bless his heart. He's as good as they come."

"Where do we find this so-called black codebook? Any hints?" Robert leaned back for the server to place his food on the table. "Before you ask. I ordered about five minutes before you got here."

"Couldn't wait, I see." She snickered. "He didn't say."

Jake drummed his fingers on the table, then stopped. "We've searched my sister's house once already. Guess we could go back and search again now that we have more details."

"Question is—" she eyed them both. "—do we want to wait until morning or go tonight?"

"We've all had a busy day," Robert said. "Let's get some rest and start fresh tomorrow."

"Agreed." Daria's nerves were on edge. Her shoulder ached a little and her head hurt. Another one of Jake's kisses might make the hurt go away. The thought warmed her heart. Maybe before they turned in for the night.

After the late-night meal, they grew silent on the drive home.

The living room lights were still on in Robert's house. Gina must have left them on for their return. Fresh snow glistened under the one streetlight her brother had installed on their property. Tire tracks streaked the driveway, and two sets of footprints trekked to the front porch. Someone must have visited Gina while they were away.

Robert pulled into the driveway. "Something's not right. We weren't expecting company."

Jake shot out of the truck before Robert came to a full stop. Daria scooted to the edge of the seat and waited for her brother to park. They both hopped out and ran to the front door but it was locked. Jake pulled his weapon and pointed to footprints in the snow that led to the window.

Robert and Daria did likewise. This wasn't good. Not good at all. Adrenaline shot through her body like a triple shot of caffeine. One of the front windows had been knocked out.

Robert pushed past both of them with his weapon in a ready position. Jake shook his head and did hand signals to say he'd go through the window first. Robert wanted to go first. Daria was the cop. She should go first. But it was Robert's home. He unlocked the front door and eased inside with Jake and her close behind. The house was quiet.

Robert and Jake eased up the stairs. Daria checked the dining room and sunroom. Nothing. She eased into the kitchen and her heart plummeted. Gina was tied to a chair. Her head was slumped over and trickles of blood dripped on her blouse.

She checked Gina's pulse. It was steady. She couldn't yell at the guys until she knew the house was clear of the intruders. She untied her about the time Robert and Jake entered. Robert rushed over to her and patted her cheeks.

"Gina, Gina, wake up. Talk to me." He smoothed her hair back from her face. "Honey, what happened?"

Daria called 911.

Gina moaned and opened her eyes. Tears exploded. "They took Emma."

"No." Jake's hands grabbed his head. "This can't be happening." He paced in the kitchen, then stopped, took in a deep breath and studied the scene before him. Hostiles had invaded their safe zone, and it was up to him to track them down.

Robert had to care for his family, and Daria wasn't at full capacity. Sirens grew closer and flashing lights lit up the night. Isaac and Alexa hopped down the stairs, rubbing their eyes. Robert met them in the living room and explained their mom had a bump on the head. The paramedics were going to make sure she was okay.

"Did Mama's visitors do that to her?" Alexa asked.

Jake kneeled in front of her. "Who were your mom's guests?"

"We never saw them before," Isaac said. "Mom told us to go back to bed and shut our doors. She was rocking Emma, and the people wanted to talk."

Daria squatted beside Jake.

"Yeah, I wanted a drink, but Mama said she'd bring it to me when the people left." Alexa leaned against Daria. "I was really thirsty."

"I'll get you a drink." Daria eased into the kitchen, which was now filled with paramedics and cops. She was back in the living room in an instant.

Jake needed to be in the kitchen to hear Gina's story, but he needed to hear what these kids were telling him.

"Want me to take care of the kids while you go in the kitchen?" Daria pulled Alexa close and handed her the water.

How did she know his thoughts? "Yes, thanks." Jake bolted into the kitchen just as the paramedic was finishing assessing Gina and one of the officers came over to take her statement.

"Blood pressure is normal... But she can go ahead with the statement now," the paramedic said.

Gina turned to the officer. "There was a knock at the front door. The porch light wouldn't come on. Before I knew it, glass shattered. Two men busted the window and jumped inside with guns." Gina wiped tears while the paramedic bandaged her head. "It happened so fast I didn't get a good look at them. Emma was asleep in my arms, and Alexa and Isaac crept down the stairs, but I told them to go back up. One man jerked Emma away and wrapped her in the blanket from my couch. I fought with them and that's the last thing I remember."

Jake's inside boiled. His heart hurt.

"The cut on your head is superficial, but since you lost consciousness for an unknown period, we need to transport you to the hospital." The paramedic packed his supplies in his bag.

"No. I'm not leaving my family tonight." Gina grabbed Robert's hand. "I'll go see my doctor tomorrow."

Jake returned to the living room, where the kids sat on the sofa with Daria.

She looked up at him, then back at the kids. "Why don't you guys run upstairs and play or go back to sleep? I need to talk to Jake."

"I want to stay with my mom." Isaac moved closer to the kitchen.

"Is Emma coming back? Did that bad man hurt her?" Alexa asked.

Jake swallowed the lump in his throat. He placed his hand gently on Isaac's back. "Your mom is going to be okay. Your dad and the paramedics are here taking care of her." Then he turned to Alexa. "Emma is okay, too. No one's going to hurt her. Everything is under control and you guys are safe. Go give your mom a hug and you can go play."

After the kids wrapped their arms around their mom, they trudged up the stairs to their rooms, and Jake waited to hear what Daria had found out from them. Nervous energy wouldn't let him sit.

"Anything?" Jake shuffled his feet.

"According to Alexa, it was a man and a woman dressed up like a man. The description of the woman suspiciously sounds like the woman from the restaurant who told us about the flash drives." Daria's hand gripped his arm. "I never suspected her."

"What about the man?" Jake asked.

"The guy was about as tall as her daddy, but Alexa said he was skinny like Isaac. By that description, I assume he is tall and lanky."

"I'm going to my house to look for the book." Jake zipped his coat. He'd never taken it off when they entered the house. "They'll hold Emma hostage until they get what they want."

"I'll go with you." Daria headed toward the door.

"No. It's best I go alone." Jake went in the kitchen and got the truck keys from Robert. He walked past Daria, who still stood at the door. "I'll find Emma. You need to take care of your family."

Jake got in the truck and started backing around all the emergency vehicles. Daria came running out of the house holding Emma's diaper bag and coat. She ran to the passenger side. He unlocked the door and she hopped inside.

"What are you doing?" Jake's emotions were all over the place.

"I'm taking care of my family, like you said. I'm coming with you." She buckled up. "When we find Emma, she's going to want her sippy cup and giraffe."

He spun the tires, trying to move too fast. His baby was in danger, and the woman he loved had been attacked too many times already. How was he supposed to process those emotions?

"Jake, I understand the anxiety right now." Daria shifted in her seat and faced him. "We will find her. I love Emma and I love you."

His insides calmed a bit, but not the distress over Emma's abduction. He reached over and took her hand.

She placed her other hand on top of his. "You and Emma *are* my life."

"Then let's go find our baby." Jake put both hands on the steering wheel.

With little to no traffic at midnight, he made it through town faster than he'd expected. He turned into his driveway. Crime scene tape was still draped across the property. The newly installed windows still had the stickers on the glass. He parked and walked to the front door with Daria at his heels, carrying the diaper bag.

"No telling what the inside looks like." He opened the door and flipped on the light. "Not bad. Looks like it did when we left it the other day, after searching for the last piece of evidence."

"Brr. May want to turn the heat on." Daria tossed the diaper bag on the sofa. It turned over and fell to the floor with a thump.

"Was that her sippy cup that hit the floor? Sounded heavy." Jake turned the thermostat on and approached Daria.

She sat on the sofa, picked the bag up and emptied the contents. A few diapers, one sippy cup, wipes, bib, a change of clothes and her cheese bites. "Nothing heavy here." She checked all the pockets and side zipper, then dropped the bag on the floor again.

The same thud sounded.

Jake's curiosity piqued. He joined her on the sofa.

"Okay, there's something here." She stuck her hand down into the diaper bag.

"Let me see." He felt around, then knocked on the bottom with his knuckles. "You're right. There's something there." He turned the cloth of the diaper bag inside out. The bottom had either ripped, or someone had cut it and hand-stitched it closed. His eyes met with Daria's. "Could it be?"

"Rip it open." Daria scooted closer. "She disguised the flash drives. Who knows?"

Jake ripped the hand-stitched seam. A little black book came into view. He pulled it out and flipped through it. Sure enough, the book contained a list of codes that belonged to a list of names. Addresses, phone numbers, locations, bank account numbers, etc.

"We've had it with us all along." She blew out a long breath.

Jake pulled her into a hug and placed a quick kiss on her lips. "We found it. The evidence needed to put these guys away and the book those two will kill for."

Daria's phone beeped. She looked up at Jake. "Who'd text me at this hour?" She unzipped her coat and retrieved her cell from her shirt pocket. A blocked ID message arrived.

Meet before sunrise at the old dairy barn outside town and bring the book or else your little darling will freeze to death.

Jake jumped to his feet and squeezed his fists. "If they harm Emma, I will, I will… I'm not telling you what I'll do."

"You don't have to, Jake." Daria stood holding the book. "It will all work out. We will find her."

"Do you know where that barn is? I remember one being around here, but I don't know where it's located."

"I've been by there several times, cruising around in my squad car. I'll text back, 'Which building? There are three.'"

Jake sat beside her, watching for a response to her message. He clasped her hand in his. He wasn't alone. Daria had his back, and he had hers.

Her cell beeped again. She held it out for him to see.

The middle one. Time's wasting. No cops.

Daria shook her head. "No cops? Really? I am a cop and they're texting me."

"How long will it take us to get there?" Jake looked at his watch. "Sunrise is at 5:35 a.m. It's 1:15 a.m. now."

"About an hour. I'm calling Robert," Daria said. "Someone needs to know where we're going." She put the call on speaker and held the phone between her and Jake.

"Robert, we found the book," Daria said.

"Thank goodness. Do you have Emma? Have

they made contact?" An urgency increased in Robert's voice.

"No, we don't have her yet. They sent a message to meet them at the old dairy farm before sunrise and specified no police."

"You have about four hours. The police are still here. I'll inform them and they can assist."

"No. Don't send anyone." Jake paced while she talked on the phone. His body tensed. "This meeting must go exactly as instructed. Emma's life depends on it."

McDaniel got on the phone. "Jake, we understand this is a deadly situation. We are just as concerned about little Emma as you are, and we won't do anything to compromise the situation."

"Better not, or I'll hold you personally accountable." Jake wiped his mouth with his hand. He'd handled all kinds of enemy tactics during the war and had always pushed his fears aside. Could he pull himself together enough to do the same for Emma?

Daria hung up the phone. "We need to get going so we can be there before sunrise. We can sit and wait until we need to make a move. I wouldn't think they'd harm a baby, but we can't take any chances."

Jake pulled her into a hug and squeezed. "I never thought I'd need help from anyone, but your support right now means the world to me." He released her, took the book and held it in the air. "Let's go get Emma."

God, keep Emma safe. Give us wisdom and the right tactical maneuvers so no one has to die.

Chapter 13

Even though she was an experienced cop, Daria's stomach still churned. She'd never faced such an intense and dangerous case. Her nerves formed knots in her neck muscles. They were coming down to the wire in this investigation. The next few hours would determine the outcome.

God, I haven't talked to You much, but I know You're here. We need Your protection for Emma and for us as we step into the battle. Right now, we don't have a plan, but I know You do. I'm trusting You to help us end these threats.

"You're quiet." Jake drove the narrow road toward the old dairy farm.

"Figured we could use some prayer about now." Daria chewed her lip. Her hand slid to her weapon. *Still there.*

"I prayed, too." Jake inhaled a deep breath

and blew it out. "I'm not good at it, but if you prayed, maybe God heard one of us."

"Jake, God hears all prayers, including yours and mine. Prayers don't have to be perfect." Daria stared at the snow glistening from the truck's headlights. Was Emma warm? Were they so inhumane as to let her freeze? Did they hurt her?

Ugh! I can't think like that. God is in control. She had to believe God would answer her prayers.

"How much farther?" Jake swerved around a fallen tree.

"About five miles ahead." She checked her side mirror for signs of squad cars trailing behind. No headlights in sight. If McDaniel, Cramer and Evans were closing in, they would approach without being seen.

"I know you said the woman could be the one from the restaurant." He slowed over a small icy bridge. "But any idea of the man's identity?"

"I've been trying to figure it out. First off, why would the woman tell us about the flash drives, then try to kill us? Where would that have left her? If she'd remained quiet, no telling how long it would have been before we discovered the value of Emma's toys."

"Could she have been fishing for more information, thinking we'd tell her about the book?" He slowed the vehicle down. "Then she'd know for sure we had found it."

"It's possible. She seems to be the one calling the shots. The man is a puzzle to me. Maybe he's related, someone she works with or someone she hired."

Jake pointed. "Is that it ahead?"

"Yes. See the three buildings? You'll turn on the second entrance and follow the dirt, well, icy drive all the way around to the back." Daria leaned toward the window and squinted into the dark. She glanced at her watch. "It's 2:50 a.m. There's no sign of backup."

"Good. It's still early, though. Maybe they listened and will stay away, considering the sensitivity of the situation." Jake turned on the snow-covered driveway. "I remember this place. It's been so long I'd forgotten about it."

"Pull over by that rolled hay bale and park. If we sit in the dark long enough, our eyes might have time to adjust." Daria leaned back in the seat. "If the moon was out, all this snow would make it almost daylight." The silence grew eerie. She studied their surroundings as best as she could. They didn't need anyone sneaking up to the window and blasting them.

Time crept. Tension mounted by the hour as they sat there watching and listening. An ache eased into her head. Should have brought the medication, but no time to think about that now.

"Movement to the right of the building." Jake pointed and whispered so low she almost didn't understand what he'd said.

Daria watched as someone or something slowly distanced itself from the building. "That can't be him or her stepping out from hiding. Oh, it's a buck." She exhaled. "It's going into the woods. We'll give the abductors a few more minutes to make a move. If not, then we'll ease inside the barn."

"I've had to wait hours for the enemy to show their faces," Jake whispered. "Knowing we only have minutes before our encounter only increases the tension. We can do this. I've got confidence in you and your skills."

She reached over and squeezed his forearm. "And I have full confidence in your expert marine tactics."

"Wait. What's that?" Jake pointed toward the barn again.

"It's our cue to get out. Someone stepped to the opening and backed up." She reached for the door handle. "Just remember, you and Emma are going to be okay."

"Don't go saying stuff like that." Jake unbuckled his seat belt and opened his door. "We're both bringing Emma home."

Daria took the book from Jake and stuck it in her coat pocket before she stepped out of the truck and pulled her weapon. Jake held his pistol by his side. He remained by her as they walked toward the old barn. Snow crunched beneath their feet and the frigid wind cut through her clothes, sending chills over her body.

Emma. Where are you, baby?

Neither breathed a word as they approached the entrance and stepped inside the barn. Jake slid to the left, while Daria stepped to the right and moved forward. A flashlight popped on and blinded her. She threw her hand up and covered her eyes like a visor.

"You can stop right there," the scratchy female voice said. "Where's your friend?"

"Why would I answer any of your questions? You're the one in control here. You should know if I came alone or if someone came with me."

"Pretty sure of yourself, aren't you? Well,

you can quit with the cocky attitude." Her tone grew angry. "I know Jake is here. If he values that baby's life, he'll show himself." She grew quiet, like she was waiting for Jake to appear.

A rustling sound came from the woman's left, which was Daria's right. Jake had gone the opposite direction. Whoever moved around must be this woman's partner. She scrolled the light around quickly. "That you, T?"

"Yep," a husky voice replied.

Daria took advantage of the second of darkness and jumped behind a hay bale. Jake was in his element and had most likely strategically placed himself out of sight of the woman's flashlight.

"Don't try playing games with me. I can shoot through that hay, Officer Gordon. Toss your weapon or I'll shoot."

"You toss your weapon so we can talk face-to-face." Daria could have already fired at her, but she wanted to gather more information. Like where Emma was.

More rustling grew closer to the front of the barn. Daria squinted to see in the dark. Was it Jake or that man the woman called T? Her senses were on high alert.

"Give me the book and I'll give Emma back."
Frustration rose in the woman's voice.

"Not until you drop your gun." Daria rolled
against the wood fence. She spotted the dark
shadow standing a short distance away.

"Jake, I know you're here. On the count of
three, I'm going to shoot your cop friend. One,
two, three."

Thump.

Thump.

Thump.

The woman shot into the hay bale three
times. Daria pointed her weapon through a
crack between the hay and the fence and pulled
the trigger. The woman screamed and dropped
her flashlight. Daria had aimed knee level in
the darkness and wasn't sure she'd hit her target.

Silence.

If she'd hit the woman, it wouldn't have been
a deadly shot. More movement, closer to her
right, increased the already racing beat of her
heart. T must have stepped her direction.

Light filtered over the horizon, through
cracks in the wooden walls and into the barn's
entrance. They were in for a standoff, for sure.
Emma must not be close because there had

been no cries of a baby nearby. Where had they left her?

I refuse to believe they were cruel enough to leave her out in these freezing temperatures.

"Come on out, Officer," a deep male voice demanded. "Your time is up. Apparently, your friend left you here to fend for yourself."

"I'll come out if you tell me where you're holding Emma." Daria waited.

"No. Show us the book first." The woman grunted, then laughed. "You barely scraped my leg. Thought you were a sharpshooter."

"If I'd wanted to kill you, you wouldn't be talking to me right now." Daria put her hands in the air, trusting Jake was in his strategy mode. "I'm standing up."

"Toss your weapon toward us and come on out."

The man's familiar voice had her stumped. She'd heard it somewhere but couldn't place it.

I know better than to give up my weapon. But I have to, for Emma's sake. Jake, I'm trusting you.

The thought scrolled through her mind like a stuck recording. She hated to succumb to the woman's demands, but she was at a point of no return until Jake made his move. She tossed it toward them as instructed and stood.

The sun peeked higher over the horizon just enough for Daria to see the same woman she'd seen in the restaurant and "T" the man who stood by her. The sunglasses and scarf still hid her identity. She studied the man. Where had she seen him?

"Trying to figure it all out, aren't you, Officer?" He huffed.

"Guess I am." Daria pointed to the woman. "You said your name was Liz Colton and you worked with Amanda, right?"

"Sort of. Things aren't as they seem, my dear. Amanda worked for my husband. She stole his files. I told him not to use his office computer, but he was all about Excel spreadsheets." She removed her sunglasses and unwrapped the covering from her head.

Daria recognized her right off. She fumed for not demanding the woman to show her face when they met at the restaurant.

Caroline, the banker's wife. A fine respectable lady, or so I thought.

Caroline blew on her fingernail and repositioned her weapon. "I suppose you've figured out that I'm the brains behind this embezzlement scheme, and I don't mind owning up to it. I worked hard to formulate the perfect retirement plan. But that Amanda girl stuck her nose in the wrong place, and it cost her life and the life of her husband. So sad." Her laugh held no remorse.

"Is he your hired help, because I know he's not your husband." Daria sized the man up.

"Shut your mouth and hand over the book." He shoved his gun toward her. The way he held his weapon told Daria he was not an experienced shooter.

"Where's Emma?" Heat rose in Daria's cheeks. This back-and-forth had her blood boiling.

"The book," Caroline demanded. "Tony, get it from her. I'll cover you."

Tony? Tony Schneider? Wasn't that the father's name of that kid she'd arrested? He stuck his weapon in his waistband and walked toward her.

Daria spotted movement back behind Caroline. Either Jake or one of the cops was about to intervene. Despite telling them not to interfere, she wouldn't be surprised if they showed up anyway. They would have entered from an alternate direction. The closer Tony got to her, the more she prepared herself to tackle him and prayed it was the right move.

Tony stepped closer. "Now give me that book."

Jake stepped behind Caroline. Daria decided it was now or never. She tackled Tony. A second later, Jake tackled Caroline.

A shot fired. Tony dropped to the ground, yelling and holding his shoulder. Jake pulled Caroline's hands behind her back and secured her weapon.

Daria scooped up Tony's weapon, retrieved her pistol, then returned and pulled Tony to his feet. He bellowed in pain.

McDaniel, Cramer and Evans made it to the scene just as Daria and Jake subdued their threats. "Cuff them," Daria said.

Jake stepped in front of Caroline. "Where is my baby? What have you done with her?"

"Wouldn't you like to know?" She sneered. "You messed up my life. Now I'll mess up yours."

Daria motioned for Jake to join her. "Our weak link is over here," she said. "Tony isn't a true criminal. He'll crack."

Daria approached Tony, who was in obvious pain. "Where is the baby? You know Caroline will try to pin everything on you and make everyone believe you arranged the kidnapping, too. You're looking at life in prison if you don't tell us where to find Emma."

"I'm not supposed to tell." He rolled his head back and groaned.

"The sooner you talk, the faster you'll get to the hospital." Daria stepped back and eyed him. "Where is the baby?"

Jake stepped forward and lifted his fist.

Tony cowered under Jake's threat. "Okay, okay. The little girl is in a cabin out in the woods. I don't know the area, but it's close to a power line. Caroline's housekeeper is watching her and keeping a fire in the woodstove until we get back."

"You're Tony Schneider, aren't you?" Daria clenched her fists.

"How nice of you to remember me." He rolled his eyes. "You arrested my son a while back. We were none too happy for your intrusion on our father/son vacation. Mrs. Caroline saw what happened. She agreed that you were out of control and offered us a job. She paid good. I didn't know it involved a kid."

Jake pulled him up by the collar. "Which way from here?"

He nodded behind them. "About two miles into the forest."

Daria and Jake took off running to the truck. Robert stood there with the driver's door of his truck open, waiting for them with the engine running.

"How'd you get here?" Jake asked.

"McDaniel picked me up. Officers are watching my house while I'm gone." Robert got in the driver's seat.

"A cabin about two miles east." Daria opened the passenger door and hopped in.

"I could trek through the woods and get there faster." Jake balked at getting into the truck.

"We know the area, Jake. Get in. We can hike once we reach the top of the ridge." Daria motioned him into the vehicle.

He hesitated. "Emma must be okay if they have someone watching her." He let out a huff and slid in beside Daria. "At least we know she wasn't left out in the cold."

Robert turned the heat thermostat and fan on high. "I'll get you to the ridge in record time." He rolled away from the dairy farm.

Jake drummed his fingers on the dash. His body was still in search-and-rescue mode, but his insides were aching to hold his baby. How could he have gotten so attached to this little person so fast? He imagined her soft hands patting his cheek. He swallowed the emotion, trying to break him down.

"There are three cabins in the area Tony mentioned." Daria reached out and stopped him from drumming his fingers. She squeezed his hand. "We'll check them all unless we see one with smoke coming from the chimney."

Robert stopped in the middle of the icy road. "Here you go. I'll wait here for a text, then I'll drive on around to the gravel road and meet you there. Wouldn't want to alert anyone of our arrival by taking you closer."

"Got it." Jake hopped out of the truck and waited for Daria.

She tossed Robert the black book. "You should hold on to this for us." She turned back to Jake. "Let's do this."

Jake walked beside Daria until the forest thickened. He stepped ahead of her. She gripped his arm. "I'm still the law and I have jurisdiction."

"Don't go pulling rank on me right now." Jake stiffened his lip. "We're in this together, and we're rescuing Emma."

"I know, but we still have to use caution and do everything according to the law, or it might get thrown out of court." She pushed a snow-covered branch out of her face, knocking the snow on her coat.

Jake's big hand reached over her and held the branch back until he passed. "Unless there's no one left to take to court."

"Jake Fisher, I'm going to ignore that comment."

Jake focused ahead. "There in the middle of the valley. Look through the trees. Three cabins. Two have smoke drifting from the chimneys."

"I see. But which cabin?" Daria's breath fogged in the frosty air.

A flag went up in his gut. Was this a setup? Were there armed guards hiding out? He stopped and squatted. Daria did the same.

"What is it?" She eased her hand up and pulled at the branches of a snowy bush. The snow fell off and sprinkled to the ground. "Did you see something?"

He couldn't help but notice her big brown eyes searching the area. He trusted her and couldn't see himself raising Emma without her by his side.

"Something tells me we're walking into a trap." He pulled his weapon again. "I could be wrong, but my gut is usually on target."

"Okay." Daria retrieved her weapon. "How about we ease around to the back of the cabin on the left and check it first?"

"You've got it." Jake turned, still in a bent position, and crept through the forest as Daria suggested. He stopped and threw his hand up for her to stop.

"I saw that." Daria squatted lower. "Two armed men. They could be deer hunters."

"But look at the guns." Jake leaned close to her ear. "Those are not deer rifles."

"You're right," she whispered. "I could walk up and knock on the door while you stay hidden and cover me. Might be nothing. Maybe we're being too cautious."

"Did you just say that? Can a cop in an investigation ever be too cautious?" He eyed her.

"That's not what I meant. If they see us out here tiptoeing through the snow, making tracks everywhere, they will wonder what we're up to and could shoot without asking. We don't know if those men have anything to do with the case."

"You're right. Maybe I look for enemy activity too much." He dropped his shoulders, but his mind stayed on alert. He wasn't buying it at all.

"Let's go peek in the window. If there's no evidence of wrongdoing, I'll go to the front door."

"I'm not comfortable with you putting your life on the line like that." Jake put his hand on her back. "Maybe I should go."

"Jake, stop. Let's just move and see how it plays out." She hunched over and ran to the side of the cabin by a window.

He followed suit and stopped on the opposite side of the same window, then eased up and peeked inside. Not two, but three armed men were inside. One man stood at the side of the front window, holding the curtain so he could look out. Another disappeared into a room carrying his weapon. The third man walked toward the window where Jake and Daria were.

Jake widened his eyes at her and pressed himself against the log cabin. Again, Daria did as he did. He prepared himself for battle.

"Hey, Joe, maybe Caroline did away with them." One man's voice carried through the cabin's wall.

The man turned away. His footsteps clomped across the floor. "That would save us from having to do the job."

Daria stared at him. Her nostrils flared and her lips tightened. She nodded toward the forest.

He eased up and checked the position of the men. Only the one at the front window remained in position. Could be a good thing or a bad thing. Before he could swing around, snow crunched behind him.

"Well, who do we have here, but the cop and the marine who have caused all the problems with our operation." The man's bushy eyebrows lowered and almost covered his deep-set, dark eyes. His rough, stocky exterior exuded killer experience.

Another man reached around Jake and Daria and took their weapons. "Making things easier on us, ay?"

"Not intentionally." Jake broke his silence and looked at Daria. He motioned with his eyes for her to watch the other guy until the timing was right to fight back.

Daria gave him a slight nod. Smart girl. She understood.

Jake evaluated his next move. If he allowed the men to take him and Daria inside, they'd either be killed or beaten and left for dead. He couldn't let that happen. Now was their chance to overtake these two men and pray the third didn't show up and put a stop to it all.

"Inside." The two men walked behind Jake and Daria toward the front door.

Jake's eyes met Daria's. He nodded slightly and spun, ramming his shoulder into one man's diaphragm. Daria had knocked the other man down, and they were rolling on the ground, fighting.

"Hold your hands up or I'll shoot." The threat came from the third man who had been in the cabin.

The fighting stopped. Jake had to come up with another plan.

"No, you hold your hands up or *we* will shoot." A demand from a familiar voice came from the edge of the woods.

Jake straightened and turned around. He'd never been so relieved to see Robert standing there with his gun, plus McDaniel, Cramer, Evans and two other officers. They cuffed the men and put them in their squad cars.

"Boy, are we happy to see you guys." Daria patted her brother on the back. "Thank you for showing everyone where to find us. Your timing was perfect. Now we've got to find Emma."

Jake took his and Daria's weapons back from

the men. He handed her pistol to her. "Emma must be in that other cabin with the smoke coming from the chimney. I'm not waiting any longer."

"I'm going with you." Daria caught up with him.

"You're not leaving me out on this one." Robert fell in beside them.

They traipsed together through the snow and uneven terrain to the other cabin with their weapons in a ready position in case of additional trouble. Before they reached the front door, a young woman opened the door, holding Emma wrapped in a thick fuzzy blanket.

Daria kept her weapon pointed at the lady. "Hand over the baby and back away with your hands up."

Jake ran and took Emma from her arms. Emma kicked her feet and squeezed him around the neck. This is the reunion he'd imagined. She loved him. His heart melted for his little niece.

"What's going on?" The young girl's eyes held fear. "Caroline hired me to babysit her niece. You can't take her."

"You've been misled." Daria handcuffed the

girl. "This child was abducted and is now back with her family."

"I didn't know." The girl burst into tears. "I didn't know."

"The officers will take you to the police station and question you. If they determine you are innocent of the crime, they will let you go," Daria explained.

Jake cuddled Emma in his arms as he watched the young girl get in the back of a squad car.

Daria stepped up beside him. "It's tough watching someone young get arrested. Just remember, she's innocent until proven guilty."

"I know. I'm certain they used her." He looked down at Emma. She held a dirty, scarred sippy cup out to him. He cringed at the sight of it and took it from her. Instead of crying, she patted his face with both hands and kissed his nose. What a relief to see her unharmed and smiling. He'd hand over her clean cup when they got back to the truck.

Daria's hand gripped his forearm. "We need to get Emma out of here. Somewhere safe and warm."

Chapter 14

After getting Emma back to Robert's house and enjoying everyone doting over her safe return, Daria received a call to come to the station. Disappointed at the interruption, she dismissed herself and headed toward the door.

She eased out of the house and hopped into Robert's truck. The passenger door opened just as she slid into the driver's seat. Jake sat smiling at her.

"Did you think you could just walk away and not be noticed?" Jake placed his hand on her arm. "You were spectacular today."

"Wasn't all me." Daria cut her eyes over at him. "We worked together as a team, and with the help of my colleagues, it appears we've solved your sister and brother-in-law's murder, arrested everyone involved with Emma's abduction and those involved with the bank's embezzlement scheme."

"Where are you headed now?" Jake buckled his seat belt. "Emma is in safe hands with your family."

"They want me to come down to the station. I suppose they want me in on the interrogation. This entire case has been so bizarre." Daria backed out of the driveway and drove down the road. "Do you really think we caught everyone? I keep getting this gnawing in my stomach that we're missing someone."

Jake's stare and pursed lips let her know he was pondering her comment. She could be wrong. Regardless, listening to the men explain their involvement might put all the pieces together and put her at rest.

"Are you thinking of a hired source or someone else at the top?" Jake turned and faced the street. "Could be a hidden source like in the war. Once you think you have everyone, there's that primary target slipping away unscathed. I'll have to trust your lead on this one. You are the law."

Daria laughed. "It's about time you admitted my status."

"I've known my limits all along. I just wanted to see you stand your ground. I love how tough and outspoken you've become over the years."

"Tough? I don't see myself like that." She turned on Main Street and headed to the station, yet again. "As much as I love my job, I'm not married to it. It has its upside and its downside, like any job does."

Traffic was calm. The slushy streets began melting with the sun's rays beaming down. Her thoughts drifted. She'd lived in Kimbleton long enough to know the weather could change in a matter of minutes. Christmas was only two days away. More snow would come, and she hadn't finished her shopping.

"Look, there are a lot of squad cars at the station. Is there some kind of special meeting going on?" Jake's comment brought her back to the present.

"I don't know." She pulled into the parking lot. "Let's go see."

Her stomach knotted. What could be so important that most of her coworkers gathered at one time, and no one told her? Was it another stab at her incompetence?

Jake opened the door for her. She stepped inside. McDaniel and Cramer greeted her. They ushered her to the conference room where other officers sat and stood around the walls. They had saved a seat for her at the table.

"What's going on, McDaniel?" Her pulse increased as she readied herself for more hazing and embarrassment. The serious look on Jake's face told her he was uncertain, too. He moved through the crowded room and stood over her. He rested a hand on her shoulder.

The room grew silent, which made perspiration form on her brow. Maybe she was going to be fired in front of everyone. She sat tall in the chair and waited.

McDaniel cleared his throat, and her eyes met his. "Your fellow officers and I realize what an outstanding and intuitive officer of the law you are, Daria. You've been steady and devout in your job and shown mercy in cases that shouldn't have received mercy. Then you stepped into the biggest, most corrupt case in our tourist town's history."

"That's true on all counts," Cramer interrupted.

McDaniel continued. "Because of your concerned comment earlier about how something still wasn't right, I took it on myself once I returned to the office to watch our security camera's recording of activity inside the office."

Daria cocked her head and looked up at him. "Security cameras inside the office?"

"Yes. Cramer and I suspected a rogue officer, so we installed hidden cameras." McDaniel looked around the room. "Sorry, everyone, we had to find the leak."

"We all know Lieutenant Jeffers played a big role in this entire ordeal, and at first, we thought we'd nailed the responsible party."

Daria sucked in a breath when Jeffers stepped into the room. Had he been released? Would her heart stop from shock? She must have really messed up.

Jeffers walked over and shook Daria's hand. "Things weren't as they seemed. That's why I permitted the security cameras. You and your marine friend helped draw out the rogue officer. After they took me into custody, and just before Jake spotted the flash drives in Cramer's office, the camera captured Evans sneaking around and tossing them inside. He threatened my family a few weeks ago and said if I told anyone about large sums of money randomly deposited into my account, my wife and kids would pay."

Daria couldn't believe what she was hearing. Evans, the rogue agent? No way.

Jeffers continued. "He had pictures of my kids getting on the school bus, my wife at the grocery store, my family and I enjoying time together at a restaurant. I was uncertain how to stop his harassment because he had people on the outside I was unaware of."

McDaniel chimed in. "We're all a team here, covering each other's backs. We want to thank Officer Daria Gordon and her marine friend, Jake Fisher, for their persistence in this case and for forcing Evans to expose his involvement on camera. Everyone's dismissed."

My marine? She liked the sounds of Jake being hers. Daria's stomach churned. She didn't deserve the recognition, but thankfully her intuition was right. There had been one last person. Why did it have to be one of their own?

Several of the officers walked by and either shook her hand or gave her a fist bump or a high five. One officer stopped and handed her a bottle of shaving cream.

"Here, we don't need this anymore, Officer Gordon. Fine job."

By the time they'd all left the room, Daria sat and stared at the wall. It was over. Finally, over. A calm washed over her. She'd been fully accepted by her team. What a satisfying feeling.

Jeffers stuck his head back into the conference room. "Daria, get a car off the back lot and take that few days off I suggested. Get some rest. Enjoy your Christmas."

"Yes, sir. Thank you." Daria stood and faced Jake. "Let's go back to Robert and Gina's where we can share the good news with them and celebrate over a big cup of hot chocolate with lots of miniature marshmallows."

"How about we stop and have a few uninterrupted moments at the diner before joining your family?" Jake took her hand. "I'd like to have some quiet time with just you."

Daria's cheeks warmed. Had she blushed? Maybe he didn't notice.

"Sounds nice. I'd love to." She exited the police station. "Do you want to drive Robert's truck? I'll meet you there in one of the unmarked cars."

"Sure thing." Jake hopped into the truck and drove away.

Daria sat in her new police car for a moment and took in some deep breaths. Saddened by Evans's deceit. Thrilled over Jeffers's return. Glad the case was over. Now she needed to talk to Jake, and meeting at the restaurant would be the perfect time.

December in the mountains was always a beautiful sight, even though clouds had rolled in and blocked the afternoon sun. The added layer of snow made it really look like Christmas. She pulled out onto the busy street with a whole new outlook on her life. God had made a way for her far above what she'd ever imagined.

Jake parked in the restaurant's empty parking lot and waited for Daria. His life lay before him, raising his sister's beautiful daughter, and that was a heartwarming fact. Although he'd like to add Daria to his life permanently, he didn't want to push her. They'd both just come through an emotional and dangerous ordeal. Maybe tonight wasn't the night to talk.

He spotted her turning into the parking lot. She pulled in beside him. He hopped out and met her at her car door. Something he enjoyed doing. She stood and their eyes met. He couldn't help himself. He put his hands on both sides of her face and gave her a quick kiss.

"Just to congratulate you on a job well done." He took her hand as they walked inside together.

"Thanks, but you should be congratulated, too." She squeezed his hand.

There was a definite connection between them. He escorted her to the booth by the window, noting no one else was there except for one server. Maybe the kitchen crew, but he couldn't see them. Where was everyone? Too early for the dinner crowd? Christmas music played in the background. He hadn't been big into the holidays for the past several years. Amanda was the festive one. Well, his mom had been, too, when she was strong enough to move about freely.

He picked up the menu. "Do we want dinner or a snack with coffee or hot chocolate?"

"Hmm, I think dinner would be nice." She pushed the hair from her face.

They placed their orders. Daria asked for hot chocolate and made it sound so tasty. He ordered one, too. It wouldn't be like Gina's, filled with miniature marshmallows, but he'd go for it, anyway.

Daria folded her hands and placed them on the table in front of her. "Such a great idea to come here. I can finally relax and breathe."

"Speaking of relaxing." He smiled. "I thought this would be a good time to have a serious conversation." He reached over and put his hand on top of her folded hands. "Are you up for it after all we've been through?"

Her eyes fell on his hand, covering hers. "I think so. What do you want to talk about?"

"Us." Jake swallowed hard. "Me returning to Kimbleton and meeting up with my best friend from middle school cannot be an accident. We were always together having fun."

Daria moved her hand on top of his.

His heart thumped hard against his chest. "I know having Emma in my life now puts a unique twist in a budding relationship."

"Jake." Daria's eyes sparkled with the blinking lights around the window.

"Daria, I need you to hear me out."

The server delivered their hot chocolates.

He continued. "I know I've only been back in town a few days, but I feel like it's been longer." Frustration crawled over him. Why couldn't he just say it? He loved her and wanted her in his life forever.

Just tell her.

A woman slowly entered the restaurant all bundled up with only her weary-looking eyes peering above the thick multi-colored scarf covering her face, and a floppy, wide brimmed hat that barely exposed her brown hair. Her movements appeared wobbly. She glanced around before turning toward them and approaching their table. Cautiously, she slid into the booth beside Daria and put a small handgun to Daria's head. "She's coming with me."

"No. She's not." Jake stiffened. He wasn't about to make any quick moves. The lady might pull the trigger.

"Yes, she is. And don't try to stop me." Her eyes narrowed.

With the table dividing them, Jake evaluated his next move. This person was the enemy right now. He curled his fingers into a fist. His knuckles whitened.

"Don't think for one minute I don't know what you're planning." She grabbed Daria's arm. "Come with me if you want to live."

Jake's eyes met Daria's.

You know I'll come for you, right?

Daria had to know he wouldn't let her leave the property with this woman. He'd settle these threats once and for all. The pulsating rushing through his body screamed attack, but he must wait for the right moment.

"It's okay, Jake," Daria said as she eased from the booth.

Her controlled tone relaxed him, knowing she had her head together. She was a trained police officer and could handle the situation. Right? He wouldn't let her out of his sight.

"Yes, as long as no one gets in my way, she might make it." The woman stood tall and determined, still pressing the pistol to Daria's temple. "So, don't get in my way, Jake."

She backed out of the restaurant with Daria and shifted the weapon to Daria's side. Jake jumped to his feet and stood by the booth, waiting for the right moment to make his move.

I need Your wisdom, God.

Patrons began filling the parking lot and trailing inside. Why now when he was trying to keep his eyes on Daria? Once the woman moved out of sight from the window, Jake darted out of the restaurant's back door and around to the side of the building. There were too many tourists and children trailing into the area. He couldn't counterattack. It was too risky.

The woman made Daria get in an old station wagon. Not a smart getaway vehicle. While the woman walked around to the driver's side, Daria dropped something out of the window. Why didn't she try to run when the woman walked away from her door? Guess she had her reasons. The car pulled toward the exit, but traffic blocked their immediate escape. Jake eased around the parking lot. What had Daria dropped on the ground? He searched until he spotted her car keys almost buried in the snow.

Smart move.

He hopped into her vehicle and fell in line with the parking lot traffic. The station wagon pulled in front of another car and onto the street. Jake kept a keen eye on the vehicle. He couldn't lose them. Who was this woman? They thought they'd solved the case.

Jake chewed his lip while some people weren't focusing on driving. Their fingers danced across the tiny keyboard of their cells. Irritation arose. His lack of patience in a desperate situation teetered on anger.

Breathe. Stay calm. Think.

The car was getting away, and he couldn't lose sight of it. He pulled out of the parking lot's traffic line and found an opening at the corner of the asphalt. The car bounced as he drove off the curb. A horn honked behind him, and the man shook all kinds of hand gestures at him. But he'd made it onto the street, and no one had gotten hurt. Only two cars behind Daria.

That's what I'm talking about. Smart maneuver if I do say so.

The car in front of him turned onto another road, leaving one car between him and Daria. Where was the woman taking her? Did she plan on harming Daria? Jake slid down in the driver's seat just enough to drive safely and in hopes of not being identified by the abductor.

Their vehicle eased across the slushy road and made a slow turn into a neighborhood. The woman wasn't much of a getaway driver. She eased down the street and made another turn into a cove. Jake made slow turns and pulled to the curb close to the cove.

He stepped out of the car and walked up the sidewalk. The woman pulled into a garage and closed the door. He crossed the street and sneaked up to the house. Car doors slammed. Then another door slammed. Why a neighborhood home? He eased around to the back of the house and peeked inside the living room window. The light-colored sheers kept him from seeing clearly, but at least he had a view and could catch most of what they said.

Daria sat on the sofa while the lady tossed off her hat, scarf and long coat. She sat in a chair across from Daria, still holding the gun. Her grip on the weapon wasn't proper, nor was her finger on the trigger. No apparent threat there, but one couldn't be too relaxed in any armed situation.

The faint laughter of kids met his ears. The lady slid her weapon between the cushion and armrest before two small children ran into the room and jumped into the woman's lap. They laughed and hugged her. Their mom? The whole abduction didn't make sense. She wrapped her arms around the kids while Daria watched.

A man entered the room from what looked like a hallway and crossed over toward the woman. His wife? His family? Jake stiffened. He looked familiar. When the man turned and faced the woman, Jake blinked and stared inside as best he could. How had Officer Evans made it home when he was supposed to be in jail?

Chapter 15

Daria studied the scene before her. Evans? Why put his wife at risk of getting hurt when she could have simply asked her to come over? After all, they'd met a few times even though they hadn't talked in a while. She looked pale.

"Evans, what's going on?" Did he have a weapon? She didn't feel threatened. "How'd you get out of jail?"

"My wife borrowed money from the equity of our house and bailed me out." He stared at her, then shoved his hands in his pockets. "It was a really dumb thing for me to have my wife kidnap you in her condition, and I'm the blame for it. She could have gotten hurt." Evans rubbed his wife's shoulder with one hand. "The department thinks I went rogue, but you should know things aren't the way they seem."

"I've heard that before, but I'm listening." Daria maintained her composure when she spotted Jake through the sheers. He'd found the car keys and followed them like a good cop or marine would.

"You remember I told you Karla hasn't been feeling well?" He paced. "I didn't explain her condition. I just brushed it off as a stomach bug or something."

"I remember, but what does that have to do with anything?"

"The doctor diagnosed her with lymphoma a few months ago. She's been losing weight and tired all the time. Fever, itching and coughing." His daughter ran and grabbed his legs. He picked her up. "Gregory Hall sent a message for me to meet him at the coffee shop. He'd heard about Karla."

Daria scooted to the edge of the sofa. "Did you meet with him? What did he want?"

Evans let the child down and sat in a chair closer to Daria. "He said he'd looked at my bank account and knew I didn't have the funds for chemo treatments and he'd like to make a donation. I was stunned. Did he have a right to look at my account?" He rubbed his forehead. "I accepted a large 'donation' from him. A really large donation. Something about it didn't sit well with me."

Blackmail? Money laundering? Daria figured it out before he completed his story. She couldn't believe Evans was involved in the case, but the evidence in that security video was hard to ignore. Gregory Hall used him, then threatened him and his family.

Where did Jake go?

She squinted at the window. Jake wasn't there. Evans looked toward the window and jumped up.

"What is it? Someone there?" He ran over and scrambled for the pistol his wife held earlier.

"Just me." Jake stepped into the room from the kitchen.

Evans spun and pointed the pistol at him. "How'd you find us?"

"Evans, stop," Daria said. "Jake is on our side. This entire investigation started with his sister, who was killed, along with his brother-in-law."

Daria filled Jake in on what Evans had already shared. She turned back to Evans, who had put his gun on top of the bookcase away from the kids' reach.

"Go ahead and finish your story." She needed to hear him say what had happened.

"When Gregory realized his files went missing, his wife became furious. Caroline, I believe. I'm not sure which one of them was more involved because she was in his office almost more than he was. She may have started the whole donation thing to pull me in since I'm a cop and use me for their schemes.

"Those toy flash drives were an ingenious idea by your sister, Jake. She was a smart and brave lady, and I'm sorry for your loss. Anyway, Gregory suddenly demanded his 'donation' back." He made air quotations with his fingers. "I gave him back as much as I could, but it wasn't enough to satisfy him. I'd used part of it for medical bills. That's when he said if he got caught, he'd point a finger at me and make it look like I went rogue. As you can tell, he succeeded. I'm a cop and I don't know how to clear myself."

Jake slammed his fist into his other palm. "That's the way it goes with traitors. Daria and I will figure it out."

"Evans, I need you to come down to the station to give your statement." Daria stood. "I'm not going to press charges, but I need this information documented."

"I can't do that. You can record my statement here, but I'm not showing my face until

I'm cleared. I appreciate you not arresting me or pressing charges."

"You're her friend." Jake walked over and stood by her side.

She glanced at him, then looked at Evans and his wife. "We've been in the department together for years and friends for a long time. Jake and I will handle things from here. You stay put. We'll be back to get your statement."

"One more thing. I owe Cramer and the department a huge apology. After Gregory started threatening me, I bought some of those rubber flash drives and tossed them in Cramer's office trying to save myself. Those drives are empty. You can check them." Evans walked them to the door. "I'm sorry for the trouble I've caused everyone. I really didn't mean any harm, but you've always been a reasonable cop. I knew you'd listen before judging me."

Daria walked outside, joined by Jake. "How could one case get so entangled in greed?"

"The world is filled with all types of people with different values in life. Some are good and, well, some aren't." Jake pointed toward the street. "I'm parked just around the corner."

"Let's run by the station and go back for his statement." Chills rushed over her body after being inside Evans's warm house. "I'd like to get this case straightened out before Christmas."

"Me, too," Jake said. "We've got a lot to talk about."

Daria paused and studied him. "I suppose we do."

Hope it's about our future. Together, that is.

By the time they reached the car, her fingers were almost frozen. Jake tossed her the keys. She barely caught them. A warm car, a cozy house and a good night's rest sounded delightful, but first things first. She couldn't leave Evans hanging. His interview was top priority.

As the day ended—after the trip from Evans's home to the station, back to Evans's, then finally to her brother's house for a hot dinner and restful evening—Daria's thoughts swirled with questions.

How should she approach Jeffers about Evans? Would he be open to hearing Evans's side of the story? Would his friends, especially Cramer, at the department welcome him back or would they see him as untrustworthy? Would they put him on probation or charge him? Could they possibly find compassion for Evans and his family?

She and Jake pulled into her brother's driveway. A leaning snowman, disturbed clots of snow and small footprints in the front yard showed the kids had had a blast in the wintry weather.

Gina opened the front door, holding Emma. Daria and Jake got out of the car.

"I saw you drive up," Gina said. "Dinner's ready."

"You are amazing." Daria hugged Gina and kissed Emma on the way inside. "And I'm starving."

"I'm ready for some grub. Smells good." Jake scooped his baby from Gina's arms and went straight to the kitchen.

Isaac and Alexa ran and hugged her around the waist. One day, she prayed she'd have a family of her own to run into her arms.

"We're waiting." Robert's voice trailed into the living room, drawing Daria back from her dreams.

She joined everyone around the kitchen table and breathed in the spicy aroma. Homemade chili with shredded cheese was a perfect meal for a frosty, snowy night. Isaac and Alexa rattled on and on about how much fun they'd had building a snowman, then running and tackling him. Emma slapped her little hands on the table.

"Here. Let me put her in the high chair," Gina said as she took her from Jake.

Daria closed her eyes at the first bite and savored the flavor. "So delicious. I needed this. Thank you, Gina, for all your hospitality. No wonder I love you so much. My brother could never cook. Good thing he's got you."

"Aw, it's the least I can do to help all of you during this dangerous situation," Gina said.

Daria finished her meal, then rinsed hers and Jake's bowls and placed them in the dishwasher. "Robert, when you have time, we need to speak with you about our latest findings."

"I have something to discuss with you, as well." Robert placed a toothpick in his mouth, pushed back from the table and crossed his legs.

Her curiosity piqued. What information would Robert have after staying home all day? He should have enjoyed his snow day off work and spending time with family.

"I'll finish cleaning up the dishes." Gina cleaned off the table and wiped down the counter. "Okay, kiddos. Go to your rooms and play." She gave Robert a kiss, then wiped Emma's hands and face before taking her out of the high chair and leaving the kitchen. "I'll be in the living room."

Daria leaned forward and placed her elbows on the table. "We need to talk about Evans."

"Just the person I need to talk to you about." Robert uncrossed his legs and leaned toward her. "Word on the street is he was framed, just like Jeffers. Only Jeffers discovered the money and confronted Gregory Hall. That's when Jeffers started receiving threats on his family's life if he exposed the embezzlement operation."

"Whoa. Do you believe the rumor?" Jake asked.

"I received an email from four police officers who were on a different shift from you, Daria. They requested an online meeting with me since I'm in investigations. So, I set it up. We met early this afternoon. They didn't believe Evans went rogue even though that video incriminates him as he tried to place blame on Cramer. Both are exemplary officers. Jeffers, too."

Jake drummed his fingers on the table. Daria reached over, placed her hand on top of his and stopped the noise.

"Evans is out on bail. His wife borrowed against their equity to get him out," Daria said. "And I have a recorded statement from him about what happened. It implicates Gregory

Hall, and his wife, Caroline. And get this—they had hired Richard, that kid I arrested, and his dad, Tony, to help get rid of Jake and me."

"I'm proud of you, being so efficient. My baby sister, the cop, pulling the case of a century in Kimbleton to a close." Robert's smile showed his approval.

"She is amazing, isn't she?" Jake took her hand.

Her cheeks warmed as Jake and Robert smiled at her. She'd proven herself as a dedicated, successful police officer, and the two men she loved approved of her actions. What more could she ask?

Robert stood and stretched. "If Evans's story matches the online meeting information I received today, his bail money will be refunded. Then outside of court hearings and sentencing of all the guilty parties, the case will be closed."

Daria played Evans's statement as they drank coffee and munched on peach cobbler à la mode. Robert nodded and made notes and Jake sat quietly as if he were devouring every detail even though he'd already heard it.

"Evans is now worried we will charge his wife for kidnapping." Daria took the last bite of her cobbler. "I'm not pressing charges. In fact, we need to take up a donation for her treatments. What do you think, Robert?"

"No harm was done. And Evans's statement is consistent with the CI's and with those of the officers I met with. The charges against him will be dropped, although he may get probation over trying to implicate Cramer."

Daria leaned her head back and closed her eyes.

Thank You, God, for answering my prayer and bringing out the truth.

Jake stretched his arms back and popped his neck. "Where is my little munchkin? I need some more Emma snuggles." He went into the living room where Gina sat reading a children's book to her. She looked up, slid from Gina's lap and ran to him.

He picked her up and tossed her in the air.

She giggled. "Again."

He did it again, then kissed her on the neck. Hearing her laugh made his mood even lighter. Emma straightened her legs and leaned toward the floor.

"I know, little lady, you want down." Jake softened his deep voice. "I'm learning what you like and don't like."

A weight had lifted from his shoulders. His sister and brother-in-law's murderer was behind bars. He could now grieve their loss and enjoy the part of them left behind. Emma.

Daria stood by the fireplace, laughing as Emma laughed. Such a pleasant sound. The two ladies he loved enjoying themselves. Would Daria consider a closer relationship? She'd said she loved him. They still needed to talk.

Daria's cell rang. He focused on her as she talked. A sparkle appeared in her eyes. What? Something good for a change? He surveyed the room and noted each person's location. Something he'd done daily in Afghanistan. One never knew when he'd have to protect them.

"Jake." Daria tapped on his arm. "Did you hear me?"

Of course he did, but he was in protective mode. "Yep, I heard you."

Her hands plopped on her waist. "What did I say?" Her smirky smile meant she didn't believe him.

"You said the windows have been replaced, and the walls repaired. My house is ready for us to return home." He winked. "See, I can multitask, too. Guess I could get packed up."

"It's late. The slush on the streets has frozen over again." Daria stepped in front of him. "You may as well stay another night here and enjoy some relaxation for a change."

Jake had the urge to pull her into his arms, but with Gina and Robert in the room, he figured it wouldn't be appropriate.

"Sounds good. Tomorrow it is." Jake slid his arms into his coat and picked up Emma's coat. "Come on, Amanda junior. Let's go to our apartment."

Gina rose from the sofa and moved toward him. "Why don't you leave her here and get yourself a good night's sleep before you leave tomorrow?"

"I want to spend time with her regardless of whether she sleeps or not." Jake picked her up. "I've been away from her long enough. We need more bonding time."

Daria took Emma's coat and put it on her, pulling the hood up over her head. "I'll walk you two over there."

Jake stepped outside in the frigid weather. He ducked Emma's head and pressed it against his chest until he reached the top of the apartment stairs. Daria stood on the step behind him. He unlocked the door and stepped into the warmth with Daria on his heels.

Emma straightened her legs and wanted down. She ran from room to room while Daria and Jake sat on the sofa. Emma brought back a pink pillow and tossed it on the floor, then tried to sit on it. She slid off and placed her head on it, rubbing her eyes.

"Looks like someone is ready for bed." Daria got up and retrieved a pair of warm pajamas for Emma. "Do you want to change her, or would you like for me to do it?"

"Uh, I'll let you." He would practice the changing of clothes when no one was around. It wasn't the same as dismantling a weapon and putting it back together. The gun didn't wiggle around as his niece did.

While Daria tended to Emma, Jake turned on the gas fireplace and went to the kitchen to make hot chocolate. He went back to the living room and placed two cups of hot chocolate on the small coffee table. In a matter of minutes, Daria had Emma changed, her bottle fixed and placed her in her bed. He lifted his eyebrows. She was a lady of many talents.

"That was fast. I know who to call when I need help with Emma." His heart rate picked up speed. Now would be the perfect time to have that serious talk.

"You know I'll help anytime you need. Oh, you made us some hot chocolate. Nice." She sat back on the sofa, holding her drink with both hands. "Thank you for all of your help with this case. In fact, if it weren't for you, we may have never known about the criminal activity taking place right here in Kimbleton."

"It all worked out. I inherited a baby, met up with you again, and I succumbed to your authority." He held his cup up. "A toast. Miracles never cease in this marine's life. Semper fi."

She laughed and bumped her cup to his. "That means always faithful, right?" She placed her cup on the table.

"You've got it." He put his cup down beside hers. Bravery was his specialty, but confronting the love of his life about his feelings for her almost had him cowering.

Why am I so nervous? God, help me remain calm.

Jake took in a deep breath and slowly released it. He turned his focus completely on her. Their eyes met. He reached over and took her hand in his. "Daria, you know I love you. I never dreamed my life could be so complete this soon after returning from overseas."

Silence.

She stared at him and didn't say anything.

He searched her beautiful face, waiting for a response.

She placed her other hand on top of his. "Jake, I lost you once, and I don't plan on losing you again. I've already told you that I love you, too."

He wrapped his arms around her and pulled her close.

Thank You, God.

Her arms wrapped around him about the time his lips pressed against hers. Smooth and warm. The moment he pulled back and looked at her, she placed her hand on his chest.

"I'd better go. We both need our rest after all we've been through. I'll help you and Emma get settled in the house tomorrow. Then we can talk some more."

"Emma and I will be over in the morning for breakfast with everyone before we leave. I'll see you then." He kissed her again. "I love you."

"And I love you." She stepped out onto the porch. "See you in the morning."

Jake watched as she walked down the outdoor steps and into the side door of her brother's house. He went back inside and fell across his bed, thinking. Who knew two strong-willed childhood friends could see eye to eye as adults and fall in love? A trained marine and a skilled police officer raising his sister's baby together.

His body sank deeper into the mattress and his eyes grew heavy. Silence ruled the night. He rolled over still fully dressed.

God, You have done the unimaginable. Thank You for protecting us.

Morning arrived much too soon. Emma sat in her porta crib, jabbering and playing with her giraffe. Jake stepped inside her room and picked her up.

"Whoa. We need a hazmat team in here. Where's Daria when I need her?" He held Emma up under her arms and away from his body to keep from being contaminated, searching for a safe place to lay her down.

"Back to your crib, you go. I've got to prepare myself for this task." He left the room, curling his nose. "I can do this."

He gathered the supplies necessary to change Emma's diaper, along with a trash bag, and tackled the unfortunate problem. The clean diaper hung on crooked, but it stayed put.

"Oorah. We did it, Emma." He picked her up and gave her a light squeeze. "Love you, sweet girl. Let's go find Daria and have break-fast. Then we can go home."

"Bite." Emma reached her arm out, opening and closing her hand.

"Exactly where we're going."

He pulled his coat on and put Emma's on her. A blistery wind blew, rustling the trees beside the house. Gray clouds covered the sky.

More snow coming. Guess we'll have a white Christmas.

Daria opened the side door to the house. "Good morning. Come on in where it's warm."

Jake didn't waste any time getting Emma inside. She kicked her legs and stiffened. She wanted down. He took her over and Daria helped set her in the high chair.

The aroma of bacon frying made his mouth water. He glanced across the table at Daria and smiled. He never dreamed he'd have an instant family.

"After we get you and Emma packed up, I'll help you move back into your home, if you'd like." Daria continued eating.

"Sure," Jake said. "I'd like that. It'll be nice to be back in my own place. Robert, I appreciate the hospitality you and Gina have given Emma and me. I owe you."

"We're glad things got settled before Christmas." Gina poured Jake another cup of coffee. "Tomorrow is Christmas Eve. Maybe you'll have time to put up some decorations."

Decorate? Not sure where to start. Maybe next year after I'm settled.

"We'll see. My mom always took charge of decorations while I helped eat all the desserts." He pushed from the table. "Thank you, again, for everything. I'll run and get my things."

Within the hour, Jake stood at Daria's car, waiting for her to pop the trunk. She emerged from the front door with Emma, the diaper bag and another bag. He heard her cell beep, but she had her hands full and didn't check it. They loaded up and Daria drove them home.

Jake started a fire in the wood fireplace. He drew in a deep breath. Memories of growing up in his parents' home flashed through his mind. A pleasant, comforting thought. He glanced at Daria. Her love for Emma showed in her caring actions.

Daria's cell rang the same time as someone knocked on the front door. Jake exchanged glances with Daria and shrugged his shoulders.

She answered her phone as he walked over and opened the door.

A man stuck a shotgun to his abdomen.

"We have unfinished business."

Chapter 16

Daria's adrenaline skyrocketed as McDaniel warned her of Tony Schneider's escape and his threat against her. "He's here now," she whispered.

"Put that phone down," Tony yelled.

Daria sat on the sofa, holding Emma. She placed her phone on the coffee table. His hostile behavior and angry tone put her on high alert. She pulled Emma close to shield her should shooting start.

"What do you mean, we have unfinished business?" Jake's feet shuffled on the tile floor.

"Not you, her."

"You're supposed to be in jail." Daria pushed to her feet. She eased over to the porta crib and set Emma down. "What do you want with me, Tony?"

"Yeah, and what else is new?" Tony squared his shoulders. "I finagled my way out of those handcuffs and used them to break the back window out of the squad car. I ran into the woods before they knew I was gone. Figured you'd be here. Same place I found you before."

"You were one of the shooters who blew the windows out in Jake's house and risked the life of a baby. How could you have lived with yourself if the child died?"

"Enough talk. I need to settle a score, and if you make any sudden moves, I'll blow a hole in your friend's belly."

Daria exchanged glances with Jake. He didn't appear to be nervous. She looked at Emma before moving farther away from her crib. In case of an attack, Emma should be in the clear.

What are you thinking, Jake?

Tony poked Jake in the belly with his shotgun. "Back up."

Jake backed up. Daria stayed put. Tony closed the front door.

"Who hired you to find me?" Daria took a step forward.

"Stay put." He shuffled the weapon from Jake to her, then back to Jake. "Caroline left me a bag of money so I can escape to Mexico. All I have to do is make you pay for destroying her life and business. Besides, Richard is still suffering from humiliation after you arrested him. Teaming up with Gregory and Caroline is the most profitable business deal I've ever made."

"You don't really think I'm going to let you shoot her, do you?" Jake towered over Tony like a streetlamp over a park bench. His tone was steady and smooth.

"I'll shoot you first, then her, if you want to throw threats." Tony spat on the floor.

Daria fumed at his arrogance. Jake spun, and his foot came around and smacked him on the side of the head. Tony dropped to the floor, along with his gun.

"Did you knock him out?" Daria rushed over and felt for a pulse.

"Guess I did. I didn't kick him that hard." Jake huffed.

"His pulse is stable, but he's going to have your boot print on his face."

Another knock at the front door had her pulling her weapon. Jake opened the door. Evans, Cramer and McDaniel stood there with their weapons drawn. A freshly cut spruce tree had been tossed on the lawn.

"Whoa. Don't shoot. It's just us," Cramer said. He pointed to Tony lying on the floor. "Looks like you've taken care of him."

Evans stepped forward, pulling out his hand-cuffs. "We were already on our way over here when we got the alert of Tony's escape. Did you get the message?"

Daria retrieved her cell and glanced at it before dropping it into her pocket. "I heard the phone's alert tone that I had a message, but we were loading the car and our hands were full. So, no, I didn't get to read the update. I'm glad you called."

Daria explained how the incident went down. McDaniel assisted Evans, handcuffing their intruder.

"We will take care of him. You guys grab the tree we brought and try to enjoy the rest of your Christmas holiday." McDaniel walked out, helping Evans get Tony into the car.

Cramer paused. "You're safe now." He walked out and closed the door behind him.

"What just happened?" Jake threw his arm up. "Is this case over or not?"

"It's over. What I'm shocked about is seeing Evans and Cramer together. Jeffers must be working overtime to smooth things out and put the department back together."

Emma let out a squeal. She reached over the top of her crib and threw her giraffe on the floor.

"I think she wants out so she can run around." Daria reached up and hugged Jake. He put his arm around her. A sense of security and warmth rushed over her. She backed away. "You just saved my life. I wasn't sure how I would take him down, but I would have taken a bullet for you and Emma."

"You would have figured something out. Besides, I'm the marine in the house. You should never have to take a bullet for me. Let me go get our tree." He kissed her on the cheek and went outside. A moment later, he dragged the spruce inside. "Let's get this tree up."

Daria picked Emma up and followed Jake to the garage. He'd left the tree laying on the living room floor.

"I see three boxes up on that shelf marked Christmas." Daria held Emma close and wrapped her arms snug around her. "It's too cold out here. I'm taking Emma inside."

In a matter of minutes, Jake walked into the kitchen carrying all three boxes. He pushed the door closed with his foot. Daria reminisced about the fun they'd had in their early years. Could her future with him be even better?

He took the boxes into the living room. "There has to be a tree stand in here somewhere." He opened one box. "Here it is. I don't know much about decorating a tree or raising a baby, but with your help, I guess I'll figure it out."

She put Emma on the floor and opened the other boxes while Jake added more wood to the fireplace. She pulled her phone out of her pocket and located some Christmas music. Emma shuffled around as she tried to dance.

They got the tree up and put lights on it. Using an artificial tree in the mountains didn't seem right. Enjoying family time and finding an actual tree always helped set the mood for the season. She hoped next year they could go out and find a real tree together with Emma.

"Now for the decorations." Jake reached in and started hanging silver balls on the tree. He lifted Emma and let her drop a small plastic icicle near the top. She stared at the lights and giggled.

Daria hung a few ornaments, bumping elbows with Jake occasionally. The setting was right for a perfect evening. She pulled out something wrapped in tissue paper.

"What's this?" She used caution unwrapping it. If Amanda thought it was that special, then she would be extra careful handling it.

Jake picked Emma up and stepped by Daria's side as a small picture in a Christmas frame fell into her hand. His eyes widened.

"I remember that day. We had fun decorating the tree while Mom took our pictures, but I did not know Amanda made a Christmas ornament out of it." Jake shook his head. "There's Amanda, you and me standing in front of the tree. And look, there in the background is my dad."

"What a treasure. Who would have known we'd be here right now, years later, and find this photo?" Daria slipped her arm around Jake's waist.

God, You orchestrated this reunion, didn't You?

Jake looked down at her and pulled her close. "Tell me. What did you mean when you said you weren't married to your job? What is your dream?"

Daria kissed Emma's little hand, then looked up at him. "You are, Jake. You and Emma are my dreams come true."

He leaned over and brushed his lips against hers. Emma pushed at his face and laughed. He placed her on the floor in front of the twinkling Christmas lights, then faced Daria.

Daria's heart fluttered.

He lifted her chin with his finger and kissed her. She pulled back and looked into his eyes. Her life was complete. She'd renewed her faith, redeemed herself with the department and discovered that the missing piece from her life was Jake.

God knew the plans He had for her. What more could she ask for?

Epilogue

"Can you believe how much she's grown in the past eight months?" Jake picked Emma up and put her on his shoulders. He walked the paved trail toward the children's play area at the Mountain Top Park. "Life took a 180 after Amanda and Tom died. Emma has challenged me and made me learn to think of others above myself. I love her as my own. Reconnecting with you was a blessing I hadn't expected."

"Isn't it amazing how life takes a shift when we least expect it?" Daria handed Emma her cup. "Who knew I'd fall for an armed marine in the Marketplace parking lot who stirred up a hornet's nest of crime? You sure turned my world around."

The playground came into view. Colorful animals mounted on large springs, a bright red mini slide and a swing set with baby seats in different shades of blue.

Emma kicked her legs and shook her arms. Juice spilled from her cup and landed on Jake's head.

"Hey." He took her off his shoulders and put her down. "That wasn't a dripless cup, was it?" He brushed at his wet hair.

Daria bent over, laughing. "No. That was the new one you bought her."

"It's not funny." Jake chuckled. "Remind me to toss it when we get back to the house."

Emma took off running toward the park.

"Emma, wait." Jake picked up his pace with Daria trailing behind him. "Wait for Uncle Jake."

She stopped and pointed to the horse on a spring. "De, ride horsey."

"Yes, you can ride it." Daria caught up with her, took her hand and helped her up on the brown-and-white horse with a painted-on green saddle.

Jake found peace knowing Emma loved Daria and vice versa. "De" had become Daria's nickname since Emma couldn't say her name. He found himself calling her "De." He joined in and helped his little sweetheart ride all the animals, slide down the slide and swing until she became fussy.

"Is it nap time already?" Jake picked her up. She placed her head on his shoulder and patted his back. A tender feeling he'd never forget.

"There's a picnic table over there under the tree. I'll go get the basket and the blanket so she can take a nap." Daria left and came back with their lunch.

Jake had hoped Emma would go to sleep while they were at the park. He wanted some uninterrupted time with Daria.

"What did you pack in here?" Daria placed a tablecloth over the concrete picnic table and got the sandwiches and canned drinks out of the basket.

"I packed what Emma likes. What else, but peanut butter and jelly?" Jake laughed as he put Emma on the concrete bench. "She's almost too small to sit there."

Emma slapped her hands on the table. After a few bites, her eyes rolled and her jelly-covered hand rubbed her hair. Jake picked her up and moved her to the blanket they'd spread out on the ground.

Now I can talk to Daria. Why am I so nervous?

They cleaned up their trash and tossed it in the park's trash can. Jake sat beside Daria on the bench and took her hand.

"I love the mountains and the open air," Daria spoke softly. "Do you remember when your family and mine used to come here on Sunday afternoons after church? I don't think I admired the view then as I do now. So serene."

"I know. That's why I wanted us to come here." Jake swallowed the nervous lump in his throat and turned to face her. "Daria, we've talked about the future many times in the past few months. Emma loves you and I love you. I think it's time to make *us*, our relationship, permanent." He reached into his pants pocket and pulled out a small box. "Will you marry me?"

"Yes, yes, I will." Her eyes sparkled.

He put the diamond on her finger and kissed her. "Because of you and Emma, I am a better man."

"And because of God's perfect plan for us, we are a perfect family." Daria placed her hand gently on his cheek. "I love you, Jake Fisher."

"And I love you." Jake blew out the breath he'd held. "I'm glad that's settled. Now I have something else to tell you."

"Guess I'm going to have to teach you how not to destroy a romantic moment." She laughed. "What's so important?"

"I heard from Jeffers yesterday. I'll start working investigations at the police department with Robert next week."

"That's wonderful. I want to be a stay-at-home, full-time mother figure for Emma. After we're married, I'll turn in my notice."

"Sounds like a plan to me." Jake put his arms around Daria and kissed her again. Emma sat up and rubbed her eyes. "Our girl is awake."

★ ★ ★ ★ ★

Romantic Suspense

Danger. Passion. Drama.

Available Next Month

Colton's Dangerous Cover Lisa Childs
Peril In The Shallows Addison Fox

Operation Rafe's Redemption Justine Davis
The Suspect Next Door Rachel Astor

LOVE INSPIRED
Alaskan Wilderness Rescue Sarah Varland
Targeted For Elimination Jill Elizabeth Nelson
Larger Print

LOVE INSPIRED
Dangerous Texas Hideout Virgina Vaughan
Wyoming Abduction Threat Elisabeth Rees
Larger Print

LOVE INSPIRED
Deadly Mountain Escape Mary Alford
Silencing The Witness Laura Conaway
Larger Print

10 brand new stories each month
Romantic Suspense
Danger. Passion. Drama.
MILLS & BOON

Keep reading for an excerpt of a new title
from the Intrigue series,
COLD CASE KIDNAPPING by Nicole Helm

Chapter One

Grant Hudson had been well versed in fear since the age of sixteen when his parents vanished—seemingly into thin air, never to be seen or heard from again. So, as an adult, he'd made fear and uncertainty his life. First, in the military with the Marines and now as a cold case investigator with his siblings.

Privately investigating cold cases didn't involve the same kind of danger he'd seen in Middle Eastern deserts, but the uncertainty, the puzzles and never knowing which step to take was just as much a part of his current life as it had been in the Marines.

And if he focused on seemingly unsolvable cases all day, he didn't have time to think about the nightmares that plagued him.

"Your ten o'clock appointment is here."

Grant looked up from his coffee. His sister was dressed for ranch work but held a file folder that likely had all the information about his new case.

Hudson Sibling Solutions, HSS, was a family affair. The brainchild of his oldest brother, Jack, and a well-oiled machine in which all six Hudson siblings played a part, just as they all played a part in running the Hudson Ranch that had been in their family for five generations.

They had solved more cases than they hadn't, and Grant considered that a great success. Usually the answers weren't happy endings, but in some strange way, it helped ease the unknowns in their own parents' case.

Grant glanced at the clock as he finished off his coffee. "It's only nine forty-five."

"She's prompt," Mary agreed, handing him the file. "She's in the living room whenever you're ready."

But "whenever you're ready" wasn't part and parcel with what HSS offered.

They didn't make people wait. They didn't shunt people off to small offices and cramped spaces. Usually people trying to get answers on a cold case had spent enough time in police stations, detective offices and all manner of uncomfortable rooms answering the same questions over and over again.

The Hudsons knew that better than anyone—particularly Jack, who'd been the last person to see their parents alive and had been the only legal adult in the family at the time of their disappearance. Jack had been adamant when they began the family investigation business that they offer a different experience for those left behind.

So they met their clients in the homey living room of the Hudson ranch house. They didn't make people wait if they could help it. They treated their clients like guests… The kind of hospitality their mother would have been proud of.

Grant had made himself familiar with today's case

prior to this morning, but he skimmed the file Mary had handed off. A missing person, not out of the ordinary for Hudson Sibling Solutions. Dahlia Easton had reported her sister, Rose, missing about thirteen months ago, after her sister had disappeared on a trip to Texas.

Dahlia Easton herself was a librarian from Minnesota. Dahlia was convinced she'd found evidence that placed Rose near Sunrise, Wyoming—which had led her to the HSS.

Ms. Easton hadn't divulged that evidence yet, instead insisting on an in-person meeting to do such. It was Grant's turn to take the lead, so he walked through the hallway that still housed all the framed art his mother had hung once upon a time—various Wyoming landscapes—to the living room.

A redhead sat on the couch, head down and focused on the phone she held. Her long hair curtained her face, and she didn't look up as Grant entered.

He stepped farther into the room and cleared this throat. "Ms. Easton."

The woman looked up from her phone and blinked at him. She didn't move. She sat there as he held out his hand waiting for her to shake it or greet him in some way.

It was a strange thing to see a pretty woman seated on the couch he'd once crowded onto with all his siblings to watch Disney movies. Stranger still to feel the gut kick of attraction.

It made him incredibly uncomfortable when he rarely allowed himself discomfort. He should be thrilled his body could still react to a pretty woman in a perfectly normal way, but he found nothing but a vague sense of unease filling him as she sat there, eyes wide, studying him.

Her hair was a dark red, her eyes a deep tranquil blue on a heart-shaped face that might have been more arresting if she didn't have dark circles under her eyes and her clothes didn't seem to hang off a too-skinny frame. Like many of the clients who came to HSS for help, she wore the physical toll of what she'd been through in obvious ways…enough for even a stranger to notice.

He set those impressions and his own discomfort aside and smiled welcomingly. "Ms. Easton, I'm Grant Hudson. I'll be taking the lead on your case on behalf of HSS. While all six of us work in different facets of investigation, I'll be your point person." He finally dropped his hand since she clearly wasn't going to shake it. "May I?" he said pointing to the armchair situated across from the couch. His father had fallen asleep in that very chair every single movie night.

"You look like a cowboy," she said, her voice sounding raspy from overuse or lack of sleep, presumably.

The corner of his mouth quirked up, a lick of amusement working through him. He supposed a cowboy was quite a sight for someone from Minnesota. "Well, I suppose in a way I am."

"Right. Wyoming. Of course." She shook her head. "I'm sorry. I'm out of sorts."

"No apologies necessary." He settled himself on the chair. She didn't look so much out of sorts as she did exhausted. He set the file down on the coffee table in between them.

"I have all the information Mary collected from you."

"Mary's the woman I talked to on the phone and emailed. I thought she'd…"

"Mary handles the administrative side of things, but I'll be taking the lead on actually investigating. I can get Mary to sit in if you'd feel more comfortable with a woman present?"

"No, it isn't that. I just…" She shook her head. "This is fine."

Grant nodded, then decided what this woman needed was to get some sleep and a good meal in her. "Have you had breakfast?"

"Um." Her eyebrows drew together. "I don't understand what you're…"

"I'd like you to recount everything you know, so we might be here a while. Just making sure you're up for it."

"Oh, I'm not much for breakfast."

He'd figured as much. He pulled his phone out of his pocket and sent a quick text to Mary. He wouldn't push the subject, but he wasn't about to let Dahlia keel over either. He slid the phone back in his pocket.

"I've got your file here. All about your sister's trip to Texas. The credit card reports, cell phone records. Everything you gave us. But you said you had reason to believe she ended up here in Wyoming."

"Yes," Dahlia agreed, putting her own phone into a bag that sat next to her. "Everything the police uncovered happened in Texas," Dahlia said. "But she just… disappeared into thin air, as far as anyone can tell me, but obviously that isn't true. People can't just disappear."

But they did. All the time. There were a lot of ways

to make sure a person was never found. More than even Grant could probably fathom, and he could fathom a lot. Which was why he focused on one individual case at a time. "So, there's no evidence she ever left Texas?"

"She took one of those DNA tests, and it matched her with some people in Texas," Dahlia said earnestly, avoiding the direct question. "She was supposed to go to Texas and meet them. She never made it to the people— at least the police there didn't think so. When all the clues dried up, I decided to look at Rose's research. The genealogy stuff that prompted her to take the DNA test. I researched everything she had, and it led me to a secret offshoot of the Texas family that wound up in Truth, Wyoming."

Grant tried not to frown. Because, no, there wasn't proof Rose Easton had left Texas, and also because no one in Sunrise particularly cared to think about Truth, Wyoming. "Ah" was all he said.

"It's a cult."

"It was a cult," Grant replied. "The Feds wiped them out before I was born." Still, people tried to stir up all the Order of Truth nonsense every few years. But there was no evidence that the cult had done anything but die out after the federal raid in 1978.

"Doesn't everything gone come around back again?" Dahlia asked, nervous energy pumping off her. "And if this line of our family was involved then, doesn't it mean they could be involved now?"

Grant studied the woman. She looked tired and brittle. It didn't diminish her beauty, just gave it a fragile hue. Fragile didn't cut it in these types of situations, but here she was. Still standing. Still searching.

She was resting all her hopes on the wrong thing if she was looking into the Order of Truth, but she believed it. She was clearly holding on to this tiny thread for dear life. So Grant smiled kindly. "Let's see your evidence."

HE DIDN'T BELIEVE HER. No different than any of the police officers and detectives back home or in Texas. Once Dahlia uttered the word *cult*—especially one that had been famously wiped out—people stopped listening.

Grant Hudson was no different, except he was placating her by asking for her evidence. Dahlia didn't know if that was more insulting than waving her off or not. Honestly, she was too tired to figure out how she felt about much of anything.

She'd driven almost eighteen hours from Minneapolis to Sunrise in two days and had barely slept last night in the nice little cabin she'd rented. She was too anxious and tangled up about this strange connection. Too amped at the thought of *hope* after so long.

"I think you probably have all the evidence you care about," Dahlia said, trying to keep her tone even. "I know investigators are obsessed with facts, but facts haven't helped me. Sometimes you have to tie some ideas together to find the facts."

Grant studied her. It had been a silly thing to say, that he looked like a cowboy, but it was simply true. It wasn't just the drawl, it was something about the way he walked. There were the cowboy boots of course, and the Western decor all around them, but something in the square jaw or slightly crooked nose made her think of the Wild West. The way he hadn't fully smiled, but his mouth had *curved* in a slow move that had left her scrambling for words.

"We are investigators, and we do have to work in the truth," Grant said, still using that kind veneer to his words, though Dahlia sensed an irritation simmering below them. "But I think you'll find we're not like the police departments you've dealt with. I'll admit, I think the cult is the wrong tree to bark up, but if you give me reason to change my mind, I'll bark away."

The tall slender woman who'd let her in the house entered the room pushing a cart. She wore adorable cowboy boots with colorful flowers on them and Dahlia had no doubt when she spoke, it would be tinged with that same smooth Western drawl Grant had.

It was easy to see the two were related even if Grant was tall and broad and…*built*.

There was something in the eyes, in the way they moved. Dahlia didn't have the words for it, just that they functioned like a unit. One that had been in each other's pockets their whole lives.

People had never been able to tell that about her and Rose, aside from being named for flowers. It took getting to know them, together, to see the way they had learned how to deal with each other and their parents. The rhythm of being a sibling.

Dahlia had been turned into an only child now, and she didn't know how to function in that space. Not with her parents, who had given up on Rose when the police had. Not with her friends, all of whom were more Rose's friends than hers and who wanted to be involved in a tragedy and their grief more than they wanted answers.

Only Dahlia couldn't let it go. Couldn't hold on to her old life in this new world where her sister didn't exist.

Not dead. Not gone. She didn't *exist*.

"I told you I'm not a breakfast eater," Dahlia said sharply and unkindly. She might have felt bad about that, felt her grandmother's disapproval from half a country away, but she was tired of caring what everyone else felt.

Grant apparently felt unbothered by her snap. "So consider it lunch." He looked at his sister. "Thanks, Mary."

She nodded, smiled at Dahlia, then left. Grant immediately took a plate and began to arrange things on it. Dahlia figured he'd shove it at her, and she had all sorts of reasons to tell him to shove it down his own throat.

Instead, he set it next to the file folder. Picking a grape and popping it into his own mouth before pouring himself some coffee.

Dahlia knew she'd lost too much weight. She understood she didn't sleep well enough, and her health was suffering because of it. She'd seen a therapist to help her come to terms with Rose's disappearance.

But no amount of self-awareness or therapy could stop her from this driving need to find the truth.

She didn't know if Rose was still alive. She was prepared—or tried to prepare herself—for the ugly truths that could be awaiting her. Namely, that Rose was dead and had been all this time. Her sweet, vibrant sister. Murdered and discarded.

It wasn't just possible, it was likely, and yet Dahlia had to know. She couldn't rest, not really, until she had the truth.

And if you never find it?

She simply didn't know. So she'd keep going until something changed.

Grant continued to eat as he flipped through papers that were presumably the reports and information she'd emailed to Mary.

Dahlia wasn't hungry, but she hadn't been for probably the entire past year. Still, food was fuel, and this food was free. She could hardly sidestep that when her entire life savings was being poured into hiring Hudson Sibling Solutions and staying in Wyoming until the mystery was solved.

She finally forced herself to pick a few pieces of fruit and a hard-boiled egg and put them on a plate. She'd been guzzling coffee for days, so she went for the bottle of water instead.

"Tell me why you decided to come all the way out here." He said it silky smooth, and whether it was the drawl or his demeanor, he made it sound like a gentle request.

She knew it was an order though. And she knew he'd ignore it like everyone else had. It was too big of a leap to take, and yet...

"Rose found out our great-grandfather was married before he married our great-grandmother. And he had a son from this first marriage. A man named Eugene Green."

Grant's expression didn't move, but something in the

air around them did. Likely because he knew Eugene Green to be the founder of the Order of Truth.

"That's not exactly a close relation, is it? Something like a half great-great-uncle. If that."

"If that," Dahlia agreed. Her stomach turned, but still she forced herself to eat a grape. Drink some of the water. "But it was in Rose's notes."

Grant flipped through the papers again. "What notes?"

Dahlia moved for her bag and pulled out the thick binder she'd been carting around. "After the police decided it was a cold case, they returned her computer to me. I printed off everything she'd collected about our family history. *That's* what took her to Texas. She had a binder just like this. With more originals, but she scanned and labeled everything. So I recreated it. The Wyoming branch and Texas branch of the family are one and the same. It connects."

Grant eyed the binder. "Ms. Easton…"

"I know. You don't believe me. No one does. That's okay." She hadn't come all this way just for someone to believe her. "And you can hardly look through it all. But there is this." She pulled out the piece of paper she'd been keeping in the front pocket of the binder. "The picture on the top is from security footage of the gas station in Texas where Rose was last spotted. That's Rose," she said pointing to her sister. "No one can identify the man with her, but he looks an awfully lot like the picture on the bottom. A picture of Eugene Green from my sister's notes."

Grant didn't even flick a glance at the picture. "Eugene Green is dead."

"Yes, but not everyone who might look like him is."

Grant seemed to consider this, but then people—law enforcements, investigators, even friends—always did. At first. "Can I keep this?"

Dahlia nodded. She had digital copies of everything. She wasn't taking any chances. If HSS took all her information and lost it, discarded it or ignored it, she'd always have her own copies to keep her going.

"Did you have anything else that might tie Rose to Truth or Wyoming?" Grant asked.

No, she hadn't come here thinking HSS would believe her, but she'd…hoped. She couldn't seem to stop herself from hoping. "No, not exactly."

"Can I ask why you couldn't have told us this over the phone?"

Dahlia looked at the picture. Every police officer she'd talked to about it told her she was grasping at straws. That the Order of Truth was gone, and all the Greens had long since left the Truth area. That the man in the picture wasn't *with* Rose. He was just getting gas at the pump next to her.

"I'm not sure I could explain it in a way that would make any sense to you, but I needed to come here."

Grant nodded. "Well, I'll look into this. Is there anything else?"

Dahlia shoved her binder, sans security picture, back in her bag and then stood. He was dismissing her now that he understood her evidence was circumstantial—according to the police.

She was disappointed. She could admit that to herself. She'd expected or hoped for a miracle. Even as she'd told herself they wouldn't care any more than anyone else had, there'd been a seed of hope this family solving cold cases might believe her.

She should end this. The Hudsons weren't going to do any more than the police had, and she was going to run out of money eventually. "If you don't have anything new in a week, I suppose that will be that."

His eyebrows rose as he stood. "A week isn't much time to solve a cold case."

"I don't need it solved. I just need some forward movement to prove I'm paying for something tangible. If you can prove to me the Order of Truth has nothing to do with this—irrefutably—that'll be enough."

He seemed to consider this, then gave her a nod. "You're staying at the Meadowlark Cabin?" Grant asked as he motioned her to follow him.

Dahlia nodded as she retraced her footsteps through the big stone-floored foyer to the large front door with its stained glass sidelights. Mountains and stars.

"How long are you planning on staying?"

Dahlia looked away from the glass mountains to Grant's austere face. "As long as it takes."

Again, his expression didn't quite move, but she got the distinct feeling he didn't approve. Still, he said nothing, just opened the front door.

"I'll be in touch," he said.

She forced herself to smile and shake his outstretched hand.

Just because he'd be in touch didn't mean she was going to go hole herself in her room at her rented cabin in Sunrise. No.

She planned on doing some investigating of her own. She'd come here hoping the Hudsons could help, sure, but she'd known what she really needed to do.

Help herself.

NEW SERIES COMING!

RELEASING JANUARY

Special EDITION

Believe in love.

Overcome obstacles.

Find happiness.

For fans of Virgin River, Sweet Magnolias or Grace & Frankie you'll love this new series line. Stories with strong romantic tropes and hooks told in a modern and complex way.

In-store and online 17 January 2024.

NEW NEXT MONTH!

There's much more than land at stake for two rival Montana ranching families in this exciting new book in the Powder River series from *New York Times* bestselling author B.J. Daniels.

RIVER STRONG

In-store and online January 2024.

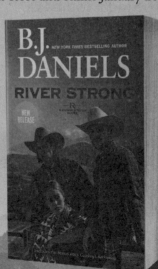

Subscribe and fall in love with a Mills & Boon series today!

You'll be among the first to read stories delivered to your door monthly and enjoy great savings.

WE SIMPLY LOVE ROMANCE